SOMETHING
UNREMEMBERED

SOMETHING UNREMEMBERED

a novel by
Della Dennis

Stonehouse Publishing
www.stonehousepublishing.ca
Alberta, Canada

Stonehouse Publishing Inc is an independent publishing house,
incorporated in 2014.

Cover image is titled "Portrait of a Lady"
by Rogier van der Weyden (1400-1464)

Cover design and layout by Anne Brown
Printed in Canada

Stonehouse Publishing would like to thank and acknowledge
the support of the Alberta Government funding for the arts,
through the Alberta Media Fund.

Government

National Library of Canada Cataloguing in Publication Data
Della Dennis
Something Unremembered
Novel
ISBN: 978-0-9950645-4-6 (paperback)
First Edition

To my children Kirsten, Hannah, Simeon, and Gregory
—my joy and inspiration.

And to Monique—my very intentional friend.

PROLOGUE

I have just recently arrived in Beauvais, a small city in northern France. I am sitting in Eglise St. Etienne—the gothic St. Stephen's Church—facing the southwest side of the nave near the main entry. Before me is a crucifix. The figure on the crucifix is a woman. A fitted bodice sets off her small round breasts, the folds of her skirt fall gracefully from a slender waist. Saint Wilgeforte—crucified Holy Virgin. She has a beard. I didn't expect to find *her* here. I came looking for someone else.

Wilgeforte. She has other names. "Maid Uncumber" in England, I know. Some say she evolved from the robed and crowned crucifix at Lucca—that over time, when the practice of clothing the corpse died out, subsequent generations reinterpreted the image. Her cult flourished in the fifteenth century. It was suppressed in 1969 and her feast day removed from the calendar. But here she hangs, large as life.

As the story goes, the beautiful Wilgeforte was one of nine daughters of the pagan King of Portugal. She became a Christian and vowed to serve God as a consecrated virgin. Regardless, her father arranged to marry her off to the King of Sicily. Wilgeforte prayed that God would so transmogrify her beauty that this pagan suitor would reject her. Miraculously she grew a full beard and mustache. The King of Sicily, horrified by her appearance, immediately renounced the engagement. Furious, Wilgeforte's father crucified her.

But I didn't expect to find her here at all. It seems pretty serendipitous. Traditionally, misunderstood and unappreciated wives invoke her, offering bushels of oats in exchange for deliverance from their husbands. *Where will I find a bushel of oats?*

PERSPECTIVE

I would advise you against defensiveness on principle. It precludes the best eventualities along with the worst. At the most basic level, it expresses a lack of faith… The worst eventualities can have great value as experience. And often enough, when we think we are protecting ourselves, we are struggling against our rescuer.

—Marilynne Robinson, *Gilead*

This is a new beginning. Several chapters along I realized my first "first" chapter won't do at all. It was quite defensive and making excuses. It also demonstrated the absolute antithesis of what I said I believed. I wrote about the importance of faith. Faith, as the apostle has it, the substance of things hoped for, the evidence of things not seen. I called it my peculiar gift. Wishful thinking. I didn't believe it for a minute. I hoped to talk myself into faith. I'm beginning to think faith has more to do with letting go. So I am trying to follow this thing as it unfolds without setting it up.

Part of the reason I came to Beauvais was to fix the first chapter and tie all my notes and observations together. I am writing everything into this one notebook—my notes, my chapters, my sporadic journaling, my travel diary. This big, blank notebook is bound, not coiled, so nothing can go missing. The story is taking time. I started by writing in fits and starts because that's how it came to me. I have no idea how it will end.

I'm not really a writer, as I imagine writers to be at any rate. Good writers have the ability to make the familiar extraordinary. I want to make the extraordinary familiar or at least believable. But finding words to do that is hard work. Writers must have a better relationship with words than I do. If they don't, I have no idea why they write at all.

I've never had writer's block. In a witness statement, you report on yourself and on what you saw—where you were when the event occurred, your vantage point, and your involvement, if any, in the events as they happened. If you have nothing more to say, it's not a block. It's just finished. This story is more like a witness statement. That said, when I started to write, I expected in time there would be more to tell. I hope I will know when the story is told out. I hope I will know when to let it go.

I began to knit these witness statements together the summer after Marilee and Jessica moved out. I was a little bitter by then. Things had been going quite well, much better than before. But things fall apart, as Yeats says. The centre, if there ever was one, did not hold. My approach to the story shifted too. At first I thought maybe a researcher would arrive at the same place I did if I faithfully gave the exact references and context. Now I know the most expedient approach is to report as things turn up, cite my source if I can, and leave it at that.

If anything, I'm a historian or *an* historian if you prefer. History was my major in college. For a while I expected to make a career of it, which I haven't done. I planned to give scholarship a shot, thinking I could be tolerably proficient. It's just as well that fell through. I couldn't have endured it anyway. When I did my history courses, I always got hung up on the details. I looked for stories about people working out the intricate patterns of their lives, hoping to find my own pattern—stories about how people dressed their daily rounds of eating, drinking, living, dying. But there was just too much of everything else to remember. I remember Aethelred the Unready, but I don't remember how he got the name. Well, he got caught off guard by some attacking warriors. But I forget when, where, why, and how that happened. Now if there were more to the story—and of course there has to be—I would have remembered, but I have little inclination for dates and battles. I usually forget those details. And I forget what difference his defeat, which I presume it was, made to the course of history. If I had known his oldest son went into battle with him and was slaughtered, for example, I may have remembered. If I had known that his family were starving and the youngest child was lame, I would have remembered. I would have remembered why the battle was important and should have been won, or why Aethelred the Unready had no business being where he was in the first place. Or how he brought it on himself. And I would have remembered the bitterness of his men and his loss of repute with kinfolk. But if the importance of history is power, and who wins it, justly or unjustly, or politics, and who makes choices for whole populations, I get uneasy, as if remembering gives that sort of power and influence the right to exist. So I forget. I forget details about lineage and, for example, where or whether France or England dominated. I do know that not so very long ago the boundaries of France were not drawn as they are today—that England ruled over large tracts of continental Europe.

I still read history from time to time. Some may say it's not really history at all, what I do—stringing stories together to make larger stories of lives in other places and other times. Nothing about me, nothing relating to my personal history. I read scattered details about the way people treading the measure of bygone days and weeks and months and years found a little joy to balance their affliction. I piece together bits of meaning. This is not escapism, what I do. It's perspective. Maybe that's about me.

All historians make choices. That's why it's often hard to find the stories. It seems so many histories don't care to find the stories or haven't bothered to tell them. The historians we read when I was in school preferred to propose organizing systems to chart the ethos of an era. Maybe they just did that for undergrads, to help us out. They presented the big picture, as they believed it to be, or wanted it to be. Stories are often a problem for big pictures. That by itself should tell you something about conventional strategies. Dates and lineages and battles and governments generalize. Stories are particular. Stories help you understand how someone in a certain part of the world living in a certain era made sense of life, or didn't, while battles and lineages will tell you who had the power to make him or her miserable. As a rule, if the task of the historian is to retrace the tracks of human activity, these general pieces of information have been the linchpins they use to hold the wheels in place on the axles of their wagons. Wheels can roll almost anywhere, but a wagon can only hold so much information. This is why I prefer to read on the margins of the historical canon. I am more interested in finding out what fell off the wagon or where the wheel rolled when the linchpin worked itself loose—finding other ways of doing history—histories in ditches.

* * *

I have a bookshelf where I keep histories of this sort that fall my way. It's my history hoard, as precious to me as the hoards of treasure guarded by old Saxon heroes. In my living room, across from a large overstuffed sofa and my husband's black leather recliner, is a small rocking chair that I found in a used furniture store. I had it rebuilt and upholstered in Belgian mohair—forest green. It is perfect for me. Beside my green chair is this bookshelf. I can reach several of the books on it without getting up from the chair. I have other shelves for old textbooks, anthologies, novels, Ellis Peters mysteries, poetry, dictionaries. But on this shelf I put the few books I have collected over the years that don't really take me anywhere—except perhaps down a garden path. I've not read these books cover to cover, but I have read parts of them over and over. Often I will page through one of them when I need a new landscape, when I feel crowded by the unsettled world of teenage sons, the relentless progress of technology, the wars and rumors of war, the impossible problems of poverty, the cold comfort of a stale-dated marriage.

The collection is quite random. Some of the books are practically historical artifacts themselves. Although I have developed a great fondness for these books, I didn't go looking for most of them. For example, *The Medieval Stage* by Sir Edmund K. Chambers. Two years after I graduated from college, my favourite history professor retired. I heard about her farewell reception after the fact, so I showed up in her office the following week instead. She was packing up her things, planning to move east to be near family. She seemed surprised but genuinely happy to see me. I had not really taken the time to thank her or say goodbye at the end of my last semester. I should have brought a gift. Instead, as she was taking two worn volumes from the shelf—no doubt planning to put them in the box she was packing—she handed them to me: "I think you will enjoy these." At the time I thanked her politely, thinking I would never read them.

I have read them, though. I have often picked up a volume to browse while waiting for water to boil, or sons to come home, or important calls to be returned, or the will to wash a soaking pot. The more I read, the more I wonder why my professor parted with them so readily. I can only imagine she was thinking more of me than herself at the moment and later regretted it. I really like Sir Edmund Chambers. Even though *The Medieval Stage* seems to have been cited all over the place since its publication in 1903, in the preface Sir Edmund says it is "the work of one who only plays at scholarship in the rare intervals of a busy administrative life." He goes on to say "I shall not, I hope, be accused of attaching too much importance in the first volume to the vague and uncertain results of folk-lore research." Not by me, Sir Edmund. The only problem I have *with vague and uncertain results* is that sometimes they disappear altogether. This is most certainly true.

The Medieval Stage is the first place I ever encountered Madeleine. It is also the only place I ever found a bibliographic citation to her. After the preface and contents, Sir Edmund provides a twenty-eight page "List of Authorities." Once, on page xxx between:

Maclagan. The Games and Diversions of Argyleshire. By R.
 C. Maclagan, 1901. *and*

Magnin. Les Origines du Théâtre moderne, ou Histoire du
 Génie dramatique depuis le Ier jusqu'au xvie Siècle. Par
 C. Magnin, 1838.

I found:
La Madeleine Voilée or The Life of a Lady of Beauvais, in
 English, dating about 1600 AD being the translation of an
 undiscovered French manuscript from the fifteenth century. Edited by S. H. Roud, 1826. [Society of Antiquaries
 of the Continent.]

It should come as no surprise then, that Madeleine made several
appearances in *The Medieval Stage*. In the book, not on the stage,
to be clear. Well, except maybe once riding a donkey. It depends on
how literal you are in defining "stage."

*   *   *

My home is in Flatfield, a burgeoning town on the prairies.
From where I live, I can walk to the edge of town in a few minutes.
The street that travels past my house disappears into a vast sea of
clover, bees, and revery, to borrow Emily Dickinson's tableau. It is a
short walk past a thicket of saskatoon, past the final row of houses
lined up along one side of the road, lined up as if the shimmering
flood of grain licking the ditch across the road would wash over
and swallow them had they settled nearer the fields. This has been
my ocean. This is where the tides heave in land-locked Alberta, for
me, at any rate.

I often wonder why the story chose me. Or if not that, how the
story came to occupy the place where I live. It may have something
to do with the gift of faith, but that's doubtful. My life, however lacking in some dimensions of human relationship, was busy enough
and, to be truthful, blessed enough—children, friends, more than

he think? Incredulous, I answered with my own question: "Aren't *you* planning to accept yours?" What else could he be thinking to do while I was in school? Yes, apparently he was planning to accept the scholarship. He intended to follow through. But he seemed to think I would reconsider mine. That I would—or should—change my plans. This was confusing for me. Was he annoyed that I had been awarded a little more money? It wasn't significantly more, really. Did he think maybe I wasn't graduate-school material? Did he think I belonged in the home? Was he really that traditional? Why didn't I ask these questions? Why did I let him make these vague assumptions about me? I don't know. I just don't know. I was too confused to challenge him. Finally, mid-February, he spit it out. I found out where he was going with all this.

Well, I didn't really tell him how his decision sat with me. I cried, that's all. Partly because there was a lot going on for me, too. I was sort of counting on getting married. I meant to do the right thing. Maybe I should have given my perspective—but he didn't ask and I was a little in awe, I suppose. To think my own Jim would someday be a priest. One thing was fairly certain. Jim was choosing the greater good—to use St. Augustine's reasoning.

Augustine's philosophy was on my mind those days. Jim and I were taking a course in Christian medieval philosophy. Father Fulbright taught the course—an ancient, balding man. I mostly liked him. He laced his lectures with pithy comments and homely illustrations. My notes were full of them. Like when he spoke of Augustine's understanding of good and evil. Since God created the world, everything in it strives toward the good. But, Augustine goes on to say, God did not make all things equal. The multiplicity of creation, the variety of substances, requires the subordination of one thing to another. You can't just have woolly lambs—that's how Father Fulbright explained it. The challenge for human beings is to seek the greatest good. Obviously, it is good to serve God. This is Augustine's point, really. You can't go wrong, there. So if Jim wanted to commit to dedicated service to God and set everything else aside, well, that's pretty good, alright. It just didn't feel very good to me.

So much for goodness. As for evil—this is where Augustine blew me away—evil does not really exist. Since everything that exists is created by God, all substances are good. If evil were a substance it would be good. Therefore, it is not a substance at all. It doesn't exist at all. Evil is just a big nothing. But substances can be corrupted. Only to the degree that something is good can it be evil. Fulbright said that only a good nuclear bomb can do harm. If there were no good in it, it could not be corrupted. Evil deprives the good, prevents creation from reaching the perfection for which it was intended. This is called privation. And at this point I really began to understand something about evil. Or experience it, at any rate. A big nothing.

I found the idea of a good bomb confusing. If I understand him correctly, Augustine argues that something good and complete should also be considered in light of its potential. The bomb's potential to do harm and deprive life gives it a capacity for evil. It can cause a lot of nothing. This subordinates it to benign things. Potential is also the difference between the human foetus and that of a pig. They look alike at six weeks gestation but their potential is different. A human infant would be a very unsatisfactory thing to a pig. A woman giving birth to a perfect pig would feel deprived. No question. I actually dreamed something like that when I was pregnant. I gave birth to a rabbit. I was definitely disappointed. So the value of anything, the hierarchy of goodness, is informed by potential.

There is also a difference between privation and absence. A penguin has wings, but can't fly as other birds do. This is absence. There's no harm in absence. A womb can be perfect, and still never carry a child. This is absence, too. This is not evil except, obviously, if you want to get pregnant and can't. That could be privation, maybe. Augustine didn't go there—nor did Fulbright. But if you break that penguin's wing, that's privation. The wing is no longer the perfect thing it was meant to be, even if it was perfectly useless to begin with.

I have thought about this a lot. The nothingness still haunts me.

I go along from day to day and suddenly there it is. Nothing. Take my rose bush, for example. I have a huge rosebush in my garden. Every year its branches generate brimming buds, full of promise. I can smell the roses as soon as I walk into my back yard, their fragrance is one of the sweetest signs of summer to me. This redolent shrub never fully blooms—the roses never open. I have puzzled over this, I have tried everything. Compost, Rotenone, Safer Soap. Augustine says nature inclines to express itself completely. A rosebud that doesn't open never completes its life cycle. This is privation in being, when something falls short of its own fulness. Every summer I confront the big nothing when the buds droop and die unopened.

Later on I discovered the problem of the rose. The petals form perfect buds. But when I cut the buds and coax them open in a rose bowl the inside is eaten away. There is nothing at the heart of the bloom except a browning emptiness. I could have asked Denise. She has a greenhouse. She would have known, but summer is her busy season. We rarely see each other in the summer. So I did my own research and I found out about a little insect called the rose curculio or—rose weevil. I should have guessed! It's right there in the name. Evil eating the bloom into nothing—that pretty much sums it up.

A weevil is maybe a quarter of an inch long, bright red with a black underside, and a long snout. These weevils make tiny holes in buds and deposit their eggs at the heart of the rose. Small white legless grubs hatch from the eggs and feed within the buds. When they are finished feeding, they drop to the ground where they overwinter in the soil. There's no way to get rid of them, except by plucking the buds and destroying them. One year I prepared a little hell-fire for those bugs—even though they were being the best bugs they knew how to be. Of course, that meant I had to destroy the buds as well. There were no sweet smells that summer and the next year the weevils were back regardless. They are good weevils, which is why they can do harm. The good weevil corrupts. The rose bush, deprived of perfection, aborts the bloom. How about that? It's back to subordination. For me there's more potential good in a rose than in a weevil.

Despite this corruption, though, I have to admit my rose bush is perfectly fragrant. Biotech companies have developed magnificent large-bloomed long-stemmed roses to last for days in water. Their blooms are absolutely perfect. They have no smell at all, those perfect long-stemmed roses. It's not just a problem of absence, either. They have suffered corruption. Some really big nothing has messed with the rose and packed off with its scent. My roses, on the other hand, give me a holy scent even when I know they will disappoint, even when I know they will never open. Sometimes the appearance of perfection isn't enough. And sometimes an empty promise seems pretty much the best you'll ever get.

I finished the term in a fog, but I graduated. Jim and I remained "friends." He was solicitous about my well-being. He asked pleasant, hollow questions about ordinary, mundane things. If I'd had the perspective I do now, I probably would have realized that I was just a detour for him. To give him credit, he tried to will that detour into a thoroughfare for awhile, but in the end, he didn't manage it. He had contemplated the cloth long before he knew me. He just wasn't sure about it until he seriously considered not becoming a priest.

After that, I didn't go to church again, except maybe once or twice, until I got married. I figured if that's the way God wanted to work, fine then. But God couldn't expect me to just deal with it and be thankful. Even if Jim was choosing the greater good, there were some pretty negative implications for me in all this. But that wasn't the point, I guess. Priests don't marry. For some reason priests shouldn't have kids. I got the message. The relationship with Jim was over. I pretty much stopped worrying about my faith—I lost interest in going to church at all. That was Jim's baby, really. Not that I was completely uninterested. But once Jim had extracted himself from my life there didn't seem to be much point in going. Not at least until I had babies of my own.

GREEN

It seemed to me that you had put on a green tunic as well, a symbol of your grace which is never dried up but always flourishing and green in the lowly valley of humility.

—Gertrude of Helfta

I know nothing, except what everyone knows—if there when Grace dances, I should dance.

—W.H. Auden, "Whitsunday in Kirchstetten"

I wasn't sure what to do after graduation. Had I done a graduate degree, the next two years would have been sewn up. I would need a summer job, just a summer job—nothing more. Graduate school would have deferred long-term decisions for a while longer. But the more I thought about it, the more the idea unnerved me. A new city, a new campus, where to live—that was intimidating enough. But Jim around every corner? I couldn't bear the thought. Instead, I took a job on campus—a clerical job, typing and editing for the alumni association. I had not intended to continue the job into the fall, but there wasn't any reason to quit. I had student loans to pay and I was planning to move out on my own anyway.

It was a dry and dusty summer. The heat made me listless. The drought quickly swallowed up every little spit of rain that came.

I spent my walk to work scanning the sky for wisps of clouds to pray into rain. It was a lonely summer. The campus kept busy with conferences, seminars, a music camp, but my friends had graduated and moved on. Denise was away, too—off falling in love somewhere in Kansas, although ostensibly learning the greenhouse business from her aunt. By that time, Gil had a job in the city. He often came home on weekends to see Mom and me, but he spent most of his time hanging out with Miles Weir, an engineering friend who had taken a position in town—a position Mom thought Gil should have applied for. Gil's regular visits offered some relief to an otherwise dreary pattern. I looked forward to those weekends.

There was one other deviation from this pattern. Jim paid a surprise visit mid-August. He showed up unannounced, as if the long months since he last stood on that threshold had evaporated into the searing sky. When I opened the door to him, he took me in his arms and held me. For a moment I lost myself there in his embrace. I even cried. We took a walk to the edge of town down that prairie levee going nowhere. He said he'd been thinking. He'd changed his mind. He couldn't face such a long lonely road. Maybe he could look into ministry in the Anglican or Lutheran church. Or maybe he could teach. Would I please go with him to Ontario?

The catch in my chest could have been anger. Or maybe grief. I don't know. Maybe love. Maybe anger and grief and love, all of the above. I couldn't answer at all. It was too late. *No, no. I don't want that on my head. I will not be the occasion for your inevitable misery. A vocation is a vocation. I carry enough of a burden from the whole business.* I found my voice and said no. What's gone is gone. That was all. I don't know how I did it. We walked back, hopelessly. Several times I almost spoke, almost retracted. I wanted to comfort him, I wanted him to live happily ever after. I don't know where my resolve came from. I don't know how I could be so hardhearted. It may have had something to do with forgiveness or the lack of it. Jim left me at the door and walked hesitantly back to the dry road and away. Inside I cried.

That was Friday. The weekend lasted so long. Thank goodness,

Gil was around. We did a few of the usual things—miniature golfing, an evening at the lake. Sunday afternoon, Gil went out with Miles to the water tower. Gil figured Miles needed an initiation into local culture. An engineer should have some practical knowledge of hydraulics. Miles needed to climb the water tower. Every town kid did it at one time or another. Miles was a city boy.

I read for awhile and helped Mom get supper on—something quick— hamburgers, garden tomatoes and yesterday's potato salad. I stood outside, minding the grill. The air weighed heavy. It hardly moved at all. Gradually the sky grew dark. I watched the west, where most of our weather comes from. On the horizon I could see the dust rising to the rain. *Thank God*. I scooped up the burgers and brought them inside. I went outside again to sit on the stoop and wait for the storm to blow in. In whistled the wind, snatching up scraps of paper, dry leaves, a forgotten garage sale sign and discarded grocery bags. Away they blew.

The rain came hard and heavy. I lingered a moment in the battering downpour, then ducked in the back door just minutes before Gil and Miles came blustering in the front. They were soaked and laughing, water dripping everywhere. I got towels to help them dry off before supper. Gil changed and offered some dry clothes to Miles. No thanks, he said. He didn't mind this at all. He'd been wanting to get wet all summer. He sat at the kitchen table on one of the sturdy old chrome chairs, the ones with the grey simulated-marble plastic seats. His dampness certainly wasn't going to hurt the furniture. I sat in my usual spot around the corner to his left. Miles rested his arm on the table inches away from me. I began to watch a drop trickling down his arm. It detoured around a curve of muscle moving toward a small hollow at the bend in his arm. Like a rivulet through a field, it rippled between the little standing hairs on his arm. Follicles stood erect at the roots, brandishing hairs like swords. Goose bumps formed little mountains. The drop bent around them, spilled into the crease at his elbow and dribbled onto the table.

Gil invaded. "Whatever are you staring at, Janine?"

I smiled up at Miles, ran my finger against his skin down the path the drop had taken, then stroked once along his arm with my hand, gathering up the damp, collecting the moisture. "You're wet."

He laughed. I was embarrassed for a moment. I did it so spontaneously. *Whatever was I thinking? Where did that come from?* But when he turned to me, I knew it was okay. His eyes sparkled. So refreshing. He had such an uncomplicated way about him. Odd that I hadn't noticed how attractive he was. And what nice arms. You wouldn't think a man's arm could be so—appealing.

I brought my thoughts back to the table. I passed the salad to Miles. Despite a bit of awkwardness, I felt a kind of exhilaration. There was something so clean and fresh about him. I'd known Miles for quite awhile, in fact, but there was no history. That was attractive too. I don't really know what it was, after all, maybe the weather, but that trickle of water was all it took. That's how I came to marry Miles. Obviously not just then and there. I think it was that furious rain after the barren heat of my last encounter with Jim that set me up. And the long hot summer. And the lonely lunches at deserted picnic tables in the quad.

Maybe it was a bit impulsive. Well, it was. But I had been at such a loss. There was something so nice and predictable, so safe, so stable, so local, about Miles. So what if I had dreamed of travelling to do graduate research somewhere—maybe in France? What was the point of that? I probably wouldn't have come up with anything worthwhile regardless. Besides, Miles was anxious to have everything settled—his work, his household, his kinship, his future. My mother found this admirable. And there's something to be said for being swept away in the moment. We were married the following May.

I'm not sure any of this is important—to the story, I mean. Of course it has importance for me. It's my life, after all. But Madeleine's story entered my life without any point of reference, so far as I can see. I had decided I didn't need to do history. I wasn't trying to revive old dreams. I don't recall having any feelings about that at all. But because of the way the story came to me, it's hard to extract it from my daily orbit.

After Miles and I married, I continued with my job at the college. When Adam—named for my father—was born three years later, I began to work at home instead, typing papers and conference presentations for the academic staff of the college. It was a good arrangement. Adam seemed to take comfort in the clicking of the typewriter and would sit in his little chair fingering a toy or teething on a carrot for an hour at a time. I didn't know, until Kit was born, what a cooperative little fellow he was. With two little ones, especially because Kit was a more spirited—some would say difficult— baby, it was much harder to get the work done. I mostly worked at night when the boys were sleeping. But it pleased Miles that I was contributing even though I was usually exhausted. We had built our house just down the street from my mother's and the debt load really made him uncomfortable. We weren't in over our heads or anything, but that's Miles for you. He prefers to pay everything up front. Life isn't pay-as-you-go for Miles.

This was a problem when it came to holidays. Miles was not interested in wasting time and money for no good reason. His idea of a holiday was to drive to the city for Thanksgiving dinner with his family. For the first few years I was okay with this, but eventually I realized that even my mother on her small income had made a point of taking me and Gil on outings for a change of scenery. I began to plan one or two vacation days a month, finding things to do in the city or spending a day at a provincial park in the summer time. Miles didn't think much of it, but soon appreciated the fact that he didn't have to be home from work in time for supper when I and the boys were busy elsewhere. By the time Kit was three, I took it up a notch and rented a lakeside cabin for two nights. It was cheap enough and everything I spent came from my personal allowance. After that, I made a point of taking these little holiday trips several times a year. It was good recreation for me and the boys enjoyed it. Eventually, I realized I also liked getting Miles out of the picture.

I never travelled more than a day's distance with the boys. Small children aren't easy riders. In many ways it was more work to go than it was to stay home. I took great pains to ensure the boys had toys, books, paper, crayons, snacks and little surprise presents to open. Still the inevitable squabbles bubbled up. At those times, I sang songs with them, especially rounds or songs that add an element with every verse to keep them—and me—alert and interested. My sons learned a fair number of songs this way until they developed the signature self-respect of school boys that won't tolerate such questionable homespun entertainment.

There was a lot of green in those songs: "Oh, I had a rooster, and my rooster pleased me, I fed my rooster 'neath the greenwood tree…"

— "The green grass grew all around…"

— "Come follow me, to the greenwood tree…"

— "Green grow the rushes, ho."

I would drive and sing: "I'll sing you one-ho!" Adam and Kit would join in singing:

"Green grow the rushes-ho!"

"What is your one-ho?" I sang back:

"One is one and all alone and ever more shall be so!"

"I'll sing you two-ho!"

"Green grow the rushes-ho! What is your two-ho?" my little choristers chortled back.

"Two, two the lily-white boys, clothèd all in green-ho! One is one and all alone and ever more shall be so!" I wondered about those lily-white boys. I wondered about the numbers, all of them, but about those lily-white boys clothèd all in green-ho in particular.

I'll sing you three-ho!

Green grow the rushes-ho! What is your three-ho?

"Three, three, the rivals! I'll sing you two, two the lily-white boys…"

I researched the song. There are several versions. A Latin manuscript from 1630 explains "two" as the Old and New Testaments of the Christian Bible, "three" as the patriarchs. They don't say which patriarchs and why they are rivals. I think it's just as likely the song dates from the papal schism in the early fifteenth century when the pope and anti-pope were replaced by a third pope, but the other two wouldn't step down.

They don't explain how you get the Old and New Testaments out of two lily-white boys clothèd all in green-ho either. The key is probably in the colours. Colour symbolism was a pretty big deal a few hundred years ago. White—purity, innocence, truth—the pure clear light of revelation shining through stories of great spiritual struggles and adultery, treachery and murder. Those last three are probably the clothèd-all-in-green-ho part. Green—youth, spirit, joy, abundance, fecundity—had a lot to do with passion—mostly amourous passion—in the Middle Ages. The body of words is white—wrapped in human desiring.

Perhaps. My research wasn't exactly definitive. And the information highway didn't exist back then. So I drove along with my two small sons crooning from the back seat continually asking what my one or two or three-ho could possibly be. But there's something very solitary about spending time with small children. However much you love the child, it's not always easy to love the level of discourse. So I would sing together with them, but my thoughts travelled solo. I had lots of time to mull over all sorts of problems. Lots of time to think about those colourful imponderables or the layers of meaning in the symbolism of medieval art.

When Kit was a baby, I took the boys on a day trip to a book sale in Edmonton. The university was weeding its collection. I know—not the most amusing outing for children, but we only stayed an hour and we went downtown to the children's library too. I made a great find: *Religious Art in France XIII Century: a Study in Mediaeval Iconography and its Sources of Inspiration* by Emile Mâle. The university had other copies in their collection. The pages in my copy are so brittle they crack if you read them too fast. It was published in 1913. It's one of the biggest books in my history hoard. For a while I would read nothing else. That's how I came upon my own theory about those lily-white boys, clothèd all in green-ho.

I figure those lily-white boys are the two Adams. Given the

medieval love of symmetry and of Old Testament images prefiguring New Testament events, I think those lily-white boys really represent the Adam of Genesis and the new Adam of the Gospels. After all, what could be more pure and innocent than a new creation in a fresh, brand-new world? There's definitely something green about Adam, something youthful and desiring. Absolutely. And Jesus, the green shoot from the stem of Jesse with white for all things made new—the second Adam. Clothed in green, God fully human; Adam, the image and likeness of God, wrapped up in human desiring. Two ways to think about being human. It was all there in the song for me. Like the programs of stained-glass windows in gothic cathedrals, you have to ruminate around the subject awhile before you see what's sparkling before your eyes.

These may not be the usual preoccupations of a mother of two small boys. I felt a little parched, I guess. Marriage and motherhood had lost their freshness, which is probably why I remember so exactly the day I first encountered her—Madeleine. It was my tenth anniversary. I should say, it was *our* tenth anniversary. I had made reservations for dinner at the Homesteader, a snug little restaurant close to home. Around three o'clock that afternoon the babysitter called to say she couldn't make it. She said she was coming down with something. I said I hoped she felt better soon and I would work something out. Not that there was anything to work out. My mother would be at work until 8:00, or later. Miles's parents were an hour away in the city. So I just canceled the reservation. I was, in fact, more relieved than disappointed. It was less stressful to stay home anyway. I felt a little guilty for that. To compensate, I decided to make a nice meal and we could celebrate at home. I called Miles at work. He said he would be working late. That was fine with me. We would have dinner after Adam and Kit went to bed.

I got Kit bundled up—we met Adam coming home from school, and walked the three blocks to our neighborhood IGA. I picked up fixings for dinner. When Miles got home just after eight, the boys were in bed, the table was set, dinner was ready. I had even changed into my silk charmeuse blouse. It looked pretty sexy with my good jeans.

I plated our dinner and brought it to the table. We didn't talk much. Miles said it was good.

After dinner, I got up to make coffee for dessert.

"No coffee for me," Miles said. "I have a full day tomorrow."

Well, fine, my crème caramel is good enough to stand alone. I served it in the delicate crystal bowls we got from his aunt as a wedding gift. I set one before Miles, one for me, sat down and tasted it.

"What are you grinning at?" Miles asked.

"Oh, just that it's perfect."

"What's perfect?" As if "perfect" was a dirty word.

"The crème caramel."

"Oh." Neither of us would have known what to do with a perfect anything else. When we'd finished, I began to clear the dishes.

"I guess I'll turn in," he said, and stood to leave.

"How about a kiss goodnight?" I asked dutifully. It was, after all, our anniversary.

"Oh, of course." He gave me a peck on the cheek and disappeared upstairs.

I cleared the table, put away the leftover dessert—Adam and Kit would be happy, they love my crème caramel—washed the dishes and left the pots to soak. As I performed these rituals I found myself feeling a familiar heaviness—a little bored and angry, a little sad, a little desperate. Well, so much for that. So much for having it all— house, children, husband, income—*the full catastrophe*—to quote *Zorba the Greek*, more or less. Zorba also said, "As for women, you make fun of me that I love them. How can I not love them? They are such poor weak creatures, and they give you all they've got." Well, wasn't that the truth—at least the part about who does the giving. But I'm fairly certain Zorba didn't turn in early. At least not by himself.

I wasn't about to give Miles the satisfaction of my company at this juncture, even if he wanted it. I curled up in my mohair chair instead and took a book from my history hoard. I think it was the first volume of *The Medieval Stage*. I wasn't really paying attention, but it has to have been "Village Festivals" that I fell upon, the chapter that begins:

> The central fact of the agricultural festivals is the presence in
> the village of the fertilization spirit in the visible and tangible
> form of flowers and green foliage or of the fruits of the earth.
> Thus when the peasants do their 'observaunce to a morn of
> May,' great boughs of hawthorn are cut before daybreak in
> the woods, and carried, with other seasonable leafage and
> blossom, into the village street.

Following that, I read the account of Madeleine, a young—
perhaps she would have been thirteen or fourteen—high-born
woman, who, falling in with the common folk, decked herself cap-
à-pie with leaves and flowers to bandy about in the greenwood
gathering the May. Masquerading thus she passed in the mist of
early morning unremarked by the general population. I can't
remember what Sir Edmund meant to illustrate by this example.
The upshot of Madeleine's escapade was that, perhaps by design, a
young fellow, also of noble birth, encountered her there and played
Robin to her Maid Marian. At cockcrow this Guy de Roquehautain,
as he was called, planted a bough of hawthorn at the feet of
Madeleine. I later came to understand that for Madeleine, this act
constituted a betrothal. Did people of gentle birth ever betroth
themselves this way? I am quite certain the manner of courtship and
betrothal generated by these gatherings in the woods was a highly
unusual or at least an irregular arrangement for classes of people
who traditionally regarded marriage as a means to protect property
and expand their sphere of influence. Such a carefully negotiated
marriage was Madeleine's expectation, too, but a marriage to de
Roquehautain would no doubt have served the ambitions of both
families. These issues were of no concern to Sir Edmund, however.
He was busy documenting the links between festivals and the
development of theatre. The thing that caught my imagination
at the time was Madeleine's unguarded and fearless errand in the
dark wood. I could feel the sappy green growth crowded in her

embrace—gathering May. I wish I had written it down, what I read that evening. Or maybe I don't. There is something about the wash of that memory—something so *green*.

Fair enough. It was May, after all. I do remember thinking about the coincidence of the month (although May shows up everywhere in that book). I do remember reading fifty pages past this spot where Sir Edmund says "…the desire of the queen and her maidens to dance alone, recalls the conventional freedom of women from restraint in May, the month of their ancient sex-festival." I found that bid for women's autonomy appealing, dancing alone as I seem to do anyway. *Tra-la, it's May. As if. As if any of that lush revelry has anything to do with me.* Whatever it was I read then, I haven't found it since—anywhere. There's plenty about Jacks i' the green, and May-poles, and the mixing of pagan practice with the rites of the church, and wooing good weather for the crops, and courting rituals. Yes, the rest is all there.

This is how I remember it. I did not think I needed to take notes. The wonderful thing about owning a book—or so I thought—the wonderful thing about setting it on your shelf, is that it is always there for you. It may take awhile to find the page, but you can find the words, you can find thoughts already formed and expressed. You can find them again and again, if you really want to. Only, I've looked again and again and never found that part about Madeleine.

UNIVERSALS

I am not young enough to know everything.

—Oscar Wilde

By the time Kit was in grade five, Miles was getting impatient with my home-based business. From my point of view, it was the perfect arrangement. I was able to see the boys off in the morning and to meet them after school and walk home with them. As far as work goes, it was interesting to read the ideas of the local academics as I typed. Trying to make sense of someone's handwriting is also a good way to learn. Amazing what you come up with. Phone calls to the authors to clarify various points gave me a sense of collegiality, even if it wasn't always a mutual thing. I felt my work was valuable. If anyone asked me how I spent my time, I didn't say I was a stay-at-home mom who typed papers for pay. I said I ran a business called Scribe Secretarial Services. And I was accomplishing more than just loving my kids and making dinner.

When I was typing those papers, I learned to make sense of language, terminology, categories and other things from several disciplines. For example, it would not have occurred to me to describe myself as an "esthetic character." But when I typed up one professor's lecture on Kierkegaard, I began to wonder about it:

The esthetic character can be best described as the ego-centric who lives in the moment for the moment by the whim of his impulses, placing the meaning of life in whatever catches his eye at any given moment. The esthetic life includes the epicurean as well as "all mediocrities, in so far as their lives are determined essentially by the contrast between the agreeable and the disagreeable" (169, Swenson).

Don't know who the Swenson person is. I kept the excerpt, but didn't bother to note the book cited. At any rate, if anyone had ever called me an esthete before I typed that paper, I think I would have been complimented. But to think of myself in company with "all mediocrities" just because I prefer to live an agreeable life, well, that seems a little harsh. Who doesn't? Besides, I was pretty sure I could also qualify as a somewhat ethical character, given the description:

The ethical character, on the other hand, ideally lives in canon with every other law-abiding citizen, and by more rigorous values than esthetic values. These ethical values we may assume to be universal values that hold for all people at all times.

As a law-abiding citizen, it follows that I do embrace *more rigorous values*. The author didn't bother to say what qualified as a universal value. I couldn't say either. I supposed life would be one. Also a means of living, I would think. What was clear is that Miles thought our means weren't adequate and my values of enjoying my work and being home for the boys, however agreeable to me, were whimsical in the larger picture. So Miles wanted to know what I planned to do with my time. Surely I didn't intend to continue my contract typing and editing? It seemed a little precarious to defend my position based on the fact that I found it agreeable, knowing what I did about esthetes.

I tried to talk seriously with Miles about it. I told him I remembered what it was like to come home to an empty house every day after school. I thought it was good for the boys to feel loved and secure and to have someone to talk to—and to feel free to invite friends home with them. I even suggested that this sense of security for children constituted a universal value. Miles raised his eyebrow at that. I hate when he does that. It's as if his right eyebrow has a marionette thread attached in the middle and some great puppeteer in the sky tugs it whenever I say something preposterous. Not that I say preposterous things, only that Miles and the puppeteer think so.

And though he was serious about me finding some other occupation, Miles wasn't ready to offer any ideas about how exactly I should go about doing this. Perhaps I should go back to school and get a master's degree in history? I suggested. I could commute to the city. I found the idea quite appealing.

"Come on, Janine! Do you really think that would pay? Stop farting around." Obviously, Miles didn't think getting a master's degree was a useful plan. I found his comment particularly offensive. It was as if the more agreeable something seemed to me, the less likely it was that Miles would find any value in it. I began to comb the want ads in the daily paper. The prospects were pretty limited. I had no intention of becoming a gas jockey. As disagreeable as that may be to me, I was somewhat certain that Miles would concur at least on this point. Still, I didn't risk telling him about jobs like that. Besides, I was getting a lot of secretarial work just then, and I didn't have time to do much more than scan the ads every day. And, of course, make dinner, do the laundry, help the boys with their homework—the usual.

Then one day a more promising ad appeared. "Receptionist/Secretary. Agreeable, organized person with pleasant telephone manner, good secretarial skills and ethical character. Must be able to take direction and willing to perform a variety of tasks as required. Daytime hours, some evenings." There it was again, the idea of ethical character. They were clearly looking for someone with rigorous values. I had only recently typed that Kierkegaard paper; otherwise I may have thought they just wanted someone trustworthy. The agreeable part seemed to be a bit of a contradiction in terms. I thought I may bring that up if I got an interview.

I quickly wrote up a cover letter and sent my resumé to the post-office-box address. I mentioned it to Miles at dinner that evening. I told him I expected my knowledge of terminology and typing experience from the past few years would stand me in good stead. I did not mention the part about the ethical character since his right eyebrow was already twitching a bit. It seemed to do that whenever I expressed a little confidence in myself.

I didn't have to wait long for the phone to ring. Postal service is pretty good in town. I figured that since I mailed my application on Monday, the soonest I could expect to hear anything would be Wednesday. Sure enough, it was just after one o'clock on Wednesday that a Sister Colette phoned to arrange for an interview. Could I come tomorrow? I hadn't anticipated the job would be in a church. I wasn't counting on my rigorous values having to withstand the scrutiny of a nun.

Thursday morning after Kit and Adam were safely off to school, I surveyed my closet and took out the only option that presented itself—a medium length grey woolen skirt with a nice sweater jacket. I didn't want to wear dress pants—not that it's unchristian or anything but I thought a skirt would give a better impression. I based all my sartorial savvy on the wardrobe of a professor in the psychology department who I think someone told me was a nun, although I couldn't be sure since she was always called "*Dr.* Susanna Bell." It seemed to me that the grey outfit was the only one in my closet that she would have deigned to wear to work. ·

My interview was at ten-thirty. I arrived ten minutes early and found Sister Colette and Father Eugene already waiting for me. "I owe my success in life to having been always a quarter of an hour beforehand," Father Eugene stretched out his hand to greet me. "I'm Father Eugene," he continued. "Do you know who said that?"

"Pardon me. Father Eugene?"

"Yes. Do you know who said that?"

"Excuse me, who said what?" *Good Lord, Janine, pay attention.*

"Do you know who said, 'I owe my success in life to having been always a quarter of an hour beforehand'?"

"Oh! Well, you did, Father. Just now, as I was coming in the door."

Father Eugene shook his head indulgently. "I was quoting Lord Nelson."

"Um, oh!" I got nervous thinking he would now want me to tell him who Lord Nelson was. This gave me a sinking feeling. At that moment I couldn't remember a thing about Lord Nelson except that he fought in the Napoleonic Wars. The one thing I associated with Nelson, rightly or wrongly, was that he lost an eye in battle somewhere. I winced, and unconsciously rubbed my eye.

"Did you get something in your eye?" he asked.

"Oh—no. I was just thinking about Lord Nelson getting shot in the eye…" I was going to continue by saying I wasn't sure about that, that Nelson is not my era, but Father Eugene interrupted.

"Well, that's interesting. I didn't know that."

I couldn't explain myself before Sister Colette, a gaunt woman with short, straight, salt-and-pepper hair, interjected, "And I'm Sister Colette. It's nice to meet you, Janine." She seemed to be doing her best to make me more comfortable. "Come this way, please."

I followed her and Father Eugene into an office, where things went from bad to worse. They quickly reviewed my credentials and references. They seemed satisfied with this. But did I know anybody in the parish? "Oh, I'm sure I do." I responded, hoping they wouldn't ask for names.

"Can you give me a few names, for example?" said Father Eugene.

I thought, dismally, for a moment. I should have done my homework. I could have asked at the grocery store about who are the pillars in the church. Surely someone would have known. And of course I'd met parents in the school who attend. But I couldn't come up with any names under pressure. "Um, nobody comes to mind just now, but I'm sure I must know some people in the parish. This is not that big of a town, you know."

"True enough," said Father Eugene. This didn't seem to bother him as much as I thought it would.

"Oh, there's Marilee. Marilee Clark. She goes here," I volunteered. *Good going Janine. Pick the teenage mom who lives with her parents and babysits once in a while.*

Father Eugene turned to Sister Colette. "Do you know Marilee Clark, Sister?"

"Yes, I do. She's a sweet girl."

"Of course, my family came here for our sons' baptisms," I offered. As if that would help.

"Oh, so you're Catholic then." This seemed to be good news.

"Well, my husband isn't but our sons go to the Catholic school." *Why didn't I think of that sooner?* "Actually, Mrs. Olcott is a parishioner. I know her. She's my son Kit's teacher."

"That's good. That's just fine." Father Eugene seemed in a hurry now. I suppose it was getting on to a quarter of an hour beforehand for his next commitment. "Sister Colette, will see you to the door." Then he was gone.

"Father Eugene is a bit brusque, but he's a good man," said Sister Colette hoping to soften the impression. There was no reason for her to apologize. She had been perfectly polite. It wasn't her fault if Father Eugene was a busy man. I doubted he was very impressed with my application. Why didn't they just advertise the position in the parish? How could they expect an unsuspecting applicant to know who goes to church?

Sister Colette saw me to the door just as Father Eugene had said she would. She shook my hand and gave me an encouraging smile. I took this as confirmation that I had no hope of getting the job.

I told Miles about the interview at supper. "I think I would have done better if I'd gotten there earlier."

"What were you thinking? There's no excuse for being late to an interview."

"I wasn't late," I countered. "I just said I think it would have gone better if I'd gotten there earlier. Father Eugene is always a quarter of an hour beforehand. I was only ten minutes beforehand."

Miles seemed skeptical, as much about the odd turn of phrase as at my explanation, I suppose. I didn't elaborate.

* * *

The next evening while I was clearing the supper dishes, the phone rang. It was Father Eugene offering me the job. "Will you accept?"

"Certainly," I answered.

"Wonderful!" He sounded genuinely pleased. "And can you begin a week from Monday?"

"Yes. What time would you like me to be there?"

"9:30 is fine," he said. I wrote 9:15!!! in bold strokes on the calendar. Peculiar and strange. They must not have had any other applicants.

* * *

I thought that if I were going to be working at the church, I should probably attend mass from time to time—and it wouldn't hurt to show up once before I started work. On Sunday, I went to the nine o'clock mass. I got there at twenty to-. Father Eugene was chatting with an elderly lady but nodded approvingly as I came in. I sat toward the back of the church, off to the side, watching people come in, genuflect, and take a seat. The Kellys came in. *The Kellys! I could have mentioned the Kellys. Such a happy couple.* And their youngest son Stephen, the star student in Adam's class. *No points for bringing Stephen to church, though.* They sat down just a few rows in front of me, sitting properly close together, their sleeves just brushing. Within seconds, Pat stretched his left arm along the pew beside him, slightly turning his right shoulder away from Fiona. Soon Fiona similarly stretched her right arm along the back of the pew turning her left shoulder away from Pat. I don't know why I noticed this. Fiona was looking absently toward a plaster relief of one of the stations of the cross. Pat was checking out the people passing in the aisle. He began to run his thumb along his ring finger, catching his wedding band with his neatly trimmed nail, pushing it up to the tip of his finger and sliding it back down again. Back and forth, again and again. *Oops. Almost pushed it off!* Why was I so heartened to observe this? I don't know. I kind of liked the idea of there being tension between them—of Pat maybe feeling a little restless, wondering how it would feel to be single again. They'd never done anything to offend me, really. *They are always so damned pleasant. I just don't believe it.* Then Pat leaned over and whispered something in Fiona's ear. They both smiled, brought their arms back to their sides and sat comfortably together. Then Pat casually stretched his right arm along the back of the pew behind Fiona resting his hand on her shoulder. *Oh well.*

At about five minutes to nine a young woman wearing a tight-fitting black sweater approached the microphone. "The psalm response for the first Sunday in Lent can be found on page…" I dutifully found my place and tried to sing along. We sang the response once and she sat down again. This was just a rehearsal. Soon the organ bellowed out a few notes and we sang the opening hymn as Father Eugene and company processed down the aisle.

An old man, who must have been in his late eighties, manned the organ. He did a good job with that hymn, rocking himself forward and back as he played. He was also pretty good accompanying the black-sweatered singer when she led the psalm. He played a rousing—if somewhat sloppy—acclamation before the reading of the Gospel. But later in the liturgy, when Father Eugene said "… and so with all the choirs of angels we join in their unending hymn of praise," we just stood waiting to join those choirs of angels. And waiting. The church was silent. The young woman at the microphone was ready to begin. She looked over to the organist whose eyes were fixed on Father Eugene. Father Eugene returned his gaze and nodded repeatedly to go ahead. The organist continued to stare absently at the priest. "Mr. Fletcher—Mr. Fletcher" the singer whispered audibly. "'Holy, holy', Mr. Fletcher." He sat transfixed. "Paul!" she hissed, "play the 'Holy, holy!'" Paul startled, gave himself a shake and began to play. *Well, thank goodness. You don't have to be perfect to work here.*

After mass, Sister Colette greeted me warmly. The Kellys were

delighted to see me. "Do come downstairs for a pancake breakfast,"
they urged. "Stephen's youth group is raising funds for famine relief." I could hardly say "Oh, no. I have to go home to wake my
sleeping sons and make them Sunday breakfast." I just said I was
so sorry to miss it, but I really did have to run. On my way home, I
wondered about universal values. What was the difference between
raising money to feed the hungry and rousting your children even
before their stomachs growled so you could make a special breakfast for them? I began to think about the fact that I found our Sunday breakfasts agreeable. Mercifully, the boys were already up and
quite hungry when I got home. And remarkably, Miles was starting
the sausages.

Breakfast was good. Adam and Kit were animated and even
Miles seemed relatively happy. I know it pleased him that I was going to start my job soon. Me being away when he got up hadn't
hurt, either. He likes to have the house to himself. Yes, breakfast was
good. I decided to go along with Augustine in this regard. There was
no apparent privation, no apparent absence. So breakfast was good,
even if it was just because I didn't know better. For the moment I
was content to let Stephen Kelly worry about the greater good.

A week Monday I arrived at my new job at nine o'clock sharp,
planning to arrive fifteen minutes early. I only remembered that I
had already allowed an extra fifteen minutes after I got there. Sister
Colette answered the door and led me into a small room off the
reception area. The staff were in the midst of Morning Prayer. They
didn't stop to say hello or anything. My interruption was just that,
and tolerated. Sister Colette motioned me to a chair beside her. Everyone kept their noses in their prayer books as a disheveled old
priest read a psalm. Then Sister Colette shoved her book toward
me and pointed as they read, "Adore the Lord in his holy court."
Just as I found the place, she flipped several hundred pages to a red
ribbon marker. Now Father Eugene was reading. I followed along
and even managed a few of the words in the section called "Re-
sponsory" when Sister Colette flipped again to a white ribbon and
everyone started reading together, "Blessed be the Lord, the God

of Israel..." It was hard to follow. Father Eugene was at the head of the pack, uttering every word a heartbeat before the others got to it. The old priest and another man I recognized, old Mr. Bergman, brought up the rear, a rumbling echo to the others in the group. Since I couldn't keep up with anybody else, I plodded along with them. Then another flip back where we'd been. Father Eugene led the intercessions. Sister Colette played with the ribbon marker in her breviary, running it between her thumb and forefinger—up and down—straightening the crease that seemed permanently pressed into it. My eyes followed her fingers—up and down. *If she wet the ribbon and ironed it, the crease would come out. I should offer to do that for her.* It was hard to pay attention. It was all so foreign to me.

After the final prayer, Sister Colette introduced me to the slow-going Father Francis who greeted me warmly. Then he and Father Eugene excused themselves.

Sister Colette turned to the other older gentleman. "This is Walter, our custodian. He can fix anything."

"I know Mr. Bergman!" I said. "I spent a lot of time on his farm when I was in school. A lot of us kids used to go skating on their pond."

Walter nodded matter-of-factly and smiled. "Yes. I tied a lot of skates back then. I'll have to tell Dan I saw you. You two were thick as thieves as I recall."

"Oh! Yes. How's he doing? I haven't seen him in years." Dan and I were good friends from kindergarten all the way through to high school.

"He's working the farm now. He'll be tickled to know I saw you."

"Well, say hello from me."

"Will do—but I best be getting something done around here. See you later." With a quick nod, Mr. Bergman disappeared out the door.

Finally Ann, the woman I was to replace, met me with a weak handshake. She was not very congenial. As she showed me around the office, Ann told me I was lucky to get this job as there were some highly qualified applicants. She didn't seem convinced that

my expertise and experience were anything to write home about. I
let it drop that I have a BA in history. Ann was not impressed. By
the end of the day, I realized that she was a friend of someone else
who had applied—Agnes, a parishioner who had served for years
in various volunteer positions. Agnes had several years of office experience and had taken courses in pastoral ministry at the college.
I was uneasy to say the least, and more uneasy the following night
when I unexpectedly met Agnes at the monthly liturgy meeting. I
was supposed to take minutes.

I arrived even earlier than fifteen minutes beforehand, hoping to
meet people as they came in. I didn't want to have to interrupt the
meeting to ask names for my notes. Sister Colette, who, among her
other duties, served as sacristan, arrived first. "Father Eugene will
be here right at seven," she informed me. "He never cuts his dinner
hour short—however much his success in life may depend on it." I
appreciated her camaraderie. Then a pudgy, balding, self-import-
ant man, with narrow eyes and a sparse, wispy strawberry-blond
mustache strutted in. He was The Musician. I should have known,
I guess. His was clearly a consequential presence. I shook his limp-
ly offered hand. His name was Al, for Aelred, of all things. Rose
and Mike came in together. Mike, a waggish, grey-haired old man,
walked with a cane, although by his bearing he seemed to suggest
he only carried it as a dapper accessory. He introduced himself
and turned to introduce Rose. "This is my girlfriend, Rose. She
says she'll take me wherever I want to go, but we always end up at
church." Rose, a soft-spoken woman, younger than me, smiled and
said, "He calls me his girlfriend because he's too cheap to tip the
chauffeur." Sister Colette, Al, Rose, Mike. I wrote the names down
on my steno pad.

As I did this, in sashayed Agnes. I looked up from my notes to
see a sturdy, flushed, squared-faced woman ogling me. Her wide-
set eyes seemed to bulge from the sides of her temples and focus
independently. "So you're the marvelous new feather in Father Eugene's cap! Welcome to St. Ignorant of Loyalty parish!" I disliked
her immediately. She wore a loose-fitting tawny pilled sweater with

orange-red pants. A loud, sheer scarf splashed with orange, red, brown, gold, and yellow swathed her shoulders. "Hello," I responded demurely. *Who is this bitch? And why do I never have a comeback when I need one?*

"I'm Agnes! As in Agnus—lamb, in case you don't know Latin—lamb, as in sacrificial."

"Take it easy, Agnes. It's not her fault." I looked gratefully at Mike, my protector.

"Agnes was a very good candidate for your job, Janine," Sister Colette added tactfully, "but I know Father Eugene had good reasons for hiring you, too."

I looked around the room, trying to read the group. Al was nervously turning his pencil, tapping it on the table at the end of each revolution. Rose took an agenda from the pile I had placed in the centre of the table and tried very hard to concentrate on it. Mike had walked over to Agnes and rested his hand on her shoulder. "Hello, Father Eugene," said Sister Colette.

"Hello, everyone," he responded in the hollow silence that met him. A few spiritless murmurs answered him.

The meeting was called to order by Mike. Rose reported first on the Eucharistic ministers. They currently had enough volunteers but the man who insists on intinction was creating confusion. The previous pastor had advised the ministers simply to accommodate him but Father Eugene said "Send him to me!" I was embarrassed to have to ask how to spell intinction. Mike obliged me and began to offer a definition but Father Eugene loudly read out the next item on the agenda: "Music!" Mike sat back unperturbed, crossed his arms preparing to enjoy the show. Al blustered importantly. Music was great at *his* mass, and he had lined up a replacement for Mr. Fletcher at the 9:00 but Mr. Fletcher wouldn't step down.

"Send him to me!" said Father Eugene.

Agnes reported dispassionately on the lectors. Nothing in her manner suggested the vitriolic person I'd encountered minutes earlier. Then Father Eugene added that the Prayers of the Faithful were not to be amended in any way. "They are to be read as written." He looked pointedly at Agnes.

"It seems to me that if we pray in good faith for 'vocations to the priesthood, religious life and lay leadership,' it's only appropriate to also give thanks for the ones we already have," Agnes responded.

"You know that's not what I object to, Agnes," Father Eugene countered impatiently. "When you pray 'teach us to use the vocations you have already given us,' you are trying to validate something the Church doesn't recognize."

"So shall I pray 'Help the Church to *recognize* the vocations you have already given.' I suppose you're right, Father, that would be better." Agnes looked triumphantly at him.

"Read the prayers as written, Agnes, or find something else to do on Sundays—Parish Mission!" he barked. By now Father Eugene was quite agitated. He had my sympathy, having to deal with such an annoying woman. Sister Colette spoke breathlessly as she reported on the final preparations for the mission. From what I could see, Agnes set everyone on edge, except maybe Mike, who seemed to relish all the commotion. It was pretty easy to figure out why I got the job.

But what a week. What an appalling start to a new job. I had no time to find my feet. The next afternoon, Agnes came to the office to ask for her tax receipt. I said I knew nothing about it and referred her to Sister Colette. "Oh dear," said Sister Colette, "didn't Ann take care of all that before she left?" Apparently not. The next Sunday would be February 28 and no one had bothered to get the charitable donation receipts out. If I'd known, if I'd realized, if I'd ever done this type of job before, I would have asked about it. I also felt set up. I suspected that Ann intended to put me in a bad light. I doubted Agnes was really waiting for her receipt. She was just rubbing it in. I clearly didn't know my job.

Sister Colette went to get Father Eugene while I looked in the files where she told me to look for the records of contributions. Agnes just hung around. She seemed to be savouring every moment. Father Eugene called a temporary secretarial service, but there was no one available to work until Friday. In the meantime Sister Colette told Agnes we would do our best to have her receipt available on Sunday. She would get it sooner that way, than if we mailed it out Friday afternoon.

"I can help," said Agnes. "I've done it all before." *Great. How to make a bad situation worse.*

"Great! That would make the best of a bad situation!" said Sister Colette. "How's that with you, Father Eugene?"

"Whatever it takes, Sister," and he left.

It was all quickly arranged. The tallying, the receipts, the addresses, the stuffing. I called home to say I'd be late. Agnes got straight to work. She didn't seem to have much to say. I was surprised by this. The next day, Agnes recovered some of her fervour. At lunch she railed on about the administrations of parishes—this sort of thing wouldn't happen if the priests didn't have to run the show—the priests should busy themselves with pastoral work and the sacraments and leave the administration of parishes to the community where it belongs—every time we get a new priest, we get a new administrative model and still the community does the work—you don't have to be ordained to run a parish—

Just put a sock in it. She was getting on my nerves even though I realized most of her venom wasn't about me. Father Eugene had been assigned to the parish in September. Neither Ann nor Agnes liked his style. It was just as likely that Ann left the receipts undone out of spite for Father Eugene. But Agnes knew what she was doing—and we definitely needed the help.

Still, it was a relief to go to work the following Monday knowing Agnes wouldn't be there. And Monday is Father Eugene's day off, so it was just me and Sister Colette. Sister Colette commended me for showing such restraint with Agnes. She told me a bit about Agnes—her husband is in a nursing home because of an industrial accident. Agnes works there as an LPN. This allows her to spend time with her husband during breaks. But Agnes was finding the work exhausting. Working shifts all hours of the day and night was taking its toll. She would have been grateful to have the comparatively regular hours of my job, Colette continued.

"I feel sorry for her. Really I do. I think there's something missing in her life. And she's trying to fill it with God, you know. Not that that's a bad thing, really. She's just gone about it all wrong."

"I know what you mean." But I didn't. Agnes was certainly going about something all wrong from my perspective, but what in heaven's name would a sister find wrong with filling a void with God, however you do it?

"I thought you would," Colette continued. "Agnes creates her own unhappiness. She knew full well that completing a master's degree in divinity is not a ticket to ordination. You have to be male to be a priest. There's never been any doubt on that point."

"She has a Master of Divinity degree?"

"You didn't know that?"

"No."

Colette could see my discomfort. "It's not as if that would qualify her for your job, you know. You don't need a master's degree in anything to type the bulletin."

"Well, there's definitely something missing," I agreed uncharitably. Over time, I got used to Agnes. She showed up all the time, whenever volunteers were needed, whenever there were special services and often with cookies or donuts for coffee. But I always found her irritating—like a pebble in a sandal—not the sort of irritant that makes pearls, that's for sure—and so lacking in subtlety.

As for the job, I realized that when they advertised for someone with ethical character, they just wanted someone trustworthy after all. This in no way conflicted with being agreeable. Father Eugene was just hoping to find someone who wouldn't be perceived to be either his ally or Agnes and Ann's. For my part, I didn't have any trouble working with Father Eugene. At the beginning it was fine having someone else make all the decisions—not to be asked to contribute except in very concrete terms. I was content to let him determine the work that needed to be done. And as I began to attend mass fairly regularly, I was content to let that shape my faith as well—I hadn't bothered to do it on my own, after all, and musing about universal values hadn't really got me anywhere.

As it turned out, my paycheck amounted to little more than what I had earned when I was self-employed. Subtract the amount I paid Marilee Clark to be at the house when the boys got home and get supper started and it pretty much came out even. In retrospect, I have to give Miles some credit, though. Within another five years or ten at most, my secretarial business probably would have dried up, since so many academics were getting their own computers by then.

NEXUS

The figures that float across these pages are like shadows dancing on the walls. They show that life is crowded with realities and flooded with radiance, for without substance and sunshine there can be no shadows.

—F. W. Boreham, *Shadows on the Wall*

I suited the job well enough. Father Eugene was generally content, if a little impatient and explosive when his expectations were not well anticipated. Sister Colette was pleasant for the most part. And I had a friend in Walter. Like so many farmers of his generation, Walter wore bib overalls—Osh Kosh B'Gosh. If his hands were empty he habitually crooked his thumbs under the straps where the metal button hook meets the bib. This was his time-biding stance. It expanded his chest to allow room for the wisdom of his observations. It also balanced the habitual forward bending of these same muscles when Walter cradled the fiddle he had played for as long as he could remember. Often he would bring his fiddle to work and the strains of "Red Wing" or some old Swedish folk song would come wafting through the ventilating system at lunch hour. Walter wasn't above taking a drink or two on a Saturday evening with the boys if there wasn't fiddling to be done somewhere. But no point in overdoing it, he said. He was a clean liver and didn't hold with staying out late and leaving the wife at home to fend for herself. And now Dan had the farm. Walter filled me in about that a few days after the tax-receipt fiasco.

"For years we worked the farm together, me and Dan, from the time he was big enough to climb onto the tractor by himself. Awhile back Dan got this notion of 'free range' chickens in his brain. Well, I just went along with it. Nothing wrong with keeping the hens happy, I figured. But when the boy got it into his head to stop using fertilizers and weed killers and other improvements, that was past my power of reckoning. I commenced to thinking it was time we parted company. Dan had kids to raise. Clara and I could do just fine in town without the bother of chores and keeping the peace. So now we go down to the farm for dinner after mass on Sundays. And they come to us whenever they take a trip to town which is often enough."

"And that's your land all the way up to the south end of town?"

"Dan's."

"Really. And he has no intention of selling it off to developers? It must be worth a fortune."

"Naw. I figure good farm land should be farmed and so does Dan. He's doing okay. He won't be selling it any time soon."

"You should thank him for me. I often walk on that road running along your fields. It's my favourite retreat."

"Well, sweetheart. If that's how you like it, we'll just keep it that way."

Walter's a dear. But the redeeming grace of the place was Father Francis, a stooped, older man with wild wisps of grey hair taking off in all directions. Likewise his luminous eyes seemed in constant motion, searching, as if to settle would be to miss half the view. He was semi-retired and nearing his seventy-first birthday when I started. As the associate pastor, he did little administration apart from signing a few cheques now and then, but he carried on with his pastoral ministry visiting the shut-ins and sick, counseling, hearing confessions and presiding at mass. He also served as a chaplain in the federal prison down the highway. The wonder of Father Francis, however, was his uncanny ability to make me feel as though I was the loveliest person on earth. Every day he greeted me as if my presence were pure gift. At first I believed this had to do with the tensions between Father Eugene and Agnes—a kind of gratitude for my adaptable and agreeable nature. But gradually I began to realize that his response to Sister Colette, Father Eugene—and even Agnes—although not the same as it was to me, was equally gracious and attentive.

I had never met anyone like him. When he looked at me, he saw someone I hardly recognized. All the goodness in me came bubbling up when I spoke with him. I even typed better when he was around. He reminded me a bit of a wonderful confessor, Blessed Jean de Beaumanoir. I read about him in Butler's *Lives of the Saints*. Butler included legendary testimonials about this holy man, about how even as a child he demonstrated sympathy for the law of the Church. I told Father Francis that he must be the same sort of saint "who, as an infant, showed marked abstemiousness at the breast on Fridays."

He laughed. "Probably only to make up for the excesses of Thursday, but please, don't call me a saint. I wouldn't know how to behave." In April, for Secretary's Week, he brought me flowers and took me out for lunch.

I looked forward to going to work on the days I knew he would be there. In some ways he became for me the father I never knew. I could talk with him about anything. I didn't have to try to be better around him. I only had to be me. But in an odd way I was more me than I could ever remember being. I became preoccupied with what I could do for him. I baked cookies, pies, or squares to serve at coffee. Miles and the boys appreciated this turn of events because, of course, I couldn't carry off all those goodies to work without sharing them first with my family. I didn't mind doing that either. I enjoyed watching Kit and Adam help themselves to a pile of oatmeal-chocolate-chip cookies or a slice of saskatoon pie. Not that I hadn't baked before, but it had been awhile since I kept a regular supply of goodies on hand.

Father Francis had the capacity to measure the true weight of a situation. The world didn't come crashing down for him when a crisis arose. One day it did for me. It was about a year after I started working at the parish. Marilee was supposed to have gone to my house to start supper and keep the boys company. Adam called me at work to ask when she was coming. She should have been there already. Sister Colette hovered while I called Marilee at home to see if she'd lost track of the time. Marilee was not at home either. Her mother thought she was at my house. Although Marilee would usually bring Jessica with her when she came over, the baby was still napping when it was time to go, so Marilee had asked her mother to listen for Jessica and left without her. It just didn't add up. Something was wrong. I quickly put my work away. The boys would have been fine on their own. When I was their ages, I was the one making supper after all. But I went home anyway.

In the meantime, Sister Colette told Father Francis the situation. By the time I got home, checked on the boys, and went over to see Mrs. Clark, Father Francis was already there. Mrs. Clark had called the police but they did not consider the disappearance suspicious so nothing could be done until Marilee had been missing for twenty-four hours. Father Francis wanted to look for Marilee. He had a hunch he could find her but it would take awhile. Could he have a photo? Father Francis slipped Marilee's grade 10 school picture into his wallet and promised to call the Clarks sometime between nine and eleven. Then off he went. In the meantime, Mrs. Clark —Eleanor—made several phone calls while I entertained Jessica. Then the two of us tried to remember the last few conversations we had had with Marilee. Neither of us had noticed anything unusual. When Marilee's father got home, we chatted a few more minutes, agreed to stay in touch by phone, and I went home to make supper. After supper, Miles took the boys for a ride around town to see if they could spot Marilee. I stayed home waiting for the phone to ring.

Waiting. Wandering from task to task, finishing nothing. Checking the clock to see if the battery was dead. Finally, to take my mind off everything, I pulled Sir Edmund Chambers' Volume I from the shelf. The book fell open to page 287:

> It seems probable that this was... something of the nature of a Processional, and that it was identical with the *codex 500 annorumi* from which the same Benedictines derived their amazing account of a Beauvais ceremony which took place not on January 1 but on January 14. A pretty girl, with a child in her arms, was set upon an ass, to represent the Flight into Egypt. There was a procession from the cathedral to the church of St. Stephen. The ass and its riders were stationed on the right side of the altar. A solemn mass was sung, in which *Introit, Kyrie, Gloria* and *Credo* ended with a bray.

A footnote mentioned that "Clément, 158, appears to have no knowledge of the MS except for the reference he found in Ducange..." It continued : "Ducange was certainly aware of Roud's introductory comments on the practice as related in *La Madeleine Voilée* where Madeleine was herself selected to ride the celebrated ass in procession for the festivities."

A hollow fear in the pit of my stomach made the account hard to follow. I could only think of Marilee's flight. But there was no child in her arms. Her sweet little baby was left behind. Marilee, a devoted, adoring mother, deserting her baby. How could she? Had she been abducted? If not, what had come over her? Miles and the boys returned with nothing to report. I resisted the urge to call the Clarks. They were waiting for news. They had promised to call me if they heard anything at all. They knew I wanted to hear, even if it was the middle of the night. A ringing phone would only raise expectations. I set out a night-time snack—some milk and oatmeal cookies from a batch I'd brought to work that morning. The boys and Miles helped themselves and went along to bed.

I returned to Sir Edmund. It seemed to me this Madeleine holding a child in her arms must be the one I had read about several years before. I paged back to a chapter entitled "The May Game" hoping to find the section on gathering the May. It wasn't all that familiar, the parts about round dances taking place at weddings and funerals. I was disturbed by a passage about the custom in Flanders to dance at the funeral of a young girl, where "a very charming chanson is used:"

> *In den hemel is eenen dans: Alleluia.*
> *Daer dansen al' de maegdekens:*
> *Benedicamus Domino, Alleluia, Alleluia.*
> *'t is voor Amelia: Alleluia.*
> *Wy dansen naer de maegdelkens:*
> *Benedicamus Domino, Alleluia, Alleluia.*

> *In heaven is a dance, Alleluia*
> *There all the maidens dance:*
> *We bless the Lord, Alleluia, Alleluia.*
> *It is for Amelia, Alleluia.*
> *Who now dances with the maidens:*
> *Bless the Lord, Alleluia, Alleluia.*

I hope this isn't an actual foreshadowing. I hope that Marilee is still dancing this side of heaven. I jumped when the phone interrupted my dark ruminations. "God forbid," I muttered. I had a dreadful premonition about the call. Yes, it was Eleanor. Father Francis had called just after eleven. He was in the city, and he hadn't found Marilee yet, but he was pretty confident about a lead he picked up. Eleanor sounded optimistic. I tried to be optimistic too, and not to think about it. *Her name is Marilee, not Amelia. Don't dwell on it.*

The reference to Madeleine was obviously not in "The May-Game" chapter anyway. I skimmed the opening paragraphs of several other chapters and settled on "Village Festivals." It's amazing how time speeds up when you can't find what you're looking for. Still, I watched the clock. I decided I would go to bed at two even if I hadn't heard anything by then. I was heading upstairs when the phone finally rang again. I answered fearfully.

"Janine—he found her," Eleanor informed me excitedly. "He's

bringing her back to town with him."

"Thank God." I spluttered and began to cry. *I can't even hold it together as well as her own mom. Must be that Amelia thing.* "What a relief. It's so good to know she'll be home tonight."

"Oh, not tonight," Eleanor answered. "Father Francis said she will sleep in the guest room at the rectory tonight. That was the deal, he said. Marilee doesn't want to come home yet."

"Did he say where she was?"

"No, he just said he found her, that she's okay, and we'll talk tomorrow. I have to be content with that."

"And Jessica? Will she stay with you tonight?"

"Oh, I won't wake Jessica. I'll just go downstairs and sleep in Marilee's bed until Jessica wakes up in the morning. That's a small price to pay for a happy ending."

The next morning I was not at work a quarter of an hour beforehand. Father Eugene, Sister Colette, and Walter were nearly finished Morning Prayer. Without the gravity of Father Francis to slow them down, they read at quite a clip. Father Eugene gave a chastening glance in my direction. I barely squirmed, sitting silently, waiting them out. I had arrived early enough, under the circumstances.

None of them knew there was a guest in the place. When they were done Father Eugene said "Spring fever, eh?"

I didn't point out that I was not even a minute late. "It was a late night, that's all." He didn't ask for details.

It was almost ten o'clock when Father Francis appeared. "We have been visited by an angel," he announced. "She's sleeping in the guest room."

"We have? Who is it?" Sister Colette had heard nothing after she left work the night before.

"Marilee," I answered in unison with Father Francis. He said only that Marilee needed a night's respite, and, please, would we let him know immediately if she showed up in the office? He then went to Father Eugene's office, poked his head in the door with the same communication and disappeared down the hall and into the rectory.

I waited, wanting to see Marilee and tell her I was glad she was okay. The clock laboured through the morning. When it finally inched toward noon, Father Francis appeared again, asking a favour. Would I please knock on the guestroom door and go in if there is no answer? He was a little concerned—thought Marilee should be stirring by now even though it had been a late night. "Yes, I know," I answered, "I waited up until I heard you found her."

"You're so good, Janine." I had nothing to say to that. He was glad to know I cared, I think. I set off to check on Marilee.

I walked through the bleakly furnished rectory living room, past the kitchen door, down the hall to the guestroom door, and knocked. "Who is it?" Marilee snapped.

"It's just me, Janine. Father Francis wants to know if you're all right."

"I'm fine."

I waited to see if she had anything else to say. She didn't. "He wants to know if you'd like a little breakfast." *I'm sure he does.*

"I'm not hungry."

"I see." I waited awhile longer. "I'm glad you're okay," I added lamely.

"I'm not okay."

Well, you said you were fine before. "I mean, I'm glad you're here."

"*I'm* not."

Good going, Janine, now what? "May I come in?" *What was I thinking? The last thing I want is to go where I'm not wanted.* No answer. *Fine with me.*

Just as I began to tiptoe away she said, "I'm not stopping you."

Too slow. I tried to turn the handle. "It's locked."

"Okay, just a minute."

My crazy beating heart echoed in my ears. *What on earth will I say to her?* I heard the lock turn. I heard her walk away.

"It's open," she said.

I turned the knob and walked in. Marilee sat on the bed, fully dressed. The bed was made up, not slept in at all from what I could see. Marilee's eyes were red and swollen, her face a patchwork of blotches. I sat down near her on the only chair in the room. I said nothing. She sat, looking down, saying nothing too. I tried to think of something to say. *Should I mention how her baby must miss her? No. Should I tell her how worried we were? No. Should I tell her she needs to be more responsible, she's a mother now. No, of course not.* I couldn't think of a thing. Finally, just when I decided it was best not to say anything, I blurted, "That sure is an ugly bedspread."

She looked slyly out of the corner of her eye. She seemed mildly amused. "When they can't sell something at the St. Vincent DePaul Store, they must send it here." We sat silently again.

"I hate my parents."

No, you don't. They've done so much for you. They've supported you and your little girl, they've made a special suite in their house just for you and Jessica, they hardly talk to your aunt because she was so mean to you. I didn't say anything though. I wondered if I would get a lunch break if I spent my whole lunch hour with Marilee. *Well, Janine, you're not as good as Father Francis thinks.*

"They just don't get it."

"What do you mean?" *You could do worse for parents.*

"They think that I'm still their little girl. Only I've got a baby now, my own little girl. They think they can plan my life for me, make me do whatever they think I should do."

After a long silence, "Like what?"

"Like babysit for you, go to church, go to school."

I was taken aback by this. "I arranged the babysitting with you. I didn't even know your mom before you started babysitting."

"Who wants to babysit when the only thing you ever do all day is take care of a baby? And go to church where everyone glares if she makes any noise."

"Not everyone…" I started.

"And go to school with kids who were in junior high when you started high school and where everyone your age has graduated."

"You're not in school right now, Marilee."

"Not if my parents have their way. They want me to go back to school with all those stupid little brats. Or else I have to move out and get a job."

"Oh— I see." And I thought I did. I was beginning to think I understood the problem. "Maybe we can find some alternatives."

"Like what? I'm not going to school."

"Not to *that* school at any rate." Who did I think I was kidding? I had nothing to say about Marilee's life. So what? I promised myself I would see to it that Marilee would not have to endure high school as a returning student with a one-year-old child.

"What do you mean?"

"I haven't a clue. But I don't think it's fair to expect you to go back to your old high school if you don't want to do that." Her face relaxed a bit. "You know, it's my lunch hour. Why don't you come have something to eat—for my sake? I'm ravenous."

"I don't want to talk to anyone."

"How about I go ask everyone to clear out of the kitchen and we'll have something to eat there?" She was okay with that. So was Father Francis, who had already prepared something for Marilee, and even me, God bless him. He removed the place he had set for himself and took his lunch to his room. Marilee and I sat together at the rectory table not saying much, keeping our thoughts to ourselves.

Finally this: "I want to see Jessica, but I don't want to go home."

"We can ask your mother to bring her."

"I don't want to see my mother."

"I'll talk to Father Francis. You don't have to see her yet. Maybe he can arrange something."

"I don't want to see her *ever*." She was going a bit overboard about this, but I made sure Father Francis knew how she felt. Within the hour Eleanor brought Jessica with all her gear as well as an overnight case for Marilee. She came in wearing her Sunday smile, expressing her gratitude for Father Francis's hospitality. She looked weary and not a little embarrassed. "Don't worry," I told Eleanor, "Marilee just needs a little retreat." What else could I say? Bad call about the school business? Hardly. Marilee hung out in the guest room waiting for her mother to go and for me to bring Jessica to her.

When we'd said our goodbyes, Eleanor passed Jessica to me. Jes-

sica screamed as I carried her away from her grandmother. Father
Francis brought the bags. I went into the guestroom and handed Jessica to Marilee. "Oh, my baby!" She jostled her little girl in her arms,
smothering her with kisses. "What am I going to do with you?"
Tears of frustration sprang at the creases of her resolutely smiling
eyes. Jessica stopped crying and smiled back. Marilee sighed. However warm and affectionate she could be with her baby, Marilee
clearly wanted to be seventeen—the free and easy seventeen. No
fixing or changing that. Mothers twice her age sometimes feel that
way. But seventeen, single, a mother with a grade-ten education, a
few elders at hand to coax and encourage. Not much to recommend
it. All the same, Marilee seemed happier and more relaxed with Jessica in her arms. No question.

We left them to themselves. "You're wonderful, Janine," said Father Francis as we walked back to the office. For a moment, I practically believed it. I almost forgot that he was the one who went to
find Marilee in the first place.

The rest of the afternoon was taken up with Marilee and Jessica. Father Francis went to do his rounds at the hospital. Marilee
was still not inclined to talk, but seemed relieved to hang out with
someone other than a priest or nun. Father Eugene blustered a bit
about my wage not including child care, but there was no urgent
business for me to do anyway, except to handle phone calls. This I
could do in either the office or the rectory. The time passed pleas-
antly enough, but very slowly. I really wanted to get home, get supper out of the way, and take a closer look at what I'd read the night
before when I had been too fraught to focus.

* * *

It took forever to get dinner ready. When we finally sat down,
Miles and the boys wanted to know how things had gone with
Marilee—more after-dinner chatter than we've had in years. Finally
the guys settled in to watch hockey and I was free to re-read that
section from Chambers. There it was on page 287—all about the
Beauvais ceremony. And there I was again, looking for a reference

that seemed to have disappeared altogether. There was no mention of S. H. Roud's comments on the practice as related in *La Madeleine Voilée*. But I remembered the reference as if it were on the page. Before this, any encounters with Madeleine had been random and unrecognized. During the night of vigil for Marilee's return, I began to recognize the nebulous shape of a personality coming to me from the past through pages of histories. I did not find confirming evidence that night. But I encountered the image of a young Madeleine riding a donkey in procession right up to the altar of a gothic church and could not suppress the notion that she was the same Madeleine who gathered the May. That night I discovered a memory for a shadow, the veiled significance of something unremembered. I began to wonder how to find her. I had only one clue. At one time she took part in a ceremony that took place in Beauvais. I checked my medieval history text. Apart from references to rise of the *Jacquerie* in 1358 which involved the peasants of the Beauvaisis—the region surrounding the city of Beauvais—I found little. There were a few bishops of Beauvais who merited a line of text. And there was a Vincent of Beauvais, a thirteenth-century encyclopedist who, from his cell in a monastery at Beauvais, compiled a massive reference work listing all the knowledge of the age. That was all.

AS IF

The rule for all of us is perfectly simple. Do not waste time bothering whether you "love" your neighbour; act as if you did. As soon as we do this we find one of the great secrets. When you are behaving as if you loved someone, you will presently come to love him.

—C. S. Lewis, *Mere Christianity*

The church rectory is no place for a real live mother and child. Marilee and Jessica had the temerity to be fashioned of flesh rather than plaster. Father Eugene was manifestly uncomfortable with their presence in the rectory but Marilee absolutely would not consider returning to her parents' home. Regardless, after Marilee and Jessica's second night in the guest room, Father Eugene pressed Sister Colette to find alternate accommodation for them. In short order she had it all arranged. I went as messenger to the room where Marilee was walking with Jessica hoping to settle her for a nap.

"Marilee, Sister Colette has found the perfect place for you and Jessica—they have a granny suite and no granny! And since they only have boys—they never had a daughter—the family are really excited at the possibility of having you and Jessica stay with them."

Marilee showed guarded interest. "Is it in town here?"

"Yes! Just three blocks from my house."

"Who are they?" I couldn't blame her for being a little wary.

"The Kellys. They're a really nice family."

Marilee blanched. "Oh…" she breathed, "I can't go there." She collapsed on the bed. Jessica clung to her mother and started to cry. *So what's her problem? The Kellys are nice enough people, even if I find them a little cloying. You could do worse than the Kellys.* I sat down beside the two of them. Marilee was sobbing now too.

I put my arm around her shoulder. "Marilee, Marilee, it'll be okay."

"No, it won't be okay. Nothing is okay." She shook my arm off her back.

"You don't need to stay forever, Marilee. It's just a place to stay until you find something better."

"I can't go there, Janine. Believe me, I just can't go there. Not even for a day."

Clearly she wasn't going to say why and there would be no point in asking. I was at a loss. *This is not in my job description. Somebody else should be dealing with this.*

"Where's Father Francis? I need to talk with Father Francis."

Yes! "I'll go find him." I gratefully closed her door behind me, took a deep breath and set out to find Father Francis. He was not in the rectory. I went to the office.

"Where's Father Francis?"

"At the prison."

"Of course! I forgot. Today's Friday."

Sister Colette smiled. "I have good news for Marilee. Fiona Kelly will come by to pick her up at three." She was pleased things were working out so well.

"Oh dear. Oh no!"

"What's the matter, Janine?"

"Tell her there's been a change of plans. Marilee doesn't want to go to the Kellys."

"Really! Beggars can't be choosers, you know. Marilee may just not have a choice in the matter."

I hadn't figured on defending something I didn't understand myself. "She's not a beggar. She's a child who happens to have a child of her own. She needs to feel safe and secure if she's going to be a good mother. I don't know why she doesn't want to stay with the Kellys, but the prospect clearly upsets her."

"She needs to accept responsibility for her situation."

"Well, it will be hard for her to do that if she has nothing to say about where she goes." I hadn't counted on locking horns with Sister Colette. We'd gotten along fine so far. Sister Colette sputtered something about me not having the last word.

"No, I certainly don't have the last word. Marilee wants to talk to Father Francis. Maybe we should let him handle it. In the meantime, would you like me to call Fiona?" I amazed myself. I did not mean to patronize Sister Colette, but under these circumstances, sending Marilee and Jessica off to the Kellys' wasn't going to solve anything.

I did call Fiona. I apologized to her, saying we had not conferred with all interested parties. I thanked her for her generous offer and said we would contact her when a decision had been reached. Then I asked Sister Colette to send Father Francis to us when he got in. I returned to the guest room.

Marilee sat wearily on the bed, her arms cradling her sleeping baby, her eyes questioning as I entered. "Father Francis won't be back for another hour, Marilee. I called Fiona Kelly and said you won't be coming." Marilee said nothing. "Will you have some tea?" I took her shrug for a "yes" and headed to the kitchen. I came back with tea, cookies, and some playing cards. I didn't consider going back to my desk. It was a work day, to be sure, but filling in for Father Francis ought to count for something. And however cool Marilee's reception of me, the ambient temperature in the office with Sister Colette would certainly be colder.

We played several games of rummy. She beat me every time. I was probably more preoccupied than Marilee was, waiting for Father Francis. She was relaxed, intent on the game. For her, it was as if the crisis were already averted. I was not so sure about that. Where else could she go? I didn't discuss it. It didn't seem possible to reason with her.

Finally Father Francis knocked on the door. "Hello there! You asked to see me?"

I stood to excuse myself. "No, no, Janine. Please stay. I understand you told Mrs. Kelly Marilee won't be coming, and that's just as it should be. Certainly Marilee needs to be a part of any decision about where she will go. For now, what we need is an interim arrangement, a place for her to stay until she figures out what will work for her and Jessica." He looked at Marilee. "Do you mind if Janine stays to help us sort it out?"

"I guess."

"I understand Father Eugene feels the rectory is not the best place for you. Do you have any ideas about where you could stay for the next few days?"

Marilee shook her head.

"Do you have any friends you could stay with?"

"Not now. Not since Jessica was born. Only Janine."

God forbid! I suppressed a gasp. Father Francis's benevolent eyes fell on me. The idea of having Marilee and her baby in my house was unthinkable. I hedged. "I doubt Miles will agree to it, but I'll ask." Miles could be depended on to refuse. I was sure of it. For once I was grateful for his stubborn territorial nature.

"Well then, I'll let Father Eugene know we're working on it, but Marilee and Jessica will stay here tonight."

It was close enough to quitting time. I needed the walk home. To tell the truth, I had not taken much interest in Marilee before all this happened. She filled a need in my household. She was an unimaginative but decent cook for a teenager and a satisfactory presence in the house— not too demanding, not asking much for herself. The boys were happy. That was good enough for me.

The drama of her flight changed all that. Father Francis seemed to think my interest in Marilee's predicament rose out of selfless compassion and concern for Marilee's well being. He got that wrong. Of course I was concerned about her and her baby. I certainly wished her well and hoped for the best. But I had no intention of getting involved. My interest had nothing to do with helping her out. The fact is, Marilee's flight provided the occasion that brought Madeleine to consciousness. However illogical the process, I connected that consciousness with Marilee. Since I was intrigued with Madeleine, I was willing to engage Marilee. But taking her and little Jessica into my home, that was a different story.

* * *

At dinner I brought up the subject, just as a formality. I had said I would.

Well, wonder of wonders! Miles was enthusiastic. I have no idea why. "I'll move the hockey table out of the rec room and we can set them up in there." *Really. You must be kidding.* But no, suddenly Miles became an open-handed, generous supporter of the disenfranchised. What could I say?

"Are you sure?"

He was. As for Adam and Kit, they thought it would be cool to have a little kid around the house. And they really liked Marilee. I had no choice. But it would keep overnight. I was in no hurry to call Father Francis.

* * *

I didn't call on Saturday morning, either. Instead, I kept my coffee date with Denise.

"Sure you have a choice," Denise scolded. "It's your home and you have to be comfortable there. You haven't agreed to it yet. Just say no."

"You're right." Sometimes I think Denise knows me better than I know myself. "But—" I sighed.

"But what, Janine?"

"Where else can they go?"

"That's not your problem, Janine. You can't save the world, you know."

"Marilee's not the world. It's not as if she's a stranger to me."

"It's not as if she's your daughter, either. This is something for her to work out with her parents."

"That's not going to happen."

"It will if she has no choice. It all comes down to who's left holding the bag. Either you have no choice, or she has no choice. Since this is her problem, she'll have to deal with it—but where's the father in all this? Who is he? Why doesn't his family do something?"

"She won't say who he is. The father wanted her to abort Jessica, that's all I know. Marilee said she wouldn't and her parents supported her in that. As far as Jessica's concerned, the father's out of the picture."

"She won't go to her parents and she won't go to the Kellys. Hmm. Sounds like she doesn't want to stay with either set of grandparents…"

"Really, Denise. Do you know something I don't?"

"Well, Marilee was willing to consider the nice family with the granny suite until she found out who they were. Why else would she react that way?"

"Can't be. Their boys are really good kids. Luke's the only one even old enough to be a possibility, and he's away at university. He's not even in town."

"Well, not anymore. Jessica's well over a year old now, you know. And, come on, Janine. Good kids have the same urges as the bad kids, whoever *they* are."

"Yes, but I doubt Luke would ask her to do that."

"It doesn't matter, Janine. I just had a hunch. I could be way off. Maybe Luke and Jessica's father are friends. Maybe the father works for Pat Kelly. I don't know. It's none of my business, but it's not your problem, either."

"Right. We're going to have to find some other alternative." I thought awhile and drank some of my coffee. It was already cold. This whole business was so damned inconvenient. "Sister Colette said 'beggars can't be choosers' when Marilee refused to go to the Kellys."

"That's a little harsh, don't you think?"

"Yes, I thought so at the time. But now it doesn't seem so very different from what I'm thinking."

"But you're willing to listen to Marilee's point of view."

"Which is that she has no other friend besides me."

"You're not exactly her peer, you know."

"Which puts me in a better position to respond to her."

"There you go again, Janine, supporting one side of a question so you can argue the other."

"Maybe so. But Denise, I think maybe it *is* my problem. The more we talk, the more I realize I'm going to do it. Not for long. Just a few weeks. Just enough time to help Marilee make some good choices without other pressures influencing her. That's what Father Francis asked me to do in the first place. I can manage that much. The guys are all for it. And for a few weeks, it won't just be me with the cat for female company."

FACTS AND FIGURES

Looking for something irrelevant, I found I couldn't find it.
—John Cage

Overall, Marilee's stay wasn't the disaster I expected it to be. Marilee did her best to be useful. Jessica was becoming a handful though, grasping, climbing, devouring everything in sight, except dinner, which she merrily tossed off the highchair tray. The boys adored her. My mother dropped by regularly on her way to work just to spend a little time with her. Miles looked for her the minute he came home, gathering her up in his arms, taking her for a jog on his shoulders or saddling her on his ankle for horsey rides. Jessica squealed in gleeful anticipation whenever he walked in the door. Miles was far more attentive to Jessica than he had ever been with his own babies. Some men are just meant to be grandfathers, I guess.

As for Marilee, I helped her get set up doing high school by correspondence and she went to work on her grade-eleven courses. I also found a young mothers group for her. That wasn't such a success. Marilee said all the other moms could talk about was how over-the-moon-in-love-with-their-babies the daddies were. Her impression was probably exaggerated, but it was an elephant in the room for Marilee. She only went twice. She herself made no effort to find friends. She had nothing in common with anyone close to her age. Only one friend from school still kept in touch with her, but she was off at university in British Columbia.

Although the Clarks were bewildered by Marilee's refusal to live at home, they accepted her decision. From Marilee's perspective her parents were too eager to decide how she and Jessica should live. She said they would always treat her as a child if she didn't make the break. However, Marilee did go home for dinner once or twice a week, and whenever her older sister came to town for a visit. When she began to work as a volunteer in the rec centre for a few hours on weekends, her mother babysat. They also contributed to her support.

And so it continued, far beyond the few weeks I'd anticipated. Marilee was a good mother to Jessica, was fairly diligent with her school work, and enjoyed her shifts at the centre. She was willing to share the housework, and to talk, and to ask about my day at work. She often came to mass with me, greeting Father Francis like an old friend. She was even warm with Sister Colette and Father Eugene, who liked her well enough once she was removed from the rectory. But at first Marilee had no interests that I could discover, apart from boys. She wanted nothing more than to have a boyfriend. For awhile she dated someone she'd met at the centre, but when she told him about Jessica, the relationship fizzled. It took awhile to get past that one. Otherwise, she settled in comfortably with our family. She liked to watch hockey with the guys. That's when I snatched a little time for myself from our crowded menage. I put the game schedule on the fridge and prayed the Oilers would make the playoffs.

I spent game time reading and re-reading my treasured old histories. And so it happened to be hockey season when I established the source of my encounters with Madeleine. I was mulling over her elusive presence and paging through the "List of Authorities" at the front of Sir Edmund Chambers's *The Medieval Stage*, when I saw it on page xxx:

La Madeleine Voilée or *The Life of a Lady of Beauvais*, in English, dating about 1600 AD, being the translation of an undiscovered French manuscript from the fifteenth century. Edited by S. H. Roud, 1826. [*Society of Antiquaries of the Continent.*]

This was the title Clément cited from Ducange when he documented the Flight into Egypt as celebrated in Beauvais! I quickly jotted it down. It was uncanny. For awhile after that I could almost *book* an encounter with Madeleine based on the hockey schedule. She seemed to be showing up all over the place.

Soon I began to recognize other relevant facts and events that revolved around Madeleine from before I ever knew Marilee—details I hadn't connected at all. It was a little late to retrace Madeleine's trail at that point. How do you piece together something so ephemeral? If I'd realized what was happening when it all began, at the very least I would have kept track of the places I found her—and probably the dates and circumstances in my own life, just as a point of reference. But how many people, having read something of interest in any history, go back to read it over and over? Psychologists would call that obsessive behaviour, at least when it comes to secondary sources. Primary sources are different. You can learn a lot from mulling over original documents. I was in the foolish position of mulling over secondary sources that at one time or another referred to an original document that apparently doesn't exist, or no longer exists, or at the very least wasn't known to many of the authors of the books where I found references to it.

I can't think of particulars in my own life that may have occasioned the earlier encounters. I have no idea where they came from. I believe my own situation was neither fraught nor happy. This is why I dismiss the possibility of these appearances being a form of psychosis. I think people would react differently to me if I really were crazy. However, I am certain Marilee and Jessica's stay with us had something to do with the spate of Madeleine's appearances that ensued during *Hockey Night in Canada*.

I thought perhaps I was developing a very peculiar intelligence.

By intelligence, I mean the Latin sense of the word—**intellègo** lĕgĕre -lexi -lextum (inter/lego) *to distinguish, discriminate, perceive.* (1) by the senses: (2) mentally, *to understand, grasp, become aware of.* The word lost its amplitude in translation. In English, "intelligence" refers almost exclusively to a mental grasp of things. Sensory awareness is not often dignified with the word. This peculiar intelligence leans more to the Latin, including both sensory perception and mental understanding. The root words of *intellègo* make it clear: "**inter**: *between, among, amid*" and "**lego**: (1) *to pass through, traverse* (2) *to survey, scan*; esp. of writing, *to read, peruse.*" Passing through, between, and among. Surveying amid, reading between. Reading between the lines. That is what I was doing. Reading between—both mentally and by the senses.

I wondered if this kind of intelligence is fostered by faith: faith, as the apostle says, the substance of things hoped for, the evidence of things not seen—even if I didn't know what I hoped for. It is a sort of second sight—witnessing the evidence of things not seen. I have never found a name for this phenomenon. It is not hindsight. What I found was in the spaces between the words—words from the past and words about the past. I was not aware this was happening at first. I began to be aware of it when second looks did not substantiate my second sight. After a time, I learned to be intelligent about the way I approached the text, to read between the lines, and to accept my knowledge of it.

I began to catalogue the encounters. At first I did it for my own sake. I wanted to put the story together, to make as much of a picture of Madeleine's life as I could from the pieces I could remember. And I needed to prove to myself that this was not all a vague fantasy. I included the places that seemed to lie on the periphery of her life. Eventually I wrote notes for scholarly purposes as well—in case other forms of substantiation finally came to light.

These are the recollected facts and events I encountered before Marilee's arrival. For the sake of accuracy, I will describe every revelation in the order I found it. This is not the sequence of Madeleine's life. There was a bit of foreshadowing, if you will.

To my knowledge, no reference to Madeleine's story preceded the gathering of the May. I believe that's where it all began. The first encounter after this was in Eileen Power's *Medieval People*, first published in 1924. Madeleine is certainly not the subject of any of those chapters. She was just a footnote in "The Ménagier's Wife: A Paris Housewife in the Fourteenth Century." The chapter is based on a book written between the years 1392 and 1394 by a Parisian householder, an aging, wealthy man who married a young wife, a fifteen-year-old, and took a paternal interest in her instruction. Eileen Power begins: "The men of the middle, as indeed of all ages, including our own, were very fond of writing books of deportment telling women how they ought to behave in all circumstances of their existence, but more particularly in their relations with their husbands." The relevant footnote occured a few pages into the chapter after this:

And because the care of outside affairs lieth with men, so must a husband take heed, and go and come and journey hither and thither, in rain and wind, in snow and hail, now drenched, now dry, now sweating, now shivering, ill-fed, ill-lodged, ill-warmed and ill-bedded; and nothing harms him because he is upheld by the hope that he has of his wife's care of him on his return, and of the ease, the joys and the pleasures which she will do to him, or cause to be done to him in her presence; to have his shoes removed before a good fire, his feet washed and to have fresh shoes and stockings, to be given good food and drink, to be well served and well looked after, well bedded in white sheets and night-caps, well covered with good furs, and assuaged with other joys and amusements, privities, loves, and secrets, concerning which I am silent, and on the next day fresh shirts and garments.[11]

I am certain it was note number 11 for chapter 5—eleven, the medieval number symbol for marriage. Any unwitting reader seeking this reference now would follow note 11 to Power's comments on the Ménagier's allusion to the three things that "drive the good-man from home, to wit, a dripping roof, a smoking chimney, and a scolding woman." I have reconstructed note 11—as I saw it the first time:

> 11. The ideal deportment of a wife was asked of, but not so freely given by, the indomitable Madeleine of Beauvais. As a young wife married to her father's creditor, she provided the marks of affection and service expected of her, but took little pleasure in it:
> I heard him entering the antechamber, slapping his legs and wheezing, fresh in from the cold. I must attend the old man. I gathered the stockings warmed on the grate against his arrival, and hurried down the stairs.
> "There you are, my little wife!" he greeted me. Indeed. I did not speak.
> "No words for your long gone husband?" he asked.
> "Welcome, my lord," I bowed my head and curtsied, as is seemly for a wife.
> "Let me see your eyes, dear wife. Can they smile?"
> "They can look to your comfort," said I, kneeling at his feet to remove his soaking boots. His stockings were wet quite through. I drew them off carefully, minding the swollen bunions and sodden blisters. "The weather has rendered unkind service to your feet, sir." See *La Madeleine Voilée*, ed. S. H. Roud (1826), II, p. 12.

"See *La Madeleine Voilée!*" Why had I made no connection between this reference and the Madeleine gathering May? Because the man who consorted with Madeleine in the greenwood seemed just as lusty and eager as she was, a young buck, not an imperious old man. That's why. I can remember very well the sense and tone of this citation, which is why I wrote much of it down. I remember the wheezing. The little wife. The unsmiling eyes. I have pieced it together quite accurately, all things considered. The details resonated for me even though Miles is only two years older than I am, and has never called me his "little wife," except once when I proudly announced I had finally reached my pre-pregnancy weight just after Adam's first birthday. But I also remember how much I waited on Miles after he broke his leg—bringing cups of coffee to him as he sat watching TV, running up and downstairs to fetch and carry whatever he wanted, and most disagreeable of all, pulling a sock over his clammy foot in the morning, and taking it off at night, helping him wash it and even rubbing it when it cramped.

Even if any part of this story did show up twice in the same place, it would be hard to confirm the next encounter. It happened in one of those conference papers I was typing for a Professor Phibbs. I don't remember her first name. The title was "The Lot of the Ladies: The Impact of War on the Status of Noble Women in Fifteenth-Century France" or something like that. The basic premise of the paper, as I recall, was that the war resulted in considerable social mobility within the second estate. In some domains, lesser nobility improved their status through service to the king or by buying up feoffs that fell vacant thanks to the casualties of famine, the Black Death, debt, and battle, while in other districts, established houses could not withstand the plunder and destruction of war combined with demands of service and revenue required locally and by the king. In situations of advancement it appears the women benefitted much as the men did, but the paper demonstrated that when a house suffered demise, the status of the women of the household was often more degraded than that of their male counterparts.

Madeleine was born into the house of Brout, a family whose influence and prestige were rising at the beginning of the fourteenth century. However, situated in the marches between territories held by France and England, the House of Brout suffered terribly during the interminable Hundred Years War. By the beginning of the fifteenth century, the war had taken its toll. Peasants attached to the land of the demesne were lost to famine and plague, seriously diminishing the revenues of the house. Lucien de Brout, Madeleine's father, was obliged to supply and equip a certain number of men-at-arms to fulfill his duty to his seigneurial overlord, the King of France. Lucien, with his son and his retinue, saw battle at Agincourt in 1415, and none returned.

Lucien was survived by his wife, Marie Christine, and his daughters, Agathe and Madeleine. Agathe was the first born, and fortunately, well-married to some sort of lord before her father's death. Madeleine, on the other hand was no more than fourteen when her father died— marriageable age, to be sure, for nobility at least, but after her father's death her mother found no suitable match—so many of the eligible noblemen of the Beauvais region had fallen at Agincourt. Nor did the dignity of Madeleine's lineage compensate for the fact that much of her family's assets—which amounted to a name and vast tracts of burnt and barren rubble— had been feoffed-to-use to a local burgher for payment of debts. The family's holdings within the walls of Beauvais allowed for modest elegance in residence, but provided no revenues. Madeleine's prospects were grim. There was not money enough to endow her entry into a marriage, or her reception into a reputable convent, for that matter. Marie Christine was understandably grateful when a wealthy local burgher proposed marriage to her daughter, the same feofee who had in so many other instances provided much needed solvency. This wealthy man ensured the endowment of Madeleine in the face of the church, which would have made the union binding, except that Madeleine apparently did not consent to the arrangement. Madeleine protested that she was already betrothed to another more desirable suitor. In good faith, her mother sent to the University of Paris where Madeleine's young nobleman was said to be in residence to enquire as to his intent. There was no timely response, indeed, no response at all, which Madeleine blamed on the treacherous route the errand must follow to Paris.

The paper reflected on a telling exchange between the desperate mother and her equally desperate daughter. The mother insisted Madeleine should marry this gentleman. Madeleine said, in fact, he was no gentleman, she would not marry beneath her station, and furthermore, he was dour and gloomy. She would have nothing to do with him. If her mother thought so much of him, she should marry him herself. Dr. Phibbs posited that the mother, who was likely only forty, would likely have been pleased to marry this man, but the potential of a young bride to produce children could not be discounted. The suitor was, after all, probably only in his thirties, a widower, and the father of one surviving daughter. Marie Christine also assured her daughter that a man whose bonhomie was so bruised by the passing of his first wife was no doubt a good and gentle husband, a rare prize indeed. In the end, Madeleine was married, whether or not she consented. Jacques, bless his heart, was not anxious to consummate a marriage with someone so young, especially since she was not compliant. He was of no mind to hurry her into maturity. The paper presented Madeleine as a fortunate woman who, in circumstances so abased, still managed a good marriage to a man who, by acquiring a title through marriage, actually preserved her noble status as well. Maybe this is so, but I do know that Madeleine wasn't the least bit happy about being rescued in this manner.

Madeleine is not the focus of the next piece of information. I was browsing the shelves in the college library when I came upon Butler's *Lives of the Saints* and, out of curiosity, decided to read all the entries for that day. It was sometime in late January or early February. My mother was looking after the boys while I went to the library to verify some of the citations in yet another paper I was typing. The entry was for BD JEAN DE BEAUMANOIR. "Bd" stands for "Blessed," which is to say, he was not canonized. Nevertheless, Blessed Beaumanoir was locally recognized and venerated for his holiness. It was generally known in that region that Jean de Beaumanoir had shown remarkable piety even in early childhood, to the extent that as an infant he displayed his "sympathy for the law of the Church by a marked abstemiousness at the breast on Fridays." I noted this quotation, and had it in mind when I joked with Father Francis about it, but I digress. Obviously, I thought it a charming observation, if a bit extravagant, showing the preoccupations of the age—which was the early fifteenth century.

The entry went on to recount a brief history of the life and ministry of Blessed Jean de Beaumanoir. As parish priest, Father Jean demonstrated a wonderful capacity to hear confessions and, with a few words, transform the vicious, depraved and bitter impulses of his flock into a redemptive response to the grace of God. The Fourth Lateran Council (1214) ordained that a "priest be discreet and cautious that he may pour wine and oil into the wounds of one injured after the manner of a skilful physician, carefully inquiring into the circumstances of the sinner and sin, from the nature of which he may understand what kind of advice to give and what remedy to apply, making use of different experiments to heal the sick one." And so it was with Blessed Beaumanoir. To demonstrate the restorative power of his counsel, Butler offered by way of example this priest's intervention in the well-known case of Jacques Mouton. Through the guidance of Blessed Father Jean, the violated husband was mollified and prevented from beating and possibly killing his wife, or at the very least, repudiating her, all of which would have been expected and excused under the circumstances. I doubt anyone, knowing what I did at the time, would have realized the wife in question was Madeleine.

I have looked up Beaumanoir since. There was another Beaumanoir in that region who wrote among other things, *Coutumes de Beauvaisis*. He flourished in the thirteenth century. Perhaps Blessed Beaumanoir is a descendant of this man. I have not found any other reference to the blessed one, however, and predictably, the original reference has disappeared from Butler's *Lives*.

I have forgotten where I read about *madame* and Marie-Josephte, Jacques's daughter by his first wife, walking in the streets of Beauvais in the early evening, lingering at the pannier of an *oublier*, a pastry seller, dicing for an *oublie*. An oublie—obley in English— was a small wafer made by pressing a mixture of flour, honey, and water between two hot hinged iron plates. The anecdote I remember was about Marie-Josephte tossing the dice and losing the throw. *Madame*, however, won her throw and gave her crisp golden wafer to the girl. This modest gesture established the beginning of a good rapport between the young woman and the girl, something that had not really existed before. *Madame*, I now know, was Madeleine, who became more a friend and companion than a mother to Marie-Josephte. Marie-Josephte was, after all, only five years Madeleine's junior. I can see how this happened. It was probably similar to the relationship I have with Marilee.

I have puzzled over the practice of dicing for an oublie. As a rule, dicing was believed to be, as Peter of Blois described it, "the mother of perjury, theft and sacrilege." There was no end of legislation against gambling in the medieval era. The sole exception to these anti-gaming laws granted oubliers the right to throw dice with prospective customers, a winning throw yielding the customer a free wafer. Because the gamble was for a wafer and the good will of the customer, and not for money (although apparently some legislation was necessary to make this point absolutely clear), the practice was generally accepted and condoned—a medieval precursor to promotional advertising, I guess.

I have thought about this custom and I don't think it is a coincidence that oublie was also the term used for the unconsecrated eucharistic host. In the fifteenth century, the whole service of the Eucharist was often referred to as an oblation. Communion oublie were similar to the pastry seller's wafer, except made without the honey and with some appropriate image or text pressed into the wafer. In John's Gospel, after the crucifixion, the soldiers fulfill the scriptures as "they divide my clothing among them, they cast lots for my robe." Since the wafer is the material accident (to use the medieval philosophical term) of the Eucharist, I would think this custom recalled the crucifixion and reminded the pastry purchaser of the free gift of grace. Just a thought. The line between the secular and the sacred wasn't as firmly drawn in the medieval period as it is now.

Infact, almost every gesture and custom was charged with layers of meaning; daily events and actions were raised to the rank of mystery and "embodied in expressive and solemn forms." That's what Johan Huizinga says on the first page of *The Waning of the Middle*

Ages. Only a few pages into the book Jacques Mouton shows up again. Huizinga writes about the power of the spoken word when, at the end of the Middle Ages, itinerant preaching friars would visit cities and towns railing against luxurious indulgence and dissolute living, preaching repentance, and inveighing against bad government. People would "hasten to bring cards, dice, finery, ornaments, and burn them with great pomp." It was one of these preachers who happened to be holding forth in the market place near the church of St. Etienne when Jacques Mouton passed by in a rage because of the knowledge his young wife had given him. He meant to return to her and exact a just punishment on her. But the preacher called out to him:

"Stop! I say, stop! What is your unholy errand? Will the passions of your heart serve your soul? Why do you cherish your wrath? What a bitter birth for your immortal soul, to nurse in the lap of the everlasting fire. As the venom of the adder slays a man's body, so will the venom of sin slay your soul."

This was the challenge that turned Jacques from his mission and toward the church instead. He was no less angry, but now not a little fearful of where his anger may take him. Approaching from the east as he did, he walked beneath the Wheel of Fortune sculpted on the bay of the transept and carried his dark thoughts through the northwest door into the church. This is where the redemptive encounter with Blessed Jean de Beaumanoir occurred.

Perhaps I chanced upon more particulars of the story before I realized what was going on. Browsing in the college library, I often found books on the shelves that interested me, but after I carried them home, thinking I'd discovered something intriguing, the books proved to be absolutely academic or tedious or both, and I couldn't remember what attracted me to them in the first place. Even if I couldn't say what I was looking for, I certainly knew when I hadn't found it. Perhaps the something got lost on my way home. The somethings that didn't get lost, though, were unmistakable, even before I knew they were all of a piece. Here is a short list of these early encounters:

1. Sir Edmund Chambers, *The Medieval Stage*, most likely "Village Festivals": Madeleine gathering the May. Guy de Roquehautain, plants a bough of hawthorn at her feet.

2. Eileen Power, *Medieval People,* footnote number 11: Madeleine attends to her husband's cold wet feet.

3. Professor Phibbs, "The Lot of the Ladies: The Impact of War on the Status of Noble Women in Fifteenth Century France":
Madeleine's father, Lucien de Brout, killed at Agincourt in 1415. Estate reduced to rubble. No response when her mother sent to Paris to inquire if the young nobleman Madeleine believed to be her fiancé had indeed committed to a marriage. Madeleine of the House of Brout married to wealthy local burgher against her will.

4. Butler's *Lives of the Saints:* Blessed Jean de Beaumanoir counsels Madeleine's husband Jacques to forgive her. When I found this I had no idea what provoked his anger.

5. Source unknown. Possibly another academic paper: Madeleine and step-daughter Marie-Josephte dice for oublie.

6. Johan Huizinga *The Waning of the Middle Ages*: Railings of an itinerant preacher in market place near the church of St. Etienne send Jacques Mouton to Bd. Jean de Beaumanoir for confession.

7. Sir Edmund Chambers, *The Medieval Stage*, "The Feast of Fools": Footnote mentioning Roud's introductory comments on the Beauvais ceremony as related in *La Madeleine Voilée*. This is the citation I saw the night Marilee fled. This is the reference that connected the six that preceded it.

The next step was to try to remember several places I had found
Madeleine since hockey season began. Number eight on my list was
note no. 22 on page 115 of *Medieval Marriage* by George Duby. This
was the first time I found Madeleine after Marilee moved in. Duby's
note number 22 reads as follows:

> According to Andreas Capellanus it was normal for a knight
> to take a peasant woman, a servant girl, or a prostitute en-
> countered by chance in a meadow. "This is tolerated because
> it is their habit and because their sex has the privilege of
> doing everything in this world that is dishonourable by na-
> ture." Such an attitude is condemned only if it is indulged
> too frequently or if the predator attacks a woman of higher
> social standing. But the shameless noble woman who gives
> herself to several men is to be rejected from the company of
> ladies. *The situation had not improved three centuries later,*
> *during the Hundred Years War, when the "companies"—un-*
> *employed men-at-arms— roamed the countryside in search*
> *of entertainment and took it where they found it. The famous*
> *example of Madeleine de Brout establishing a house for victim-*
> *ized and forsaken women attests to the continuing prevalence*
> *of the endemic sense of entitlement enjoyed by armed men in*
> *the fifteenth century.*

Madeleine had a lot of time to establish her hostel. The war went
on interminably. I knew when I found this that I had my first entry
into a later stage of her life. The first part of the note is still there
in Duby's book. The part in italics only survives in my own notes.

The most compelling discovery, the citation of *La Madeleine
Voilée* in Chamber's "List of Authorities," came shortly after that. I
gave it number nine. Number ten is now a conundrum to me. I was
so diligent in writing it down—the reference to Madeleine—that
I completely ignored the source. I'm embarrassed to say it. It was
another book on medieval marriage, I know that. I found it in the
same section of the college library as Duby's book. The books were

overdue. I dropped them off and paid the fines at the circulation desk on my way to work the day after I read it. As an alumna I was considered a "special borrower." Such transactions were not yet part of the computer system, so they kept no record of the books once I had returned them. I tried to find the source on the shelf. Predictably, it didn't show up again.

But, much to Madeleine's pleasure, Guy de Roquehautain *did* show up again—right on the pages of that book. He came to Beauvais for the twelve days of the Feast of the Nativity and stayed on for the Flight into Egypt ceremony—the *Festum asinorum,* the Feast of the Ass—on January 14. This would have been only a year or two after the feast when Madeleine took centre stage. Madeleine's husband was conveniently absent, whether on a merchant errand, which I doubt given the time of the year, or simply away from home for some other reason, I can't say. Madeleine slipped out, lost herself in the periphery of the crowd, and followed the procession from the Cathédrale St. Pierre to Eglise St. Etienne. And there in the crowd she ran into Guy. They were immediately swept up in each other's company. When the procession arrived at St. Etienne's, they made no effort to enter the church but stepped around the bell tower into the recess of the doorway of the tower. Soon they were locked in an impassioned embrace. In Madeleine's words: "Then I knew he meant to keep his promise to me. Even so I asked for his signet, which he urgently pressed to my bosom." She wanted some kind of token. While the noisy celebration continued inside the church of St. Etienne, Madeleine and Guy warmed the winter air outside. When the festivities came to a close, Guy withdrew and left an elated Madeleine to make her own way home. The following afternoon she sought him out at his brother's town house.

Madeleine believed she was betrothed to Guy. As far as she was concerned, her congress with him constituted a marriage bed. She had been given to Jacques against her will. In the eyes of the church, a marriage is only valid if both parties consent to the match. This was common knowledge. Chroniclers of the era make much of the happiness of brides at their *disponsia*—their betrothal ceremonies—

to make it certainly known that the marriage contracted is agreeable to both parties. Madeleine knew this. Jacques's willingness to give her time to adjust to the marriage before consummation had as much to do with his desire that the notion of abduction should not compromise the arrangement, as with his good will toward a powerless orphan—a dead father was all it took to be an orphan in the fifteenth century—and her mother.

I can't speak for Guy. He may have taken Madeleine in good faith, but his own fortune was so decimated by the war that he could not be considered a good marriage prospect for her. As the second son of debased nobility in the Beauvaisis his choice was to find a vocation in the church or to join the "Companies" —a frequent resort of unmarried younger sons who would not inherit the means to stability and a ticket to mischief when their services were not needed in battle, which was most of the time. Guy de Roquehautain was too ambitious to lose himself to the vagaries of war. He was apparently studying for the clergy at Paris. When Madeleine presented herself at his brother's door, Guy stepped outside with her and whispered hotly, "Why did you come? What are you doing here?"

"Oh, Guy! I am so glad to see you. Since we came together yesterday I have devoted my thoughts and hopes entirely to you."

"Foolish girl! You are a married woman. I can have no intentions toward you."

"But you can! The marriage is not consummated. It can be annulled. My would-be husband has let me be. The marriage is as nothing in the eyes of God and the Church."

"Then you will have to make something of it. Surely you remember, I am an ordained subdeacon—I will espouse myself solely to Christ and His Church."

"This you have most certainly forsworn by your congress with me!"

"Nonsense. I am tonsured, that is all. The other vows will follow."

"But you took me for love! By all that's good, would you dishonour me by the act?"

"The events of the feast are an abomination to me now. I want no part of it."

"You already have a part in it."

"God forgives."

"And if you have got me with child, what then?"

"You are a married woman. Go home, and fulfill your debt to your husband. If you like, I will see to your absolution."

"Despicable serpent!" she spat. "As if you could!" Raging and in tears, she turned on her heel and hurried away.

ETHICS

The first step in the evolution of ethics is a sense
of solidarity with other human beings.

—Albert Schweitzer

Denise was right. Luke Kelly is the father. I couldn't give her the satisfaction of having figured it out because Marilee told me in confidence. She told no one else, except Father Francis who heard her confession. That's how he knew where to find her when she took off in the first place. He knew about Luke and had some idea of his haunts. Of course he could not ask anyone else to go see what had happened, to see if Marilee had gone in anger or desperation to find Luke. Luke was horrified—that's the word Marilee used, horrified—to see her on campus. She begged him to let her stay with him until she found a job and a place to live. He wouldn't suffer the distraction.

Luke was a serious student, already going places. He had dated Marilee briefly when she was just beginning grade ten—a short fling to console himself after his high school sweetheart broke up with him in grade twelve. It was soon over, except not for Marilee. This became clear when Marilee picked up the community paper from the kitchen table one Saturday morning, scanned a feature article, then let the paper fall limp in her hands.

"What's the matter, Marilee?"

"Oh, nothing."

"I know what you mean. I've seen a bit of nothing myself."

"Huh?"

I didn't intend to get all Augustinian on her, but there it was. "The void, the nothingness. It's not easy."

"How do you know?"

"Oh, I don't know. You just look as though the sky fell. I haven't read the paper. Is there some bad news?"

"Just this."

She pointed to the article: "Local Scholar Wins Top Prize." It didn't seem so terrible to me. "That looks like good news for *somebody*.

—Oh, I see. It's Luke Kelly. Well, good for him!"

I read on. Apparently Luke won the largest entrance scholarship available in the Faculty of Law. The article wrote about his prodigious intelligence, excellent work ethic, athletic achievement in Triple A hockey, and wonderful sense of humour. I looked up. Marilee drooped.

"What's it to you, Marilee?" But I knew. I think I would have known even if Denise hadn't already guessed it.

"It's him. He's Jessica's father." She started to cry. When I took her in my arms, she shuddered.

"It's not fair, is it. He moves on as if nothing has happened and your whole life is changed."

"Yeah. He's going to be a lawyer, make lots of money, get married—and I'll be alone with Jessica and have to depend on friends and family just to get by."

"No, you'll finish high school and explore lots of possibilities—you've just begun. You're doing so well. Who knows what's in store for you?"

"I can't do anything without allowing for Jessica. Not that I don't want her. But I can't just take off and do things. He gets all the breaks. He just goes ahead and does whatever he feels like doing."

"He's just a selfish prig. It won't serve him well in the long run."

"No, he's not. He's a nice guy. Everyone likes him."

"Nice guys don't ditch pregnant girlfriends."

"We broke up before he found out. He wasn't trying to take advantage of me. He was just heartbroken at the time. I know. I always liked him and just wanted to be with him—but it was the first time he ever noticed me. I just wanted to make him happy."

"And you? Was there anything in it for you?"

"I thought so then. But he wouldn't even consider me having our baby. He said if I decided to carry the pregnancy, he couldn't stop me. But he wasn't ready for it. He wanted nothing to do with it. And now he's free to have the kids he wants and the wife he should have— someone more his equal."

"Well, if you like him, don't wish that on him!"

She laughed little gasps like sobbing children do at the end of a cry. "Yeah, right."

"You're better than his equal, you know. You made a hard decision and followed through—by yourself, without any support from him. If he's as good as you say, some day he'll grow up and realize that." She wasn't convinced. She started to cry again.

"You still really like him, don't you."

"Yeah. I just wanted him to like me back. I didn't ask for much. I don't know what's so bad about me."

"Maybe he's the one with the problem."

"But I tried to be everything he wanted."

"Maybe its better just to be everything you are. But that's harder to do."

"I keep hoping he'll want to see me again."

"What are the chances of that?"

"None."

* * *

He saw her soon enough. On Sunday Marilee and Jessica came with me to the nine o'clock mass. We sat one pew from the back on the right, as usual. It's not far from the door which makes it easier with Jessica. Pews aren't assigned, but everyone knows. The Kellys were already there in their usual spot several pews in front of us.

Beside them sat Luke, all deserving and brilliant.

I don't know when Marilee saw Luke. Throughout the liturgy she cuddled Jessica and responded impassively to the mass. If she saw him, she gave no sign. In procession at communion, I watched Luke out of the corner of my eye. His head was bowed. No response.

After mass, the Kellys were making their way to the back when Fiona saw Jessica. "How's our dear little Jessica today?" With her comment, Luke saw us and recoiled, completely caught off guard. "*Whose* little Jessica?"

"Oh, sweetheart. This is Marilee's little girl. Such a darling. Isn't she lovely? And look! See how beautifully the back of her head curves down to her neck, just so. Just like my own babies' did."

I don't know which of the three of us was most uncomfortable. Marilee, and I, and a gaping Luke saw the obvious conclusion to be drawn from this observation. But Fiona seemed blind to it and continued, blissfully unaware. Stroking Jessica's beautifully curved head she said, "Someday maybe I'll have a granddaughter just like you!" Then turning to me: "You know what I mean, Janine, don't you?"

"N-not really," I stammered. *Did Luke tell her?*

"Well, you have two sons. Don't you hope for a granddaughter some day too? I love my boys, of course, but little girls are so special."

"Oh, I see! Well, right now it feels like I already have both a daughter and a granddaughter—Marilee and Jessica have been with us quite a while, you know. But, you're right, Fiona. They are pretty special." I gave myself a pat on the back for that one. Both Marilee and Luke looked relieved. I changed the subject directly. "And I hear congratulations are in order for you, Luke!"

"Huh?"

"It's quite an achievement."

"Oh, that. You mean the award."

"Yes. You're doing pretty well for yourself!"

"Thanks. I don't know…"

"Yes, we're so proud of him." Fiona chimed in.

On the way home Marilee and I discussed just exactly what it might have been that Luke didn't know. Marilee thought he was demurring at the praise, suggesting he would make some excuse for why he should be the lucky one. Marilee is definitely more forgiving than I am.

*   *   *

On Mondays Agnes often came into the office to help with the Sunday collection, a tedious job I gladly shared with anybody. That week she came in wearing a garish NDP button supporting Olga something for the upcoming provincial election. Good old Agnes. Just like her to pick a party that clashes with what she wears. I ignored it. Help is help. Agnes got right to work.

Sister Colette walked in. "Agnes, what's this?" She flicked Agnes's button. "You can't be serious?"

"About what? Shredding the offering envelopes? I'm trying to be playful, but the shredder hasn't figured that out yet."

"Come on, Agnes. You know what I mean. Your button. You don't support a party that promotes abortion, do you?"

"The party has a lot more to it than that, Sister. I hope I'm supporting a party that supports women with children."

"They all do that, Agnes."

"You must be kidding. None of them do. But at least Olga cares about the issue. The best way to mess up your future is to have a baby. Especially if you haven't finished school or if the father's out of the picture."

"That's not always true, Agnes. Take Marilee, for example. She's doing pretty well."

"No thanks to the Conservatives. She's managing because she's lucky enough to have the emotional and financial support she needs. For now, at any rate. It will be a long time before that little girl of hers is grown and on her own. Where would she be without her parents and Janine?"

Just leave me out of it. I just want the whole issue to disappear. Abortion is an ugly word. I don't even like to hear it said. It's not a rational reaction. I wouldn't impose my feelings on someone in a difficult situation. But the word makes me feel small. I just want it to go away. And the last thing I wanted was to talk politics with Agnes and Sister Colette. No chance of that. They were both on a mission.

"When you make something legal, you affirm it. If it's legal to do it, people think it's moral. Once people accept something as legal, it is accepted as something good."

"Gambling's legal. So's war, apparently. I know lots of people who think neither one has anything to do with goodness."

"And I know lots of people who support both because the government says it's okay."

"Well, you can't legislate ethics. The only way you're going to see a difference in the number of abortions is by making real choices available to mothers—housing, childcare, education, a supportive community—and by giving young people good information and teaching personal responsibility."

"That's asking a lot. That's impossible."

"It's asking a lot to expect someone to carry an unwelcome pregnancy or parent a child when they have no money, no support, and no place to go. That leaves desperate women bleeding to death after primitive coat-hanger procedures. Not exactly pro-life if you ask me."

"If they make good choices, with God's help they will manage."

"How many unwanted pregnancies are the result of good choices? Young people need good education and support to learn how to make better choices. They need to know their community will see to their education and support their ability to take care of themselves and their children."

"I don't think the government can be held responsible for that."

"All of us are responsible for that. Government is a big piece of it since we worthy citizens have dropped the ball—" she glanced sidelong at me, "—Janine excepted, of course. Lots of governments take responsibility for the well-being of their citizens. If you're going to hold the government responsible for ethics or morality, then you damn well need to make them responsible for social welfare. In the Netherlands, public education focuses on sexuality and family planning. Teachers help youngsters understand how to take charge of their personal well-being long before puberty. As a result, teenagers become sexually active later, the rate of teen pregnancies is several times lower than here, and they have the lowest abortion rate in the industrial world. In addition, parental leaves are longer and supports for children are universal in several countries in Europe. But if you refuse to support women in pregnancy, childbirth, and motherhood, they take desperate measures to survive."

"God forgive them."

"God forgive us all."

They worked silently for a while, but Agnes couldn't leave well enough alone.

"Well, if the government can't figure out a way to support our most vulnerable, perhaps the Fertility Gods can farm all the extra embryos and foetuses they're producing, make sausages out of them and feed them to the poor. Then everybody wins. You can't argue against that!"

Sister Colette gaped in disbelief. Agnes grinned devilishly.

"What's the matter Sister? Try telling a hungry child that you could feed her, except you would rather support some greater good. It's pretty obvious, really. Sometimes expedience is the noblest choice."

Sister Colette was appalled. I had to help her out. "Agnes is saying you have to meet basic needs before you can expect more of people, that's all. You have to have life before you can choose it. Agnes is just a little cynical."

"Well, thank you Janine. I didn't think you were listening."

"How can you even think such things, Agnes?" Sister Colette was recovering her ingenuous rigour.

"I'm trying to be part of the solution!"

"She's not serious. She's just making a point." *And she can't leave well-enough alone.*

"She sounds serious to me."

"When have I ever not been serious? Our politics would be

much improved by a little seriousness—and creativity, maybe. Or by taking recreativity seriously. Everybody wants to reduce life to a logical exercise. What's to choose between moralism and rationalism? Either way we lose the human face of it. We've got a lot of bathwater and no baby."

Finally Sister Colette figured it out: no comment, no extrapolation. She changed the subject. "Speaking of Marilee, how's she doing?"

The encounter with Luke aside, Marilee was doing well. That spring, Denise offered her part-time work in her greenhouse—late afternoons and evenings. No one was more surprised than Marilee at how much she enjoyed helping customers and working in the dirt—mixing soils, seeding, transplanting. And she was good at it. Besides, Denise kept several young people employed this way including her own kids. Marilee craved the camaraderie and relished the change from parenting and school work. It was good to be off on her own and in the company of other young people while Jessica amused the grandparents.

It was good for me, too. I had evenings to myself even after hockey season. More or less. The boys had lots to do, and I did as much as middle school moms do, driving to soccer games or dropping them off to visit friends on the other side of town. But it was an easy rhythm. After gardening season was over, Marilee continued work on her high school courses and got her diploma. She stayed with us another year beyond that, working at the greenhouse whenever Denise needed her and taking courses by mail from an agricultural college. Marilee really caught her stride, and Jessica blossomed, too.

EVIDENCE

*But of course, religious faith begins with the discovery that there is
no "evidence." There is no argument or trail of evidence or course of
experimentation that can connect unbelief and belief.*

—Wendell Berry, *Life is a Miracle*

Bit by bit the shape of Madeleine's story appeared in the three
years Marilee and Jessica lived with us. Madeleine's dalliance with
Guy began at the Feast of the Ass in the year she played the part of
Mary and rode on a donkey in procession from the cathedral to
the porch of the church of St. Etienne. Traditionally the role was
filled by a "young girl from the village." I don't know how the girl
was chosen. I do know that the young Madeleine was quite capable
of having her way. She would have been about thirteen years old at
the time.

The donkey and his gentle rider remained on the church porch
while the ceremony began within. After the assembly chanted an
inaugural prose, *Kalendas ianuarius solemne,* the doors swung open
to admit them. The year Madeleine rode the celebrated beast, Guy
was the subdeacon who took the bridle to lead them in procession
up the centre aisle of the nave to the altar. As they made their way,
the high-spirited crowd sang *Orientis partibus.*

Orientis partibus	*From the regions of the east*
adventavit asinus,	*came an ass,*
pulcher et fortissimus,	*beautiful and very strong,*
Sarcinis aptissimus.	*fit for burdens.*
Hez, Sir Asnes, hez!	*Hey, Sir Ass, oh hey!*
Hic in collibus Sychen	*Here in the hills of Sychen,*
iam nutritus sub Ruben	*nurtured by the Rubenites*
transiit per Jordanem	*he crossed the Jordan;*
saliit in Bethlehem.	*and leapt into Bethlehem.*
Hez, Sir Asnes, hez!	*Hey, Sir Ass, oh hey!*

The "Prose of the Ass" goes on for several verses, celebrating the remarkable strength and agility of the ass, expanding on his hearty appetite, until finally—

Amen dicas, asine	*Say Amen, Ass!*
Iam satur ex gramine	*Now you are filled with grass,*
amen, amen itera	*amen, amen again*
aspernare vetera	*to spurn the old.*
Hez, Sir Asnes, hez!	*Hey, Sir Ass, oh hey!*

As a central figure in the celebration, Madeleine would have been censed with smoking black pudding and sausage—*hac die incensabitur cum boudino et saucita*. Madeleine and Guy volleyed playful exchanges between them throughout the mass. Together they brayed their amens with the congregation. When the final threefold bray marked the end of the ceremony, beast and burden recessed.

Tradition has it that this was a feast to honor the beast that carried young Mary to Bethlehem. References to other donkeys including the one that carried Jesus into Jerusalem, and Balaam's ass, also grace the liturgy. Similar feasts were celebrated throughout the Christmas season in other parishes in Europe; collectively they are referred to as Feasts of Fools. Chambers calls them *tripudia*—

primeval religious dances, although I haven't read anything about dancing at the Feast of the Ass. At Beauvais there was a drinking bout on the porch of the church (probably the point at which Madeleine and Guy disappeared around the corner and engaged in their own excesses the following year). The minor orders—subdeacons and company—ran the show. Solemn and sacred rituals became the occasion for outrageous pontification and burlesque buffoonery, inverting hierarchy and order. It threw all that was held dear and sacred into relief—for the initiates, a kind of social safety valve releasing pent-up energies and frustrations with regular life and the process of initiation, and for townspeople, an opportunity for insubordinate revelry.

In the same year, on the other side of Lent and Easter, Guy planted the hawthorn at the feet of a very green Madeleine. There may have been other encounters throughout the summer. It was sometime early autumn Guy de Roquehautain packed himself up and went off to the University in Paris, needing to see to his own advancement.

As for Madeleine, all hope of material and financial recovery for the de Brout family perished with the death of her father at Agincourt on October 25, 1415. Her mother, Marie Christine, went quickly about the urgent business of settling her younger daughter. Their fortune plummeting, there was no time to lose. It could be that Madeleine's marriage to Jacques Mouton was sealed within weeks of the French catastrophe. At the very most, she was married within the year. Accordingly, I have placed Madeleine's birth date in the summer of 1401 and her wedding to Jacques close to Christmas in 1415.

I have inferred what I can about Jacques's métier. He was probably a draper—he had something to do with textiles, certainly. Likely he was one of those merchants who made his fortune by "putting-out," purchasing wool from places as far away as England, arranging for householders to card wool and spin, then providing this product to weavers who worked on looms in his own establishment. This would account for his lengthy journeys from Beauvais.

He traded in the ports north and east of his base of operation—both to purchase wool and to sell his finished cloth. He may have made trips to Calais, which was held by the English.

I am not sure about his loyalties in the war. Beauvais had been part of the royal demesne long before the war started. But as early as 1411, the bishop of Beauvais, Pierre de Savoisy, ordered allegiance to the Burgundians. In autumn of that same year, John, Duke of Burgundy, even sheltered in Beauvais one night. Not that the townspeople ever fully aligned themselves with the bishop and the canons of the cathedral. Nevertheless, Jacques's livelihood depended on the textiles market which would no doubt incline him to sympathize with the Burgundians who wanted to protect trade with England. Since his business seems to have continued with reasonable success, or at the very least, did not provoke worry to warrant attention in my sources, he must have maintained a tactful reserve on political matters. At first I didn't connect Jacques Mouton with Madeleine. He married a daughter of Lucien de Brout, a name I didn't recognize at the time. Of course, when I did finally realize how Jacques figured in Madeleine's life, he could no longer be found on all the pages where I had encountered him. I would say his evanescence confirms his place in the story. He was, by this cameo portrait, a respected citizen of Beauvais, wealthy and influential among his peers, an important parishioner of Eglise St. Etienne.

I doubt Jacques got what he hoped for when he married Madeleine, at least at the beginning. He surely thought this spirited girl would become a lovely, lively companion. His return from an excursion early after the marriage gave rise to the encounter in note 11 of Eileen Power's *Medieval People* where Madeleine washed his feet and freshened his stockings. Jacques persisted in good will but she was in no way biddable, even though Jacques was gracious not to urge himself into the marriage bed of his sullen wife.

In France, the times were dour as well. They were nineteen years into a truce with England that was regularly broken by piracy and *chevauchées*—destructive raids on territories held by the enemy. The French King Charles VI—Charles the Mad—had fewer and fewer moments of sanity. When he was insane, the Dukes of Burgundy, his uncle, Philippe le Hardi—Philip the Bold, followed by his cousin, Jean sans Peur—John the Fearless, were his regents. When he was capable of assuming royal duties, Charles relied on his brother, Louis, Duke of Orleans, until Burgundy's men sprang on Louis as he was mounting his horse, lopped off his arms, and did away with the defenceless man. This was done after years and years of excesses and offenses between the feuding parties, mind you. But there it is. Jean sans Peur justified the act as "tyrannicide." The murder only increased hostilities between the two great houses of France. Charles of Orleans, Louis's son and heir, and his father-in-law, the count of Armagnac, breathed vengeance. Across the channel, except he never stayed home, Henry V was on the throne of England. After his victory at Agincourt, Henry began calculated military campaigns to conquer and occupy Normandy.

The church was also in confusion. An attempt to resolve the claims of two rival popes in 1409 led to the election of a third pope... *three, three, the rivals!* In 1415 the Council of Constance convened. This council had an ambitious agenda: to suppress heresy, reform the church, and to end the papal schism. The most notorious result of the council was their condemnation of John Hus as a heretic. The council handed him over to the Emperor Sigismund, who burned him at the stake. As for church reform, there was much debate with little result except to require the convening of several future councils to address the problems. Consequently, festivals such as the *Festum asinorum* continued in sturdy abandon. But the council did ultimately succeed in ending the schism. By 1417, one pope, Martin V, enjoyed general approbation. Of the three rivals, only one intransigent held on until 1423. He died without heirs.

Meanwhile, Guy de Roquehautain devined the way the wind was blowing. He quietly aligned himself with Burgundy when he went off to Paris. For years Paris had been under siege from within, falling alternately into the hands of the Armagnacs and Burgundians, but by this time, the Burgundians and English held the upper hand, as they would for twenty years to come. Guy slunk to the ferment like a dog to carrion. When he returned to Beauvais for the Christmas festivities, he was quite full of himself and his loyalties to Burgundy explicit. Who knows what he was thinking when he encountered the married Madeleine? Perhaps he was quite taken with her—or thought no harm done, since she was willing.

It would have been all over, except Madeleine conceived. Had she paid her marital debt to her husband, that would probably have been the end of it. But Madeleine couldn't bring herself to seduce a husband she so readily scorned before. She soon suffered bouts of nausea and extreme exhaustion. Jacques, like a worried father, thought she had contracted a terrible disease and would waste away before his eyes. Finally, she told him. He came to her room one morning when she was particularly indisposed. Other householders were all about the kitchen seeing to breakfast and the order of the day. Standing well back so as not to be afflicted with what ailed her, Jacques drew aside the curtain of her bed and asked what could be done for her.

"Send me to my sister for the year and I will recover well enough."

"Oh, dear child. I cannot send you so far afield in such dangerous times."

"I will do better if I go away."

"That cannot be done with you sick as you are."

No doubt Madeleine's dismay at her predicament contributed to her poor health. And Guy's unceremonious repudiation of her must have made her miserable as well. She looked up at her husband and benefactor: "You will not want me here when I am well. Better to let me go now."

"What can you mean by that?"

"I am with child."

Jacques smiled indulgently. "My dear, except for Our Blessed Lady, these things don't happen to virgins." She stared back at him, saying nothing. As he stood silent, the import of her words settled. Then rage devoured him. "Flesh of the devil!" Before she could turn from him he lunged at her and delivered a stinging blow to the side of her face. Madeleine stifled a scream. He kicked at the

bedstead. "Wallowing sow. You will hang. And that's a kindness."
He went storming out of the room meeting Nannette, his old servant and former nursemaid, in the stairwell. "See she doesn't escape
the room. If she's gone when I return, there will be no mercy for
anyone."

Jacques had no idea where to turn. What he wanted was to exact
a little justice. He could repudiate Madeleine—he was well within his rights there. But that would only give her what she wanted. Had he lived in the Holy Roman Empire under Frederick II,
he could have had her nose cut off, but alas, that practice didn't
last. Public lashings had fallen out of favour too. Madeleine was
lucky, I suppose. But Jacques was not worried about the law. The
thirteenth-century *Coutumes de Beauvaisis* excuses husbands for
injuries they inflict on their wives, as long as they neither kill nor
maim them. Even so, were Jacques to kill her for adultery, the court
would certainly show clemency. He was a man of importance in
the community and had no declared enemies. He raged along the
streets of Beauvais looking for some friend or confrere to hear him
out and advise him, or perhaps for some villainous lowlife to take
Madeleine to hand.

To Jacques's hindrance and much to his aggravation, the marketplace was crowded with activity when he tried to cross it. The
crowding was due to the presence of a half-crazed friar preaching against the ills of the age. It seemed the more Jacques pressed
against the tide, the more the masses surged against him. Thus he
attracted the notice of the preacher who read Jacques's resistance as
a threat to his immortal soul. Jacques wondered how he knew, how
the preaching friar could so readily read his intent. But the preacher
made his mark. Jacques began to think about his own end. If he did
away with Madeleine, how would his own life unfold? Where would
he spend eternity? However angry he was, the terror of nursing in
the lap of the everlasting fire overwhelmed his wrath. So it happened that when he escaped the crowd he headed directly toward
the church of St. Etienne passing underneath the Wheel of Fortune
now turning treacherously to bring him down.

Jacques retreated into the shadowy nave and collapsed onto a short joint stool tucked away in a stone-cold corner. This was more than he could endure. He had done well by Madeleine. She was lucky to have both wealth and kindness in a husband, but what had she done with it? Ungrateful strumpet. Would that God strike her down! She was the one should suffer for this, not he, who only asked for justice.

He sat, bent and confused, not knowing what to do next, when a lively head popped out from the curtain of the confessional. "Are you ready now, brother?"

"Excuse me, Father. Ready for what?"

"To make your confession, of course!"

"Not at all! I have nothing to confess."

"Then I must surely speak with you. What a grace for me!" The animated man trotted over to Jacques. "May I?" He pulled up another stool to sit beside Jacques, who grunted something that passed for consent.

After a halting beginning, Jacques poured out his heart. I wish I knew what passed between them—what the Blessed Jean de Beaumanoir said that worked such a change in Jacques. It may have been no miracle at all. Blessed Jean may have just brought Jacques to his senses and reminded him of who he was. Jacques needed to remember that his generous spirit and good will were only good and generous in proportion to how he responded to situations beyond his control. Even so, that is something miraculous I suppose, healing a choleric and malevolent humor in such a fraught state.

Finally the cavernous silence of the old church enveloped the two of them huddled there. It was the feast of the Annunciation. When time came for the mass, Jacques stood well away from the gathered assembly. Blessed Jean took the opportunity to remind the congregation that at first the news of Mary's pregnancy did not sit well with poor Joseph, but even before he had word from the angel, he resolved to treat her with discretion and honour. The words of the mass settled. After the faithful had come and gone, Blessed Jean invited Jacques to join him for a bite to eat. "A day without bread is a long day, my man!" Jacques followed him to a small cell, off and around the corner, where Blessed Jean de Beaumanoir poured a bowl of cider and broke a small loaf to share.

There are no details about Jacques's return home—only that Jacques forgave an unrepentant Madeleine and that it was not generally known in the household or anywhere else that Jacques was not the father of the son she bore. Jacques tenderly welcomed the child as his own, and named him Jean-Etienne. His daughter, Marie-Josephte, on the other hand, resented her supposed half-brother. Enough that Madeleine demanded so much of the energy of the household—now her upstart son looked to usurp Marie-Josephte's place as the hope and joy of the family.

In time Madeleine resigned herself to a situation that could have been much worse. Having born her child in safety, Madeleine softened toward the household and began overtures of friendship toward Marie-Josephte—with no success at the outset. Marie-Josephte would have been eleven. She had lived with Madeleine for well over a year and had learned to stay out of her way. Even had the girls been sisters, the confounding effects of early puberty for Marie-Josephte and Madeleine's premature passage into adulthood may well have frustrated their friendship. But whatever the errand that took the two of them out togther, dicing with the pastry seller for an *oublie* shifted the humours. The crisp golden wafer won by Madeleine and shared with her step-daughter somehow acted as a remedy for accumulated bitterness.

Madeleine was sixteen when her marriage to Jacques was finally consummated. By then Jean-Etienne was almost a year old. In short order Madeleine gave birth to another son, little Jacques-Lucien. His father was euphoric. Jacques opened his arms to the universe and everyone within the scope of his embrace. And Madeleine came to cherish his kindnesses.

This same grace of peace and rapprochement eluded the larger community. In April of 1417, the son and heir of mad King Charles VI died. His second son, also named Charles, thus became the dauphin at fourteen years of age and was named lieutenant general of the kingdom. He and his mother, Queen Isabeau, were not close. After the murder of Louis of Orleans, she consorted with Louis's murderer, Jean sans Peur of Burgundy. I suppose the dauphin thought it would be easier to keep his mother on side if she were imprisoned, but Jean sans Peur, with a bit of derring-do, rescued her. He and Queen Isabeau escaped Paris with the mad king in tow and set up court at Troyes in opposition to that of her young son. This was the year Jean sans Peur signed a pact with England, and the year he entered Beauvais in August greeted with welcoming shouts of "Noël!"—Good news!—by a crowd hoping for tax relief and letters of protection. Instead, as it turned out, the duke was bad news for the city, exacting hefty taxes to support his personal ambitions.

Meanwhile, the English took advantage of the French political mayhem and renewed their assault on Normandy. The pièce de résistance of this campaign came in July of 1418 with the siege of Rouen. Henry V built four fortified camps connected by trenches and fed his armies with food shipped from England. Within the walls of the city, the citizens were soon reduced to eating horseflesh. At length, the defenders expelled some 12,000 "useless mouths" from the starving city. Many of these were people from the countryside who had fled to safety from Henry's advancing soldiers. But Henry V denied these hapless wights passage beyond the cordon of the siege. They were trapped within the fields of battle. It was a horror. An appalled English soldier serving under Henry wrote a lay describing their desperate condition:

> "There one could see a piteous spectacle—
> one could see wandering here and there
> children of two or three years of age begging for bread,
> for their parents were dead.
> These wretched people had only the sodden soil under them,
> and they lay there crying for food—
> some starving to death,
> some unable to open their eyes and no longer breathing,

others cowering on their knees as thin as twigs.
A woman was there clutching her dead child
to her breast to warm it,
another child sucking the breast of his dead mother,
and a weeping bride cradling the corpse of her young husband.
There one could easily count ten or twelve dead to one alive,
who had died so quietly without call or cry
as though they had died in their sleep.
John Page wrote this story without fable or falsehood
in rough and not in polished rhyme
(because he had no time to do this).
However, when this war is ended,
and if he is alive and has the inclination,
he will put this right.
May He that died for us upon a tree
bring His blessing to those who have heard this reading;
for charity's sake let us say, 'Amen.'"

But—bless his heart—for the Feast of the Nativity, Henry V sent food to the starving masses by way of two priests, the only emissaries the defenders of the city allowed.

Some fifty miles to the east, people in the region of Beauvais were better off, to be sure. But it was no great advantage to be under the protection of Burgundy. They could escape the walls of their city and glean what they might from uncultivated lands and ravaged fields, and hope the bells of the city would ring out in time to call them back from marauding soldiers and other imminent threats. Food was scarce and disease rampant. It was all Jacques could do to keep his household. Madeleine was weary with caring for the unrelenting needs of their sick and the aged who had no health to hold them. And she had two suckling babes. Jean-Etienne was just two years old and Jacques Lucien not yet a year. Old Nanette died of consumption. Jean-Etienne had a terrifying bout with fever. Into the midst of these troubles came an unwelcome request from Blessed Beaumanoir. Would they take into their home a young woman whose husband had died in the shadow of the walls of Rouen? "Do not worry about providing for yet another soul. God knows your needs," he said. Madeleine balked. *Let the day's own troubles be sufficient for the day. There are beggars enough at the door and travellers in the hall.* But Madeleine could not say no to the holy man.

As is often the case, the idea was more burdensome to her than the reality. The young woman who came was the weeping bride of John Page's lay. I have not seen John Page's "rough, unpolished rhyme" other than the excerpt above which I found on page 22 of Fowler's *Hundred Years War*. Perhaps the line about the weeping bride can still be found in the original, but I am surely the only one ever to have seen it in Fowler's book. Her story only came to light when Blessed Beaumanoir presented her on Madeleine's threshold, weak and wasted and pregnant. When Madeleine saw her— *la pauvrette!*—she immediately took her in hand, nursing her as if her every breath were a benediction. La Pauvrette rallied for awhile, but when her little boy—P'tit Beau she called him—was born, she hemorrhaged and died.

Madeleine was overwhelmed with grief, as much for the orphaned P'tit Beau as for La Pauvrette and for what she believed to be her failure in caring for the young woman. She herself took P'tit Beau to her breast and nursed him as if her own life depended on it. He began to thrive. With three busy little boys about, Madeleine took some delight in their endless adventures and discoveries. However, she found little consolation in the reasonable abundance of her larder, the health of her children, the equanimity of her husband, the relative comfort of her life. These things stood in stark relief to the life and death of La Pauvrette. Madeleine could no longer shut out the moiling misery of the world outside her doors. It gnawed at her sensibilities and she responded as best she could, despite the busyness of her household.

And so it continued. As did the war. The year 1419 opened with the fall of Rouen. Even so, France appeared to be pulling things together. In the summer, at Corbeille, the dauphin Charles and the Armagnacs met with the Burgundians led by Jean sans Peur.

The meeting seemed promising enough and the parties agree to meet again. Come September, they met on the bridge spanning the Yonne at Montereau. When Jean sans Peur knelt to pay homage to the dauphin, an Armagnac attacked him with a battle axe. Tit for tat. Louis of Orleans was revenged. Hope for reconciliation between the parties lay hacked to bloody bits on the cobbles.

In December of that year, Philippe le Bon—Philip the Good, son of the murdered Jean sans Peur, cast his loyalties across the water and formed an alliance with Henry V. In May of 1420, with pomp and ceremony, Henry V made his way through the French country-side to St. Denis, the pilgrimage destination of French kings, where he stopped to pray. Then on he went to Troyes to meet with Queen Isabeau and her mad king. Here Isabeau disinherited the dauphin Charles, claiming him to be the offspring of an extramarital affair, making her daughter Catherine the king's only legitimate heir. The Treaty of Troyes betrothed the English King Henry to Catherine, thus Henry became the heir and regent of France. France's King Charles signed the document, apparently not even knowing who Henry was. A wedding for Catherine and Henry followed in short order. The happy couple made their marriage bed near the battle front and Henry spent his honeymoon laying siege to Sens.

On August 21, 1420, Pierre Cauchon, a chief negotiator of the Treaty of Troyes, was named bishop and count of Beauvais and thereby made an ecclesiastical peer of the kingdom through Philippe le Bon, who attended his investiture. The city remained under the supposed protection of the duke of Burgundy, although ravages by both Burgundian and Armagnac troops continued not-withstanding.

It was about this time that Guy de Roquehautain finished his studies at the University of Paris, was ordained, granted a pre-bend, and came back to Beauvais as Guy Monsieur le Chanoine de Roquehautain, a canon of the cathedral of St. Pierre. This did not come as a surprise. Several prominent families of the region had dominated the chapter of canons at the cathedral for generations and Guy was no doubt connected to one of these families. More than forty canons served the cathedral. But unlike canons regular, they neither lived in common quarters nor shared regular meals. They lived near the cathedral in their own houses, supported by the revenues of their prebends. Guy's house was directly south of the cathedral, on the street leading most directly from the cathedral to the church of St. Etienne. His revenues must have been relatively small in 1420, so many lands of the region lay in waste. But canons had rights of justice over mills in their prebends and the rights to hear cases of larceny and even the right of excommunication. This suited Canon Guy just fine.

No doubt Madeleine was aware of his return. Her orbit, however, in the church of St. Etienne and his orbit, at the cathedral, rarely intersected. It was years before any interaction of note passed between them. Madeleine managed her household and continued her works of mercy as occasion presented them. She had much to be thankful for—more children, a daughter and two more sons all surviving infancy, and an easy joy in her life with Jacques.

TURNING

I know this now. Every man gives his life for what he believes. Every woman gives her life for what she believes. Sometimes people believe in little or nothing yet they give their lives to that little or nothing. One life is all we have and we live it as we believe in living it. And then it is gone. But to sacrifice what you are and live without belief, that's more terrible than dying.

—Jeanne d'Arc

Marilee finished several distance courses from Foothills Agricultural College before she applied to go into a full-time program with a focus on woody plants and trees. She had done well and was readily admitted for the fall term. The situation was ideal. Marilee's cousin, Blythe, lives in the town. She and her husband regularly rent a room to students of the college. Marilee secured the room and arranged childcare with her cousin for times when Jessica was not in kindergarten. I was so happy for her.

Mid-August Marilee packed up, full of hope and expectation. My mother came over for breakfast and to see them off. "My girls," she called them. She had become quite attached. "Of course, this is 'au revoir' not 'adieu.' You'll be back again and again and I will make a feast every time!" she said.

Miles offered his truck for the move. We all loaded it up after breakfast. The Clarks arrived and settled Marilee and Jessica into the back of their car. Miles was to follow them down the highway. At the last minute, Adam and Kit decided to go along to help unload at the other end. Mom and I stood on the sidewalk and waved them off. There would have been no room for me in the cab, had I hoped to join them.

"It was good what you did for them, Janine."

"It was good what they did for us, Mom. We're all going to miss them." In fact, I was a little afraid of how we'd do—left to ourselves. Mom came in to help clean up breakfast, then went to work her Saturday shift. I met Denise for coffee as usual and finally came home to a very empty house. A day to myself. How often I had thought I wanted one.

Surely something needed doing. I worked a bit in the yard, but Marilee had mostly seen to that. The perennials were trimmed, the weeds under control, and the rose bushes pruned to perfection. No question—she had a gift for growing things. Inside I wandered from the laundry to the dishes and browsed the paper. *Odd how it turned out. How much I resisted her coming and now it seems the whole reason for living went out the door with her and Jessica. Our life is over like a sigh. Our span is seventy years, or eighty for those who are strong. And most of these are emptiness and pain.* Monday's psalm. Father Francis had the reading of it. Father Francis would soon be seventy-five. If *he* experienced emptiness and pain, I didn't see it. *Well, Janine! You have your boys, your work, your home, even Madeleine, wherever she's got to.*

I decided to make bread. I love baking bread—coddling the leaven, keeping it warm, feeding it something sweet so it will grow. And the flour, folding it into the leaven sponge, then working in more flour more heavily. Finally turning it all onto a floured surface to knead it, turning and pressing the formless mound with the heels of my hands, drawing it up and pushing it back. With every turn it responds with elastic impertinence, bouncing back more and more active and reactive until it rests, a smooth round sphere of dough that will rise to double its size.

I couldn't have done anything better with my afternoon. Bread and dinner were ready when the boys and Miles returned home full of the day. Kit, who had just got his learner's permit, drove the first 50 kilometers or so and Adam had driven the rest of the way back. The bread warmed the conversation and filled the hollow inside. I felt better than I expected to.

It took awhile to settle into the vacancy. At first both Miles and I maintained a certain civility. When the girls were with us, I had seen a tender side of him I had forgotten, a side he had been reluctant to show for some time. I tried to keep the things he values at the forefront: economic restraint, orderly household patterns, and early bedtimes. I was playful, but not to excess. Miles tried too, I think. He sat longer at dinner, as he had done when Marilee and Jessica sat with us. He let the boys be the first to excuse themselves, which they often did early as they rushed off in other directions. Miles continued to help clear the table as he had begun to do when the girls moved in. It took a while to renew old hostilities. The truth is, however, that although Miles and I had put our differences aside to make room for our guests, we never really let them go. The insidious reticence wormed its way between us again. It wasn't long before Miles didn't bother to drive above an hour's distance in order to be home on weekday evenings. When he worked out of town, he stayed out of town, as he had always done before. Even with little or nothing to keep us kind, wherever it goes, life goes on, I suppose.

As if the girls' going wasn't enough, at the office we celebrated Father Francis' seventy-fifth birthday and he officially retired. Father Francis planned to continue his work at the prison after an extended vacation visiting family out east. At least his absence was only temporary. He would remain at the rectory since his replacement would not be needing accommodation. The new associate pastor would be joining the faculty at the college and only serve part-time in the parish.

Farewells said, I prepared for a dismal fall. In two weeks the boys were off to school— Adam to begin grade eleven, Kit, grade nine. The summer quiet in the office began to ravel. Liturgy and council meetings started up, as did the choir rehearsals. Our new pastoral associate would come to us mid-September, giving him time to settle into his teaching schedule first. The day he was expected began much as any other. The remnant, Father Eugene, Sister Colette, Walter and I, were hotfooting through Morning Prayer. I was flipping along with the rest of them—so much has become second nature to me. We had begun the intercessions:

We bless you, Creator of all things,
—for you have given us the goods of the earth and brought us
to this day.

when the bell rang. Sister Colette went to answer the door. We rumbled on without her.

Look with favor on us as we begin our daily work,
—let us be fellow workers with you.
May our work today benefit our brothers and sisters
—that with them and for them we may build...

Sister Colette returned with the newcomer. They stood in the doorway behind me, repeating the *Our Father* with us and remained standing for the benediction. I turned for the introductions.

"Janine!"

"Jim! What are *you* doing here?"

"Such a welcome!" He took my hands. "It's good to see you again. Are you a member of this parish?"

"I work in the office here. But, yes. I am."

"Oh. That's lovely."

"Do you know Father Eugene?" They nodded and shook hands. "This is Walter, the custodian and a wonderful fiddler." Another handshake.

We explained we had done our undergrad together. Then Father Eugene whisked him off to show him to his office and take a tour of the building.

Hard to say how I felt. Apprehensive to be sure but it seemed quite auspicious. *Father Jim. How will I ever call him that?* Although Jim may have changed over the years, I knew him to be as good-natured and caring a person as anyone. I hoped he wouldn't be aloof or impersonal with me. No need to worry. We all ate lunch in the rectory. Jim was talkative and engaging. I think Father Eugene's estimation of me improved when Jim enthused about my academic career.

* * *

Miles wasn't quite as keen to hear about our new priest. "How long is he likely to stay?"

"I have no idea. Could be a year. Could be ten. But he'll be good, I know. As a pastor, in homiletics—everything."

"Oh, *everything*. Your priest is pretty much perfect, I suppose."

"*Miles,* he's not *my* priest. It's just a relief to have somebody who's good with people. Father Eugene's competent, but he comes across as perfunctory and cold."

"And now you've got someone to keep you warm. Well isn't that nice."

"No. I don't have anyone to keep me warm. That won't change. I'll just have to keep shivering along as best I can."

"I don't know how you bear it."

"Neither do I."

This may have been what set off the old familiar rhythms. How was I to know? Why should I even expect Miles to care? Still, I tried to be sensitive to his obvious discomfort. I made sure Miles knew Jim was at the parish just two weekdays and Sundays and I learned to mention Jim—Father Jim— only in terms of a larger group. Which was mostly how it fell out anyway. What more could I do?

* * *

Marilee and Jessica came home for Thanksgiving. The Clarks' home, I mean—as it should be. But they spent Saturday afternoon with us. Jessica—so clever and such a little flirt—had a heyday.

Miles and the boys couldn't get enough of her. She presided as reigning princess over her adoring subjects. They were enthralled. Marilee was full of news. Her courses and teachers were everything she had hoped for. She'd made several friends among students, and, best of all, she'd found a boyfriend, Shane, who liked Jessica almost as much as he liked her. They spent more time together as a three-some than the two of them did on dates.

The girls were to come for brunch after mass on Sunday, before we set out for the city with Mom to have our holiday dinner with family there. Brunch was mostly ready when Kit and I left for church. Miles took charge of final preparations.

Kit and I sat with the Clarks in the usual pew, second from the back on the right. The Kellys filed by just as we were settled. Behind them came Luke, who looked our way, mostly at Jessica, nodded briefly and passed. "Well, that was a little more civil," I whispered to Marilee. It wasn't often we had enjoyed his shunning over the years, our paths crossed so rarely. But this was the first time he had voluntarily acknowledged us and it was the first time I had seen Marilee become aware of his presence with such composure.

After mass, as we collected ourselves, chatting with friends as they passed, the Kellys came along. Fiona stopped to say hello. "And how Jessica's grown! How old are you now, sweetheart?"

"I'm five! And I had a birthday party. And lots of kids came. And Katy spilled ice cream all down her dress!"

"My, that sounds like quite a party!"

"And the dog licked her all over…"

Jessica continued her saga, but lost her audience when Luke turned to Marilee, said hello, and asked would she like to go for coffee?

Marilee was stunned. She glanced at me and answered, "I'm not sure. We're going to Janine's for brunch."

I couldn't read her face. I didn't know if it was with regret or relief she made her excuses. "Brunch will hold, Marilee. If you want to go for a half hour, that's fine with me. I can take Jessica if you like."

"Oh, no. Jessica will come with us—if that's okay with you,

Marilee." Luke was intent and unequivocal. They were off in a heart-beat. Fiona stood staring after them. Pat took her arm, bid us a happy Thanksgiving, and guided her out the door.

The Clarks had occupied the far end of the pew. Eleanor came over to me. "Well, good for him. It's about time he took an interest!" We shook hands with Father Eugene, and went our separate ways.

"What was that about?" The implications of what passed weren't lost on Kit.

"You'll probably know soon enough."

We walked home crunching leaves underfoot all the way. The trees were bare: two weeks of colour, then leaves brown on the ground, but the crisp autumn air still brilliant. The phone was ringing as we entered the house.

"Hello, Janine?" It was Fiona Kelly.

"How are you, Fiona?"

"I'm a little worried."

"Yes?"

"About Luke. I don't know what to think of Luke going out with a girl like Marilee."

"He's meeting her for coffee, Fiona. What's the problem?"

"Well, you know…"

"No, I don't."

"I'm just not sure about her—standards—her—well, we all know about Jessica."

"That Marilee's taken responsibility and doing a good job raising her little girl?"

"Well, yes. I mean, no. I'm just not sure she's right for Luke."

"Marilee is as lovely a person as he's ever likely to meet."

"But he needs to think about his reputation, especially in *his* field."

"I assure you, Fiona, his reputation is improving by the minute with me. I'm glad he's taking time to renew old acquaintances."

"I think you'd feel differently if he were your son."

"Relax, Fiona, I'm sure Luke just feels free to be sociable now that he's finished school. Besides, Marilee has a boyfriend who is wild about her and Jessica."

"She does? Oh. That's great!"

"I doubt she'd be interested in Luke even if he did want to date her."

"Well, it *is* nice of Luke to take her out for coffee. I'm sure she appreciates it."

"I'm sure she does."

"So then! I want to wish all of you a wonderful Thanksgiving!"

"Thanks. You too, Fiona."

* * *

Marilee and Jessica were not long. Luke saw them to the door and went on his way. Marilee hurried Jessica inside, shut the door, backed against it as if to prevent the escape of—I don't know what— "You just won't believe this!"

We were all attention. "What? What is it?"

"Luke gave me a support agreement for Jessica! And cheques for a year. He said he isn't doing it to be nice. It's his legal obligation. I'm supposed to look over the agreement and if I want to change anything I can call him. And he will pay retroactive support as well when he finishes articling. And he wants to visit Jessica—with me— at least until she knows him better. And he's going to tell his parents. Not yet. Maybe at Christmas. He wants time to get to know Jessica first. He'll drive down in two weeks for his first visit."

The boys stood silent, grasping the sense of what she said. The import of all this settled uneasily on Miles. He fidgeted awhile then left the room.

Brunch had long been ready. I called Miles back as we arranged ourselves around the table. Marilee leaned over and whispered, "What's the matter with Miles?"

"I think he's a little jealous. He's been a bit of a father figure for Jessica, you know."

"Well, that won't change."

* * *

Come Christmas, Luke was as good as his word. He let the Feast of the Nativity pass, waiting until Boxing Day to herald his own child. Fiona took it hard at the beginning. She needed awhile to adjust but she came around. Pat mostly kept his stride. "Kids can get into worse trouble," he said. But they were a little surprised at the people who came forward with congratulations on their new grandchild and with admiration for Luke for owning up. I know Marilee was never so wholeheartedly championed. The best part was that Jessica's village was larger. But it meant there were even more people to see when they came to town. Bless her heart, Marilee always made as much time as she could in Jessica's schedule for an unspeaking but grateful Miles.

We waited expectantly for every one of Marilee's visits that year. She and Jessica helped us tolerate each other better. Me and Miles, that is. I must say that although Adam and Kit felt the tension between the two of us, they did their best to walk the wire. And perhaps it is a grace that while we turned away from each other we turned toward our sons for ease and friendship. It doesn't always happen that way.

VOICES

Why do they shut me out of heaven? Did I sing too loud?
—Emily Dickinson

Not being heard is no reason for silence.
—Victor Hugo, *Les Misérables*

Father Francis never returned. On New Year's Eve he, his sister, and two of his nieces went skating on an outdoor pond and returned home for hot buttered rum before bed. The next morning, he didn't come to breakfast. Full of years, he lay emptied of life in his bed. His great heart had finally failed. He died as close to home as a solitary celibate can.

He was to have come back to us the next day. It was a blow to the whole community. Only Father Eugene remained dispassionate it seemed, except he lost patience with the littlest thing and often wandered into the general office area for no apparent reason, shuffling through papers or scanning the bookshelves. I tried to be sensitive, cosseting him a little, baking treats for coffee. I don't know that he appreciated it. I often took the brunt of his confusion and ill-humour. We planned a memorial mass for the middle of the month. That helped a little.

I felt like a part of me died with Father Francis. No one had seen the goodness in me as he had. I was accustomed to my failures. Miles certainly had expectations that I had no hope or inclination to fulfill. Not so with Father Francis. He seemed to think me capable of more than I ever dreamed of. And yet, I was never aware of any expectation from him until I had already exceeded it.

After Father Francis died, Agnes didn't come around as often as she had before. Not that I missed her, but the days at work seemed to last interminably. Any disruption was welcome. She showed up for liturgy meetings, however, and continued to take responsibility for scheduling and training lectors. Late in January we began to plan for the three-day cycle that begins on Holy Thursday and culminates in the Easter Vigil—the *Triduum*. Agnes was not happy about the previous year's observance. "The Gospel for the day reads: 'standing near the cross of Jesus were his mother, and his mother's sister, and Mary Magdalene.' So why were all the servers for the veneration of the cross men?" Father Eugene mumbled something about not needing to take everything so literally. Agnes didn't hear him. Just as well.

One pattern held. Agnes showed up at the office for lunch the day after the liturgy meeting pitching her usual budget of grievance and injustice, Colette and I her reluctant audience. "It's not as if the faces of women have eclipsed the glory of God—or the glory of men, for that matter." On she went about the blindness of the clergy, about their remarkable ability to ignore the gifts and vocations of women except to serve their own purposes.

Finally I'd had it. "If you are so unhappy in the church, why do you bother with it at all?"

"This is *my* church, Janine. You don't move out of your house just because the roof leaks or the sewer backs up. You fix it. 'What is lame may not be put out of joint but rather be healed.' Sometimes you even have to break bones to reset them. Otherwise you lose the chance for redemption."

"You're called to redeem the church?"

"Well, that has a nice ring to it. I think we all are."

"I doubt you'll see much change in your lifetime."

"And you think that's a good enough reason to give up?"

"I don't know. I'm not sure things are all that bad."

"Perhaps not. As long as you're content to let a small, select group of men interpret faith and experience for the whole community. Well, I was anointed at my baptism to participate in the prophetic, priestly and kingly offices of Christ. 'Like good stewards of the manifold grace of God, serve one another with whatever gift each of you has received. Whoever speaks must do so as one speaking the very words of God.' That's Peter. Can't argue with him there."

Walter came clattering in with a ladder. "Hello, ladies. Where's the culprit?" I pointed to a burnt out light in the corner of the office. He set up his ladder, climbed up and began to unfasten the cover.

"Well, Agnes," Sister Colette replied, "Saint Paul says we should 'have unity of spirit, sympathy, love for one another, a tender heart, and a humble mind.' Don't you think it's a little divisive to continually question the authority of sacred tradition?" It was beyond my ability to quote scripture and argue as they did. *And Denise thinks Lutherans can quote chapter and verse. These two could take a Lutheran any day.*

"What aspect of our tradition do you mean? The one that calls all of us a 'chosen race, a royal priesthood, a holy nation, God's own people'?" Agnes was on a roll. "What's divisive about forwarding Paul's own contention that we are no longer Jew or Greek, slave or free, male or female?"

"He also said women should be silent in church."

Climbing down the ladder Walter slipped and missed the final step. He landed shakily on his feet but the ladder crashed to the ground. He grinned sheepishly. "Ladies, you should be careful what you say when an old man is tottering nearby." He picked up the burnt-out lightbulb from the shelf where he'd left it, bent over slowly to pick up the ladder, perched it on his shoulder and walked out muttering something about unsafe working environments. Agnes and I smiled. I could see Sister Colette would like to have had that last comment back but Agnes wasn't going to let it pass.

"I'm sure you know, some scholars believe that passage was a late addition to the original text. Why would Paul tell women not to speak except if they already were? Maybe after a few administrative failures he got impatient. The world was a little older by then and the earliest practice more distant. Paul, or perhaps a scribe, looked around and said, 'Aha! There's our problem! Christians recognize women as equal heirs to the kingdom. Well, we'll have to fix that.' Gradually they reinstated cultural norms that bound women to silence and submisson."

Just then Father Eugene came blustering in. "Where is the file for the Cabrelli wedding?" I jumped up to fetch it. It wasn't in the drawer where it should have been. I checked the file folders before and after the slot. No luck.

"I just saw it. I know I did. Didn't I give it to you yesterday?"

"No. It's not on my desk."

Sister Colette came over and anxiously began to sort through my papers. "Please, let me do that." I wedged between her and my desk. I don't appreciate people messing with my stuff. It wasn't there anyway. Father Eugene paced and fumed while we ransacked the office. "When's your appointment?" I asked.

"In a quarter of an hour. What have you done with it?" The edge in Father Eugene's voice only distracted me more. "I can't abide this kind of carelessness, Janine! Those are confidential documents." All this under Agnes's quiet observation. Colette and I kept up the flurry a while longer. There was no place else to look. It just wasn't to be found.

"May I check your office, Father?" My voice faltered.

"It's not there, Janine. You've lost it."

"Sometimes a second pair of eyes..."

"This is none of your business, Agnes!" Now he was really in a flap.

I tried to settle myself and think of what to do. "Why don't you go back to your office while I get you a cup of tea, Father?"

"You're just wasting time, Janine."

"No. It will help me think." I rushed into the rectory before he could answer. The water was still hot from lunch. It only took a minute to boil. I hurried back with the tea to Father Eugene's office and found him sitting at his desk, perusing the Cabrelli file.

"I found it," he said sheepishly.

"Where was it?"

He jerked his head toward the credenza.

"Here's your tea." I set it before him.

"Thanks." That was all. I got back to the reception area just as Sister Colette was inviting the wedding couple to come in. She glanced sidelong at me.

"Don't worry. He found it," I whispered.

Sister Colette announced the couple, led them into Father Eugene's office and came back to her desk. "Well, that's a relief. Where was it?"

"His inbox."

Of course, Agnes couldn't let *that* pass. "I hope he apologized."

"He's been having a rough time of it since Father Francis died. I don't think he realized how much he depended on him—or how much he cared for him."

"And for solace he bullies you?"

"I wouldn't call it bullying. He's just sad and impatient and lonely."

"Case in point. We should be better able to care for one another. With a proper diaconate we would have dedicated men and women to lead the way. And not just to take care of women and orphans, but battered old priests too. Obviously, they could do with a little ministering themselves."

"That's what I'm trying to do, Agnes. Why else would I put up with it? Just because we're not ordained doesn't mean we don't minister."

"Well, why do we need holy orders at all then? If ordination sets priests apart for the work, it should also apply to dedicated men and women."

"I'm not exactly dedicated."

"And the diaconate has always been an order for men." This from Colette. She should have known better.

Agnes was off again. "'I commend to you our sister Phoebe, a deacon of the church at Cenchreae'—Romans 16:1! But, not now. Can't have that! There is no brooking any woman's voice, much less a dissenting one. All discussion and debate and discernment in the church come from the minds of men. For the love of God, one would think by now they would want to hear from us."

"Some do. The clergy don't all agree on this point, I think." I knew Agnes to be wrong about this. Father Francis used to consult with me and Sister Colette all the time.

"Sure, they disagree among themselves, but only by degree. Back in the day people would parody stuff like that. The courts had fools. The medieval church had feasts of fools and other ribald ceremonies to siphon off the surfeit of self-importance. But the Church quashed that."

"Yeah, those feasts were finally condemned by the Council of Basel in 1435. The Pragmatic Sanction issued by Charles VII in 1438 made those decrees ecclesiastical law in France."

Agnes raised an eyebrow. "You surprise me, Janine. How would you know that?"

"I have done a little history, Agnes. And it's my era."

"What's your era? Those feasts were kept for centuries."

"Well, mostly the High Middle Ages. Things were in a big mess then, you know. For the church, I mean. Well, all over Europe. And those celebrations got more and more out of hand. Whatever catharsis the feasts may have provided for the minor orders and laity was probably offset by the damage done by their excesses. The papal legate to France tried to clean it up a bit at the turn of the thirteenth century. But it was tolerated until the fifteenth century."

"And then thoroughly suppressed."

"Not immediately, I think."

"How would I know? I do know that nothing since then has ever done much to flout the juridical severity, canonical intransigence, and righteous posturing of the hierarchy."

"Not counting the Reformation, I suppose. That left the Church feeling a little defensive."

"Touché."

JUDGEMENT

Such small exercises in moral agility still came easily to him,
where the need seemed to justify them.

—Ellis Peters, *The Rose Rent*

Surprisingly, Agnes dropped by again the next day. "Have you heard this?" She held up a CD by the Boston Camerata: *Noël, Noël!* She opened to a page in the liner notes and shoved it under my nose. Halfway down the page I read: "Christmas Week in Beauvais."

"May I borrow this?"

"Of course. I brought it for you. The fourth track is music from one of those Feasts of Fools."

I quickly scanned the CD booklet. There it was. *Orientis partibus.* I thanked her effusively, brought it home and listened to the raucous performance until I could sing it from memory.

This was a nice coincidence, nothing more. I had read something relating to the feast just before my conversation with Agnes. That is why I had two dates to hang the prohibitions on. In fact, I could have said more. I could have told Agnes the exact session of the Council of Basel—session xxi, June 9, 1435—and the date of the French Council of Bourges that ratified the decrees—July 7, 1438, but that would certainly have aroused suspicion. I would not have remembered such detail had I not that same week mulled over a footnote in *The Medieval Stage,* citing the documents. I wanted to figure out how old Madeleine would have been, and especially how old her first born, Jean-Etienne would have been at the time. If, as I calculated, he was born late in 1416, he would have been twenty-two years old when he was called to account in January 1439 as the instigator and leader of that year's celebration of the *Officium* for the now prohibited *Festum asinorum.*

A few things happened before Jean-Etienne got there. In the early part of the fifteenth century, France was still losing ground. Cities in the north fell to Henry V of England like so many dominos. Articles in *The Recovery of France in the Fifteenth Century* mostly concern the later half of the century. One chapter, "The Devastation of Rural Areas during the Hundred Years War..." by Robert Boutruche, gives a glimpse. Through it I became aware that, as much as possible, Jacques directed his trips for trade through parts of the country that had grains and root crops to sell. Thus he kept his family and Madeleine's little band of wayfarers fed. Somehow he avoided major calamities in his rounds. Nothing short of a miracle, it seems to me.

As I mentioned before, on August 21, 1420, Pierre Cauchon, a chief negotiator of the Treaty of Troyes, was named bishop and count of Beauvais. Shortly after that, Guy de Roquehautain was granted a prebend and became a canon of the cathedral. This grant was approved, if not instigated, by the new bishop. Monsieur le Chanoine Guy de Roquehautain quickly made himself indispensable to the bishop, willingly serving in any capacity where he was wanted. Therefore, Canon Guy was at hand when, in 1425, the bishop led the starving people of Beauvais in a procession to the four points of the compass to pray for rain and for a harvest fruitful and unscathed. Subdeacons and deacons in dalmatics carrying crucifix and banners led the procession followed by secular clergy in their finest regalia. Next came the canons wearing ceremonial rochets and finally the bishop fully arrayed with cope, crozier and mitre. At each of the four points they offered up a reading from the beginning of one of the four Gospels followed by a litany and other prayers.

Madeleine, Marie-Josephte, and a servant set out with the children in hopes of joining the procession as it passed near their home. The three older boys, now eight, six, and five years old, bounded toward the crowd ahead of the women and infant children, reaching the procession just as the bishop passed. P'tit Beau squealed with delight. Jean-Etienne hushed him, saying he would have a flogging from Bishop Cauchon himself if he didn't settle down.

"Cochon?" cried P'tit Beau. "A pig! Why do you call him a pig? Is he ugly or is he greedy?"

This brought a howl of laughter from the crowd. The bishop, who had not heard the child, asked about the commotion. Some of the attending canons assured him it was a child's outburst of no consequence and the procession moved on. But Canon Guy would not let it lie. He broke rank, briskly seized the young offender and carried him off. Jean-Etienne and Jacques-Lucien hung on the canon's sleeves but could not stop him. I don't know what Guy would have done with poor P'tit Beau but just then he came face to face with the child's indignant mother.

"Set him down!" Madeleine glowered.

"He shall be punished," Guy retorted.

"He-shall-be-set-*down*." There was something so frightening, so unworldly, in Madeleine's eyes, that the pathetic canon simply obeyed and turned tail. The two older boys stood tall and proud, glad to be part of their heroic mother's triumph. P'tit Beau clung to her, not quite sure what to take from the experience. The family then fell in with the procession, praying in earnest with the townsfolk for the relief so desperately needed.

Naturally, this event did not warm Canon Guy to his erstwhile sweetheart. Other events may have made matters worse. There was tension enough to go around in Beauvais at the time. The bishop and the canonry were decidedly in the pocket of Burgundy and England, but most of the townspeople did not embrace that alliance. In only a few years, however, something quite miraculous awakened a new hope in the hearts of the citizens. Since October of 1428, Orléans, a southern city bridging French- and Burgundian-held territory, had been besieged by a legion of English soldiers. Its duke, Charles d'Orléans, a prisoner in England since the battle of Agincourt in 1415, was powerless to do anything but write poetry. The duke's half brother, Jean Bâtard d'Orléans—John the Bastard of Orleans—arrived with a small army to defend the city. But after several months the city was on the point of falling. Then, in the spring of 1429, came word that a seventeen-year-old girl from Domrémy, Jeanne d'Arc, had been sent by God to raise the siege of Orléans. Affectionately known as Jeanne La Pucelle—Joan the Maid—she was answer to the dauphin's prayer. He had prayed that if he were indeed the true heir to the House of France, God would protect and defend him. Equipped by the dauphin with a military entourage, La Pucelle set out for Orléans. However, without Jeanne's knowledge, the party was diverted past the city to avoid the English positioned at the outskirts of the city. When La Pucelle learned how they forestalled her approach, she was not pleased. Discovering Jean Bâtard to be the author of the plan, when she met the man, she rebuked him. Jean Bâtard recorded his first encounter with The Maid:

"Are you the Bastard of Orléans?"

"Yes, I am, and I rejoice in your coming."

"Are you the one who gave orders for me to come here, on this side of the river, so that I could not go directly to Talbot and the English?"

I answered that I and others, including the wisest men around me, had given this advice, believing it best and safest. Then Joan said to me:

"In God's name, the counsel of Our Lord God is wiser and safer than yours. You thought that you could fool me, and instead you fool yourself; I bring you better help than ever came to you from any soldier to any city…"

All this you'll find in Pernoud and Clin's *Joan of Arc: Her Story*. You'll also find other instances where these wisest men would have done better not to second guess her. They never quite had faith in her, despite unhoped for victories under her leadership. After the liberation of Orléans, La Pucelle set her heart on seeing the dauphin crowned. The coronation took place at Reims on July 17 of the same year, whereupon Beauvais submitted to the king and drove the English and Burgundians from the city. As it happened, Bishop Cauchon had been visiting Reims when Jeanne and her dauphin approached the city. He did not stay to attend the coronation and bear the royal mantle as prescribed for the Bishop of Beauvais, a peer of the realm. Instead he returned quickly to his bishopric only to be driven from the city because he was no friend of the people.

But Bishop Cauchon retained his seat *in absentia* while serving the English on several missions. His most prominent claim to infamy is as the man who launched the trial of Jeanne d'Arc. On May 23, 1430 at Compiègne, a city in the diocese of Beauvais, English and Burgundian soldiers had come on in force. To protect the retreat of her company, Jeanne took up the rear. An anxious captain raised the drawbridge of the city too soon leaving her stranded outside with only a few of her men. She successfully repelled several attacking soldiers, but finally an enemy archer took hold of her doublet and pulled her to the ground. This exulting lieutenant took her prisoner. She was now in the hands of Philippe le Bon of Burgundy. It was a matter of several months before the English paid a "ransom" of 10,000 pounds for The Maid. That is to say, the English wanted the power to exact justice as they saw fit. Bishop Cauchon, now in exile, was the principal negotiator in the deal. He also argued successfully that since La Pucelle had been captured in his diocese, the position as presiding judge fell to him. Next he appointed the officers of the court. But the Bishop of Beauvais had to be granted a "commission of territory" by the ecclesiastical authorities of Rouen—at the express urging of the English Duke of Bedford—in order to try her outside the boundaries of the diocese of Beauvais. And so it was that in January of 1431, this peasant girl was brought to trial—without charge—in the English-held city of Rouen. In May, the University of Paris, examining the evidence, concluded that she was guilty of 'being a schismatic, an apostate, a liar, a soothsayer; suspect of heresy, of erring in the faith, and of being a blasphemer of God and the saints.' Much of this was drawn from the fact that she dressed as a man in full armour. On May 30, in the public marketplace of Rouen, La Pucelle was burned alive at the stake. A crowd of witnesses stood by. "I would that my soul were where I believe this woman's soul to be," murmured the Canon of Rouen. "We have burned a holy woman." As for Pierre Cauchon, he died in 1442. He was interred in the Chapel of the Virgin in Lisieux. Apparently, there is no substance to the popular legend that his body was later exhumed and thrown into a common sewer.

I have no evidence Monsieur le Chanoine Guy de Roquehautain had anything to do with the trial of Jeanne d'Arc. At most he may have served as a personal secretary to Cauchon. But I do know that, despite persisting devastation, his prebend in Beauvais still held promise and he retained his position. Nonetheless, the bishop's exile left the Beauvais chapter of canons orphaned for a time. Canon Guy rattled around Beauvais keeping a low profile. When the eminent Jean Juvénal des Ursins was appointed bishop and count in 1432, Canon Guy demonstrated appropriate reserve. Over time he was reconciled to his situation and found ways to regain some of his former influence.

Canon Guy happily assumed a disciplinary role in the community. This I know from his action *ex-officio* against Jean-Etienne when, in 1439, in spite of the interdict, the young man took it upon himself to observe the traditional *Festum asinorum* as had been done in the city for centuries. Of course, he couldn't have managed it by himself. He had confederates and a lot of popular support. But they needed someone to preside, and Jean-Etienne qualified. In 1436, Paris had been taken by siege from the English and shortly after that, Jean-Etienne went there to further his education. He had studied at the University of Paris and taken minor orders.

Thus, on the fourteenth of January, the celebration of the *Festum asinorum* took place with as much abandon as it ever had before. Just as the unsanctioned ceremony drew to a close, Jean-Etienne was apprehended. This did not bode well for his future in the clergy. He was held overnight in a cell near the cathedral. Madeleine may not have been aware of what her son was up to, but reports from her other children came thick and fast. Since Jacques was out of town, she took it upon herself to seek out her son. She went to the cathedral and was informed that he would be held until Monsieur le Chanoine de Roquehautain had opportunity to question him. "Could she see Jean-Etienne first?" she asked. The intermediary did not refuse her since she was a member of the nobility and wife to a wealthy and influential townsman. Madeleine negotiated a time for her visit and went home. At the appointed time, she saw him. Jean-Etienne was somewhat chastened but in good humour and perhaps still a little cocky. Madeleine took him to task, warning him that this inquisition could well destroy his prospects, at least in Beauvais. When he was somewhat subdued, she helped him prepare a defence to see him clear.

Later that day, Jean-Etienne stood before his inquisitor. Canon Guy was aware of the family connections of the young cleric. He noted something of the mother's eyes and saucy demeanor in the fellow's bearing.

"You, fool! Are you ignorant of the decrees condemning what you have done?"

"No, your reverence."

"Then why did you do it?"

"For my sister's sake, sir."

"Your sister?"

"Yes, sir. She was chosen to ride the donkey in procession this year. I could hardly deny her that since she waited a full twelvemonth for her turn." This was true. His little sister, Blanche, had been chosen according to custom at the end of the celebration the year before—

"And I repent, your reverence. I will not do it again."

"How am I to believe that?"

"You have my word, sir. And I give you this token of good faith from my father." Jean-Etienne offered a small packet to the canon.

Canon Guy took the parcel and slowly unwrapped it. Jean-Eti-

enne watched curiously and closely as the canon took a little velvet
envelope from the wrapping. He had no idea what his mother had
sent with him. When Canon Guy opened the envelope, Jean-Etienne could not interpret the peculiar expression that passed over
the man's face. The canon examined the token thoughtfully. It was
his own signet. He turned his gaze on the young man standing before him. Finally, after a long silence, the canon spoke.

"This is from your father, you say?"

"Yes, your reverence."

"And what of your father? What does he think of your behaviour?"

"He doesn't make much of it, sir."

"Did he go to the *festum*?"

"No, sir."

"Will he forgive you?"

"I'm sure he already has, your reverence. It is in his nature to
forgive."

"He has said so?"

"He is from home at present."

"Then whence this token?"

"My mother brought it to me."

"And why don't you say it is from your mother?"

"Perhaps she thought it would be unseemly, sir, as a woman, to
offer such a gift. I only know I was to tell you it is from my father. I
am certain he would approve."

"Very well." The canon absently surveyed the gift for a time.
"You have a brother?"

"Four, sir, all younger."

"And you plan to enter the priesthood? That is a little untoward.
As the eldest, you should, by rights, inherit your father's estate and
holdings."

"I have worked in my father's occupation several years, sir. It
does not suit me. I believe it runs more in my brother's blood, so he
shall have it. For myself, I prefer the life of the mind and my father
blesses my endeavour. I will have some of the inheritance, as fairly

and justly as can be arranged."

"But you will want to marry."

"I did, sir. I loved a young woman once, but her father saw her married to another man. I went to the university to turn my mind from grief. In time I was taken up with my studies. I believe I have found my vocation."

"To defy the authority of the church and the king?" Canon Guy had finally collected himself and recovered his role as inquisitor.

"No, sir. To keep a promise, as I did for my sister, and to keep faith with God, which I will do with all my heart from this day forward."

It remained for the canon to judge and prescribe penance for Jean-Etienne. Surprisingly, the penance consisted almost entirely of assisting the canon at mass and other offices, as well as the necessary daily invocations for pardon and forgiveness—nothing significantly out of the line of Jean-Etienne's usual duties in Beauvais, except that his service was rendered almost exclusively in company with the canon. He performed his penance with fidelity and vigour until he returned to Paris to further his studies with an aim to full ordination as priest.

As for Canon Guy, he could now account for the young man's tall, elegant frame and his aquiline profile. He knew the mother to be petite and her husband to be a rather square, muscular man with round, full features. Jean-Etienne could not so easily account for the clemency he enjoyed from the canon, a man he knew by reputation to be severe in judgement and rigorous in duty. He attributed this unexpected mercy to his mother's prudent counsel. She had known the man in his youth, she told him. And she was a good judge of character.

CONFESSION

Now I see that the opposite of fact may not be fiction at all, but something else again, something hidden under layers of color or conscience or meaning. If I were a visual artist, I might call it pentimento. If I were a historian, I might call it a palimpsest. But I am a writer and I call it the place where literature comes from.

It is a place akin to those known as "thin places" in Celtic mythology. Like the thin places in both palimpsest and pentimento, these are threshold bridges at the border between the real world and the other world, still points where the barrier between the human and the divine is stretched thin as a membrane that may finally be permeated and transcended.

Now I see that the opposite of knowledge may not be ignorance but mystery; that the opposite of truth may not be lies but something else again: a revelation so deeply imbedded in the thin places of reality that we cannot see it for looking: a reverence so clear and quiet and perfect that we have not yet begun to fathom it. Thanks be unto God for his unspeakable gift.

—Diane Schoemperlen, *Our Lady of the Lost and Found.*

Spring came early. Rather, winter broke early. The weather was dry, the sloughs parched all April. Shallow-rooted plants lay dormant. I uprooted several of these, thinking they were dead. Fortunately, I was too busy to be thorough so other plants survived, and leafed in time, and bloomed.

Agnes had her female attendant at the Good Friday service that year. Father Eugene asked Rose to be thurifer. Close enough. Women brought spices to the tomb; Rose brought incense. After Easter, Father Eugene went to the pastors' annual retreat in the Rockies leaving Father Jim to care for the parish. It is a slow time of year— the second week of Easter—summer activities yawning and stretching, soccer season in the wings. Despite the drought, townspeople plan their gardens and farmers get ready to seed. Still the weatherman reports risk of frost. It is too early to plant.

Father Jim had also to deal with end-of-term papers and exams. Even with the lull, the work of the parish is a full-time job. He was feeling quite pressed. As usual, his strategy was to slow things down. At morning prayer he read the psalm in an unhurried, hypnotic rhythm:

You care for the earth, give it water, you fill it with riches.
Your river in heaven brims over to provide its grain.
And thus you provide for the earth; you drench its furrows,
you level it, soften it with showers, you bless its growth…

I thought about my dusty excuse for a garden at home. Father Jim read on. At the final "Amen" Jim was the picture of tranquillity. As for me, I was trying not to worry about the drought. Colette and Walter went off to work, but Jim followed me to my desk. "May I help you?" I asked as I sat down.

"Yes. Would you do me a favour, Janine?"

There was nothing much going on. I had planned to use the week to reorganize several file drawers that needed attention. I don't like being asked to shift my plans so unexpectedly. Regardless, I asked what would he have me do. He had a mostly handwritten draft of a paper he would present at a conference the following week. Could I clean it up a bit and type it for him?

"How long is it?"

"Just a minute." He went to his office and came back with a fist full of note paper, all helter skelter.

"Jim! You have a computer, don't you? This is a mess!"

"I know, Janine. I'm sorry. I've done most of the work in the library or at supper. I just haven't had time to deal with it properly."

"This will take all day."

"Could you just do your best to pull it together and type it? I'll revise and finish it later. Don't worry about the details."

"You know that's impossible. I can't do it piecemeal."

"Yes, I know."

"And that's what you're hoping for, isn't it. You're asking me to rescue you."

He didn't even hesitate. "Would you, Janine? I don't know how it will get done otherwise."

I shrugged. "Fine, I'll do it."

"Thank you so much, Janine. God bless you."

"You're the one who's blessed at the moment."

"Absolutely! No question."

"Well, go away then. Looks like I have a lot of work to do."

"Thanks again." And off he went.

"You're quite forward with Father Jim, don't you think?" I started. I'd forgotten Sister Colette in the other corner of the office.

"You know we were in college together, don't you?"

"Yes, but…"

"Well, I used to type his papers all the time. He would amass quantities of research, write up some commentary, then count on me to make sense of it. It's not an easy job to do, and he knows it."

"I see."

"But I think he probably has enough to do this week even without Father Eugene gone. So I'll do what I can."

I took awhile to sort through the bundle. Working with Jim's peculiar scratches again, it seemed time turned twenty years back—

except I had the forgiving technology of "cut and paste" to help with the project. I figured out his thesis and argument and got to work. Jim called his paper "Healing the Heart: The Confessor's Art." It was about the rite and practice of penance and how confessors mediate this grace. His illustrative examples included stories of confessors and redemption from centuries of Catholic Christianity. I half expected Blessed Jean de Beaumanoir to show up somewhere. I hadn't finished by the end of the day. Before I went home, I printed off the first fifteen pages and put them on Jim's desk. The next morning he was all smiles. "Thanks so much, Janine. This is great. Will you be able to manage the rest today?"

"I'll see what I can do." It was Wednesday, Sister Colette's day off, so I had no one to relieve me from the phone and the door. On the other hand, I didn't have to respond to her comments or overhear her calls.

The next section of Jim's paper began with practices of confession and spiritual healing falling outside the conventional understanding of the rite. One example was of Gertrude the Great (1256-1302) who lived in community at the Saxon monastery in Helfta and distinguished herself as a scholar, spiritual director, and intercessor. Very little writing by or about her survived the destruction of books and manuscripts during the Peasants' Revolt of 1525, except the five books that comprise *The Herald of God's Loving-Kindness*. Citing the first book, Jim discussed her reputation among her sisters as well as in the larger world. Gertrude herself continually wondered at the special graces and miracles that took place through her counseling and prayers. So she asked God the reason why:

The Lord replied: "Does not the Church's faith rest universally on the promise I once made to Peter alone when I said, 'Whatever you shall bind on earth shall be bound also in heaven?' And does not the Church firmly believe that this has come about to the present day through all the ministers of the Church? Therefore why do you not believe with equal faith that I am able and willing to do anything, prompted by love, which I promise you with my divine mouth?" And touching her tongue he said: "There! I have put my words in your mouth, and I confirm in my truth every single word that you might speak to anyone on my behalf, at the prompting of my Spirit. And if you make a promise to anyone on earth on behalf of my goodness, it will be held in heaven as a promise that has been irrevocably validated."

Fascinating. And still in the calendar. I wonder if Agnes knows about Gertrude. Of course she does. As for Gertrude, she didn't know quite what to make of this. She worried that she may respond inappropriately or fail to minister fittingly. But God assured her that many people would be blessed through her.

Even more irregular was the practice that developed in the Middle Ages of confessing to a layperson in cases of necessity. Jim presented some of the historical *sic et non* arguments from theologians. Whatever their conclusions, the debate ended with the Bull of Martin V, "Inter cunctas," of 1418 saying that the Christian is bound to confess "to a priest only and not to a layman or to laymen however good and devout." This posed a problem in times of extreme emergency when no priest was willing to attend, or there was no priest alive with jurisdiction to pronounce a valid absolution. Of course I thought about the situation in France in 1418 with so many villages vulnerable to attack and so many people dying in extreme circumstances.

I got it done by noon. Jim had just come in from an early lunch. He was visibly relieved when I handed him the last several pages. I went back to clear my desk and set up the answering machine for my lunch break. Just as I stood to go, Jim came to my desk with an odd smirk on his face.

"What?" I was a little abrupt. I figured I had done enough for him.

"I should thank you for your contribution. But if you must add material, I will need a citation."

"Pardon me?"

"The instance of the fifteenth-century female confessor you added. What's her name— Madeleine de Brout?"

"Let me see that." I snatched the paper from his hand. "Where? Where is it? Show me." I rifled quickly through the pages.

"Relax, Janine. It's not a big deal. I'll find it." He wrestled it away from me. "It's here— somewhere—just let me have a look."

I was far too agitated to leave him to it. I crowded beside him, trying to scan and turn the pages all at once. He pulled back in exasperation.

"Please, Janine! What's gotten into you? It's not a problem. I really don't mind."

"I need to see it, that's all."

"Well, sit down and take a deep breath. It's just a few pages. It won't be that hard to find."

I tried to be patient. He shuffled through the pages. "Somewhere around here—I think it started near the top of— hmm—I seem to have lost it."

"Damn!"

"Excuse me?"

"Sorry. I was afraid of that."

"What?"

"That you wouldn't be able to find it—that it would be lost."

"Well, I'll find it. It's not going anywhere."

Little do you know.

"Oh—here it is." He pointed to a paragraph on page seventeen.

"Can I have that?" I grabbed it, glanced at the paragraph, and went to the copier. To my amazement, the machine spit out a perfect copy. "I can't believe it!" I was ecstatic.

This completely bewildered poor Jim. "What—is going on? Are you okay?" He stared at me as if I were some sort of changeling.

"I'll keep this copy and print the last four pages for you without that part."

"No, Janine. I'm really interested in this. Can't you just give me the citation?"

"There is no citation, Jim. I made it up."

"You don't expect me to believe that."

"Well, you're going to have to. I won't be able to find a citation if it isn't already on the page."

"Janine, you're not making any sense."

"I'm sorry. No, it doesn't make sense at all, does it? Not something you'd expect from a rational human being. That should tell you something."

"Why don't you go for lunch and we'll talk about it when you get back."

Gladly. I went to the rectory kitchen. Before I unpacked my bread and cheese and apple I straightened the paper on the table. It stuck to a spot of breakfast's marmalade. Delusions don't stick. The paper was real. I took out my sandwich and began to read. Just after the section about the "Inter cunctas" of 1418 I read:

> Despite the Bull, there is the remarkable case of Madeleine de Brout of Beauvais, a woman who opened her home to some of the hapless peasants who flocked to the city for refuge in the bleak years of 1437 and 1438. When "la famine, la peste, sinon les deux à la fois" reduced multitudes of poor folks to sudden death, she heard the confession of a desperate woman. De Brout had sent for a priest to no avail. Not one dared enter a place so full of disease and death. Her hospice avoided, her pleas ignored, she took it upon herself to see the poor woman reconciled before she died. She said nothing of this to anyone, but since "famine, plague, if not both at once" so marked those wretched years, once she had undertaken the task, she was called upon again and again to counsel and console. Her final words were always the same: "God forgives." Except, alas, when followed by *"Requiem æternam dona eis, Domine, et lux perpetua luceat eis"*—"Grant them eternal rest."
>
> Her reputation grew. As if Madeleine de Brout had inherited the mantle from the Blessed Jean de Beaumanoir, people came to her door seeking counsel. Today we would probably

call her a therapist. In the medieval era she was acknowledged as a woman who later in life enjoyed the gift of tears,
a gift inducing spiritual and psychological transformation.
Madeleine, however, not only experienced her own transformation but was honoured as one who imparted this same
gift to others. Even so, a certain canon of the cathedral heard
of her reputation and, believing her to be apostate, threatened her with excommunication. He fancied this to be well
within his rights, since much of her family's estate—however
devastated—lay within his jurisdiction. Fortunately, when
she appealed to Bishop Jean Juvénal des Ursins, he advised
the canon to show restraint. "The people are brought low," he
said, "surely we must countenance such acts of kindness as
help them bear it."

I reread the section several times, wondering how on earth to
explain it to Jim. There were dates and references I could not account for. I do know now that 1437 and 1438 were terrible years
in Beauvais, but this was the first I'd heard them singled out. And,
no question, Juvénal des Ursins was the bishop then. *How am I to
tell the truth? I don't have to—not in such a circumstance. Jim won't
believe it anyway. Who would be hurt by a lie? No one. Except maybe Madeleine if I do. And my credibility if I don't. Does Madeleine
really figure in the equation? I just don't know.* I struggled through
my sandwich and apple. I made a pot of coffee. Someone's Easter
chocolates were on the counter—probably a gift to Father Eugene.
*Does he really think they'll be here when he gets back? He shouldn't
have left them out. If I'm going to lie, I may as well steal too.* I took a
chocolate. Then I saw the note beside the box: "Please help yourself.
Fr. E." *Hmh. Saved from myself. Well, I'll take that as a sign. I'll tell
Jim the truth, as little of it as possible. But I won't fabricate anything.*
Jim was obviously waiting for me when I came back.
"Come in, Janine." He motioned me to one of the arm chairs in
his office and took the other. I sat down. "Well, then?" I screwed
up my mouth at this as I instinctively do when I'm in a quandary.

"I can see you're uneasy, Janine. Why on earth should I think you made it up?" I didn't know what to say. "It's none of my business, if you really don't want to tell me. I just thought, since you included it in the paper, that you figured it was relevant and I'd want to include it. And it *is* relevant, and I *do* want to include it."

"You have a lot to do this week, don't you? Maybe another time would be more convenient."

Jim smiled indulgently. "Well, I'm not so pressed as I was. Somehow my paper came together in spite of myself. I feel much relieved and positively at leisure."

I thought quietly, trying to figure out where to begin. Jim was in no rush. "You're going to have to treat this as a confession, Jim. You can't tell anyone about this."

"Absolutely!" But he was perplexed.

"I have no memory of typing that section on Madeleine de Brout."

"That's understandable. You've been in a maze of typing for quite awhile."

"No, I mean I have never heard of it before—what I wrote."

Now he really looked puzzled. "But clearly you have heard of Madeleine de Brout before. Otherwise you would not have reacted so strongly when I mentioned her name."

"Yes, I have. I have encountered Madeleine many times before, but not in any tangible way. Well, not in any permanent way, I mean."

Jim nodded slowly. He didn't have a clue.

"The first time I encountered her was several years ago, long before I started to work here. I was reading Chambers' *The Medieval Stage* about May Day celebrations and there she was on the page. Except the next time I looked for her she was gone."

"I don't follow…" This was not helping.

"I was reading *The Medieval Stage* and came across an account of Madeleine all decked in leaves and flowers to celebrate May Day. A young man, probably the canon referred to in the passage I typed for your paper, planted a bough of hawthorn at her feet, and by this sign Madeleine fancied herself engaged to him. As it turned out, he abandoned her and Madeleine's mother arranged for her marriage to another man. It's a long story."

"And all of it is in *The Medieval Stage*?"

"Oh, no! Not at all. I've found bits and pieces of her story over the years in all sorts of places, mostly cultural history books."

"Hmm. But I've never heard of her. One would think…"

"No, of course not. That's my point. I encounter references to her but when I return to the same place in the book, she's gone."

Jim was beginning to regret his persistence, I think.

"Believe me, Jim, I thought I was going mad. It happens just often enough for me to wonder if I'm losing my mind. And at first I didn't connect all of the appearances to the same person. But eventually I decided to note the fragment and the page it was on as soon as I encountered it, so I wouldn't forget. And so I could be sure I wasn't mistaken about the place I found it. And then I started looking for her, wondering where she would show up next, where I would find another part of her story. This photocopy is the first hard copy I've ever retained. And you're the only person I know of besides me who has ever witnessed Madeleine's appearance."

I heaved a big sigh and stared at the flecks of dust sparkling in the light shining through the window. *Well, it's done and I haven't lied at all.* Jim mostly looked at the floor, but peripherally I saw him steal a glance in my direction. Finally he spoke.

"Have you thought about why this may be happening?"

"Really, Jim!"

"Well, I mean, what the point of it could be."

"Of course I don't know. Sometimes I think maybe her story is important to history, but I'm not sure why. I doubt it adds anything new to the record. It may be a little less charged with the usual bias."

"Well, it's an interesting and unusual case. And it may confirm something less unusual than we think. I wouldn't mind adding her story to my paper."

"You can't do that, Jim. You can't cite 'Flatfield, Alberta, St. Ignatius Parish office computer on a dry, sunny Wednesday in April.'"

"Just watch me."

"Jim, you promised!"

"No, relax Janine. I know I can't use it, at least not yet."

"Not ever."

"You say you've been keeping notes."

"Yes."

"Why don't you write it up and see what comes of it?"

"How can I write a history based on sources only I can see?"

"You could write it up as fiction."

"I'm not a writer. I can't write fiction. Besides, it's not fiction for me. I think it's true. I can't imagine all this coming from my unconscious. And, at the beginning, I didn't know the region or the era well enough to have made it up—though I do know a fair bit about it now."

"Even if it were fiction, Janine, that doesn't mean it isn't true. Sometimes the places we live are the lies. The world we encounter at the office or the gas pump is our invention. Or someone else's, but we go along with it. Truth is the place we meet God and recognize ourselves in God's image. It's where we learn how to be more fully human, to forgive and be forgiven our failures. You need to have faith, Janine, that the story will take you where you need to go. Faith makes life a little more real—if you allow it to."

This was unsettling. Not the truth and fiction part, the idea that I should write—the idea that I could mediate or give form to something real. "How would I do it? I can't imagine where I would begin," I demurred. "And you have no idea how hard it would be to try to do something like this at my house," I added, to seal the argument.

"Well, then go somewhere else—go to Beauvais. At least to get started."

"You must be out of your mind."

"Good. You're not alone then."

Maddening! I went home and tried not to think about it.

HOPE

It was a time when sorrow may come to the brightest without causing any great sense of incongruity: when, with impressible persons, love becomes solicitousness, hope sinks to misgiving, and faith to hope...

—Thomas Hardy, *Far from the Madding Crowd*

However Madeleine's story colonized me, the thought that it may be my ticket to lunacy held me in check. After my confession to Jim, some of the worry shuffled off. I was pretty sure that if Jim really thought I was going mad, he would at the very least have been more circumspect in his advice. He is not one to toy with people. Well, not in a case like this. At the same time, I felt defeated. On some level I had resisted the story. Were I mad, there would be no reason to take it seriously. But to be drawn inexorably to a place where I had only a trammelled inclination to go, that was something else. It seemed I would be giving up the struggle for sanity, the struggle to keep the ordinary business of living afloat.

Miles noticed a difference in me right away. He had the good sense not to draw conclusions from it but I could see it made him anxious. People often talk about how someone contemplating suicide seems more at peace when the decision is made and the method determined. Perhaps that was what made him solicitous and more accommodating. Or maybe I was just a little easier to live with. At any rate, for awhile, Miles was less irksome to me.

Oddly enough, the same event precipitated a profound sense of regret concerning Jim. Although we had been comfortable together since his return, I had kept a careful distance to avoid confusion. With Madeleine's appearance in his paper, the sense of mutual understanding came back so startlingly. He was so easy to talk with. I began to dwell on how Jim had come back and asked me to marry him after we had broken up. Of how he had been willing to consider ordination outside the Catholic Church just so we could be together. And of how readily I dismissed the idea. I was still fairly certain I had been right on that point. Even so, the regret that rested somewhere deep inside me now surfaced and would not fall back. So, maybe I was a little nicer at home, but I was also sadder.

The thing I tried not to think about was going to Beauvais, which I did anyway. I thought a lot about it. I had never been beyond Canadian borders, not even to Montana. Such an exotic idea—to range so far beyond my own orbit. It would pass. Surely. But the plan to write up my notes into a coherent story consumed me. Of course I had thought about it before and, in fact, some of my notes already had a narrative quality. I told myself I was just waiting until I knew the whole story. That was only an excuse, though. The project was daunting on so many levels. Apart from the fear of my incipient madness, on a practical and historical level, I didn't know enough of the era and the region to make sense of it.

I set these misgivings aside and forced myself to take the first step. The evening after my confession to Jim I looked through my notes. I was both appalled and encouraged; my records consisted of notes written on scraps of memo pads, backs of flyers, corners of old envelopes. It made the bundle of research Jim handed me on Tuesday look positively systematized and orderly. I had forgotten some of the things I'd noted. There was really quite a lot of material—many gaps, to be sure, but more details than I had remembered. I wished I had been more careful to file things sequentially as I discovered them. But that would have required an acceptance of the project that I was only now beginning to embrace. As I looked over the accumulated evidence, I realized that the parts I had written up more fully read like a witness statement. That's when I decided to deal with things in the order they appeared, however whimsical it may seem. At the very least, that would mean several passages were already written.

Jim came back from his conference quite animated. "I have some news for you, Janine." He invited me into his office. At the conference he encountered a friend from seminary, Edwin, who was going to Paris for a sabbatical year. He asked him to see what he could find by way of inexpensive accommodation in Beauvais. "You see, Janine, 'when I pray, coincidences happen!' I'll let you know when I hear from him." I asked how his presentation went. It was well attended with lots of discussion afterward. He said he alluded to "exploratory research of a colleague" regarding the record of a lay woman hearing confessions. "As I said, no breach of promise." He was very pleased with himself. I feigned exasperation but smiled to myself. It was good to have him around—an old friend again even though, in fact, by this time I'd worked with the people in the parish office longer than the year and a half Jim and I were together in college. But Jim was a friend I had chosen.

* * *

It did rain eventually. April's flowers bloomed late and sparse in May. Spring's promise soon faded. A baleful cloud seemed to settle over the parish of Flatfield that summer, especially for Jim. In June he went back to Ontario to help his mother and sister move his father into housing for dementia patients. The family was heartbroken to see the sphere of this once witty and productive man so sadly reduced. Jim was not back a week before word came that his mother had had a stroke. He returned home and got there before she succumbed to a second, fatal stroke. He stayed on to see his mother buried and to help his sister break up the household. He was gone the better part of a month. On his return he received a letter assigning him to a full-time appointment as professor in Toronto. As much as he loved academic life, he wasn't particularly happy at this turn of events. He'd just gotten settled into one community. Now he had a month to move, prepare courses, and settle into a new one.

Father Eugene took a week's holiday the beginning of August and Father Jim filled in again. On Wednesday he was called to a family whose son got on the wrong side of the wheel of a tractor working the summer fallow. The news of the child's death dismayed the whole community and rent the hearts of strangers. Jim came back from the hospital shaken and sorrowful. My heart broke for him, too. I knocked on the door of his office and went in. He sat at his desk, his head bowed in his hands. "The world is out of joint, Janine."

"Yes, it is." I had nothing more to say. I stood there quietly a while and finally asked, "Can I get you some coffee or tea?"

"Thanks. Coffee would be good." I went off to prepare the rite of consolation. When I returned, Jim was just as I'd left him. I set the coffee down. Not knowing what else to do, I rested my hands on his shoulders and gave him a little massage. He sighed and shuddered. At length I said, "Jim, why don't you come for dinner tonight? I'm expecting Miles back in town so I have a roast ready to go. There's plenty to go around."

"I have an appointment at four."

"That's fine. We'll eat at six. You don't need to stay long. I know you're busy."

"Sure. I'd like that."

* * *

I hurried home to get started. *I hope Miles gets back in time for me to explain. He'd better behave.* I really had no choice. I couldn't leave Jim to rattle around in the rectory in the condition he was in. Adam was home when I got there. "Dad just called. He said to tell you he won't be home tonight. He said he has to reconfigure the flow routing. He'll be back tomorrow." *I have a priest coming for dinner and my husband is out of town. Great.* "I have to get ready for work," Adam continued.

"You can't go!"

"Why not? I have to Mom. The schedule was made up a week ago."

"I'm making a big dinner. And I invited Father Jim."

"So what?"

"Have you seen Kit? He'll be here, won't he?"

"Far as I know." Adam went to put on his white shirt and bow tie and headed off to wait tables and inspire tips.

Kit was home before Jim arrived, thank goodness. "You have to stick around, Kit. I thought your dad would be here so I invited Father Jim for dinner. He's had a hard day."

"You don't trust him?" Kit grinned.

"Of course I do. It just doesn't look right. I would be embarrassed."

"Is there dessert?"

"Saskatoon pie."

"Well, why didn't you say so?"

"Maybe I'll send the leftovers home with Father Jim, so if you want some…" He got the point.

Jim arrived a little late, which gave me time to have the table set and ready when he arrived. He already knew Kit, who comes to mass with me on occasion, and said hello. I told him Miles would not be home after all.

"Oh, I'm sorry. I thought I would finally meet him tonight. I have to wonder, Janine, if he really does exist at all. He could well be a figment of your imagination. You're not making it up, this idea of having a husband?"

"Very funny." I tried not to credit the comment.

"Figment or not, as long as he lets me drive the truck, I'm okay with it," said Kit.

Jim thoroughly enjoyed his dinner. You would have thought he hadn't eaten for a week. When I got up to clear the table for dessert, so did he and—not to be outdone—so did Kit. I put on water for tea. I thought it would be best, under the circumstances. I normally prefer coffee with pie but Jim could do with some chamomile tea.

The plates and all loaded in the dishwasher, Jim set to washing the pots. It was nice to have company at the sink. My sons will do dishes if they can blast their music while they are at it. I usually retreat upstairs, which may be their object. Otherwise it's me, standing alone at the sink, evening after evening. So I enjoyed his proximity. It was nice to have the company of a man, too. Odd since I live with one. But Miles mostly avoids the kitchen. Well, he just avoids me. Anyway, I savoured the interlude at the sink—a snapshot of domestic piety. This is how marriage should be, I thought. And not many priests will wash the pots while waiting for the kettle to boil. Jim is a good man.

I made the tea and served the pie à la mode. Kit and Jim made short work of their portions. "Mmm. Lovely. Did you bake this?" Of course I had. Would he like another piece? They both did. By way of explaining his appetite, I suppose, Jim said, "I can't remember when I've tasted anything so delicious." I didn't take his compliments too much to heart, though. Most priests are such suckers for home cooking and baking, they've pretty much lost critical perspective.

Kit cleared the pie plates and went to watch TV. Jim and I took our tea into the living room. He noticed the library books piled on the table beside my chair. "Good Lord, Janine! Haven't you heard of light reading? Oh, and here's *The Crown and Local Communities in England and France in the Fifteenth Century*. I should have known you would have it."

"What do you mean?"

"Oh. I just requested it at the library. You'll probably get the recall in the mail by Friday. May I borrow it now? I'll check it out on my card and you can have it back when I'm done."

"Sure. Take it. Alumni only get two weeks anyway."

"You can't possibly get through all these books in two weeks."

"I'm just doing my usual research. I only look for the relevant parts."

"And have you turned up any more evidence?"

"Nothing. Nothing at all since your confession paper."

Jim sat down, stretching and settling into one of the cushioned corners of the couch. He sipped his tea in silence.

"Hmh. Maybe the tale's told out. You *are* writing it up, aren't you?"

"I haven't got very far. I'm mostly working through my notes. I wrote the first chapter some time ago and three more since. I've not really sorted out the rest."

"But you've started. Good. That's the main thing."

"You don't think I'm crazy?"

"Not any more than you were before."

"You thought I was before?"

"Not at all. But your approach to scholarship has always been a little eccentric, starting with details and ending up in unexpected places. Far be it from me to mess with that."

"Do you think you know what's going on with me and this story?"

"I haven't a clue, Janine."

I changed the subject. After all, I had invited Jim over for his sake, not mine. I asked about his new appointment and how he felt about living closer to his father and sister. That was the good part about the move, he said. But he enjoyed the collegiality at the school in Flatfield and felt so much at home in the parish here. In Toronto he would not have the same relationship to the community. He reminisced about the some of highlights of the year. Then he remembered the heartbreak of the young child's death. He fell into silence.

The phone rang. "I'll top up the tea," I said and went to answer it. It was for Kit. As I filled the kettle Kit said "Craig's got a new game. I'm going over to his place for awhile."

"No, you're not," I whispered emphatically.

"Why not? I can sleep in tomorrow. I don't have to work again until Saturday."

I jerked my head toward the living room. "Wait 'til he's gone."

"Mom! You're perfectly safe with him."

"That's not the point."

"Well, what is the point?"

"He's a priest."

"So what? I'll go say goodbye to be polite."

Kit walked into the living room and came directly back. "Woh! A napping pastor!" he whispered.

"He's asleep?"

"Check it out! A reverend in reverie!"

"Smarten up!"

"A dozing divine!" Kit simpered. "Now what are you going to do?"

"Now I'm going to make you stay home, Kit. We'll finish up here, then if he's not awake, we'll put a blanket on him and let him rest, I suppose. He's had a rough summer."

Kit hung out in the kitchen and put some dishes away. When clean-up was done, we crept into the living room. "Jim?— Jim?" He slept on. "Go get Grandma's afghan." Kit found it in the family room and together we unfolded it over Father Jim. I switched off the lamp. Jim lay quiet in the half light from the dining room. We left him there and went to watch a dismal documentary. The clock's hands stretched up to twelve and still Jim had not stirred. I left the dining room and front entry lights on, and Kit and I went upstairs for the night. I must say that as I got ready for bed the thought of Jim sleeping downstairs pleased me. Such an unexpected and special guest. I happily fell asleep. But if I had any dreams at all that night, I can't remember them.

Perhaps Adam's home coming sometime after midnight woke him. I vaguely remember hearing Adam come upstairs and, a few minutes later, hearing the door shut downstairs. *He's on his way.* I turned over and went back to sleep. In the morning I found a note sitting on top of the folded afghan.

Janine,
   Food for the body, food for the soul. You have been so kind.
Please forgive me. I did not realize I was so tired.

Thank you and God bless,
Jim
P. S. I took the book.

DEPARTURES

My dwelling, like a shepherd's tent, is struck down and borne away from me; you have folded up my life, like a weaver who severs the last thread.

—Isaiah 38:12

Miles was already back when I got home from work on Thursday.

"Kit tells me you had company for dinner last night."

I went up to him and gave him a hug—his arms hanging diffidently at his sides. "Hi Miles. Welcome home."

"And he spent the night. I'm not surprised." He spoke slowly and deliberately, measuring his words. "I've always been a third party in this marriage. May as well be explicit." I could not tell yet whether this would translate into retribution or shunning.

"You said you would be home for dinner last night. How was I to know? And he slept on the couch until midnight. He was just tired."

"Poor guy! Nothing like an old girlfriend to set things right." He walked away.

Shunning takes it.

I called after him. "He was upset about the accident on Ridge's farm." He turned and stood in the doorway.

"Don's place?"

I nodded.

"What accident?"

I told him what I knew. He sat down, propped his chin on his elbows and stared absently at the table. Miles worked on a project at Ridge's the summer before. He and Don really hit it off. If Miles were one to meet a friend for golf or fishing he would likely have maintained a relationship with Don. But he wasn't. He hadn't seen Don since.

"When's the funeral?"

"Monday."

"Oh." He just sat there.

"You don't need to go, Miles. They may not even remember who you are." I was suddenly aware of a strong desire to prevent Miles from invading my space.

"How can you say that, Janine? Where's your sense of decency? I remember him and I know his father. That's all that matters."

He was right, of course. "I'm sorry. It was a thoughtless thing to say. You should go if you can."

Dinner was quiet. Miles was so shaken, I couldn't help but want to encourage him. The world was in ferment for me, though. So many conflicting feelings about Miles, about Jim, about everything. At times I hated Miles and then, for this moment, I loved him. And it wasn't just about the accident. I felt terrible about that. Even though I hardly knew the family, I shuddered to think of the horror they were enduring. But my own tottering little world would not settle. The accident only highlighted the precarious imbalance.

* * *

Father Eugene returned from his week's vacation on Sunday evening. On Monday, he joined us for Morning Prayer. We were all there, Sister Colette, Father Eugene, Father Jim, Walter, and me. Walter began the first psalm. I am often surprised at how expressive his plain, matter-of-fact reading can be.

You turn men back to dust
And say "Go back, sons of men."
To your eyes a thousand years are like yesterday,
come and gone,
No more than a watch in the night.

Here he paused. His eyes still fixed on the page, he sat silent a moment, then quietly nudged me. "You do the rest…"

You sweep men away like a dream,
like grass which springs up in the morning.
In the morning it springs up and flowers:
by evening it withers and fades.

I paused, weighed down by Walter's heaviness of heart. "It's just not right," he muttered. "It was still morning. He was just a boy."

Lord, relent! Somehow I finished the psalm. *Give us joy to balance our affliction for the years when we knew misfortune.* The others in this sombre little gathering carried us through the rest of the readings to the benediction, then we slowly got up to go.

"To think I saw that poor boy a week ago at the MacDonald wedding, dancing as if his life depended on it," said Walter as we moved toward the door. "I just wish there was something I could do."

Miles came to the office to meet me before the funeral. We turned a few heads as we made our way to the church and into the sanctuary. This town isn't so small that people in the church necessarily know what my husband looks like. I felt oddly guilty for my self-consciousness about this, as if I brought him to show him off. Perhaps Jim's comment about Miles being a figment of my imagination contributed to that. And of course, Miles didn't know where I usually sit and headed straight up the middle aisle choosing a spot halfway to the front, in the Kellys' area. I don't like being so visible, or encroaching on other people's space, but I wasn't going to unseat him either. Miles sat thoughtfully as the church filled. I nodded hello to a few people as they entered.

Mass began at eleven. The church was packed, people stood in the outer aisles and at the doors of the church. Pall bearers brought the little coffin to the doors of the sanctuary. We stood for the rites at the entrance to the church. The family, acolytes, and priests gathered around to lay the pall over the coffin. Then the procession. Robed in white, the priests passed by. I realized Miles would not know which one was Jim. I was glad of that. Jim processed with a dispirited shuffle. Father Eugene, on the other hand, moved with his usual elegant sweep that some find arrogant. He does have a more impersonal ritual presence. Miles would approve of Father Eugene, no doubt. I wasn't so sure Jim would pass scrutiny.

Father Jim gave the homily—a tenderhearted reflection on the gift of life and how robbed we feel when one so young and so dear is taken from us, on how important memory is to the human experience, and on the precious bond we, the living, share with those who have gone before us. It was cathartic, and not so Catholic that the people from other churches or no church at all were excluded by it.

The Ridge family bones lie in a cemetery well beyond the limits of Flatfield where once a small rural church served the parish. We followed dozens of cars and pickup trucks out of the town, then turned off the pavement down a dusty gravel road, past fields of ripening grain, past other fields cut to stubble, with their scattered bales of green feed—desolate icons of untimely reaping. Our convoy slowed as we approached the burial grounds. The overgrown lane leading into the cemetery was hardly long enough for the hearse and the cars carrying family members. The rest of us parked at the side of the gravelled road. If you were to follow this road a little further and turn with the bend, it would lead back to my road and my landscape. I thought about my connection to this family, and this place, as Miles and I followed the procession of townsfolk and farming families down the road, and up the rise, and through the cemetery gates. As we approached, the soulful tremolo of a violin met us and accompanied our walking. I looked around to see where it came from. There at the far end of the cemetery in the shadow of a stand of spruce stood Walter pulling the plaintive "Danny Boy"out of his fiddle.

Miles and I did not talk at all on the way home. The shades of the day filled the spaces. He dropped me back at the church. Miles did not go to the reception. I did, but only briefly. The place was packed and so many people came from beyond the borders of the town. I would not be missed.

I returned to work—rare to find the office so empty and quiet, every move amplified by its solitary resonance. I felt like an actor in one of those existential movies where the echo of footsteps becomes a part of the narrative. The echo stopped at my desk. On my desk was the library book Father Jim had borrowed from me: *The Crown and Local Communities in England and France in the Fifteenth Century.* I picked it up and paged through it. A scrawled note read: "Thanks. Due back September 15." *Well, that's convenient.*

The chair scraped loudly into place and I sat down. I began to read P. S. Lewis's article on "The Centre, the Periphery, and the Problem of Power Distribution in Later Medieval France." The very first paragraph states that during the whole reign of the "impeccably 'French'" Jean Juvénal des Ursins as bishop of Beauvais, for all those twelve years until 1444, the city was "in a state of siege… sometimes literally." Lewis then quotes the bishop:

> … I have suffered much tribulation, adversity and affliction, because I am the spiritual father of the diocese of Beauvais, and I have fine lands and lordships which used to be ploughed and grazed, but the enemy and those who say they are on our side have killed the local people, taken them and deported them, robbed them and tyrannized them, and they have lost all their stock, and the region is waste and desolate, and churches and houses are burned down and collapsed in ruins, and they have murdered the poor people by imprisonment and other means, and in short I have lost land, stock and my people who are my children…

Then, also from Jean Juvénal, a letter to the king saying "that
there was not between the River Oise, the Seine and the Somme a
town in the French obedience except this wretched city, which carried the whole burden of the war, and could not rely for help neither
upon you nor anyone else, but only upon themselves." Lewis writes
of "the daily pillaging... of the merchants of Beauvais and others
victualling the town." *Here it comes.* I knew in my bones something
terrible was about to happen to Madeleine. I turned on my computer so I could type as I read it. Sure enough. After three months of
silence, Madeleine's story continued:

> As was customary, the gates of the city opened every day
> when no hostile forces were in view and people went out for-
> aging for roots or plants that may have bravely regenerated in
> some trackless ditch or furrow. Nervously they scratched for
> edibles all the while waiting for the inevitable warning of the
> bells. So it was that Jacques Mouton's celebrated excursions
> finally came to an end. Returning from one of his forays for
> trade and victuals he heard the bells of Beauvais ringing
> wildly. He hurried his horses to reach the city before the gates
> closed. He was too late. He was cut off by a passing company
> of *écorcheurs* who seized their good fortune—the abundance
> Mouton carried in his carts. They impaled the worthy man
> on the end of a lance and slaughtered his retinue. The follow-
> ing day, a servant was found, wounded but alive under an
> overturned wagon, who lived to tell the story. This was one of
> the final horrors of Jean Juvénal's tenure in Beauvais.

When will it end? Well, it has for Jacques. That interminable war. I
had read and worried about these *écorcheurs*— "fleecers"—who di-
vested travellers and villagers alike of their possessions. These bands
began to emerge after the Treaty of Arras in 1435. They could not be
contained, affronting order and the royal authority throughout the
countryside, especially in times of truce. They not only robbed their
victims, and fed their horses on people's corn crops, and made kin-

dling of the timber of their homes. They also tortured, and raped, and murdered. How was Madeleine to survive now, Madeleine and all her people? Or, rather, how did she survive or did she? *Of course not. She would be close to 600 years old by now.* I was glad I was alone. I was overcome with an overpowering sense of futility. When at length the others returned from the funeral reception, they found my reserve understandable. The day's own sorrows were sufficient for the day.

* * *

With Father Eugene back we soon settled into the regular rhythm of parish business and Ordinary Time. Jim was as good as gone. He would leave before August closed. The church's farewell tea would be held after the noon mass on Sunday. He dropped in on Wednesday to pack up his stuff. He came in buried under a stack of old cardboard boxes, looking as upbeat and happy as I'd seen him in a long time. "Janine, would you come to my office when you have a minute? I have something for you."

"Now is as good a time as any." I couldn't sit around wondering what *that* was about. I followed him down the hall into his office. The boxes tumbled out of his arms. I collected a couple and set them aside.

"You won't believe this." He handed me a piece of paper. "Read it." It was a letter from Edwin, his friend in Paris:

Dear Jim,
I have found a place for your colleague in Beauvais at the Maison Diocésaine - 101 rue de la Madeleine.

"Come on, Jim. You don't expect me to buy that, do you? 'Rue de la Madeleine.' Really! What do you take me for?" I was not impressed. I hadn't expected Jim to play such a callous and insensitive joke on me.

"Just read it, Janine."

She will have to use my name for a reference as the rooms are not usually made available to the public although a few rooms are used to house students. Bathrooms are shared. I trust this will meet her needs. I don't think you'll find a better deal than this, so I will not look further.

The letter went on to give the cost and contact person. Edwin also enclosed a train ticket to take me from the airport Roissy Charles de Gaulle to the Gare du Nord in Paris where I could catch the train to Beauvais. And a map of Beauvais. There it was, nicely circled, on rue de la Madeleine. Hardly three blocks from the train station marked with a big X. Too good to be true, certainly. And a room at the diocesan house in Beauvais! I was stunned. "I can't believe it."

"Amazing, isn't it? But of course, if you're going to find a 'rue de la Madeleine' anywhere, it would be in France. Still, it's quite a coincidence."

"Did you tell him about Madeleine?"

"Not a word."

"Hmh. And so generous. I must pay him for the train ticket, even if I don't use it."

"Well, that's already taken care of. And you should use it."

"I don't know what to think."

"I think it means you have to go to Beauvais."

"Wasn't this your idea in the first place?"

"Only by extension. I doubt you'll be satisfied with staying in Flatfield and wondering and never checking it out for yourself.

—Have you ever been to Europe, Janine?"

"I haven't been to Butte, Montana."

He grinned. "Well, think about it. You're not going to beat 1200 francs a month! That's around $200.00 Canadian, if I figured out the exchange correctly. You couldn't stay in a hotel two nights for that. And watch the seat sales—Oh! And something else." He took out a pen and wrote on a piece of paper. "Here's my contact information in Toronto. Send me a postcard from Beauvais!"

I wasn't much use after that. For every minute I spent working I'm sure I spent ten musing, looking over the letter, thinking about the possibilities. At home, I was Missing In Action. I put the vegetables to steam without water. I left the ice cream to melt after dinner.

Sunday came. And Jim went. The prospect of continuing in the office with him gone left me hollow. I was sorry to see him go. But if tears are a necessary part of sorrow, then it wasn't sorrow I felt, because I did not weep.

FROST AND OTHER WEATHERS

*As cold as everything looks in winter, the sun has not forsaken us.
He has only drawn away for a little, for good reasons, one of which is
that we may learn that we cannot do without him.*

—George MacDonald, *Ranald Bannerman's Boyhood*

Late in August came an unexpected cold snap. Unexpected by
me, anyway. I went to bed thinking about nothing but my own
comfort. That night the mercury sank three degrees below freezing.
The house was cold when I woke up. Miles was working out of town
again and got up earlier, leaving his side of the bed colder than usual. I hurried to dress and turn up the thermostat. You'd think Miles
would have had the decency to do that before he left. Still shivering, I put on the coffee and went outside to survey the damage.
Little mounds of dianthus persevered. Daylily and iris spears stood
stalwart. The rose bush, protected by the warmth of the southern
wall where Marilee and I transplanted it the summer before, had
only one bud in July. This I cut and put in a rose bowl to watch it
open. No regrets for the rose for once. Then I turned to the dahlias.
Their bursting blooms folded and fell, darkened leaves drooped. Of
course the tomatoes were hopelessly frozen. No chance for redemption there. And no use now to drape the plants with sheets and
extend the season by a few weeks. No question. Summer was gone.

I went in to breakfast and set off for work soon after.

Our new associate pastor arrived that Monday. I was quite certain that any man who aimed to replace Father Francis or Father Jim would fall short of the mark. Father Bob Golding did not disappoint in this. In fact, he far exceeded expectations. His first order of business was to make us aware of our good fortune in securing his services. He was, after all, a part-time administrative assistant at the college with aspirations to high preferment somewhere, although it wasn't clear where his ambition would take him. He seemed to have a hard time keeping busy on the days he spent in the parish. Several times a day he would come strutting into the office area asking "How goes the battle?" or some such convivial turn of phrase.

The first week was trying at best, with Father Bob interrupting, giving opinions, ruling on our thoughts, and always operating on the assumption that he was educating his audience, no matter what the topic. And always assuming we adored him. Insufferable.

On Friday I was collecting my things to go home. Walter came in to see if anything needed doing before he left for the day. "Is Father BG gone?" That's what Walter called him—"I'm sure he would prefer that to 'Father Gelding' anyway" he explained. Just then Father Bob passed by on his way out the door with a jovial "Take it easy, but take it! —I'll see you Sunday."

Even Sister Colette, who tries so hard to be positive about the parish, found Father BG's priestly investment was not quite equal to the task of redeeming him. "I wonder how long he'll be here," she mused, when he was safely gone. "It didn't take them long to move Father Jim. Unfortunately, it seems the less promising the priest, the longer it takes to reassign him. But what else can they do with him?"

"Yep. He's one in a million," Walter observed, "and to keep it that way, see to it he don't break that vow of celibacy."

* * *

It was a very dry fall. And it was cold. I should have been comfortable with that. Those are my elemental attributes. According to

Aristotle in his *Physics* of the four classical elements, earth is primarily dry and secondarily cold. I don't hold much with astrology but mine is an earth sign. It suits me. And it was too dry and cold even for me.

* * *

I should have invited the priests for Thanksgiving dinner. In my better moments I wondered if Father BG had been raised by demeaning and domineering parents or if he'd been beaten or otherwise abused. Mostly, he just annoyed me far beyond my capacity to forgive. So I left the priests for someone else to invite to dinner. I was usually out of town for Thanksgiving anyway. I hadn't ever invited them before. This was certainly not the year to start.

Dinner was at my house that year. Mom had been feeling sick again, the same headache and nausea and general malaise she'd often complained of the winter before. So Miles's parents, and Gil and his family, came to us from Edmonton. Mom hadn't been long at dinner before she began to feel better. Over turkey and mashed potatoes, we tried our diagnostic skills. Gil observed that the symptoms returned with autumn and that at present, Mom was feeling fine. "It's probably your furnace. You should get your furnace checked, Mom. When did you last have it looked at or cleaned?" She couldn't remember. Gilbert became convinced of his diagnosis and suggested that Mom should stay at my house for a few nights to see if she felt better. And she should call to have the furnace checked before she went home again.

"Oh no," said my mother, "I can stay where I am for now. I'll call the furnace people right away."

Miles was quick to counter. "Definitely not. You cannot go home until we know what the problem is. You can stay in Marilee's room in the basement. It's quite bright and plenty warm enough." So it was decided without my consultation. Mom should move in.

Mom leaned over to me. "Is that okay? It isn't right to shove it down your throat."

"Sure, Mom. I don't want you to live in a house that makes you sick." But really, who wants to live with her mother at my age?

"I know that. But here we are talking about me living in your house. That's different." I never could put anything over on my mother. "I want to talk close with you, Janine, before I say yes."

"Mom, there's nothing to talk about. You know I'll be fine with it. I just need to get used to the idea. I'll adjust."

"Yeah, we'll talk after dinner."

The conversation broke up into smaller ones. Miles asked his father about a long lost uncle who had recently surfaced in Ontario. Adam chatted with his cousin Giselle about his upcoming eighteenth birthday and the best places to go in Edmonton to celebrate. Kit bragged to his grandmothers about how cleverly he charmed and diverted his examiner in order to get his driver's licence. He didn't say a word about how hard he practised and studied the weeks before the test. Gil's wife, Amy, asked how I managed to make the buns so moist and light. I should have relished the compliments on dinner. I should have enjoyed the happy, animated company. As I surveyed the scene my eyes fell on Gil who was looking thoughtfully at me.

When all that remained of dinner were bones, I began to clear. Gil jumped up to help. So did Giselle and Amy, followed by Adam and Kit. "Thanks," said Gil, taking the plates and stacking them. "Now all of you go sit down. I can take care of this." He unburdened them and hustled the kids and Amy back into the dining room. I started the coffee, took out dessert plates and the pie server. Gil stood by. "I'm sorry, Janine. I shouldn't have done that."

"What?" I knew very well what he meant.

"I shouldn't have suggested Mom come and stay with you."

"No, that's okay. You're probably right. She's never sick at work and she's fine when she's here. We need to find out why. I'm just feeling a little dispirited. It'll pass."

"Well, I'll do what I can to get it dealt with right away."

I began to whip cream for the pies. He scraped and rinsed and turned again to me. "What's up with you and Miles?"

"What do you mean?"

"It seems you aren't even friends anymore."

"I just get a little preoccupied when I have a big dinner to do."

"I'm not just talking about today. Every time I've seen you two in the last few years, you seem unhappy with each other."

"Oh, it's nothing, Gil. He's just so cold."

"Well, you don't exactly heat up the room yourself when he's around."

Mercifully, the doorbell interrupted. I went to see who was there. Kit got to the door first and in came Marilee and Jessica. "Just in time for dessert!" I said.

Immediately half the table was up to greet them, Jessica in her element with hugs and kisses from all of us. Miles picked her up and danced her around the room. "Hello Sunshine! What do they feed you? You are so big! Pretty soon you'll have to carry me!" He brought her to the table and she settled on his lap.

"It's so good to see you, Marilee!" I put my arm around her and led her into the dining room. "How are things going?"

"School's good. And Jessica loves her teacher."

"That's great."

"Yes. She's doing well."

"And you?"

"I'm okay."

"Are you sure?"

My mother set a chair beside hers for Marilee. "Sit down. I have to look at you!" Gil and Amy greeted them warmly. I excused myself and went to finish whipping the cream, wondering what was going on with Marilee. She wasn't her usual self. Probably the barometric pressure. Seemed like everybody was feeling it. Even so, we were a lively company, ignoring for the moment the churning undercurrents turning in all directions. We sat a long time over coffee. My in-laws were the first to go. "It's a long drive to Edmonton, even on a full stomach." Miles and I saw them to the door. Miles poured after-dinner drinks and we settled in the living room. Finally Gil stood.

"Mom, let's go get you packed up."

"I want to talk to Janine first."

"Don't worry about it." I really was okay with it by then. "We'll talk tomorrow if you like. Let Gil help you put a few things together for now. I'll sleep better tonight knowing you won't be asphyxiated by morning." Gil and Mom carried their cups and plates into the kitchen on the way to the door. Miles followed along.

"Do I need two strong men to make me do it?"

"Damn straight, Mom," said Gil.

"I just want to have a look at the furnace," said Miles. And off they went.

"Why don't you kids take the first shift in the kitchen?" I wanted to nurse my drink awhile longer.

"Aw, Mom!"

"We don't know where it all goes."

"Just put all the bones in the stock pot and deal with the plates and silverware. I'll do the rest later."

Giselle was hardly more enthusiastic but she led the way. Adam and Kit followed. It always amazes me how compliant the boys become in the presence of a girl. Marilee has that effect too. They set to work laughing and joking throughout the ordeal.

In the meantime, Jessica found some of her favourite books and brought them to me. "Well look what you found, Jessica! You'll have to wait awhile though. We can read them when Miles gets back." Amy and Marilee could have kept each other company, I suppose, but Marilee was not very engaging. Bless her heart, Amy offered to read to Jessica, who took her hand and led her into the family room.

"Well, Marilee, what's the matter? You don't seem very happy."

"It's Shane."

"What happened? Aren't you two getting along?"

She shook her head. "Not really. But I don't know what to do. Shane is jealous of Luke. He says he is more of a father to Jessica than Luke ever was and what business has Luke to interfere?"

"So he's feeling a little threatened. That's understandable."

"In a way, he's right. Shane is the first guy who ever just liked me and wasn't put off by me having a kid. But now Jessica and I go out with Luke every other weekend so it cuts into the time we used to spend with Shane. And Jessica is so excited when Luke comes because he always finds something fun to do."

"And you go along?"

"Yes. Luke always invites me. Well, he just expects me to come now. Jessica likes it that way. And now she calls Luke, 'Daddy'. I can see why this bothers Shane. But I don't really know what to do about it."

"How do *you* like these outings? Do you look forward to them too?"

"Well, yeah. I do. We just have such a good time. It's always special."

"So, it's almost like dating two guys."

"Oh, not at all! Luke and I never go out by ourselves."

"But every two weeks this good-looking young lawyer shows up at your door to show you a good time."

"Yeah. I know. I mean, I don't blame Shane at all. I just don't know what to do about it."

"You could plan to spend time with Shane during the next visit."

"Jessica would be so upset."

"And you?"

"I don't want to hurt Luke's feelings."

"Is that all?"

She hesitated. "Well, no." She fingered a gold heart pendant that hung from her neck, pulled the chain up to her mouth and began to suck on it. "I don't want to be left out either."

"You've been left out of a lot, haven't you. It's not fair to ask you to give up something you enjoy so much."

"And I like seeing Jessica and Luke together. They are so alike. They really have a good time. Sometimes I laugh so hard I could cry at how funny they are together."

"Hmm." This was not getting easier. I had nothing to offer. "Nice locket," I said instead. "Whose picture is in it?"

"Oh, Jessica, of course." She snapped it open and showed me a picture of Jessica mugging impishly for the camera.

I laughed. "She's such a ham. Who took the picture?"

Marilee paused. "Luke." Then looking self-consciously at me she added, "He gave me the locket on Jessica's birthday."

"And Shane? What does he think of that?"

"He thinks I got it from my parents. They came down for her birthday too."

That's as far as we got.

"Done!" Adam announced sauntering into the living room. Giselle came running in on his heels shrieking, trying to escape the towel Kit was snapping at her.

"Can't be. That was hardly five minutes." Giselle plopped down beside me on the couch and squeezed behind my shoulder for cover. "Cool it Kit! Go finish up."

"You said just the plates and silverware. We're done."

"Fine, then."

Kit aimed for Marilee who caught his arm and wrestled him into a half-Nelson.

"Mom! Marilee's hurting me! Save me!" Jessica came bounding in to see what the ruckus was all about. "Save me, Jessica! Your mom's beating me up!" Jessica wrapped her arms around her mom's leg and tried without success to pull her away from Kit. The three toppled onto the rug. Adam pulled Giselle from safety. At once they were a churning mass of bodies tumbling and toppling all over each other. I quickly removed our empty glasses and stood watching in the doorway with Amy. The kids are so rarely together, we left them to it. I could see Marilee was relieved to escape her own predicament for awhile. In a way I wished I could join them.

When the men came back with my mother, Amy and I were still cleaning up in the kitchen and the kids—all five of them including Marilee and Jessica—couldn't seem to stop squealing and laughing and bouncing off the walls. Miles and Gil agreed that the long-neglected furnace was past redeeming. They left it on—just low enough to keep the pipes from freezing. Gil said he would arrange to have it looked at, since Miles would be on the road again after the weekend.

VANITIES

Remember the creator in the days of your youth, before the days of
trouble come, and the years draw near when you will say, "I have no
pleasure in them;" before the sun and the light and the moon and
the stars are darkened and the clouds return with the rain; in the
day when the guards of the house tremble, and the strong men are
bent, and the women who grind cease working because they are so
few, and those who look through the windows, see dimly; when the
doors on the street are shut, and the sound of the grinding is low,
and one rises up at the sound of a bird, and all the daughters of song
are brought low; when one is afraid of heights, and terrors are in the
road; the almond tree blossoms, the grasshopper drags itself along
and desire fails; because all must go to their eternal home, and the
mourners will go about the streets; before the silver cord is snapped,
and the golden bowl is broken, and the pitcher is broken at the
fountain, and the wheel broken at the cistern, and the dust returns
to the earth as it was, and the breath returns to God who gave it.
Vanity of vanities, say the Teacher; all is vanity.

—Ecclesiastes 12:1-8

As for my mother's furnace, Gil was right. It was putting out a
good deal more than hot air. The furnace was condemned. As it
stood the house was deemed dangerous and unfit for human hab-

itation. It didn't have a proper basement and the brick foundation was crumbling. We were at a loss whether to begin repairs or rebuild or sell the lot. Mom's house was the only war-time house left in our part of town. Finer, grander homes surrounded it. But there was nothing immediately to be done, so Mom continued to live with us.

This was an adjustment. Mom was not happy being underfoot. She felt awkward and unwanted. That was my fault. I tried to be welcoming but she wasn't duped by that at all. It didn't help that Miles was Mr. Hospitality. He was as attentive as a lover to her, asking how she slept, pouring her coffee, and even bringing her flowers on her birthday. He bent over backward to make her comfortable. I could tell Mom was not impressed with my response to him. She bit her tongue and encouraged my more charitable impulses.

Adam's birthday comes fast on the heels of my mother's. As usual, I baked six layers on her birthday and froze three. A little variation in glazes and fillings makes Adam's cake a different creation. Mom's birthday was on a Saturday. Adam's fell on a Tuesday. I cooked his favourite dinner with mashed potatoes and gravy. Adam made short work of the food and quickly dispensed with our domestic celebration. Having reached Alberta's legal drinking age, he and several friends were anxious to begin the youthful rites of initiation. These they would perform in Edmonton. Gil and Amy graciously agreed to shelter the young sots for what remained of the night after their partying. Giselle was the designated driver. I thought we had pretty much covered all the bases. Hopefully Adam and company would have a good time and come home safely the next day.

Mom and Miles insisted on cleaning up. I had done enough they said, which was true. So the two of them chattered and clattered away in the kitchen and I took refuge in my green chair. *How lovely. Miles does the dishes and Mom thinks he's a saint.* I needed to escape my oppressive mood. I thought I should look for Madeleine, but I was afraid to find her. It seemed my ancient companion had been visited by the same maelstrom that was swallowing up the goodness in my own life. Of course the idea was ridiculous. To think my own discontent was anything to her suffering. Still, the last thing I needed at that moment was to take on Madeleine's troubles. I tried not to imagine Jacques's funeral—Madeleine dragging herself along behind the casket, the requiem mass, whether Blessed Jean de Beaumanoir presided. Did it take place at St. Etienne's or at the cathedral? I didn't want to worry about how Madeleine was to keep alive, much less feed her family and her people. I couldn't imagine how her story could have anything but a dismal ending. I thought Mâle's *Religious Art in France* should be safe enough and took it up. I had never found Madeleine there.

However unwilling I believed myself to be, I followed the indexed references to Beauvais—again. I turned to Mâle's reflection on the significance of the Wheel of Fortune beginning with the half-wheel on the south porch of the cathedral at Amiens.

> The figures descending so abruptly with the wheel are dressed in rags, and have bare feet or shoes through which their toes appear... The subject is certainly power, riches, glory, the pomps and vanities of the world, and the wheel expresses the instability of these things. The example at Amiens is not unique. On the north porch of St. Etienne at Beauvais... the same little figures mount and descend with a wheel.

Well, that did relate to Madeleine. Her fortunes surely fell after Jacques's horrific end. But I couldn't say what brought *me* so low. On the surface, things were mostly unchanged. Except for my mother's situation and Marilee's unease. And Jim was gone. And work was a burden with Father BG in the place. And Miles was really getting to me again. He really came out of his shell around my mother. And the nicer he meant to be, the less I liked him.

I turned the page. Here Mâle considered representations of the Virtues and Vices in medieval art. Primitive Christianity used heroic, beautiful and simple maidens to represent the Virtues but soon the soul becomes a battlefield where the Virtues, now armed maiden warriors, confront their opposing Vices. The fourth century poet Prudentius depicted these allegorical battles in his poem *Psychomachia*. Mâle gave a synopsis of the poem. I read easily enough through portrayals of Faith and Idolatry, Chastity and Lust, but then I came to this:

> Patience (*Patientia*), grave and quiet, stands awaiting the attack of Anger (*Ira*). Immovable as a rock she receives the blows which rain down upon her breastplate. At last Anger rushes forward sword in hand and strikes her enemy on the head, but the helmet is invulnerable and splinters the sword. In her rage she seizes a javelin that is at her feet and thrusts it into her own breast. Thus Patience triumphs over her enemy without even drawing sword.

Anger, a self-defeating passion. Nothing new in that. The idea has been around for quite awhile. Of course, because it is a self-defeating passion, the healthy thing to do is find out where it's coming from and express it—if you have a problem with anger, which I don't. I rarely lose my temper. Nor do I lash out even when blows rain down on my breastplate, which pretty much describes the way I was feeling. I more readily identified with Patience.

But I got stuck. I couldn't seem to read past that section. *I'm not angry. I'm just a little depressed.*

— *'Depression is rage spread thin.'*

— *'Depression is anger turned inward.'*

Amazing how the mind turns things around and fastens on thoughts unbidden. I began to wish Madeleine would show up again. I was escaping to places I didn't want to be. I leafed aimlessly through other pages for awhile then went upstairs to have a bath. I wanted to cry. And for no good reason.

I should have slept, I was so weary. I lay quiet when Miles came to bed. He brushed my cheek with a kiss, murmuring, "Oh, Janine." I didn't move a muscle. I felt him hovering awhile to see if I would wake, I suppose, then he stretched out on his side of the bed and was soon asleep. Not me. I couldn't sink into sleep. My mind would wrestle and turn around and around.

I must have finally drifted off since the phone startled me awake. It was the hospital emergency room in Edmonton. Was I the mother of Adam Weir? "Your son is being treated for alcohol poisoning. His condition is unstable. I suggest you come right away." I got what information I needed. Miles was awake and listening. I told him what she had said. We both dressed quickly and got out the door. We drove worried and silent into the city.

> *Since Adam, being free to choose,*
> *Chose to imagine he was free*
> *To choose his own necessity...*

Auden's lines tumbled incessantly in my head. My eyes held to the road. Except for the occasional mesmerizing headlights—approaching, glaring, passing—the highway was clear but dark, dark as only autumn can be, when daylight is short, before the snow scatters luster to reflect the stars. There was no moon. *Why had I named him Adam? For my father, of course, but*—Miles had wanted to name him Trent, but I said "No, Trents are party animals. We don't want him to grow up to be a party animal." I'm not sure how I knew this about the name. *And I thought Adam was better? What was I thinking? Living in a perfect world with the woman who was meant for you from the beginning of time—a match made in heaven—and you blow it. No work, no sweat of the brow, no thorns and thistles, no strife, and no, that's not good enough. What could Adam have possibly needed? And Christopher. Christ bearer. What were we in for with him?* Chris. When two-year-old Adam tried to say "Chris" it came out "Kit" and it stuck. *Maybe that will save him.*

Poor Adam. Calling a kid Adam, that's just asking for trouble. Formed from the dust of the ground—dust to dust—the dust returns to the earth as it was. Such dark thoughts. We came to my favourite part of that stretch of highway. Skirting around a pretty little knoll, the road banks first to the left, then to the right. *Turning, turning, the Wheel of Fortune—power, riches, glory, the pomps and vanities of the world—and the wheel broken at the cistern, and the dust returns to the earth as it was. All is vanity.* I stared past the glass, determined to escape my thoughts. *Those who look through the windows, see dimly—and terrors are in the road—and the region is waste and desolate, and churches and houses are burned down and collapsed in ruins, and they have murdered the poor people—If only I knew Madeleine was okay, I could handle this better.—I have suffered much tribulation, adversity and affliction—Madeleine is not okay. Of course, you idiot. She's dust now. Has been for some time. But surely she found a little joy to balance her affliction for the years when she knew misfortune...*

The white reflective lines on the shoulders of the highway fore-ran us, bright ribbons unwinding, blazing the route as we sped along. Miles drives fast. That was fine with me. I stared purposefully at the lights of the city as we approached, willing ourselves already there, willing ourselves anywhere but there. I did not want to look further into the darkness of that night. *"I suggest you come right away."* *Was she keeping something from us? Is she waiting for us to be present before she delivers the unthinkable news? No, they don't do it that way. They come to you in such a situation—I think. How did Madeleine receive the news of Jacques's death? Who told her? But this is different. Here there is nothing to tell. There is no news. I pray there is no news.* Insistently I prayed and tried to believe all would be well.

Finally we arrived. Miles parked quickly and probably illegally. We rushed into the emergency reception desk and were pointed in Adam's direction. *No look of veiled significance from the receptionist.* We found his cubicle and pulled the curtain back. The attending nurse looked up. "He's out of danger."

Adam looked like a sleeping gorgon, tubes snaking all around him. I collapsed onto Miles's shoulder for a moment then collected myself. Miles was asking if Adam was unconscious. "Not now, but he's very sleepy. He's dehydrated. He'll need monitoring for a while yet."

"Can I wake him?—Is it okay to disturb him, I mean."

The nurse nodded and moved aside. Miles squeezed Adam's

shoulder. "Adam. We're here now, your mom and I. Can you say something?" Adam's eyes fluttered for a moment. He groaned and turned away.

I moved to the other side. "Adam. You're going to be okay." No response.

The nurse suggested we wait a few minutes. She motioned to two hard plastic turquoise chairs against the wall. There sat Giselle, overtaken by sleep. She stirred when I touched her. "Bless your heart, Giselle. Did you bring him in?"

Yes, and she had called her parents to let them know what was going on and that we were coming into town. We were welcome to stay there overnight. I thanked her and said both Miles and I needed to be at work in the morning if at all possible. We talked briefly. She told the story of Adam's misadventure, then I kissed her and sent her home. Attended by the hollow ticking of the clock, Miles and I took up the vigil. The IV beeped at intervals. From time to time we heard the shuffle of feet, then voices low and sometimes urgent as a gurney rolled by on the other side of the curtain. Miles began to nod off. After several minutes, the nurse looked in on us. I asked a few more questions. Adam had thrown up a lot. He had obviously had a big meal before the binge which probably saved him. She said we may as well go home. Since Adam's condition was now stable there was no need for me and Miles to wait it out. Adam just needed to sleep it off. The hospital would keep an eye on him for a few more hours and call when he was ready to be picked up. First, though, she would get the doctor to come speak with us. I went again to stand by Adam. He began to stir. Immediately Miles was up beside me.

"Adam. Are you okay?"

Adam groaned, lifted his heavy lids and tried to focus. He muttered something incomprehensible. "What was that, son?" Miles moved in closer. "I couldn't hear you."

"It's not my fault." Adam looked ruefully from Miles to me. "The guys just kept buying me more drinks."

"Did they want to kill you?" I could hear anger rising in Miles's voice. "And can't you speak for yourself?" Adam looked helplessly back at his father.

I pressed Miles's arm. "We can talk about that later. Let it rest for now."

Miles collected himself. The doctor's visit was brief and reassuring. Together we tried to comfort Adam. Miles said how glad he was that he had survived it all. I kissed my boy and told him how much I love him. Finally Miles hugged him and said goodbye. So Adam slept and we went back into the night to find our way home.

If Wednesday were not Sister Colette's day off, I would have stayed home from work. As it was, Miles and I barely slept at all that night. We were up early for breakfast. Since neither Miles nor I would be free to drive back to the city, and my mother would be working in the afternoon, we let Kit skip school to wait for the call and bring Adam home. Miles set to work writing out instructions and drawing a map. I watched the procedure over my morning coffee. It was quite a production. Miles drew highways and junctions complete with landmarks from the edge of town right up to the parking area next to the emergency room. I was surprised at the detail—of course, Miles does spend a good deal of time driving around the countryside so he is well aware of route numbers and intersections. Even more remarkable were his sketches of the landmarks en route. A pair of leaning silos, peculiar out buildings, bridges, railroad crossings, a few distinctive structures and even a glimpse of the Strathcona Hotel emerged with quick calligraphic strokes. When he had finished Miles said, "Well, if you can't find it with this, you shouldn't be driving."

Kit was aglow with the mission. To drive by himself into the city and rescue Adam!

"You should save that map, Kit. It's a work of art." I was about to suggest making a photocopy of the original and sending that along with Kit instead but Miles's clear disdain for my comment silenced me.

"Don't be ridiculous, Janine. It's a map. Just enough so he doesn't lose his way."

"You can't even accept a compliment from me?"

"Fine. It's beautiful. So frame it." He pulled on his jacket and picked up his lunch. "Pay attention to the speed limit, Kit. Slow down in the towns or you'll have a dozen tickets before you get where you're going." With that he went out the door.

"Gee. Who pissed in his cornflakes?"

"Don't talk about your father that way, Kit. We didn't get much sleep last night. It's pretty scary to think of how badly things could have turned out with Adam." I expressed more understanding than I felt. *Miles was fine until I said something personally affirming. He is so defensive. As if accepting a compliment from me diminishes him.*

* * *

Wednesdays used to be the best day at work. When Sister Colette was off, I never worried about getting in anyone's way and no one got in mine. The day was especially lovely when Father Francis was around. And with Jim, too. Father BG changed all that. He couldn't leave me in peace, nor were his interruptions gratifying or to the point. Father Eugene took to working behind closed doors on the days BG ranged. Mercifully, Walter put in an appearance from time to time. That usually put me in better humour. This Wednesday I was telling Walter about the night's errand and my concern about Adam. Walter was philosophic. "Boys will be boys. The point is to trick death—see if they can get away with it. If they do, usually they settle down. I think your boy will be fine." Heartening. Adam had always been an easy keeper. This was one event, not a narrative.

"How goes the battle?" In waltzed Father BG.

"Well, sir," says Walter, "Can't be talking about it now. It's all strategy and secret. I'll have to get back to you on that." And out he goes leaving me to entertain BG. Father BG continued undaunted.

"And you Janine—are your battles also secret?"

I could not humour him. I said the first thing that came to mind. "I assume you are referring to the inner battle of the soul and you wish to know whether the Virtues are winning?"

Apparently, from the blank look on his face, he was not.

"You know—" I continued, "—as Prudentius describes it." I let him shift a little then finally said "Yes, I would say my battles are personal and therefore not open to general discussion."

He muttered something that may have been an apology and went back to his office. *Well, that took care of that.* I felt mean and a little sorry. *I wish I didn't have to be rude to make him back off. Such a buffoon! So officious.* Still, I felt terribly guilty, knowing that at best he was probably confused and at worst, feeling hurt and uncomfortable. The trouble was, I just couldn't bring myself to apologize to Father Bob and if I were to confess it to Father Eugene, I had a feeling I would drag him down with me. Father Eugene might even enjoy it. So I only resolved to be more compassionate in the future.

GRAY

The poignant misery of dawn begins to grow...
We only know war lasts, rain soaks, and clouds sag stormy.
Dawn massing in the east her melancholy army
Attacks once more in ranks on shivering ranks of gray,
But nothing happens

—Wilfred Owen, "Exposure"

Weary as much from the day as from the night before, I hurried home to see if Kit and Adam were back. The trees were bare and the wind brisk. Overhead, geese were having a leadership crisis. They couldn't find their instinctive "V". They formed a "W"— "double V" in French of course. Proceeding with much honking and other goosely deliberations, even the geese couldn't fall in and find their place. Not surprising that I felt so out of sync.

The boys were back! I was as much relieved at their safe journey as that Adam was well and home again. Adam said little as Kit recounted his happy adventure. "And here's your map, Mom. You *should* frame it. My first drive to the city. It's a collector's item now."

I did. And I hung it in the stairwell to the basement. Mom pronounced it *charmant* and commented on it to Miles one evening before she made her way downstairs. It had hung there for perhaps a week by then. "Your drawing makes me smile every time I pass by."

"What drawing?"

"The little map you made. See? Here."

Miles followed her down to the landing. "Oh, that silly thing." Mom said little joys are the stuff of life or something like that and Miles made his way back upstairs. He made no comment but seemed somewhat forgiving of my folly. I thought this a good sign. I had already decided to give him art classes as a birthday gift. With his birthday so close to Christmas, it's not easy to come up with gift ideas for both.

November is such a gray month. The green is gone. Often there is no snow. Gray and white reminiscence of war marches across the television screen—stories of heroes and sacrifice, expressions of remembrance, and tears. The only colour for me is the resumption of weekend coffee dates with Denise. Once the growing season dies down we take up where we left off in spring. This November I finally began to tell her about Madeleine. I didn't tell the whole story. I told her the references would be considered spurious by some historians. I did not tell her they utterly disappear. I told her about Jim's suggestion that I go to Beauvais to see what I could learn about Madeleine there. Denise thought that was a great idea. At her urging, I wrote to the contact person, Soeur Lucille Claire at Maison Diocésaine - 101 rue de la Madeleine. It all felt so fanciful. I asked this Sister Lucille Claire if a room would be available for several weeks in the new year. I also made it clear that I had no confirmed plans and I was not at all certain I would be able to make the trip. I sent it off hoping she would respond saying any rental would be impossible at that time.

Other events of November were principally the steady descent of the mercury, arctic weather riding in on the wind, and at the end of the month, the first Sunday in Advent, the beginning of cycle A in the lectionary.

Pray for the peace of Jerusalem:
"May they prosper who love you.
Peace be within your walls,
and security within your towers."

Advent. Great expectations. Maybe this year will be different. After mass, I greeted a few friends and shook hands with Father Eugene. I headed for the door. And here was Agnes, handing out some sort of flyer. I don't see Agnes much anymore. If her presence in the office decreased once Father Francis died, under the current dispensation, she gave up her visits to the parish office entirely. To be polite, I took a flyer and asked her about it. "We'll almost certainly have an election this spring," she said. I looked it over. Her title was, "We Ask Too Little of Our Politicians." This was followed by two selections from the prophets:

"Justice is turned back, and righteousness stands at a distance; for truth stumbles in the public square, and uprightness cannot enter. Truth is lacking and whoever turns from evil is despoiled. The LORD *saw it, and it displeased him that there was no justice."*
—Isaiah 59:14-15

"Thus says the Lord GOD: *Enough, O princes of Israel! Put away violence and oppression, and do what is just and right."*
—Ezekiel 45:9

What followed was her usual litany of ills perpetrated by irresponsible governments. She wrote of corporate greed, irresponsible management of natural resources, the erosion of the social safety net, compromises in health care. Finally, she said "Many Catholics are reluctant to vote for parties that promote universal benefits because of their stand on abortion. The issue is a red herring. It blinds us to deep problems in society that must be addressed before we will see any change in attitude or our collective sense of responsibility around the issue. The blight of abortion will be with us as long as carrying an unwanted pregnancy is choosing poverty, social marginalization and overwhelming challenges to personal development, where dreams of education and financial stability vanish."

"Fair enough," I said as I finished and began to go.

Agnes groaned.

"What's the matter?"

"Mrs. Noseworthy took a flyer and is now delivering it to Father Eugene. Great."

I turned to see an animated Mrs. Noseworthy pointing with all importance to the fine details of Agnes's handiwork. Father Eugene scanned the flyer, thanked her, and walked over to Agnes saying, "You can't do this here, Agnes. You know we have a strict policy about distributing political material on church property."

"This is not political. This is an *apologia* in the cause of civic responsibility. It is not partisan."

"I disagree. Please take your business elsewhere."

Agnes set her jaw and stood firm.

"Agnes, please don't cause a scene," he begged.

"Father Eugene, please don't cause a scene," she countered.

The blood vessels on Father Eugene's temple dilated and writhed like snakes under a wet blanket. I didn't want to be there. I slunk into the shadow of the recess of the doorway and tried to slip away.

"Janine, where are you going?"

"Home. It's Sunday, Father." *He'd better not get me involved in this.*

"I need you for a minute."

Lord help me. This is not my problem. "I really have to go."

"No, stay!"

There was something desperate in his voice. He was out of his depth. I had never seen him like this. I don't know why it was such a big deal to him, or why he was having trouble being his usual authoritarian self. Agnes also looked quite shaken at the standoff. *What did she think would happen? Did she really think Father Eugene would give her a pat on the back for her commitment to her peculiar brand of social action?* I stood stupidly unable to move or speak.

"Talk to Agnes. We do not allow people to campaign in the church."

I like the "we" bit. Really! When has Father Eugene ever deferred to me? He seemed to beat a retreat.

"I don't know what to say." All three of us stood like idiots, no one quite up to casting the next stone. Who cast the first? Father Eugene, who could have begun by asking her to clear it with him beforehand, or Agnes who does her own thing without regard for consequences? It wasn't me, that's for sure. Finally I looked directly at Agnes and, trying to appear supportive, said "Maybe it would be better if you stood outside the doors at the bottom of the church steps." I could see Agnes balk at that. Father Eugene took a quick short breath, ready to forbid it. This was not what he wanted from me. I quickly preempted him: "That way, you both will be equally unhappy and no one will think Agnes's flyer is being distributed by the church." And I walked away. I didn't look back until I was a half a block from the church. There stood Agnes outside in the blowing cold at the bottom of the stairs handing out her leaflets. Father Eugene was nowhere to be seen. I must admit, this surprised me. I was puzzled at how much both of them—usually so convinced of their own lights—wavered. I wondered what was going on in the world. Even Father Eugene seemed to be suffering from a failure of nerve.

And why doesn't Agnes ever let it go? She magnifies everything— all the social ills and religious blind spots the rest of us recognize as the burden of a greedy and thoughtless society. Not that the status quo is at all acceptable. I don't mean that. But this isn't what prophecy looks like. Agnes is not eloquent. Agnes is not anointed. She's just a voice—crying in the wilderness. Well, I don't mean that. That's not Agnes. She's just a loose cannon. She's out of her mind.

—And I'm not? Is everybody crazy? I tried to change the subject. That's not as easy as it should be when the conversation is all in your head. I tried to think about faith. *Maybe faith is just being open to being crazy. Can't be. "The substance of things hoped for, the evidence of things not seen." I haven't had any evidence of Madeleine since Jim left. I have pretty much given up hope. I probably never had any faith at all. Not once did I ever find Madeleine by looking for her. She showed up when I was preoccupied with other things. I am no more faithful than Agnes is prophetic. We're both just nuts.*

The walk from church is short. For once I was glad to have such a deadly predictable life. Adam and Kit were still asleep. Mom was making breakfast. Miles was busily drawing up plans for an extension to the house—a three-room granny suite. "You will have your privacy and still be with us when it suits you." He turned enthusiastically to me. "There you are! I was just thinking that maybe the best solution to your mother's housing problem would be to sell her property and build an extension here. What do you think of that?"

I sighed.

"What's the matter? It would be a completely separate suite." Now Miles was annoyed.

"I don't want to have to think about things the minute I get in the door."

"Oh gosh. Miles is so *idéaliste*." My mother tries so hard to diffuse the tension. "How was church? Should I be warned?" Mom goes to the evening mass.

"Just a set-to between Father Eugene and Agnes. Nothing new. It makes me weary."

"Well, let's have something to eat." She put a fruit salad and one of her wonderful omelets on the table.

Miles set his drawings aside. "Shall I wake the boys?" He looked a little downcast. *I wish he didn't think he has to fix everything.*

"Just let them sleep. This omelet is only enough for three anyway. I'll make another one when they get up."

Breakfast was delicious. I tried not to care how glum Miles became the minute I expressed an opinion. And Mom tried not to notice.

Later, while I was putting together Sunday dinner, the heartiest meal of the week, she came to the kitchen. She set to work peeling potatoes. "Janine, I know this is hard on you, me living here, and I don't want you to worry about my problems." She clicked away with the peeler, broadcasting peels across the bottom of the sink. "I have to learn to handle it by myself, you know. As far as I can see, I just need to find a place in a lodge somewhere. Then I won't be causing all this trouble."

"Mother, you are not a problem. And you are not going to any lodge. You have your own home and you worked hard to get it. And you haven't even retired yet."

"Yes, but I can't live in my own home anymore and I've been there for so long, eh? So I don't have ideas yet. But I have to figure out something. And I will. This week. Don't you worry about that."

"How about I call Gil and we talk about it when you get home from mass? I'll tell him about Miles's idea and see what he says."

"No. That won't work. You know darn well what he'll say. He thinks a lot of Miles. He won't argue about that."

"Well, maybe Miles's idea is the best solution."

"But it isn't fair for you. I can see you are uncomfortable."

"That's just because Miles—he doesn't—the way he presents his ideas as if they are mine."

Mom opened her mouth to speak, caught her breath, exhaled—and said nothing.

ACCUMULATION

Some say the world will end in fire;
Some say in ice.
From what I've tasted of desire
I hold with those who favor fire.

But if it had to perish twice,
I think I know enough of hate
To know that for destruction ice
Is also great
And would suffice.

—Robert Frost, "Fire and Ice"

It really was the best solution. It's not as if there is a shortage of space on our property. The lots in our part of town were divided when the town was a small agrarian centre and townspeople expected to have room to grow their own produce. With money from the sale of Mom's property, we could build without incurring debt; she could claim ownership of her little apartment and still save the bulk of the equity for her retirement. We figured a small percent of this money held in trust could constitute Gil's "inheritance" if Mom didn't need to use it. The value added to our property would make up my portion. So Miles spent the early part of December drawing up plans.

We had more snow than usual that month. Often the roads are clear late into December. But roads were already packed and drifts deep around shrubs and fences when on the fifteenth it began to snow again—after a fashion. Snow lingered in the air for several days, an incessant drizzle of dry flakes that defy snowballing. On the eighteenth, the mercury plunged to -32. With wind chill it was below -40. Forty below—the fabled place where Celsius and Fahrenheit meet. Apologists for Alberta's weather will say "it is a dry cold"—presumably somehow less chilling than a "wet cold." I couldn't say. It was the only cold I knew. Regardless, even for Flatfield, it was a dry snowfall and seemed to be only getting dryer—soon it was just a frozen fog, ice crystals suspended without enough influencing moisture to flake. Eventually the crystals came to rest and did accumulate by virtue of population and application.

It was Miles's birthday. It had been a long week. The parish office was buzzing with preparations for Christmas. The aura of anticipation and excitement made Father BG only more boisterous and difficult to endure. It was Thursday. I had as much to do as done on my lists. Feeling overwhelmed, I hurried home, crystals forming with every breath. No one should be out in such cold weather. I had put the cake together the night before. Mom had switched her work schedule so she could be home to make dinner. That was a help. But I was tired and out of sorts when I got home, just the same.

Dinner was pleasant enough. I have to admit having Mom around has its benefits. I served up the birthday cake and poured coffee. Miles opened gifts from the boys and my mother and was gracious in thanking them. Then I gave him a birthday card with the art class registration enclosed.

I watched closely as he opened it. I actually thought he would enjoy something out of the ordinary. I should have known better.

He read the card. That was fine. Then he scanned the registration and seemed perplexed. Finally he looked up and said:

"What possible use is this to me?"

"After watching you draw that map for Kit, I thought you would enjoy it—your sketches seem to take shape so easily and naturally."

"Well, you know I don't do stuff like this. What a total waste of time and money."

Mom looked surprised and quickly began to clear the table. For a second I was stunned—Miles was usually so well behaved around my mother—but then I was livid. Such a small detour out of his rut and he wouldn't even suspend his misgivings long enough to say thank you. To my own amazement, I blurted back:

"Jackass! Can't you even pretend to be interested for my sake? It's all about you, isn't it. You don't want me to have anything to do with who you are." He looked startled. I continued. "You're the perfect package all taped and tied shut. If I love you, I have to love the man *you* think you are, not the man I know. To live with you, I have to arrange our life the way you imagine it should be. If I am to be happy, it can only be about things you deem worthwhile." My mother retreated downstairs. The boys gaped in disbelief. "And when it comes to me, you only care about what you think I should be. You are not content unless I meet those expectations, unless I arrange my space and time to your specifications. You only smile when there is no surprise." For once I savored his silence. Then carelessly I added: "Well, you can use your considerable talent to draw a cardboard replica of me if you like; make it large as life. That's all you want anyway. As for me, I'm going to France."

This, of course, was the first time I even mentioned the idea out loud to anyone but Jim and Denise. Miles and the boys, all three of them, stood like a choir, their open mouths forming some unworldly inaudible triad. I pulled on my coat and gloves and scarf and hat and boots and stormed out the door. As I slammed the door, I saw them still standing there probably wondering if I really thought I could go to France just like that. *They think I'm crazy. Well, it's time they knew.*

The air was so cold. The wind blew it colder. Snow hung in the air too frozen to fall. Dry snowflakes flitter and sparkle—packed on sidewalks they squeak. I hurried along the sidewalk, my footsteps sounding like some yipping imp dogging my heels. *Phantom prairie dogs. That's how they spend the winter, nasty little buggers. What came over me? They're probably laughing at me right now. How ridiculous! Why did I say that? And why did I even consider giving Miles such a thing in the first place?*

I reached the intersection. Because of the sheer volume of snow, the roads were a heaving sea of the stuff. It made for slow crossing, like walking on breakers of builder's sand. *It's just that Jim is gone, Adam is messing up, my mother needs a home, work's annoying, Marilee's anxious. And I can't find Madeleine. Still, it would have been only fair—decent—of Miles to be a little more appreciative. He didn't even try.* I walked on past where the sidewalk stops, past the last lamp in town, onto my levee, into the heaving prairie sea, my only light the reflected glow of a waning gibbous moon. I tried to follow the road. I slogged on, wading through shifting ridges of snow, trying to stay in the widest tire tracks. Icy astringent wind tightened my skin. It started to burn. *Damn, it's cold. I should turn around.* My eyes burning and tearing up, my exposed skin stinging and numbing, I kept going. *Where? There's nothing out here for miles.* Frost formed in layers on the wool where I breathed into my scarf. *Layers keep you warm.* I knew it was not a good idea to continue. If the temperature was going anywhere that time of night, it would be down. But I was just too angry and proud to turn around. I didn't want to go home—to walk in the door as if nothing had happened.

Headlights behind me. *Who, in God's name, is driving down this road tonight?* Hardly anybody used that road anymore. Even the farms along it use the paved road a half mile up. The road was unplowed, thick with shifting snow, hardly navigable at all. I slowly plodded over to the side of the road. *A slow approach. Good. Speed kills.* The vehicle rumbled along behind me. It did not pass. It just kept pace with me. I felt a seizing in my chest. *Crap! Leave me alone. What idiot would stalk on such a cold night?* The driver would not overtake me. I stumbled along, losing my footing. *If he would only get out of my way I could sit down for a minute and catch my breath.* The vehicle followed slowly. *Just pass, you jackass.* I seethed. I tried to size up my stalker out of the corner of my eye. The truck stopped. A door opened. *Shit.*

"Mom!" Kit stood on the running board yelling at me. "Mom. Get in. You'll freeze to death."

Thank God. I crossed in front of the headlights; Kit leaned over to push the door open. I got in, brushed off the snow and fastened my seatbelt. The fan was on high, the hot air so welcome. "Thanks, Kit."

"What're you doin'? Are you crazy? No one goes walking on a night like this!"

Yep, I'm crazy. No question.

"Are you okay?"

"I just needed some time out."

"Pretty far out for a time out."

I couldn't say a thing.

"Adam went to work, so Dad sent me to get you."

Kit backed up carefully in the tracks that got him to me—maybe the distance of three city blocks. It seemed an enormous distance. Finally he backed onto the slightly more navigable pavement and turned around. The truck lumbered the two more blocks to home. I sat silent beside my rescuer.

Miles was standing in the living room, waiting, when we got home. "You're back," was all he said. He sat down, maybe expecting me to join him, maybe not. I didn't answer. I didn't meet his eyes. I went directly upstairs, took a hot shower, brushed my teeth, helped myself to a sizable dose of valerian root and went to bed. I didn't feel Miles come to bed, if he did. He was already gone when I woke up in the morning.

The next day at supper he said nothing about the art class or my response to his comment. I realized he probably would take the course in spite of his negative reaction. Not for my sake, certainly, nor because he was at all interested in it, but because he was too cheap to let it go to waste. For the record, he never said any more about it, although at Christmas he was careful to say *thank you* for the drill bits and sweater I got him.

After supper, Miles and Kit sat down in the family room to watch the hockey game. Both Mom and Adam were at work. I washed the dishes, then sat in the living room browsing aimlessly through my bookshelf. I leafed through the several books where Madeleine had appeared. *What is the point? What am I supposed to do about it? Why did she show up at all? Why did she bother with me? My world is a pretty lifeless place to be. Hardly the place for someone like Madeleine to make herself at home.* In a way, I resented her. She had stirred things up. *I would never have thought to give Miles such a gift if she hadn't somehow skewed the way I saw the world. And I wouldn't be embarrassed now about last evening's expedition. I wonder what would have happened if Kit hadn't come along—maybe my fifteen minutes of fame, posthumously. Maybe not. Maybe a long recovery in hospital and a futile attempt to save my toes and fingers. Then rehab. Learning to type with my mouth so I can keep my job.* The books weren't offering any consolation. The hockey game had gone into overtime. I went to bed.

I didn't sleep well. Miles came to bed and seemed asleep before his head hit the pillow. *Typical. You hear about the walking wounded, but nobody talks about the walking sleepers. Walks through life with his eyes closed. It's all about him. Either you accept that, or you're in the way. A lot can get in your way if you don't open your eyes long enough to see where you're going.* I lay awake far too long. Finally I got up to take more of that sleeping potion. *Someday I'll write a tribute to the power of valerian root. A tribute—to valerian root. To valerian root, a tribute, a tribute, a tribute—*If the herb didn't work, the rhyme did. I finally fell asleep.

I had the strangest dream. I was dying. It was very sad. At the church, I picked out several hymns—Denise was with me. Al the musician was there. He was not impressed. Very standard funeral hymns, nothing new, nothing interesting. "Oh, for heaven's sake, Al! This is a funeral," I told him. "It's not supposed to be interesting."

After making these preparations, I left the church. Several people were making their way into the church for mass. One woman looked familiar, an acquaintance of sorts. I quietly nodded a greeting to her, then crossed my arms across my chest and briefly closed my eyes to demonstrate that I was dying. Then I opened my eyes, shrugged, and pulled my closed lips into a grave, complicit smile. I raised my left hand by my cheek and, fluttering my four fingers, gave a little wave and whispered inaudibly, "Bye."

At the funeral home, I chose a very simple coffin. It should have been solid pine, but it wasn't. It was "good one side" three-quarter inch plywood. Still it was very tasteful, painted in a dark flat matte gray with a deep blue cast to it. Smooth shiny white satin lined the box, of course. I chose a matching car. I think it was a 1954 Fiat 500, not quite like the one my mother used to drive—the one she bought used from the Fedoras—because it had a silver running board. The fenders that took off from the running board made a flamboyant swoop over the back wheels. I couldn't quite figure out how the coffin was going to fit inside.

I crawled into my coffin, crossed my arms on my chest and tried to die. It wasn't working. I shouldn't have spent so much time getting ready. I'd lost the urge. I was going to be late for my own funeral, just as my high school English teacher said I would be when I handed my paper in late—again. Oh, well. Tomorrow was a new day. I decided to come back to die in the morning.

I drove the Fiat home, parking it carefully in a parkade somewhere, manoeuvering it behind a concrete pillar so no one could dent it. I was concerned that there was already a small chip out of that deep blue-gray paint at the bottom corner of the front door. I hoped the funeral home wouldn't charge me extra for that.

The next day, I got up to go to my funeral. I drove a double-decker bus this time. It was the same deep dark blue gray as the car and the coffin. That nice blue Fiat was still in the parkade behind the concrete pillar. I don't know why I was driving a bus. There were no passengers. I bounced along a winding avenue on my way to the funeral parlor. Heading around a curve and down a hill, a couple of young fellows—maybe fourteen years old—were executing several tricks standing on the seats of their rolling bikes. I had to drive onto the sidewalk to avoid hitting them. I screeched to a halt. They hardly noticed me. The light turned red, so I couldn't drive off the sidewalk. I lost my place in traffic and had to wait until it cleared. Back on the road, I made my way down the hill. I met a neighbor driving up the hill, made the polite "hello neighbour" wave, then thought it only fair to let her know I wasn't long for this world, so again I crossed my arms on my chest and briefly closed my eyes, pulled my lips into that tight resigned grin again, raised my left hand by my cheek and fluttering my four fingers gave a little wave and whispered inaudibly, "Bye." I hoped she would understand. I didn't have time to stop and explain things.

I got back to the funeral home, climbed into my coffin, crossed my arms, each of my open hands resting palm down near the opposite shoulder. Then Father Jim came and made some ritual gestures over me. I saw my sons standing at the foot of the coffin. They looked very young and clean and tidy, their hair combed flat, still wet from a shower. They were wearing green blazers. They were trying very hard to do the right thing. Then Agnes and Madeleine appeared beside the coffin. "I know how you feel," Agnes said. Her eyes rolled a bit as she tried to focus on me. Madeleine just looked on knowingly. I closed my eyes and I tried to die. Still no luck. When I opened them, Miles was standing impatiently beside my coffin. I was no longer aware of the presence of any others.

"What are you going to do with the car?" Miles asked. I could tell, by the way he fidgeted, that he thought I should be leaving it to him. That old Fiat was a real collector's item.

"You forget, I don't own the car," I reminded him.

He hovered restlessly. "What's taking you so long?"

This irritated me. "Well, Miles," I said, "it's harder to die than you think. I'm doing my best…" On the whole, however, I had the sinking feeling I really wasn't going to be able to die after all. I *was* doing my best, but I just wasn't certain how it was done.

I'm not clear about how things were left when I woke up. The last image I remember, I was in my coffin at the back of a small chapel, trying to accommodate, trying to figure out how to die. There was music—the usual funeral organ playing standard funeral hymns.

When I woke up, I was quite relieved to be alive. I looked over at Miles, absorbed in sleep and oblivious to my experience. *As usual.*

Still, he was alive too and, oddly enough, this consoled me. *I've got to talk to Denise.*

LIMEN

Of course it hurts when buds burst.
Otherwise why would spring hesitate?
Why would all our fervent longing be
bound in the frozen bitter haze?
. . . .

Hard to be uncertain,
afraid and divided,
hard to feel the deep pulling and calling,
yet sit there and just quiver—
hard to want to stay
and to want to fall.

—Karin Boye, "Of Course It Hurts"

Thank goodness it was Saturday. I went early to meet Denise. I sat sipping my coffee and wondering how on earth to extract myself from the corner I seemed to have backed into. I watched Denise come in the door. She nodded and smiled in my direction and went to get her coffee. I went over to wait with her and muttered, "Do I ever need to talk to you!"

"What's the matter? You look like you just lost your best friend."

"Oh, I hope not. I need you now more than ever."

"No doubt."

"I'm serious."

"So what's going on?"

"That's what I need to figure out." I whispered so the barista wouldn't hear, "I think I'm going to ask Miles for a divorce."

"You must be kidding."

"I don't know. We're at an impasse. I can't seem to break through. And he doesn't even try." She got her coffee and we headed back to the table.

"Well, you don't begin with divorce, Janine. You could do a lot worse for a husband, you know."

If Denise has one fault, it's that she likes Miles too much. I don't mean she's got a thing for him or anything. She just doesn't really seem to get what the problem is.

We sat down. I told her everything—about how rude Miles was about the gift, about my embarrassing threat about going to France, about my trek in the snow, and finally about my dream. All of it.

"Whew! What a dream! You should write it down. I wish I knew more about dreams. Isn't the car supposed to represent your life?"

"That's just the point. Miles wants it and I don't own the car."

"And that's Miles's fault?"

"Denise, whose side are you on?"

"I didn't think there were sides. I thought you wanted to figure this out. This is your dream, not his. "

"Well, it's Miles who wants to own the car."

"But it's a funeral parlour that actually does. Is that any better?"

"It is my funeral, though."

"Well, isn't that auspicious!" I had to laugh. "But what about the bus? Nobody's travelling with you. Do you really feel that way?"

"Absolutely. Even my mom seems to think it's my problem—although I could see she wasn't impressed with Miles's behaviour on his birthday."

We didn't make much progress in figuring out the dream. What we did manage was to talk about Beauvais and whether I should even entertain the idea of going there. I talked at length about the Madeleine story and about how disturbing it was not to know more

about her. I told her about Jim's urging me to write it up, even as
fiction, and how that scared me.

"I'm just not a writer, Denise. If I can't find enough to support
Madeleine's story as academic research, I doubt I can write it up as
anything else."

"But you can try. Once you've done it, you will have organized
everything you can say about the story and you'll at least have an
account of what you do know."

"I'm just afraid of what might happen. And I don't want to do
anything shoddy—as research or as fiction."

"So without the guarantee, you'd rather not risk doing it at all."

"Exactly."

"Who ever did anything of value knowing beforehand what the
outcome would be?"

"Well, you would think one would have more to work with at the
outset, both in hard evidence and talent."

"You really think so! And you complain about Miles not break-
ing out of his rut. A slave with one talent—all you can think about
is your lack of resources."

"Huh?"

"You know, the parable of the talents, where a man going on a
journey trusts his property to three slaves, and two of them invest it
and repay twice what they were given when the master returns? The
third slave buries his single talent in the ground."

"Oh, I see. Well, just for the record, my sympathies have always
been with that poor guy with only one talent. He says he knows
the master is a harsh man, reaping where he does not sow. Imagine what would have happened if he lost the talent? What kind of
trouble would he be in then? So, the slave protected it and returned
it unharmed. That doesn't seem so foolish to me. What more did
the master expect? It's a pretty risky business, having to take care of
something you can't really claim as your own in the first place. Now
if the master had said, 'Hey, Joe, here's a real opportunity for you. I
know you can handle it. Go crazy,' that would have been better. A
little affirmation goes a long way. Joe would have had more confi-

dence and worried less about what was expected of him."

"Hmm. 'Having to take care of something you can't really claim as your own in the first place.' Do you hear what you just said, Janine? You don't own the car—and taking ownership is a risky business. Maybe that's your problem. The master has a point. You shouldn't make someone else responsible for your own fear. Face it. Write the story down. Since this research is already so much a part of you, you can own it. Invest in it, even if the whole idea is a bit scary."

"Yeah, and then if I do write it, and it does get published, some reviewer will say I should have buried this one. Can't you see at least how someone who has so little to work with—no experience and no hard evidence either—would hesitate?"

"Have a little faith, Janine. Begin. That's all you can do. This story has preoccupied you long enough. Burying it won't complete the work and certainly won't make it go away. Besides, if you go to Beauvais, at the very least, you'll get a trip to France out of the deal. And time to figure out what's going on with you—and what you really feel about Miles. You'll never be sure it was a bad idea until you've done it."

* * *

Well, I wasn't able to do much about it with Christmas at the door and so little time to myself. I took to sleeping on the futon in the family room. I could see this pained my mother, not just because she wanted things to be better between me and Miles, but also because she occupied Marilee's room, our *de facto* guest room. And I stopped taking communion. I couldn't have told you why. It just didn't seem right any more. It mostly had to do with Miles, I figured. Life with Miles—I couldn't face it—a future as desolate as a soccer pitch in winter. But how can you be reconciled to God when all you can think about is divorcing your husband?

I waited until after Christmas to break the news to Miles. It wasn't easy. It's hard to be convincing when you're not at all sure of something yourself. But frightening as the prospect of leaving was, the prospect of continuing in the frozen haze our relationship had become was more than I could bear. There was a moment in my conversation with Denise when I realized I probably would go to France. I was surprised at how that happened. I was so sure the idea was preposterous, and here I was, not only entertaining the notion, but preparing to act on it. I even left the radio tuned to French CBC after my mom went to work on Saturday, just to refresh my feeling for the language.

Boxing Day morning, I got up early to catch Miles before anyone else began to stir. I made coffee and a little breakfast and waited for him in the kitchen. He was surprised to see me up when he walked into the room.

"You're up early for a holiday."

"Yeah. I need to talk to you." My voice shook. I didn't expect to feel so sad. And it seemed his face began to hang heavy and took on gravity just from the tone of my voice.

"I'm going away."

"What do you mean?"

"I'm going to France."

"Just like that?" Much as he seemed a little shaken, his right eyebrow began to dance with annoying condescension. Well, that helped. Anyone who allows his eyebrow to say so much can't possibly have anything in his heart. It made me more determined than ever. And telling him I was indeed going to France made last week's announcement at my exit into that cold night a little less absurd.

"Yes, just like that. I have research I want to do there and I really need to get away from here—from you."

Miles groped for a chair and sat down at the table—all colour drained from his face. "What research?"

"I've been researching references to a fifteenth-century woman called Madeleine de Brout."

"Why?"

"Because she interests me."

"So you think you can go just because something interests you? Don't I have anything to say about it?"

"No."

"What about your commitments? Isn't this supposed to be a marriage?"

"Some marriage! We don't know how to talk to each other, we don't laugh together, we hardly ever eat together, we don't—care."

Miles dropped his forehead in his hand, closed his eyes and sighed. After a while he lifted his head, rested his chin in his hand and looked cheerlessly at me.

"Some marriage," I muttered again.

Miles decided not to pursue that course. "How long have you been doing this research? What got you started?"

"I discovered Madeleine in one of my books years ago and have been noting references to her ever since. But my resources here have dried up. She lived in Beauvais so that's where I'm going. I'll write up my notes when I'm there, and check to be sure I've got it right. I also want to see if there are any local legends about her or any folk history."

"So that's what you were doing with those stacks of library books. Why didn't you tell me?"

"Why didn't you ask?" We sat silent awhile. I got up, poured him some coffee, and sat down again.

Miles took a deep breath. "But you're not—" He hesitated. "This is only temporary. You're not—going for good?"

"Don't know." I shrugged. To be honest, much as I resented him, it was hard to watch him suffer. "I need to get away. I'm not leaving you. But I'm not *not* leaving you either. I can't see this turning around, but I'll decide when I get back. "

"And you'll keep me posted?"

"No. Not at all. And I don't want to hear from you when I'm gone. That will only confuse everything."

"When will you go? How long will you be gone?"

I didn't have a reservation yet. I hadn't confirmed anything with Sister Lucille Claire. I could only say I hoped to leave in early January and I didn't plan to be back before Easter. I have never felt so torn in all my life. Not so much about Miles. Once I allowed myself to consider leaving him, the idea of freedom seduced me. That's what made me determined to follow through. The thing that tore me apart was a fear that I would lose everything. In so many ways, I lead a blessed life. Would it still be there for me when I got home? What if I did find Madeleine? What if I didn't? What if Beauvais is a hole? And beneath all that, a fearful sense that I was the story. That was the most terrifying thing, although I couldn't imagine why. I was the one who longed to know, who ached for some kind of conclusion, even if the ending was tragic.

SEA CHANGE

Why would anyone want to be
so far from home and across the sea?
The doubts you want to leave behind
are the first companions your heart will find.
Rather leave dull ennui to chance
than fix it with a trip to France.

—Janine LaFoy, "Fool's Errand"

Well, if nothing else could induce me to act, my pride was equal to the task. There was no turning back. Telling Miles settled that. My mother was not impressed. "You have a good husband, what more do you want? Sometimes I think you'll be lucky just to stay married." Single parenting had been a lonely life for her. Why would anyone choose that? I couldn't explain it, and I didn't try.

The following Monday, I booked a flight to Paris, sent a letter to Beauvais, and went late to work. I submitted my resignation. Father Eugene was shocked. I had expressed no dissatisfaction with the job and he had been comfortable with me. I understood intuitively what he required, and he knew it. When I said I was going to France for awhile, he urged me to consider a leave of absence. I couldn't do that since I had no idea how things would unfold when I got back. And nearly six years in the parish office—that should be long enough for anyone.

The weeks between Christmas and my departure crept along, despite the hurry about getting a passport, changing money, and packing. Miles recovered himself after the initial trauma. He was mostly sullen and aloof. Mom became interested in my adventure. I think if I had invited her along, she may have come with me. Maybe next time. The boys were impressed. I had finally "exceeded expectations" on my report card from them. My flight left on the twelfth of January. "I suppose I can take the morning off and drive you to the airport," said Miles grudgingly, as if it were a great hardship for him.

"Not at all. Denise is driving me. And don't you dare think of picking me up when I get home either. Mom or one of the boys can do it. I will see you soon enough when I get back." I was quite chippy. If he had shown the least bit of generosity about it, I may have felt differently.

The morning of my departure I got up at four o'clock. Miles was already up, fixing breakfast. I wished he hadn't done that. We breakfasted in silence. After a few minutes Mom came upstairs bleary-eyed—she never gets up before eight—but she was determined to see me off. I went upstairs one last time and kissed my sleeping boys. We'd said our goodbyes the night before. Denise drove up to our door at 5:00 am. I kissed and hugged my mom, gave Miles a peck on the cheek, and away we went.

Denise was perfect. She shared my enthusiasm and calmed my anxiety. After three long weeks of waiting, the drive to the airport passed so quickly. We talked about all the possibilities. I promised her regular reports about the trip, Beauvais, my work, and any discoveries I may make. In no time at all she pulled into a parking stall and we found our way to the departure desk. I had tried to keep my luggage to a minimum so I could handle it by myself, but there were books I needed, which were heavy, and it was winter, after all, even in Beauvais, so clothes were bulky. I checked my bags, Denise saw me to the security area, I submitted to the security guard's wand, turned and waved and Denise was gone. I was alone with my adventure.

I walked along a cavernous hallway to the waiting room at my departure gate. I sat down in the middle of a row of vacant chairs and looked around at my fellow passengers. Bored or busy, this was all commonplace to them. Even a little girl travelling with her mother seemed tired and disinterested. Could no one see I was leaving my family for the first time?

We boarded. I had a window seat where I could watch or wonder or worry as much as I chose. Next to me was a lively fellow who could not keep his place. He worked as an airline steward and was on his way to a training course in Toronto. He knew all the staff and kept bounding out of his place to consort with them and bouncing back when they were too busy to be bothered. I'm not sure they appreciated him, but I did. He hadn't a care about the turbulence when our breakfast trays nearly slid into our laps. And he was very busy telling me about how they load a plane to maintain balance, or how they land it, or how east-bound flights are usually faster because they will pick up a tail wind or ride with the jet stream. His nonchalance eased my anxiety about all the terrible things that could happen because I had the audacity to leave my family and take this unnecessary journey.

By the time I found my connecting flight in Toronto, I no longer thought about what it may mean to be leaving home. By then I was thoroughly preoccupied with my final destination. I found my seat and settled beside a small, wiry man, balding on top but with bushy curly hair circling the spot like a monk's tonsure gone wild. I said a polite hello. He nodded, muttered a greeting, and made a great show of digging out a mound of papers and reading material as fortification against my intrusion. That was fine with me. I read the safety card, located the flotation device, and tried to ignore him. After takeoff, I dug the first volume of *The Mediaeval Stage* out of my bag and determined to read it quite through from the beginning—to finally consume it in courses like dinner, not nibble randomly from a buffet as I had always done before. I read impatiently of mimes and games in antiquity. I really was only interested to the degree they established practices that survived to the Middle Ages.

The book seemed to render me more tolerable to my companion. When our meal was served he deigned to chat over entrees on plastic plates and a side of salad in miniature. I soon discovered he was researching the impact of printing on the cultural trends of the fifteenth and sixteenth centuries. Of course I was interested. As far as I knew, Madeleine was still alive when Gutenberg printed his Bible in 1455. Madeleine and Gutenberg were exact contemporaries. My seatmate informed me that by invitation German printers were operating a printing press at the Sorbonne in Paris by 1470. People of rank and taste considered printed books common and unrefined, despite the fact that the first books to be printed in France were selected by the rector and librarian of the university. However, with printing, books became more affordable to the emerging middle class, which caused concern among the elite of society.

Finally, I asked my companion, "Do you know what the first printed work written by a woman was?"

"No, I don't. What was it?"

"Oh, *I* don't know. I was just thinking *you* would."

"I suppose I should. I have no idea. But I do recall hearing about the life story of a woman from northern France that may well have been the first."

"Whereabouts in northern France?" Immediately I took the woman to be Madeleine.

"I don't remember. The reference was vague. An educated guess would suggest Christine de Pisan. She was no longer alive when printing arrived in France, but I believe her work was still quite popular. However, if I'm not mistaken, the book I heard about was written in prison."

"In prison! It can't be. Don't tell me she went to prison!" This was new information. My companion looked at me doubtfully. I realized he thought I was referring to Christine de Pisan and wondering why this was such a big deal for me. I tried to recover a disinterested conversational tone. "I was under the impression that she ended up in a convent."

"Well, that's a prison of sorts, I suppose."

"But the printed work. Could the woman who wrote it have come from Beauvais?"

"Possibly. I really don't know anything about it. The little I do know comes from a comment someone made after I gave a paper at a conference several years ago."

The attendant came by with coffee. This unknown work had to be Madeleine's story. I argued with myself, trying to reason with my intuition about it. Outwardly I wrestled with the tough shell of a cream-filled pastry that passed for dessert.

My companion was doing his own mulling. He swallowed the last of his pastry and put the whole question to rest. "At any rate, scholars of the era dismiss the work, since there are no extant copies and references to it are rare and elusive. I'm sure I couldn't find the reference either—even if I went looking for it. At this point, I could as easily be fabricating the whole thing, I remember so little."

Well, that confirms it. "I know what you mean."

His eyes demurred but he said nothing. I worked busily with my plastic fork. A few more polite exchanges and the attendant relieved us of our trays and, in effect, each other's company. I went back to Chambers. I learned that you could get away with a lot if you were a minstrel or jongleur—and have easy access to the great castles of Europe to boot. *This is auspicious. Not even in France yet and Madeleine's back. Well, not auspicious. Why would she be in prison?* The characteristic shaved face and close-cropped hair and coloured cape and flat shoes of a minstrel provided a popular disguise in the Middle Ages. *She must have seen her share of minstrels in her day, although by that time their numbers were falling. I doubt there was anything to be gained for minstrels in a war zone.* The performances of popular minstrels could be well rewarded. Many were as adept at siphoning off the riches of nobility as they were at singing their praises or mocking their powers in burlesque satire. Yet in the end, minstrels died "like dogs in a ditch, under the ban of the Church and with the prospect of eternal damnation before the soul." *Well, it was a living, whatever you may say about the dying. If minstrels came to Madeleine's hospice, she would surely have let them in. Maybe she shared a cell with some in prison. How did she ever end up in prison?*

I wasn't making a lot of progress with the book. I ended up watching an inane movie that would never have tempted me into the theatres. It's truly remarkable, the speed of travel we enjoy in the modern world. But it was turning out to be a long flight just the same. I tried to sleep amid the crowding images of Madeleine, anxiety about my destination, worry about finding the right trains to take me to Beauvais, and wondering if I had left home for good. *They will be having dinner now in Flatfield. No wonder I can't sleep. We'll be getting into Paris just about the time I normally go to bed. And then I begin my day negotiating an itinerary in a strange land. I never sleep at dinner time.* I tried to breathe deeply and rest. Why pretend to sleep?

What am I doing in this noplace, next to a stuffy sleeping academic? This is limbo. The old theologians saw it coming. Neither here nor there. What an absurd position, suspended midair. "You make the clouds your chariots and you ride on the wings of the wind." It's good enough for God. Well, I'm not God. I need the ground. And here I am thinking an airy reference to an obscure possibility is relevant. You're desperate, Janine. Admit it. This is a fool's errand. I finally got sleepy, but I could not sleep. I just began to feel more and more hopeless. *This isn't helping. You're running away from your life, Janine. You're in limbo at home so you decide to extend its influence. Great. Carry it with you into the air and bring it at last to an alien place across the ocean.* I was overtired, I know. The tension building up to my departure finally caught up to me flying 500 miles per hour over the Atlantic. Perhaps I slept, fitfully, for an hour or two. It didn't help to have someone beside me sleeping deeply enough to snore but inclined to groan or grunt every time I made a move. Finally the cabin lights came on urging us awake just when I may have drifted off. Breakfast. My companion ate in cold silence. I made no attempt at civility. I was feeling out of sorts myself and anxious to be free of him.

We landed. There was no gate available for our flight so an airport bus picked us up. My seatmate was one of the first on the bus and found a place at the front. I readily moved further back. We were a quiet, sleepy bunch riding over the tarmac to the terminal. At the terminal we all crowded through the door and headed off in the same direction. It seemed somebody knew where to go to claim our luggage and pass through customs.

Finally I was cleared and on the other side and on my own. Except that the whole world was there too. Never had I heard so many languages and seen such an assembly. People from every country on earth, I'm sure, bumping into me on all sides, jabbering away in languages I couldn't identify with all the urgency of the tower of Babel. I dragged my bags through two expansive terminals, following big signs pointing the way to the trains, the last one indicating a descent down what must be the longest escalator in the world. In the bowels of the terminal, I stepped onto a wide platform that funneled the teeming horde into the gaping mouths of waiting trains. I was swallowed up soon enough, but pretty sure I was on the right train. *Surely all trains go to Paris.* I found a handhold several seats from the door and stood crowded in with all humanity, lurching and staggering with the movement of the train, trying to remain within reach of my luggage. We came out into daylight but there was nothing to see from where I stood. Then down again into the echoing gullet. I closely followed our progress on the map overhead. Was it the first stop? I don't remember. But the train soon pulled into the Gare du Nord and disgorged half its hold, heaving me onto the platform where I stood for some time, trying to recover myself. *So far, so good. I still have my bags.*

I had urgent business to attend to. My stomach was empty. I stood in three separate lines to collect a croissant, an Orangina, and a ticket for Beauvais. Then I found a washroom and paid for the privilege of using it. *Imagine being too poor to pee!*

Every hour, a train leaves the Gare du Nord bound for Beauvais. When I got to the right platform, a train stood there wheezing and ready to go. I hurried past a line of people punching in at some sort of mechanism, boarded, and muddled myself and my bags onto seats facing a small table. A young woman holding no more than a purse and a bagged lunch occupied the forward-facing seat opposite. She smiled at me as I settled. As we lurched out of the station, she asked where I came from and we engaged in short-sentence conversation until the conductor arrived.

"Votre transports, s'il vous plaît." My companion handed him her ticket while I rifled through the "documents" section of my purse to find mine. I congratulated myself for having managed things so well and began to think my French was up to this adventure too. I handed him the ticket. There was a problem. The conductor gave me an incriminating look and said something about "valider" that made no sense to me at all. My young friend came to the rescue:

"Elle n'est pas d'ici."

I gratefully assented and told the conductor I had just arrived from Canada. He then took her ticket and pointed out the validation stamp. I realized what those lineups on the platform were all about. I had assumed they were commuters with a different kind of ticket. Turned out I had jumped the queue and boarded illegally. Fortunately, the conductor was inclined to forgive. He wrote some relevant information on my ticket, signed it, and handed it back to me with assurances that just this time it would be okay. I had been validated.

Somewhere around St. Denis, we came out into the light again. So far I had managed to escape seeing anything but the underbelly of Paris. That was okay with me. I didn't come to see Paris. And I was so sleepy. I would have been happy just to watch the world go by but my companion wanted to talk about Canada—such an exotic place. Finally, she wished me well, and got off at Bornel—Belle-Eglise. I was on my own again. I switched to her forward-facing seat and began to take it all in—the mackerel sky, dormant garden plots with small sheds girded by stone walls, algae-covered streams moving slowly but not frozen and, most remarkably, naked trees ornamented with lovely green globes hanging like Christmas balls. I could not see well enough from my window to tell what sort of leaf arranged itself so festively. We stopped at Meru—a pretty little town. Towns in France are nothing like towns on the prairie. Snug.

Our towns are not snug. We moved out of the station. Rolling hills. Trees everywhere. A few cows and fewer horses. Every now and again a lovely old church. And all the scene so close and compact. *Nothing like the endless open fields at home. But no snow. How dark the nights must be.* I was getting tired. It was, after all, close to three a.m. for me. I could hardly keep my eyes open. *What on earth am I doing here? It's all very charming, but so what? It's irrelevant to me. I have all I need at home.*

—*I should have brought Mom with me. It would have been so different. She would love this. We would be laughing now. Or dozing. Probably dozing. But we would take turns keeping alert so we don't end up in the wrong place.*

—*This is definitely the wrong place. If you can't be happy at home, how is that going to change among strangers? One friend. That's all I have here. And she's dead. Very dead. Five hundred years dead, even if she lived a long life.*

I took out the map Edwin sent and plotted my short trek from the station to rue de la Madeleine. *Across avenue de la République, down boulevard du Général de Gaulle. I can do this.* I dozed again. And struggled to stay awake again.

—*Where's the sun? It's nearly noon—high noon and the place is as dull as daybreak in December. This is daylight, nothing more. There's no radiance at all. And it's getting cloudy. That mackerel sky was a ruse to keep me from getting off the train and going home when I still had a chance.*

—*Damn him. This is Miles's fault. He should be the one to go. He just sticks around as if—as if he expects to stay. As if he loves me. As if he couldn't imagine it any other way. He can't. He has no idea. I'm in his box, that's all.*

I nodded off again and again, waking myself up with a start then drooping back to sleep. One more time, the train lurched me awake. I started, looked out the window to get my bearings, and saw the city. There before me a monolithic structure rose above the place like a fortress, a mighty citadel. *How ugly! A modest skyline and this thing planted in the middle like a big old cabbage in a bed of crocus.* It was the Cathédrale St. Pierre dwarfing all its neighbours. Gradually the scene shifted until the cathedral settled a little into its habitat and finally disappeared behind the graffiti-covered walls and buildings of commerce encroaching the rails.

I was in Beauvais. Unbelievable! I scrambled off the train. Passing down some stairs and through a tunnel under the rails, I encountered a somewhat confused and bedraggled man—he had either an open sore or a wound bleeding down the left side of his face—I'm not sure—I didn't want to stare and quickly got out of his way. I wrestled my baggage up the other side and emerged with two other disembarking passengers to be greeted by nine uniformed train personnel. My ticket was checked and I was allowed to go. There seemed to be something afoot as they conferred in an animated fashion—about what I couldn't tell. I wondered if the poor man I met in the tunnel had precipitated this show of strength. Nobody seemed to notice my own confusion. *Just as well.* I lumbered through the station like a pack animal and out into the city. *Here I am! Standing on French soil. Well, French concrete. This—is concrete. I am here. I have arrived.*

I headed immediately to the east side of boulevard du Général de Gaulle, past Hôtel le Chenal, stopped to check my map, and there it was, a narrow one-way street almost directly across from where I stood. Mid-day traffic raced in all directions—lots of little cars, very few sedans and no pick-up trucks. Any trucks or vans whizzing by were commercial vehicles. When traffic cleared a little I stepped into the street to cross. A nun, her little black veil flapping in a half-opened window, roared by. Well, everyone roared by.

I crossed over and read the small cast metal sign attached to the curved corner of a brick building—a dark old sign that I could only read by the shadows of the embossed letters. "RUE DE LA MADELEINE." I made my way, slowly taking in the numbers on either side—111 on my right, 82 on my left. Then I came to 101bis. *101TWICE. Must be a second entrance.* It wasn't such a big house that it should open onto another avenue. The gate was locked. I could not open it. I was too tired to drag my bags any further so I left them there and wandered down the street to find someone to help me. For all the busyness of the boulevard, there wasn't a soul in sight on foot. Another few steps and I came to 101. *You haven't a clue, Janine. They don't give you 101a, they give you 101 AGAIN. As if there weren't enough numbers to go around on this little street.* I went back to 101BIS to gather my luggage and carry it to my final destination.

An iron gate big enough to admit a tank barred entry into a paved courtyard. Next to it was a smaller, narrower gate and on the wall beside it a row of six buttons with a sign that read:

MAISON DIONCESAINE
SONNEZ ICI

And at the bottom:

OUVERTURE DE PORTILLON.

I read the labeled buttons and chose the third, "Accueil," took a deep breath and rang it.

"Bonjour?"

"Bonjour. Je cherche Soeur Lucille Claire."

"C'est moi," crackled through the intercom.

"Je suis Janine LaFoy du Canada."

"Ah, oui! Entrez! J'arrive tout de suite."

She buzzed me in. *So here I am, turning myself in. I will finally be institutionalized.* I opened the gate and stepped into the courtyard.

LEVITY

Modern investigators of miraculous history have solemnly admitted that a characteristic of the great saints is their power of "levitation." They might go further; a characteristic of the great saints is their power of levity. Angels can fly because they can take themselves lightly.

—G. K. Chesterton, *Orthodoxy*

A collection of buildings ranged around the courtyard. Before I had time to stare and wonder which way to turn, my eyes fell on an animated figure hurrying toward me. Soeur Lucille Claire was a striking woman—petite with a kind of purposeful energy about her. A billowing knitted silvery-blue cape floated over her simply tailored shirt dress. This somehow imposing presence was crowned with the most dazzling silver hair that, short-cropped though it was, swept gracefully into a kind of halo around her head.

"Entrez, entrez! Bienvenue! Vous parlez français?"

I nodded. "I am getting a lot of practice."

She continued in French. "Good. Not many people here speak English. Now, let me look at you." With this she took my shoulders in her hands and surveyed me. Her gaze slowly took the measure of my face. "Yes, I think we will like each other. This is good." Then she cocked her head to one side to take another angle. "I wonder though—" Her voice trailed away. Then she began again with more resolve. "I think you are not as *those—qui n'ont point d'espérance.* You know what I mean surely, when I say *those—who have no hope.*" I thought I did, at least in terms of understanding the language— thank goodness she repeated it. I nodded, not because I had any idea of what she was talking about, but because I thought she want- ed me to. Satisfied with her appraisal, she smiled. Apparently rent- ing a space in the diocesan house involved a good deal more than a room and a bed. Normally I would be put off by such seeming impertinence. But there was something in Soeur Lucille Claire's reckoning of me that felt rather like a blessing.

"As you know, I am Soeur Lucille Claire, but everyone calls me Soeur Luci. Now come along." She picked up my heaviest suitcase and walked briskly to a door across the courtyard. I scrambled to keep up with her. She set the suitcase on the rise in front of the door. "We will leave your baggage here while I show you the place you have come to." I set down my other suitcase and my carry-on and turned to follow her.

"First, here," motioning to her right, "is the entrance from rue Jeanne Hachette." She opened a great door and led me into a cob- bled passageway to another arched door. "You can escape, you see, if you must!" She opened the creaking door and we stepped onto the sidewalk of a narrow street. Shutting us out, she quickly showed me the secret to unlocking the door and we were back in the dark, musty tunnel. "Now, you will want to know where you can make your meals." We crossed kitty corner, through a service door and into a shabby little kitchen. "This is where our day staff and roomers eat." She showed me where the pots, pans, dishes, and flatware were kept. There was a small fridge, an old gas stove, and a large, stained enamel sink with an extended surface for draining dishes where a few mugs and plates and a badly twisted fork were set to dry. Above the sink a sign, S.V.P. Faites la vaisselle!

"This is not perhaps the most servicable kitchen, but I think you did not come to Beauvais to learn haute cuisine? You can manage, bien sûr?"

"Yes, thank you. This will do."

"But you won't cook here today. You have no food and you must be tired. After our tour we will have a little lunch. After that you will have a few hours to yourself; then you will come to us for dinner to have a good meal before you sleep. We can't have you remember Beauvais as the place you went to bed hungry! Usually we leave our guests to themselves. For you—an exception—since you have come so far. The sisters are anxious to meet you. Besides, it will be better for you to stay awake until night, even though it is a long day. You will adjust more quickly that way." Clearly everything was already arranged without consultation. I didn't mind. I was too tired to plan my next move. Just as well someone was doing it for me.

"Now then! On to the chapel!" Soeur Luci gave me a brief history en route. "This place was originally built as a Dominican house in 1234. Its first prior was Vincent de Beauvais."

"Vincent de Beauvais, the encyclopedist! Imagine that! To think I am walking in the very place where he compiled all the knowledge of the age!"

She laughed. "You know Vincent de Beauvais?"

"Not really. But I have read about him."

Soeur Luci nodded. "And so have I, of course, since I came here." She continued on. She told me the monastery thrived for over three hundred years. Then in 1472, Charles le Téméraire laid siege to Beauvais and the buildings suffered extensive damage. The monastery was rebuilt and survived another three hundred years until it fell into the hands of the French Republic and the last of the monks disappeared. When the heyday of the Republic passed, what remained of the monastery once again housed various programs of the church, although most of the existing structures were not rebuilt until the mid-nineteenth century. The place was first a seminary, then a convent. A community of sisters used it as a school for poor girls, and then as an orphanage when the town was devastated by cholera in 1852. But with the separation of church and state in 1905, the nuns who carried out these works of mercy were expelled. The complex was used as a hospital during World War II. Eventually, it all ended up back in the hands of the diocese. Now this place is used for catechesis and education and all sorts of diocesan functions. There is a library in the oldest surviving part of the building, where the only remnants of the fifteenth century can be seen.

"So much has happened here!"

"And so many more stories we don't remember!" Well! Soeur Luci was speaking my language.

"But isn't that's a tragedy," I said, "that they are lost and forgotten?"

"Ah. But you will find the stories regardless, if you pay attention."

"I hope so! That's why I'm here."

"You will not be disappointed, I think." By now we had crossed the length of the courtyard and approached another heavy arched door. Soeur Luci opened it. "Et bien! This is our chapel." We entered. The aging, grand exterior belied the austere lines of the space inside. Soeur Luci watched me closely. "You are surprised?"

"This could be any modern church in Alberta. It is no different."

"Yes, we French are learning to be simple."

"Too bad. I like the old buildings."

"And so do I. But it is good to have a place where memory is quiet too—as an aid to contemplation. Those stories will clamour. They inhabit the details and the nicks and bruises too. The past has something to say, but we live in the present. When I come to this space, there is very little to tangle my thoughts. They roll away and evaporate like drops of water on a hot griddle. And when my mind is clear, there's more room for my heart—and my spirit."

We stood silent a moment in the chapel before we turned back into the courtyard. I thought of the slick modern buildings and the wide empty spaces back home. "We don't have many old buildings in Alberta. You would have no problem clearing your mind there. In fact, I think you would practically float away."

She laughed. "Yes, Canada is a young country."

"*My* thoughts get plenty tangled even without old buildings. My mind is often crowded even though I have no memories to speak of—I don't think my heart has benefitted either."

"How dismal! No memories to speak of. You must be tired."

"Maybe so. But I often feel like that."

"What? That you have no memories?"

"Of my sons and my mother and my brother, yes. But few of my own."

"Perhaps you will find them here."

We headed back toward my luggage. We passed a little fenced garden on our right. I noticed some green mounds of winter-hardy herbs, but mostly the plot was full of stubble and dead leaves.

"As you see, we fence and lock our garden here inside our locked courtyard. Our flowers and vegetables are quite wild! It won't do to have them running all over the place. Sometimes I leave the gate unlocked just to tempt them, but the others call me to account when I do this. So I must remember the security of the plants depends on me and usually lock them up as I should." At this she smiled slyly, an irrepressible twinkle in her eyes.

Finally we stepped up to the entry of the residence. "We have a combination to unlock the door. See here." She pushed the buttons as she told me the numbers and pulled on the door knob. Nothing happened. She wiggled the knob and pulled again. "Ah, you naughty little *mioche*. Will you never learn to behave in company?"

"Pardon?" I was confused. She had been so friendly up to now.

"Oh! Not you." She laughed. "I am talking to this tricky little miss. She can be quite stubborn, especially when she's wet and cold. "There now. I'm sorry. Let me atone." She cupped her hands over the lock and turned to me again. "I should know by now. I was too impatient. I will show you again." Soeur Luci carefully told the numbers as she pushed the buttons, then opened the door. She smiled and nodded to me, picked up my suitcase, and led me into a dark hallway and up a creaky staircase.

Upstairs we peeked into the common area for the sisters' community of three. "You will have a small *repas* with me here. But first to your room." We proceeded down the hall. Soeur Luci pointed out the shared washroom as we passed then turned into a wide, long hallway with gabled windows on the right and doors all along the wall to the left. There were no furnishings, except halfway down a desk and two chairs. An old telephone sat in the corner of the desk. Soeur Luci stopped about five doors down. "This is your room, right next to mine." She unlocked the door, handed me the key, and we walked in.

My heart sank. I had expected it to be pretty basic, but thought it may be charming. It was basic, that was all. There was a cot, a folding easy chair, a sturdier desk chair for the built-in desk top under the gable. The window was too high to reveal anything but sky, the flooring patched together with grey indoor-outdoor carpet squares. A clumsy built-in closet and a washstand area off to the side completed the amenities. I tried to mask my disappointment but couldn't repress a sigh. A little smile twitched in the corners of Soeur Luci's mouth.

"Not quite like home, perhaps?" She set my suitcase down.

"Perhaps." I tried to think of something nice to say. "But I did not come so far to find a place just like home. I just didn't know what to expect. I have never travelled before."

"There are more elegant accommodations to be found in Beauvais."

"Yes, but this is good enough and I can afford it. And you live here. I think I will like staying here."

"Good! I will set out lunch. Come when you are ready." She left me there and shut the door behind her.

Well, here I am. I made it. I sat down on the bed. It was made up with a rough grey woollen blanket, the kind we called army blankets at home. Beauvais was occupied during World War II, the base of operations for the German defence at Dieppe, hardly 100 kilometres from Beauvais. *I wonder if Canadian soldiers ever slept here? Not likely. More likely German soldiers.* My eyelids drooped. The pillow looked soft and fresh and clean. *This place isn't so bad.* I fought the urge to put my head down. By then I had been mostly awake for twenty-four hours. But I was really hungry, too. In a supreme act of will I stood, hung my coat in the closet, took out my toiletries, freshened up, and went to lunch.

A delicious aroma met me at the corner even before I approached the open door. As I tried to decide whether to knock or just walk in, Soeur Luci saw me. "Ah! vous voilà! Come in! And please be seated." She motioned to a chair at the table. Then, opening an oven door she said. "Aren't you pretty now! Warm and brown, just as you should be."

This time I realized she wasn't talking to me. She took her pretty pie out of the oven and set it in the centre of the table. "Voilà! Flamique and a glass of cider. Now you know you are in Picardy!" It was a leek pie, a specialty of the region. I don't know if it was because I was so tired and hungry, or because of a happy combination of ingredients, or because Soeur Luci is an exceptional cook, or all of the above, but it was certainly the best meal I had ever eaten.

"Mmm. This is excellent. I don't think I have ever tasted anything so good. This pie is traditional in Picardy?"

"Well, not exactly so. You have to make a recipe your own. But the fundamentals, they are traditional." Then she laughed. "When the writer Alphonse Karr was served flamique, he said it would have been awful if one had only been able to eat it!" I soon learned to credit Soeur Luci's infallible instinct for flavour and texture and balance. I'm sure she could make a peanut-butter sandwich taste like canapés nougat.

We set ourselves to the tasks at hand, eating and sampling our personal biographies. Soeur Luci once aspired to a career in music as cellist and teacher, but the life was not to her liking—too much travel and bad cooking she said. I suspected there was more to it than that. She asked about my life in Alberta. Thinking to find some common ground, I told her a bit about my job at the parish and my interest in history. She continued:

"You are married."

"Yes."

"And you have children?"

"Yes. Two sons." Just thinking about them, my heart skipped. To my surprise, I already missed them. I smiled. "They are almost grown up and such wonderful people."

"What a grace for you. There is no greater honour than to give life and nurture it."

"Yes, I do love my boys—but any imbecile can be a mother." Soeur Luci looked appalled. "I mean," I continued, "girls get pregnant all the time. And some don't think twice about whether they drink or smoke or eat poorly while they're pregnant. Then, when the child is in the world, they neglect it, or worse, abuse it. It's no great achievement to be a mother."

Soeur Luci looked closely at me, as if to discover the reason for my jaded assessment. "Our inability to honour it doesn't make the gift any less precious."

"Oh, not at all. You are right, of course. And I am deeply grateful for my children. But there are mothers everywhere, and many are good and some are less so. We have an abundance of mothers, that's all."

"We also have an abundance of sunshine but we would not live long without it." She put her fork down and sat back in her chair, folding one arm to support the other that served as a prop for her chin. Once more she looked me over, then said quietly, "I think you are probably a very good mother."

I can hardly describe the effect her words had on me. It seemed so silly to take them so much to heart. *Of course I'm a good mother. I know that. Not perfect, of course. But I do my best and my children are thriving. You can't ask for more than that.* But I wanted to cry. *You're tired and overstimulated, Janine. Get a grip.*

"I hope so," I faltered.

"I'm sure of it!" She smiled, covered my hand with hers, and stood. "We will have an early dinner. If you can keep yourself awake a few more hours, you will adjust more quickly. But do what you will, sleep if you must."

I was dismissed. I thanked her for the wonderful meal and went back to my room. I sat on the bed. *This is too much for one day. I can't bear it. I will sleep.* I stood up. *—No, I will go out and walk in the streets of Beauvais. I will walk where Madeleine walked.* I sat down again. *—Tomorrow, not now.* I went over to the built-in desk

top, climbed up on it, and stood looking out the window into the
courtyard. It was empty and cold. Not a soul in sight. I remembered
to call home, which I did from the telephone in the hallway. No one
was there but my mother, as I expected. I told her I had arrived safely. That was all she needed to know. I promised to call again when
the boys would be home on the weekend and hung up.

In the end, I did go—out through the door on rue Jeanne
Hachette. I turned right and walked up to rue des Jacobins, then
turned left. These are ancient avenues. Some of the houses lining
the street date from the fifteenth century. The cobbled sidewalk,
flush with the buildings, is no wider than a wheelbarrow. Meeting
a man coming toward me, I stepped into the street to let him pass
on my left. He stepped into the street as well, and motioned for
me to take the sidewalk. We both smiled at the awkwardness. I do
believe the faux pas was mine. He was gallant and I, a lady. Conventional traffic courtesy—keep to the right—which I had meant to
observe—did not apply in this case. His simple gesture put me into
a different world.

I soon discovered that this gallantry is no more the general practice in Beauvais than in Alberta. Other pedestrians, other men, held
to the right of way without any deference to me. But that gentleman
accompanied me in my thoughts all the way down the avenue. I
rather hoped I would meet him again some day. I walked on. The
street widened as if to prepare for the importance of what lay ahead.
I had my head down, minding the bumpy cobblestones, yielding to
oncoming pedestrians, avoiding the more and more frequent evidence of uncurbed dogs.

It rose out of nowhere. One minute I was following a vague
direction toward the city centre, the next I was looking up at the
most exquisite, formidable edifice I had ever seen, the Cathédrale
St. Pierre. It was every bit as imposing as it had been from the
train—but breathtaking and beautiful—impossibly grand. I stood
in a trance, watching the shadows play in panels of glass and tracery
that drew my eyes up from the great arched portal to a magnificent
rose window above it all. *Who could have imagined this?* My heart

followed my eyes up to the pinnacle. All the ambiguity about my adventure dissipated. *Here I am, standing on a street in Beauvais, looking at this otherworldly creation. There is no place on earth I would rather be.* I don't remember ever feeling such exhilaration. For the first time in my life, I was completely on my own, and everything so new and everything so old.

I crossed the street and went inside. I have no idea how to talk about these things. I know a few architectural terms—I could say something about ribs and pillars and vaults, I suppose, but the enormity of the impression is beyond my ability to relate. I felt small, small like a grain of sand. That was fine with me. All matter is made up of small things, and these small things come together to make bigger things, I know. But this! This place had substance. So much matter! At that moment, my smallness made me feel light. Being so small, the weight that had somehow attached itself to me could not be of much importance after all. I don't know how long I wandered in the stone sanctuary. I have never fallen asleep standing up, but I believe I did then. I was so overwhelmed and so exhausted. I walked in a dream taking everything in, remembering nothing.

I finally stepped outside where cars compete for parking, shops advertise their goods, people come and go, wrapping their coats snugly against the winter. No one stopped to cast even a quick glance at the treasure in their midst. Life scurries on. I turned back toward rue des Jacobins, dropping in at the tourist office en route to pick up a few brochures, and made my way to Maison Diocésaine. The air was cold on the way back, even without ice or snow. It was a wet cold, I suppose, although I hadn't seen a drop of rain—only a few small unfrozen puddles in low-lying areas. Nothing more. But I was shivering by the time I got back.

I made my way through the outer passage and across the courtyard. The lock to the residence opened with my first try. This small success made me feel giddy. *I can manage this. It's going to be okay.* It was warm inside, and fragrant with Soeur Luci's dinner, and resonant with music. I walked up the stairs and past the sisters' door which, standing open, released all these good things. Soeur Luci called out a welcome to me over the music. I went to my room, put away my coat and my bag and returned.

"Just have a seat," she shouted over a very busy bunch of violins. "Do you mind the music? —Corelli. —Joyful, don't you think?"

"Yes!" I shouted back. "It's fine!" Soeur Luci smiled her approval and continued working her wonders at the stove. There was no competing with the music, nor did Soeur Luci expect it. I settled back and let it all wash over me, this extraordinary world of the senses—of sound and smell and taste. And sight, of course, at the cathedral. I quivered like a seedling in spring. I could hardly contain my anticipation.

Soon a second sister came in. "Ah! La Perle!" Soeur Luci shouted out. "This is Madame Janine LaFoy. Please introduce yourself." The sister headed my direction, stopping on the way to turn down the stereo, saying "I can't listen to two things at once." I stood as she approached to shake my hand. "No, no. Please, be seated. —Bienvenue!" She held out a smooth, plump hand to me. "I am Soeur Béatrice, but since there are two of us, Soeur Luci calls me 'La Perle.' I answer to everything, in any case." She was aptly named, her round face lit like the moon by her soft, luminous skin. She was probably much older than she looked. Good skin ages slowly. She took a seat close by me, picked up some knitting from a basket on the floor and her needles were soon clicking along. She did all this without missing a beat in conversation, asking about my trip, about my family, about the weather in Alberta.

"I think you brought your dry weather. We've had nothing but rain these past eight days. And now, see? Not one drop today," her needles tick-ticking all the while. She may not have been able to listen to more than one thing at a time, but she certainly could talk and knit simultaneously—and ceaselessly.

"Was it you who knit Soeur Luci's beautiful blue cape?"

"Oh, yes. It suits her, doesn't it?"

"Perfectly. It must have taken a lot of time."

"Pas du tout! Hardly more than a month's work. I am quick, you see."

"No doubt! I've never seen anyone knit as fast as you do."

"Well, you see, at home from a very young age, we children had to knit our own stockings—even my brothers. Everyday after school we knit a half thumb's length before we could go out to play. And stockings are made on small needles, you know. It was a lot to do even when our thumbs were small. Of course we learned to knit fast. My oldest brother was the fastest, because he had the most experience, but I knit faster than him now."

In the course of our conversation, she finished off a sleeve. Soeur Luci, who had been having conversations of her own with dinner, turned to us to say, "Now where is La Belle?" just as a tall, elegant woman of perhaps seventy years walked in the door. Her face could have been sculpted marble, the bones were so beautifully articulated. This classic head was displayed on a long, smooth neck that disappeared into the flourish of a loosely knotted scarf.

"Here I am. I hope I have not kept you waiting."

"You are just in time. Soeur Béatrice, this is Madame Janine La-Foy." For my benefit, Soeur Luci added, "Since we have two Soeurs Béatrice, I call her La Belle."

"Enchantée, Madame." With a smile and a slight bow, La Belle offered her hand.

"Enchantée, Soeur Béatrice, but please call me Janine."

"So very glad to meet you, Janine." She did not ask me to call her 'La Belle.' I guess I would have trouble with that, too. *My name is Janine, but please call me 'The Beautiful.'*

We sat down to dinner. There was an easy animation in their exchanges. They all seemed pleased to have me there. La Belle had spent time in a sister house in Quebec. "I love to listen to you speak. I love Canadian French. It is so charming." Or quaint, perhaps. Somewhere I heard that, as a rule, the French find Canadian French "provincial," but apparently not every French soul shares the view of The Academy. For her part, La Belle was effusive about many things, as if her warmth of approbation must compensate for what could otherwise seem a cold beauty. When La Belle liked something, it was beyond critical review. She complimented the chef, the wine was excellent, the weather lovely—just as January should be.

At first the conversation revolved around me and Canada, but my ability to engage it was fading fast. Gradually the sisters took up their own stories of the day. The meal, every bit as good as Soeur Luci's first offering, was pretty much wasted on me. I dined in a daze. In the end, it was all I could do to move fork to mouth, chew, and swallow. And I was up to my ears in French. I had hardly missed a beat since I arrived, but eventually, whether from inattention or my lack of comprehension, the three of them could have as easily been speaking Medieval Latin.

Soeur Luci saw my predicament and took charge. "You, my dear, must find your bed. We will not keep you longer."

"Thank you. Forgive me. I am so glad to have met you all." I stood to go.

"Now come along." Soeur Luci took my arm shepherding me away and down the hall. "Sleep as long as you like. I will be here to make coffee when you wake up. After that you will be on your own." She took me to my door—just to be sure I didn't fall over on the way, I suppose. Then she was gone. I don't know how I got ready for bed. The next thing I knew, the sun was high and shining into my eyes through the unwashed window. I had slept through the night and well into the morning.

I would happily have rested there in the sunshine, reviewing my first day in Beauvais, but I urgently needed to make the trek down the hall and around the corner to the washroom. I hurried into my housecoat and set out. Again there was music. Not so loud as the day before, but enough to assure me that Soeur Luci must be somewhere close at hand. Back in my room I set up my toiletries, unpacked a few clothes, and got ready for the day. After that, I happily went to claim the cup of coffee Soeur Luci had promised. I could already smell it as I approached the common room.

"And here you are! I heard you stirring, so I made the coffee. It is just ready now—perfectly fresh. Please, come to the table." She motioned me to my place. "How do you like your coffee? With cream and sugar?"

"Just cream please."

She put a little cream in two cups, poured the coffee and set a cup before me. "Servez-vous." She offered a basketful of large buttery croissants.

"Did you make these?" At this point I believed Soeur Luci capable of any culinary feat.

"Oh no. I bought them fresh this morning. It takes a lot of time to make them. I have other work to do, you know!"

"Of course. But you have such mastery in the kitchen. I think you could do anything if you had the time for it."

"As you say." She nodded. "I do sometimes make croissants when I have a holiday. But these are very good, I think."

"They are delicious. Where do you get them? I will need to go shopping today."

Soeur Luci gave me advice about the best places to shop, about market days in Place des Halles a few blocks away. She held me captive with lively and detailed accounts of the most practical things. The best soap can be got in only one place—this soap, he loves the skin and she knows it—and fresh market eggs, they are good friends to every cook—and you will want French sea salt—he is so rich with minerals, the mouth sparkles. The list went on. I took notes.

After this extended initiation, Soeur Luci drained the last of her coffee. I jumped up to get the coffee pot and replenish her cup. She covered her cup with her hand. "Non, merci!—You have to do it right!" She inhaled dramatically for effect then continued. "First—put in the cream —which is the sweet taste of candour and innocence. Only *after* that pour the coffee, the acerbic portion of experience and wit. There you have the taste of a good life." She nodded emphatically. Then raising her hands in a profound shrug she continued, "If you do it in the reverse order all the moderation floats on top!" Then she bent her head conspiratorially and added, whispering, "And bitterness lurks forever beneath the surface."

Knowing now the metaphysical importance of the act, I carefully poured some cream into her cup. I glanced at her to be sure of the amount. She nodded. I served myself as well before adding experience and wit to our cups.

"What about café au lait?" I asked. Soeur Luci was clearly pleased to continue this avenue of inquiry.

"Ah, that is a little different! Heating the milk sharpens the appetite for experience. When the youthful heat of passion warms it, the milk of innocence says to experience 'I am ready' and the milk and the coffee are poured together." She smiled indulgently. "And it is often a happy union. But there is great danger in this because you may burn the milk which leaves a bad taste in the drink. And then you don't just have bitterness, you have bile!"

I laughed. "Well then, I can't imagine what you will say about lattés."

"Par grâce! Don't even mention the Italians! What they do to their milk! I am a nun. There are limits to what I can comprehend!" With this a silvery glissando of laughter poured out of her like so many bells. I have never met anyone with so much liveliness. Everything that enters her sphere of influence overflows with life, everything around her glows with personality, every gesture is symbolic. And she anthropomorphizes it all. Of course, speaking an unneutered language helps.

She asked what brought me to Beauvais. I had my answer all prepared. "I am writing a novel about a woman who lived in Beauvais at the end of the Hundred Years War. I came here to learn about this place and get a feel for it. And I think it will be easier to write and easier to put the parts I've already written together when I am away from home." It sounded like a reasonable explanation to me, if a little rehearsed. And it was mostly true—only with a shift in emphasis and some missing information.

Soeur Luci sat back in her chair, chin in hand as she had done when I made my "abundance of mothers" comment the day before. I felt as though she already knew why I had come, which is more than I could say for certain myself. I braved her scrutinizing eyes. I wasn't ready to express all the ambiguity I felt about Madeleine. Or anything else for that matter. I hoped she didn't think I was just running away from home, that's all. Finally she spoke.

"So! You are a novelist!"

Amazing! The only thing I said that isn't at all true and she finds it. "I don't know yet. That's partly what I came to find out." *Now, that's true.*

"Well, the important thing is that you have a story to tell. And this is a very good place to find it. Your time here will be productive, I think. You only want a little courage—and faith, Madame LaFoy!"

SAINTS AND MINISTERING SPIRITS

O Raphael, lead us toward those we are waiting for, those who are waiting for us. Raphael, Angel of Happy Meetings, lead us by the hand toward those we are looking for!

. . . .

Remember the weak, you who are strong, you whose home lies beyond the region of thunder, in a land that is always peaceful, always serene and bright with the resplendent glory of God.

—Ernest Hello

Setting out from my audience with Soeur Luci that afternoon, I could hardly believe my good fortune. Apart from a comfortable bed, what more could I want? The Soeurs Béatrice were lovely, self-assured women—good company, should the occasion present itself—and Soeur Luci, a law unto herself. And I was living in the heart of history—plaques on buildings and an odd mix of old names and newer structures. I felt a growing confidence that I would be able to find what I came for, whatever it may be. Soeur Luci had pretty much convinced me of that. *I will find Madeleine. I will put the pieces together. I will get this story written. I will finally figure out what to do about Miles.*

I had much to do the next few hours. I had to buy groceries, of course. But first, more urgent business. It was January 14, the day of the Feast of the Asses. "Why the rush?" Miles had asked. This was why. To be in Beauvais on the actual day of the celebration, to see the traces, if I could find any. I set out down rue des Jacobins, keeping a lookout for my gentleman friend who never appeared. I got to the cathedral, entered, and stood awhile taking in the vast magnificence. I surveyed the furnishings in the chapel by the south entrance that housed the baptismal font—nothing of immediate interest there—then moved on to the first chapel at the base of the choir. This chapel, once the province of Saint Nicolas, was dedicated to a Sainte Angadrême dressed "in the habit of an abbess." *Never heard of her.* The next chapel was dedicated to Saint Léonard *or* Saint Vincent de Paul, take your pick. In this chapel stood an intricately sculpted reredos that once backed the altar of the church at Marissel near Beauvais. Talk about stories inhabiting details. Eleven panels of painted figures and gilded ornament relate an account of the Last Supper and the Passion of Christ. *Over five hundred years old—but not as old as Madeleine. She would never have seen this thing. She would have been cold in her grave and this carving still a tree.*

I met a surfeit of personalities—carved in the wood of altars, choir stalls, and other furnishings, painted in tableaux and medallions, woven into tapestries, pieced into full programs of shimmering glass, chipped out of limestone and sculpted in marble. Early on I encountered one of the big guns: Saint Denis, first bishop of Paris and patron saint of France, whose inspired preaching in the third century led to his arrest by local magistrates. He was beheaded at Montmartre—the 'Mountain of the Martyr.' According to legend, he picked up his head and, preaching all the way, carried it two miles to his final resting place where the St. Denis Basilica now stands, about two miles north of the Montmartre district in Paris. Sacred art usually depicts Saint Denis holding his head in his hands.

I moved on, slowly walking around the choir, stopping at each of the chapels to meet other influencing saints and ministering spirits of the region. There were many more than the number of chapels would predict. In most cases the original occupants make room over time for other inhabitants, the axial chapel of Notre Dame excepted, which was and is primarily devoted to the Virgin and her Son.

In the chapel of Saint Lucien hangs a painting of la Madeleine turning away from a mirror, divesting herself of worldly ornaments. Not my Madeleine of course, but Mary Magdalene. Saint Lucien is the chief dedicatee of the chapel. A reputed companion of Saint Denis, he probably lived in the third century, but at some point his dates were moved backward in time to send the region's roots deeper into antiquity and give him apostolic status. Saint Lucien is deemed the patron and first bishop of Beauvais. He is also said to have lost his head, but his story is sketchy. Regardless, images of Saint Lucien are easily confused with those of Saint Denis, since they both wear their heads in their hands. They belong to the company of cephalophores. The headless horseman of Sleepy Hollow, the West's most famous representative, is the only other cephalophore I know.

Next to Saint Lucien's is the chapel of Jeanne d'Arc, originally endowed as a chapel of la Madeleine in 1256. A large marble statue flanked by bas reliefs dominates this chapel now. Commissioned in 1930 by Monseigneur Senne, bishop of Beauvais, the statue represents Monseigneur Senne himself kneeling at the feet of Jeanne d'Arc to make amends for the unjust and cruel treatment she received at the hand of his distant predecessor, Bishop Pierre Cauchon. The bas relief on the left depicts the condemnation of Sainte Jeanne, the one on the right, her rehabilitation.

I had made a full turn around the choir. I could not have imagined such a collection of artifacts. Some were exquisite, some historically remarkable, some seemed tawdry to me. But I must admit I was disappointed—overwhelmed, too, by the endless list of dramatis personae. I don't know what I thought I would find. Something about the Flight into Egypt perhaps or the celebrated ass. Or some other obscure link to Madeleine. There were lots of women, Veronica, Catherine, Barbara, and Agnes, to name a few I'd heard of before. Anything else I could have hoped for escaped me.

Finally I came to two large clocks at the bottom of the choir on the north side. The older one was commissioned by Canon Etienne "Musique," in 1302 and built into the wall of the cathedral. It stands perhaps fifteen feet tall. This clock not only marks the passing minutes and hours of the day, but tracks the phases of the moon as well. Remarkable. And close to 700 years old. I had no idea there were clocks so long ago. This clock chimed in Madeleine's day, and still does today. Now that was something. The chimes were originally set to signal the offices of the Liturgy of the Hours. Madeleine's son, Jean Etienne would have kept these hours when serving penance under the watch of Canon Guy. I was gratified to make even this meaningless connection. Next to this marvel stands a much larger nineteenth-century anatomical clock with 90,000 working parts— the pride of the place for some, but of little interest to me. I wandered back into the transept and out the door.

I tried to figure out from my map what would logically have been the route of the procession. I have lately seen a map of sixteenth-century Beauvais and am pretty sure I got it wrong. Nevertheless, I made my way south down rue Jean Vast to rue Molière then left on rue Louis Graves, across rue Desgroux, under a building set on pillars, across rue de l'Etamine and up to the porch of l'église St. Etienne. Nothing on the way suggested the route for a festival.

A well-weathered bas relief in stone arches over a pair of tall doors at the entrance to the church. I opened the door on the right and walked in. A rich baritone voice singing in grand style echoed through an empty nave. I looked for the source. It was a recording—an aria from an opera by Handel, I later found out. It seemed incongruous to me, standing in a Norman nave constructed in the twelfth and thirteenth centuries listening to something so foreign to the space. Not all the French are purists, it seems.

I walked up the right side of the nave, glancing around to see if anything may be relevant to the day or to Madeleine's story. Nothing much presented itself—halfway down the nave, another statue of this Sainte Angadrême—but nothing of interest. They were silent, the voices I was listening for, maybe because of the beautiful presumptive music filling the space. I looked idly at the stained glass windows sparkling like jewels in the afternoon sun. I crossed the nave, walked slowly down the other side, sat in a chair on the aisle—there are no pews except for the choir stalls—and looked around. It was all so remarkable, but nothing moved me. I wasn't even a good tourist. I didn't bother to learn more about the church or anything in it. There would be time enough for that. I was thinking something should happen—a connection or an event or a memory. Something I could pack up in my store of experience and carry off as proof that this was all worthwhile. I set out with high expectations. I sought the obvious course for their fulfilment and found nothing. Not Augustine's idea of nothing, of course, except perhaps absence. I was not facing evil, thank goodness. I was looking for something and it was hard to find. That was all. And I had thought I may find it on the Feast of the Flight into Egypt.

I spoke to the receptionist in a little kiosk by the door, who had sat invisible all the while. I commented on the music. She was playing it because she likes it. She enthusiastically showed me the CD booklet, pointing out her favourites. Well, opera highlights in high fidelity and digitally remastered are more exalted than a tinny radio playing the top 40. I could give her that. I took a brochure about the church, thanked her, and went outside. I stepped under the Wheel of Fortune to scan the brochure. It's a wonder—intersecting Norman and Gothic architecture, a modern French woman, and eighteenth-century opera filling the space thanks to twentieth-century technology. I took a quick look at the Wheel of Fortune and headed off to find groceries.

I'm sure I would have been a disappointment to Soeur Luci. I found a large épicerie just off rue de la Madeleine and bought everything I needed there—something easy to make for supper—eggs, cheese, and a baguette for breakfast, and coffee, of course. That was all I could manage in one trip. The store was closing as I paid for my groceries. As I stepped out the door, I heard a loud crashing noise. I nearly jumped out of my skin and dropped my purchase. Then another loud clattering. People continued about their business as if nothing had happened. I looked at the store fronts along the avenue. One shop owner was dragging a billboard off the street into the shop, another dismantling a display. A third was reaching up to unfasten a large metal grate, which jangled down to the concrete sidewalk. Another grate clamoured from across the parking lot, and another. That was the calamity—the banging, clanking, crashing of metal grates. Beauvais was closing shop. I collected my bundles and continued on. People scurried everywhere, many, like me, parading our daily bread, with baguettes carried like muskets over the shoulder, or poking out from under a clutching elbow, or strapped to bicycle carriers. I was just one in the crowd hurrying home to get dinner.

I was quite hungry. I did not bother to go upstairs, but went straight to the little kitchen, cooked up a fry of sausage, onions, and potato, and ate it with a side of tomato. It was a decent meal thanks to the quality of the sausage. And quick, which was the point. I washed up my dishes, put my perishables in the fridge, and carried the bulk of my groceries up to my room. It was an awkward kitchen, and an awkward arrangement to be sure, but nothing I couldn't weather for a season. I spent the evening in my room unpacking the rest of my things, finding space for my off-site larder, and setting up my work—my papers, notes, books and brochures. Then I ate a little bread and cheese, took a shower, and went to bed early.

That was my first full day in Beauvais. No fanfare, no grand revelations. But no family or friends, either. This pleased me. I can't remember any time in my life when I have lived so free of obligation. No one at home had any idea what I was doing that very minute. And nobody expected anything from me at that moment either.

I slept nearly twelve hours. I woke up quite rested but sluggish, and I had a throbbing caffeine headache. It took forever to take care of the morning's ablution. Finally I was dressed and ready to go make a cup of coffee. The hall was silent except for the boards creaking as I passed. The door to the sisters' common room was closed and quiet. I went down the squeaking staircase, out across the courtyard and into the kitchen. Two young women on their coffee break sat chatting at the table. They looked mildly surprised to see me standing in the doorway. I introduced myself. They offered me a cup of coffee and I joined them. Their coffee was not anywhere near Soeur Luci's standard. I resolved to get there early enough to make my own from then on. The women were welcoming and interested, but I was glad when their break was over and I could get on with breakfast.

Soon I learned to dovetail my schedule to those of the other people around me. Since I could hear the rooming students pass by my door between seven and eight, I did not start too early, which was fine with me. Nine-thirty appeared to be the staff's coffee break. So I settled on 8:15 as a good time for breakfast. But it was nearly eleven when this first breakfast and dishes and all were done. I went back to my room, picked up the brochure from Eglise St. Etienne, a notebook and pen, and headed back to the church.

This time, I resolved to pay attention, but not to look for anything. I resolved to take things as they came. I entered the church. The place was quiet except for my own echoing presence. I sat down and began to write. *I have just recently arrived in Beauvais, a small city in northern France. I am sitting in Eglise St. Etienne*—I looked up at the crucifix on the wall beside me.

How strange. I checked the brochure. *Well, how about that?* It was Wilgeforte. *I didn't expect to find her here. It seems pretty serendipitous. Traditionally, misunderstood and unappreciated wives invoke her, offering bushels of oats in exchange for deliverance from their husbands.* She had never struck me as the kind of saint that would show up in Northern France. *Wilgeforte. She has other names. "Maid Uncumber" in England, I know. Her cult flourished in the fifteenth century—Madeleine's century. It was suppressed in 1969 and her feast day removed from the calendar. But here she hangs, large as life.* I thought about Miles. *Whatever possessed me to marry him? That summer was so dry. We are just not at all suited to each other. At best, he is a scientist. I like the humanities and art. And he's so uptight. And surly.* "Note the semblance of a beard," said the caption in the brochure. I looked again at the bearded face of Wilgeforte. It borders on the grotesque. I tried to imagine her beautiful feminine aspect. It was hard to do. Still, it was a happy accident, finding her here. *Where will I find a bushel of oats?* I thought about the market. *Surely if you can get them in bulk anywhere, you can buy oats there.* Wilgeforte's blue overskirt drapes around a red slip or something. It is too short to be a dress. Would a self-respecting woman in that era show so much calf and ankle? I guess if you're being crucified, you're not worrying about that sort of self-respect. Polychrome is the word they use to describe her. They mean painted. Painted and faded and uneven. Yet the red marks of blood from the nails in her feet are still a deep red. The gold trim on her bodice and skirt are fairly bright.

"Pardon, Madame." I jumped. The receptionist had whispered up on soft soles. "C'est midi. The church will close now."

"Oh! Pourquoi?"

"C'est l'heure du déjeuner."

The church closes from noon to two every day. I was welcome to return when it reopened. I excused myself, closed my notebook, pocketed my pen and went away.

Noon hour is busy on Beauvais sidewalks. I had to pay close attention. I decided to keep in the wake of a business man walking purposefully in front of me. "Bon appetit!" he said to a man approaching. "Bon appetit!" the man nodded back. Then a pair of gentlemen approached and murmured "Bon appetit!" and he answered in kind. This congenial pattern continually repeated between people known to each other. All along the way, from every direction "bon appetit" floated like a benevolent cloud above the citizens of Beauvais. *How civilized.*

I ended up in a short-order restaurant on rue St. Pierre. The place was busy, but not crowded. I believe many of the people I passed in the street went home for dinner since service venues and many commercial venues close their doors for these two hours. As for me, I had the equivalent of a submarine sandwich. The bread was better than that, the chicken fine, but there was enough of the greasy spoon quality about the food to make me wonder if lunch would make me sick. Probably not. The proprietors do a brisk business. I thought I may soon have to surrender my seat, but I took out my notebook anyway. Happily, two tables nearby opened up and I kept my spot for another hour. I bought a coffee—could have had two for the price in Alberta. It was worth it though, even if it inspired a budget plan in the margins of my notebook.

There was no washroom in the restaurant, so off I went to find one. I was directed to a free-standing unit a block away. Two francs. I had only one franc. The rest of my change I left as a pourboire for the server at the restaurant. I asked a lady passing by if she could change a twenty-franc note. She dug into her little change purse and pulled out two francs. I offered her the note. "De rien," she said.

"But I only need one more franc," I said, trying to hand back the extra franc. She folded my hand over the change, "Servez-vous!" and walked away.

It was nearly two o'clock. I returned to Eglise St. Etienne, humming to myself all the way. *I love you a bushel and a peck, You bet your pretty neck, I do, Doodle, oodle, oodle...A bushel and a peck—Nobody uses bushels anymore—a bushel of oats—hmm. A barrel and a heap and I'm talking in my sleep about you... One of Miles's lame attempts to be charming when we were newlyweds—singing that silly song—How romantic. Well, we did laugh together at the time.* The air was cool, but hardly a hint of winter, like April in Alberta except cloudy and damp.

Inside St. Etienne's I nodded hello to the receptionist, gave a slight bow as I walked past Wilgeforte—*Don't worry. I'll be back. I'll think of something*—and up to a sixteenth-century carving imbedded in a stone column halfway down the nave, a Pieta flanked by Saint John and Saint Etienne. A miniature image of a donor to the church kneels at the feet of the Pieta. Much of the art, windows and statuary in St. Etienne's are from the sixteenth century. It seems few artists were at work in the fifteenth century during the Hundred Years War. Go figure.

Next was the large wooden statue of the ubiquitous Angadrême.

I realized I wasn't going to be able to ignore her. She lived in the seventh century at the court of Clothaire II. When she forsook the world to become a nun, her father built a convent for her, and she became abbess. Imagine that! Her own convent. Hard to think she wasn't a bit spoiled, religious aspirations notwithstanding.

I was generally more observant this time. I walked slowly around the twelfth- and thirteenth-century Norman nave and transept. Madeleine would have known these old stones. I tried to observe the differences between them and the sixteenth-century gothic choir. I imagined how this church would look without the choir, what sort of wall may have stood there at the top of the transept. And through what door Blessed Jean de Beaumanoir may have taken the dismayed Jacques Mouton to serve him a bit of bread and cider.

I spent a long time looking up at the breathtaking "Tree of Jesse" window in the choir. Deep Chagall blues form a background to the rich colours of the house and lineage of Jesse, linking Jesus to the royal line of King David. Being descended from royalty was a big deal. The window was installed in 1522. The glass work by Engrand LePrince is considered some of the finest of the Renaissance era.

To the right of this window, by the chapel Our Lady of Joy, is a stone statue carved at the end of the *fifteenth* century. *Our era. Good.* Mary, holding the Christ Child, lifts her elegantly draped overskirt as if to step down from the pedestal where she stands. Her skirt is a gold-painted brocade. Skin tones are warm and subtle. Jesus wears a full chemise painted blue with gold trim at the hem. He holds the wing of a dove in flight in his right hand. It's a family portrait— mother, child, and progenitor. I like this statue. I like its grace and movement. I study the square neckline, the tucked, fitted bodice, the intricate painted patterns on the heavy fabric—the fashion for women of means in Madeleine's lifetime.

I was diligent, noting everything. I discovered that the bell tower was added in the late sixteenth century. Something else must have stood in its place before because there has to have been some sort of niche where Madeleine and Guy resorted that fateful day. One

thing I realized. I had wondered at any protracted encounter such
as theirs taking place in the middle of January. But no risk of frost-
bite here. I began to doubt they even know what snow looks like in
Beauvais.

It was getting late. I needed to buy the day's groceries. I left St.
Etienne's and went about my business. As I entered the courtyard
of the Maison Diocèsaine, I stopped to read a yellowed notice taped
from the inside to a window just beyond the entrance.

...One cold winter day the Abbess Angadrême went to the
farrier in search of coals to heat the abbey. As she approached
she met with a blazing spray of embers but was not burned.
From that time she has been venerated as a protectrice
against fire.

In 1472, during the assault of Charles le Téméraire, the
relics of Angadrême, patroness of Beauvais *(aha!)*, were displayed on the ramparts of Beauvais as a sign of resistance
and, according to legend, the saint came to the aid of the city
in securing the victory.

The king, Louis XI, willed that every year a solemn procession recall the memory of that protection through which
good fortune covered the city. In our time, this ceremony
takes place on the Sunday closest to 27 June.

I made dinner, washed the dishes, crossed the courtyard and
went upstairs. I could hear the sisters as I passed the door to their
common room. It was as good a time as any to bring my hostess
gifts to them, since I had not unpacked them on my first evening
there. I went to my room, dropped off my things, picked up the
gifts, and made my way down the hallway only to meet all three of
them coming out the door. They greeted me enthusiastically. When
I told them I came bearing gifts they turned around and invited
me in. I brought a beautiful book on the Canadian Rockies, which
clearly delighted them, but they didn't quite know what to do with
the maple syrup. I explained that we mostly serve it with pancakes

only, of course, I had no other word for pancake than crêpes. I tried to explain the difference.

"Our pancakes are smaller and thicker than your crêpes. Sort of—" at this I tried to find a the word "—sort of like crêpes sauvages—" They laughed. "—or rather, crêpes rustiques." If they hadn't enjoyed the problem so much, I would have been frustrated by my inability to describe a simple thing like pancakes. Finally I suggested that I make these pancakes for them—perhaps for pancake Tuesday—the morning of Mardi Gras. We chatted briefly about how we observe this day in our respective places. Not much at all, as it turned out. For the sisters, as for me, Mardi Gras is simply the day before Ash Wednesday. But the occasion gave me about a month to figure out the French ingredients for the recipe.

"Now, will you join us for Evening Prayer? We were just on our way when we met up with you."

"Oh! Certainly. I hope I haven't made you late." I was thinking they must keep regularly scheduled hours in the Simple Chapel Without Memories in the courtyard.

"Not at all."

In fact, the sisters' chapel was just behind another door on our floor, the first door in the long hallway, a room much like mine. A small table beneath the window offered aids to reflection—a small icon of Mary and the infant Jesus, a few candles and some dried grasses presumably from the wild garden in the courtyard. A carved crucifix hung in the space between the window sill and the table. Chairs lined the walls on each side of the table. There we said and sang our prayer, Soeur Luci's bell-like soprano carrying us along. A far cry from the hurried approach to Morning Prayer at Flatfield parish. But this was the close of the day, after all, and the day's work done.

WALLS

Something there is that does not love a wall,
That sends the frozen-ground-swell under it,
And spills the upper boulders in the sun;
And makes gaps even two can pass abreast.
. . . .

Before I built a wall I'd ask to know
What I was walling in or walling out,
And to whom I was like to give offense.
Something there is that doesn't love a wall,
That wants it down."

—Robert Frost, "Mending Wall

Beauvais is a walled city. In the first century, "Caesar's Market," the Gallo-Roman city of Caesaromagus, began doing business at the confluence of the Therain and Avalon rivers along the Brunehaut way, an important Roman road originating in Cenabum, the city now known as Orlèans. Caesaromagus was the regional centre of the Bellovaci, a prominent clan of the Belgica tribe of Gaul. After the barbarian invasions in the third century, the city built walls and rerouted the river to create a moat at the base of the ramparts. The walls were quite deep—wide as four men walking abreast—and tall as these same four men standing each on the shoulders of the next. They were constructed of rubble and bricks and faced with small squared field stones called *pastoureaux*. Ruins of these walls can be seen today. In the ninth century, Beauvais became a countship, which passed to the bishops who became peers of France in 1013. A cathedral, now called the *Basse-Œuvre*, was built within the walls sometime around the close of the first millennium. The nave of this cathedral still stands adjoining the west wall of the transept of Cathédrale St. Pierre.

The more or less urban area surrounding Caesaromagus was first called Beauvais in the ninth century, taking its name from the Bellovaci. The medieval walls of Beauvais enclosed an area ten times the size of the walls of the Roman city to accommodate a tenfold increase in population between the tenth and thirteenth centuries. These walls served the city during the Hundred Years War and well into the seventeenth century. Their most famous defence in Beauvais came in 1472, nineteen years after the Hundred Years War finally ended. Here is how it happened:

When Louis XI became King of France, he had a falling out with his brother-in-law, Charles le Téméraire—Charles the Rash—the fourth and final duke of Burgundy in the Valois line. In 1471, the king accused Charles of treason, ordered him to appear before the French *parlement*, and seized several Burgundian-held towns in Hainault and Flanders. Charles responded by invading France with thousands of men at arms. On a ruthless campaign that earned him his epithet—the Rash—Charles captured the town of Nesle and massacred all the citizens. Nesle is only forty miles northeast of Beauvais. Rumours of his savagery undoubtedly reached the people of Beauvais well before he laid siege to their city.

At daybreak on June 27, 1472, roofers working on top of the cathedral saw the *avant-garde* of the army of Charles of Burgundy approaching. The alarm sounded by the bells of St. Pierre reverberated in the bells of all the parish churches of Beauvais. In an instant the city was on its feet. Three hundred armed men rose to defend Beauvais.

At eight o'clock in the morning, a Burgundian herald summoned the defenders of the city to surrender. Beauvais refused. Without waiting for the full battalion, the commander of the vanguard began his attack. In the assault at the porte de Bresles, a Burgundian soldier scaled the wall and planted a flag on it. Inside the walls, a sixteen-year-old girl, Jeanne Fourquet, took an axe and clambered up to challenge him. She flung herself upon the standard bearer, hurled him into the moat, wrested the banner from the battlements and carried it off to l'église des Jacobins. Heartened by her courage, Beauvais' men-at-arms rallied. Women and their daughters bolstered the defence, raining stones, boiling oil, boiling water, and flaming faggots down on the enemy. In the midst of this pandemonium the gate caught fire and soon spread to neighbouring houses. As in the crises of the Hundred Years War, the people resorted to the power of Sainte Angadrême for protection against fire and carried her reliquary to the scene. When she arrived, the fire died down. They set her bones on the ramparts for the duration of the siege.

At the opposite porte de Paris, a very different scene unfolded. Panic reigned and people pressed against the gate. Bishop Jean le Bar was among them. Mounted on a horse, equipped with spurs, javelin in hand, and surrounded by his men and officers—one of whom carried his dishes—the bishop tried to flee. The people urged him to stay, warning that his departure would bring him grief and leave Beauvais in danger. Outraged that a bishop would think to abandon his flock in distress, a townswoman, Madame Brequigny, seized the bridle of the bishop's horse and headed him off, saying he was not going anywhere, that he would live or die with the rest of them. The bishop protested that he was of more value to the people outside of the city than in it. *Quelle sottise!* In the end, he was forced to abandon his project, but not without vigorous opposition. Within two days he stole away anyway, perhaps over the walls by his garden, that is, into territory occupied by the Burgundians, where he must have managed to negotiate safe conduct away from the siege.

Meanwhile, the small garrison and the people of Beauvais held the city. By eight o'clock that evening, 200 lancers in the king's ordinance arrived and immediately took up the battle. Reinforcements for the defence arrived regularly until July 22, the Feast of Saint Mary Magdalene, when the amassed fourteen or fifteen thousand combatants finally defeated Charles le Téméraire who, as he and his armies retreated to Burgundian territory, consoled himself by burning over two thousand towns, villages and castles en route.

For the city of Beauvais, this was their moment. After more than a century in no man's land, so vulnerable to the vagaries of war, the citizens of Beauvais finally established themselves as a sturdy presence capable of first defence against a brutal attacker. It gave Holy Angadrême a chance to stretch her bones, and Jeanne Fourquet became known to posterity as "Jeanne Hachette"—"Hatchet Joan" in English. In gratitude for Jeanne's courageous act, King Louis XI instituted the Procession of the Assault, now observed on the Sunday closest to June 27. The event is celebrated by a grand procession with Angadrême's relics, costumes and re-enacted battles. Traditionally, women take precedence over men at this celebration. And in 1851, the city erected the imposing statue of a young woman brandishing an axe that stands in front of the town hall in Place Jeanne Hachette, at the end of rue de la Madeleine. Much of this account of the siege comes from Charles Fauqueux, *Beauvais: Son histoire,* the first book I bought when I arrived in Beauvais. I hope I have it right. It's hard to compress so many particulars.

Because of the siege, Beauvais became known for her secure walls. However, the vaults of the famous Cathédrale St. Pierre did not enjoy the same reputation. When the great fire of 1225 burned the cathedral now known as the *Basse-Œuvre*, Bishop Miles of Nanteuil began the work on a new cathedral, providing most of the funds for the fabrication of the new structure from his annual revenue. (Bishop Miles! Who would have guessed?) Work continued, or was suspended, over the years, depending on the collective will and the availability of funds from the bishop, the chapter, and the bourgeois of the city. At times the cathedral came to represent the struggle for power between Beauvais' bishops and the king of France. The bishops of Beauvais had no inclination to be under the thumb of Paris. The cathedral refers directly to the seat of Peter, even though most of the great gothic cathedrals in France are dedicated to Our Lady, most notably, Notre Dame de Paris. But Beauvais' cathedral was to be the grandest in all France. At over 150 feet tall, the interior vaulting was higher than any other gothic structure in Europe.

The church with the loftiest vaults in all of Christendom was never completed. There is no nave, except for the remnant of the ancient *Basse-Œuvre*. The gothic structure itself consists of the transept and choir with its seven radiating chapels. Under Bishop William of Grez, the builders decided to extend the reach of the choir. The dazzling new choir was complete in 1272. The people of Beauvais gloried in this wonder of human achievement a full twelve years before a dreadful catastrophe occurred. The choir collapsed.

Remarkably, no lowly pious soul ended up buried on the cathedral floor among monuments reserved for saints, and bishops, and people of rank. "On Friday, November 29, 1284, at eight o'clock in the evening, the great vaults of the choir fell and several exterior pillars were broken; the great windows were smashed...and the divine service ceased for forty years." This is from P. Louvet, who published *Histoire et antiquitez du diocèse de Beauvais* in the 1630s, but I found it in *Beauvais Cathedral: Architecture of Transcendence*, a wonderful book by Stephen Murray, where I read the whole story of the cathedral and the history of Beauvais, though I didn't find anything about Madeleine there.

Murray speculates about what probably caused the collapse of the choir. It has something to do with miscalculating an architectural practice called eccentric loading—in this case, those places in the vault where a significant part of the mass of the uprights of buttresses projects beyond the support. "Such eccentric loading can produce bending, resulting from pressure on the side of the support where the overhang exists, and tension on the other side." That sounds like marriage to me, all that pressure and tension. If two people lean too much toward each other, or away, the whole thing crumbles. The stresses have to be in good balance. The pillars and buttresses need to be well seated and stable. There is a limit to how much any two pillars can sustain leaning in or leaning out—one too far toward, one too far away or both leaning in a parallel trajectory, like those silos Miles drew on his map, where no foundation other than geography connects the two. They only support their own weight. They don't come together at all—two silos side by side, not falling over yet. Like us, like me and Miles.

At any rate, the restored choir stood alone for two centuries before work on the transept began in the sixteenth century. The builders ran into problems in the transept as well. Ultimately these problems precipitated the collapse of the crossing tower in 1573. But the cathedral stands today, despite the metaphorical fodder these disasters create about the classic problem of overreaching—not only in physical in terms of the height of the structure, or as a power struggle between bishops and princes, but of the weight of the established church in the face of heresies, and mendicants, and the Protestant Reformation. In eras of social ferment there were times the church just couldn't keep it all together. Instead of revisiting the foundation, it just pushed further in the same direction.

I sent Miles a nice postcard of the cathedral—told him the work had been begun by a Bishop Miles and what did he think of that? I didn't mention the collapse, or the overweening ambition of so many bishops of Beauvais.

* * *

I have been in Beauvais six weeks to the day. I am dreaming in French. I haven't done that since high school. I met a couple of tourists from England at the cathedral last week. We spoke English. It felt so strange. English has become a written language for me. I spend my mornings writing. I usually sit at the desk in the hall. There is nobody around to distract me. Tuesdays and Fridays, I return to the desk by three o'clock. Early on I discovered these are the days Soeur Luci cooks. I like hearing her music and her singing, and smelling the delicious aromas that drift around the corner. I'm sure she doesn't hear me coming up the stairs, she's so busy and buried in sound. It makes the writing more enjoyable. It makes me feel "with." Not that I'm lonely or anything. I'm still fine about the solitude, but it's good to feel connected that way twice a week. It's very hopeful. It's good to hear the sounds of someone's life percolating along. Not that mine isn't. I have pretty much written up all my notes from the first encounter with Madeleine to the present. This is as far as I've got. I have no idea what comes next.

Midday I go out. Sometimes I run into one of the sisters and am invited to join them for a little lunch. That's a treat. Often I take a hot meal in a restaurant at noon to save myself the trouble of cooking supper in the uncongenial staff kitchen. I spend the afternoon wandering the city, visiting the churches, museums, bookstores, and other shops until everything crashes to a close. I'm sure I have walked a dozen times down every street within ten blocks of the cathedral. In neighbourhoods where some fifteenth-and sixteenth-century houses still stand, the walls of private houses and commercial buildings abut streets or sidewalks without any preliminary threshold. Newer houses on other streets probably owe their redevelopment to the bombs of the Second World War. These comfortable homes stand secluded behind tall walls of brick or stone. Wrought-iron fences gate the entrances and driveways. Bare branches of trees or shrubbery creep beyond the barriers. Surely in spring they will soften these bald narrow avenues. I sometimes peek through the iron open-work to glimpse what the walls contain. I never see anybody. Of course, it's winter. In Flatfield, you don't see many people out in their yards in February, except to shovel snow or make snow angels. But there's no snow here.

Then back to my room. For supper I eat a lot of fresh fruit, cheese and bread, which is not a hardship in France. I spend the evening reading and arranging the day's discoveries—that is, the books and brochures I have picked up. I now own several books about Beauvais. I never encounter Madeleine in any of them.

I am accustomed to the way of life here, more or less, but not entirely comfortable with it. That may be because the bed sags and the bathroom is down the hall. I have to be decent to get there. I have toyed with the idea of slipping out with only a towel when I take my shower but I want to avoid scandal. I have yet to meet anyone when I go on such a mission, but there's a first time for everything.

Aline tells me all the roomers are female. She's one of them. We talk in the hall from time to time. She says the others only stay Monday through Thursday night and go home for weekends. I'm not sure they really exist. They are just phantoms creaking in the hallway.

Aline's in her fourth year at the agricultural college, one of the few institutions in Beauvais that draws people from other parts of France. Monday night I invited her into my room. I had my little supper still laid out and offered some to her. I told her how I would love to try the dinner menus at some of the restaurants I'd heard of, but I am a little afraid to go out in the evenings. She agreed. She doesn't like to walk alone after dark because of the come-ons. And the locking up—Aline also thinks it odd. It's eerie. It gives us both a sense of insecurity. They don't lock up that way in the town where Aline comes from, near France's border with Switzerland. She finds the town gloomy. She says in the first part of the twentieth century, brick-making was one of the main industries in Beauvais. Gradually, concrete blocks replaced the bricks, and unemployment depressed the town. Currently the industry of the town includes a sponge factory, a farm-machinery manufacturing plant, Givenchy perfumes, and the ambitious Nestlés Corporation, which Aline boycotts.

I ran into my gentleman friend along rue des Jacobins again. I let a smile play demurely at the corners of my mouth and dipped what I intended to be a regal nod when he chivalrously yielded the right-of-way. Our eyes fixed a second longer than courtesy would demand. He smiled broadly. As I passed by the épicerie on my way to église St. Etienne that day, I bought a half-kilo of oats. Not nearly a bushel, but it was a start.

* * *

Yesterday was Shrove Tuesday. I made my crêpes rustiques or

whatever you want to call them. La Belle was effusive, saying the ethereal-sweetness-of-the-tender-cakes-positively-vaporizes-on-the tongue. I am not making this up. And she loves maple syrup. When she was in Quebec she went to a *cabane à sucre* festival and tasted maple-sugar pie. She also remembers rolling hot maple taffy off the snow onto a stick. La Belle could not say enough about my breakfast. It brought back so many happy memories. La Perle's compliments came primarily in the form of a generous second helping. Soeur Luci pronounced the pancakes satisfying—not only to the appetite, but to the heart.

I had planned to take charge of the dishes too, but La Belle would have none of it. She shooed me and Soeur Luci away to the sitting area, promising to enjoy our company from the sink. As for La Perle, she set down her fork and picked up her knitting. The cardigans she was working on when I came had been finished long before and were already keeping two little girls in the parish warm. She's now knitting another cape like Soeur Luci's, this time in deep green. She clicked away and Soeur Luci told me their plans for Lent. First Soeur Luci will go on retreat for a week. The following week the Sisters Beatrice will go while Soeur Luci minds the shop.

"You should come with me, Janine. I can take you as far as Saint-Germer-de-Fly and you can take the bus back. It would be good for you to see the countryside, and the abbey church at Saint-Germer-de-Fly is worth a visit." Of course I accepted, and I look forward to it.

I was pleased with how well it went. We had a good time. Content and optimistic, I set off to église St. Etienne for the afternoon. A line of people—a remorse of penitents—formed along the aisle approaching the confessional—several respectable sinners, and from all appearances a more inglorious one, since he tried so hard to seem indifferent. I gave them a wide berth. I sat far back in the church and wondered if this was the very place Jacques encountered the Blessed Jean de Beaumanoir.

I don't know when I last went to confession. It's been awhile. It was before Father Francis died, maybe two years ago this spring.

He was a priest you could talk to. No advice, no judgement, just an open ear and a generous heart. Besides, I have no idea what I would confess if I tried. I feel fine at the moment. True, I often feel a little disenchanted. Does a person confess disenchantment? How can something so unlooked for be a sin? Well, it can't be. It's not deadly at any rate—pride, envy, anger, avarice, gluttony, lust, sloth. Nothing about disenchantment. The only thing I've ever heard of that even comes close is the "noonday demon" from Psalm 91—something called *acedia*—*torpor mentis*—a torpor of the mind—a soul sleeping from weariness. Gregory the Great called it sadness. Somewhere along the line they figured "sloth" captured the idea. Could be disenchantment is deadly after all.

God forgive me, now I'm down in the dumps. I am so far from my home and my family here. I like Beauvais, and I love the sisters, but I don't think I'm going to find what I came for, and I have so little waiting for me at home. Bless me, Father, since my last confession, I have been sad 638 times. Not so sad that I couldn't sometimes smile at people or laugh at a joke—even my own. I'm just trying to be accurate here. And I've been angry sometimes, mostly at Miles. It makes me even sadder. Does that make it better—or worse?

I think maybe I should just leave this place. I have been here long enough. I have had a little taste of France. I have met some lovely people. But the place is so closed in. I often remember the first person I encountered in Beauvais—that man I met in the underpass at the station the day I arrived—the man reeling and battered and bleeding. I really don't want to go there. It's absurd to think the only exit from this place is down and out. I arrived at the far platform after all. Logically the train back to Paris will leave from the platform nearest the station. There should be no need to pass under the tracks to get home.

The trouble with leaving is, I haven't achieved anything yet. I have sorted and scribbled and organized the story. I have written a lot of transitional sentences. And I've practically written my own biography in the process. If I went home now, I would only have a bigger unfinished project. When I got back to Flatfield, I would have to say I followed her story as far as I could and I never found her. Madeleine wasn't here at all. She would have been about seventy-two years old at the siege of Beauvais. She did not show up once in *Beauvais: son Histoire*—the most logical place to find her. Madame Brequigny made it into those pages, for Pete's sake. You'd think with all that hullabaloo during the siege, I would have heard something of Madeleine.

She's got to be here somewhere. Maybe behind one of these walls. I just can't seem to break through. A fortified city under siege is also a prison. Whether Madeleine ever went to prison, the fact is, she's locked up somehow. I had hoped to be her rescuer. Still, I am honoured to have found so much of her story, even if it means I'm crazy. Jeanne d'Arc heard voices. She accomplished great things as long as she trusted those voices and was not compromised by the swaggering notions of her men-at-arms. I read between the lines and have swaggering doubts. It's not all that different, except I'm trying to liberate a shadow, not a nation.

I am setting a goal. I will go with Soeur Luci next week. And I will try to make some real progress before she returns. I will find all the walls and walk around them, like Joshua and his army. I will circumambulate the old city walls, and next, the walls of the medieval city. I will find the walls that enclose Madeleine. And I will summon Joshua's trumpets and blow these walls down.

FAITH

There are only two ways to live your life. One is as though nothing is a miracle. The other is as if everything is.

—Albert Einstein

These few days pass slowly. I am so looking forward to that excursion out of Beauvais. I enjoyed the breakfast, but it left me feeling quite lonely. I wish I could be more connected with the sisters in their little community. It's as if because I want to see more of them, I seem to encounter them even less frequently than before. Sometimes I pass Soeur Luci in the courtyard, but La Belle and La Perle are practically invisible. So I have gone twice to Evening Prayer. It is some consolation. But of course, the sisters are at the end of a long day working with people. They want to be left alone I think, so I am left alone too.

I called home. I've called home every weekend since I came. I spoke once before with Miles. It was awkward at best. This time he picked up the phone and seemed so happy. He didn't try to figure out what I was up to, as he had the time before. He just said I was right about the art classes. He truly enjoys them. He said he's sorry he made such a stink about it. Then he went on about the instructor, Vikki. She's really good, apparently. Sounded more to me like she thinks he's really good.

Adam was at work. I talked with Kit and my mom. Mom said I should call back in an hour. Marilee is in town and really wants to talk to me. Mom will call her and have her come over. I suggested I just call her at the Clarks'. No, it would probably be better to call her at our house. So I waited an hour. I began to wonder about this Vikki chick and whether it was the half-kilo of oats at work and whether I had been a bit hasty.

I called back. I didn't realize how much I miss Marilee. I haven't thought of her as a friend before—not as a daughter either. More as a dependent, I guess. But here she was, needing to talk and me grateful for every minute. Marilee and Shane are not getting along. It has only been getting worse. In the meantime, Luke now has a girlfriend who resents his visits to Southern Alberta. Luke wants to arrange to take Jessica on alternate weekends to stay with him at his parents' home in Flatfield. As usual, I had no wisdom to offer. I just listened. I told her how much I miss her. Marilee really wants me to come home. That was nice. Not that my family doesn't miss me, but I think I kind of scared them off about saying anything. And I still have my pride after all, however deadly it may be.

* * *

Finally Sunday came. I went to mass at St. Etienne's, sitting in the back, as usual. I didn't go up for communion, as usual, so the sisters were surprised to see me there when the mass was ended. We rarely end up at the same service. I followed them into the sunlight. Outside a beggar lifted a small blue glass—a votive candle holder, I think. La Belle dropped a few centimes into his cup. I was not prepared. I rifled through my purse, but I had no money with me. I felt bad about not being able to put the smallest coin in the cup. "Desolée" seemed to overstate the case. I felt bad, not desolate. So I looked him in the eye and said, "Bonjour."

We walked home together. La Perle was busy confirming all the details about what needed to be taken care of while Soeur Luci was away. She seemed a little anxious. I realized that even though Soeur Luci is the youngest of the three, La Belle and La Perle look to her for direction. I have not noticed whether they ever call her "mother."

After lunch and a short rest, Soeur Luci and I set out on our little adventure. She drives a 2CV Citroën. "You know you are in France when every other car on the road is a 2CV. Now they stop making them, but that doesn't mean we stop using them. Even the archbishop of Paris drives one."

As we wove through the city streets, Soeur Luci kept up a continuing conversation with the traffic: "Alors, my little green, your turn," to a car hesitating in a traffic circle. Then to a sedan neglecting to yield, "Pardon, monsieur, c'est à moi! Oo la la!" The streets were busy for a Sunday. Many vehicles seemed to go just where she wanted to be. As we finally headed out of the city, a car cut in abruptly after a poorly judged pass. "Dites donc, coco!"

We hummed along. The sky was clear and as close to blue as I'd seen since the day I arrived in France. The countryside, still in the habit of winter, kept to conservative greys and browns except for those persisting green balls that hang from the bare branches of so many trees—the same festive ornaments I saw from the train on my way to Beauvais, and here they are again. I asked Soeur Luci if she knew what it was.

"Oh, that! It's *gui*. Do you know *gui*?"

I shook my head—no. All I could think of was Canon Guy.

"It grows mostly on apple trees. Surely you've heard of it. It is green all the year round. At Christmas, people bring it inside for a decoration. Ancient peoples thought it had mystical properties."

"Oh! It's mistletoe! I've never seen it grow in Canada. Amazing!"

"Here in the north of France—I think the legend comes from Brittany—we call it 'Herbe de la Croix.' This tradition says the wood of the cross came from a tree of mistletoe. After the crucifixion, the tree shrivelled, because it had become the instrument of death for the Giver of Life. Now it is dwarfed and depends on other trees for survival."

Soeur Luci drove as fast as anybody on the meandering strip of highway, or maybe a little faster. She slowed behind a creeping 2CV and said patronizingly, "—Allons, papa!"

"It seems not all the 2CVs are as fast as yours."

She laughed. "Non, pas de tout." At a break in on-coming traffic, she slipped quickly past him and continued on. "You see, we have mistletoe everywhere here—because we have so many apple trees."

"I think it's enchanting. Is it really such a terrible plant? I've heard it is harmful to trees."

"Mais non! The mistletoe is a wonderful plant. It only becomes a problem when it grows on a sickly tree. When a tree is in difficulty, the mistletoe will make matters worse. In a healthy tree the mistletoe is a special presence that nurtures little animals and birds. The mistletoe invites variety and difference. People often look for only one kind of productivity, but if you look at the abundance in life, there are many ways to understand the world. I think it is like the Church. When the church community is healthy those who cling to it thrive. Whether as blossoms or mistletoe, both bear fruit. Where I come from just north of here we have our own name for the mistletoe of the apple, perhaps because it is so plentiful. We call it *brout*."

"Brout? B-r-o-u-t?"

"Yes. I don't think the term is common in other parts of France."

"But this is the cider district, after all."

"Vraiment!"

"Hmh." I looked out the window. *Madeleine de Brout. Madeleine of Mistletoe. It probably means nothing more than that Madeleine comes from this district, which I already know. Sometimes a name is just a name. I once met a man named Goodenough who wasn't. And an African-American named White. And the first name of the glummest teacher I ever had was Felicity.*

Soeur Luci drove along, keeping company with her companions on the road.

— "Avancez donc, ma tresor!"

—"Pardon, ma petite!"

And Guy too, for that matter. Well, both Madeleine and Guy planted themselves quite handily on a host in a different place and era. I don't know. Maybe Madeleine was a heretic. No. She only did what she could out of love for suffering and dying people. She's not a heretic. She didn't preach that creation is evil. That's heresy. Weeping with those who weep is a kindness, especially when you could choose to do otherwise. She is just a manifestation of that varied and different expression of faith Soeur Luci talks about. If the name means anything, it means her faith and hope and love did not always follow the conventional forms. She was a great confessor because of her love and empathy. And because nobody else would do the work.

"You are very quiet. Are you enjoying the scenery?"

"Yes. —I was just thinking about *brout*. Is it ever a name? Do people take it as a surname too?"

"I don't know anyone named Brout. Are you planning to change your name? I don't think you can do better than LaFoy." She smiled on me with her usual radiance.

"Maybe not. But I don't really suit the name. Naming something doesn't make it so."

"True enough. You are known by your fruit. But are grapes gathered from thorns, or figs from thistles?" For the first time I felt Soeur Luci pushing, or at least nudging me. As far as I know she never quoted scripture to me before.

"I mean, LaFoy is not an easy name. It just reminds me of what I lack."

"Ah, I see. It is not easy to have faith. I would hope the name makes you more aware that faith is a gift from God. —But that is not enough?"

"It raises expectations. I used to think if I willed something in faith, all my questions would be answered."

"That, I believe, is the opposite of faith. Faith allows you to live in the mystery. To celebrate the miracle of life, even when you don't understand it."

"But faith is a virtue. That's a lot of pressure—to be named for a virtue. Maybe I *would* be happier if I changed my name to Brout. There's more ambiguity about mistletoe. People don't necessarily expect it to be a good thing."

"But they are related—faith and mistletoe."

"They are?"

"They are both eternally green. Green is the colour of faith, you know."

"No, I didn't know that. When I think of green I think of something fresh and young, innocent and flourishing. Or maybe humility. I know in the Middle Ages green had something to do with passion."

"And so—do these negate faith? If not green, then what would you colour it?"

I thought awhile—about good faith, and standing fast, and letting go. About the substance of things hoped for, the evidence of things not seen. Like spring. That would have to be green after all.

When we arrived in Saint-Germer-de-Fly, Soeur Luci turned onto a side road and up a rise where a good view of the abbey church could be had. In the foreground a stone-fenced pasture corralled two dappled horses that loped over to greet us. We said hello to the horses, then Soeur Luci told her car to enjoy the view, and we set off to see the twelfth-century church. A modern tractor hauling an enormous empty trailer lumbered along the road past the church. It seemed so incongruous to me. The tractor was no different from the ones around Flatfield. Despite its historic church, the town was small and seemed to serve a mostly rural population— just an ordinary town keeping company with an extraordinary building.

It was the best time, walking around the old church with Soeur Luci, often in a three-way conversation including whatever saint we encountered. She knows all their stories. She did her best to help the saints get comfortable with me and usually introduced me as one of their company. Finally, I protested. "Even if I were holy, I'm not dead yet."

"But of course. And do you suppose they are?" I am never sure of how literally to take her. She is always in earnest, but not always serious.

An arched passage leads from the church to the Sainte-Chapelle built in the thirteenth century. The church felt close and shadowy to me, but the chapel is bright with walls of windows. We sat in the light for quite awhile. After reverent musings on the history and architecture and personalities of the abbey, Soeur Luci asked me how my writing was going. I told her I have set down all I know about the story and only wait to find the conclusion.

"*Does* it have an ending? The best stories I know finally reach a beginning. Perhaps you are already there. Is the story about you?"

"Oh no. Well, it's not my intention. Only enough of my story to document how it came to be in the first place."

"I see." She may just as well have said, "I doubt it."

"But now I think the main character will be named for mistletoe."

"Voila! It is about you after all!"

The time passed too quickly. About five o'clock Soeur Luci saw me to the bus stop opposite the church. She waited with me until the bus came, then waved me off. As the bus pulled away from Saint Germer-de-Fly I watched Soeur Luci turn to walk back toward her little car, who must have been getting lonely by then.

* * *

The bus ride back from Saint Germer-de-Fly was absurdly long for the short distance. There were only two other passengers. I stared out the window trying to count all the trees with mistletoe. I thought about faith and Soeur Luci's comment. Willing a resolution—demanding certainty—is the opposite of faith. That has been my problem. I have tried to will Madeleine into existence. Since I came here, I have rarely lost sight of that goal. I have resented the intrusion of saints like Angadrême who are important to Beauvais, but who have nothing to do with me.

I hoped to find Madeleine here and I haven't. I was so sure if she could be found anywhere, it would be here. I have pretty much lost hope of ever finding her. I think I have lost hope about everything. By extension I have lost faith—the things hoped for—too. The evidence of things not seen seems to have disappeared. How was it I ever came to meet Madeleine in the first place? I doubt that had anything to do with faith. Our tenth anniversary—that was a pretty faithless effort. I was already disenchanted with Miles and my life with him—everything flat, the future folding itself up into a cardboard box with nothing inside. The fields disappearing into the horizon were just that. Flat fields. Flat and dry. A dry weary land without water. There is no ocean there, no hidden depths, no mystery. My levee is nothing more than a dusty, abandoned road.

And those other encounters. When Marilee moved in I stopped thinking about it, or my own life, or Miles. There was too much going on. I had no expectation except to be crowded and interrupted. And there she was, Madeleine, to join the party.

As for Jim's paper, I had a job to do, that was all. Her appearance was most predictable when I had no expectation. And here I am in Beauvais with the primary expectation being to find Madeleine. Of course I'm not going to find her here. This journey has not been one of faith at all. It has been my desire to contain something. To find something to put into that cardboard box and hang onto it. Well, the box is still empty. I have come looking for something that doesn't exist, and found nothing.

It was dark by the time we pulled into Beauvais. Several big men loitered by the exit to the station. I hurried past them, walking briskly along with an inordinate fear of everything that moved. There is no one to worry about me here in dark, oppressive Beauvais—if I never make it back, no one to wonder why. Solitude may be a good thing, but isolation frightens me.

* * *

I felt better when I woke up this morning. The best way to cope with loneliness is to find something meaningful to do. The best thing I can do for the story now is let it go. Perhaps it will find me. I have been preoccupied with Madeleine being locked up somewhere. It could be she is locked up because I won't unbind her and let her go free. And I, her supposed liberator.

I am not changing my plan, I just hope to change the way I go about it. I have mapped the walls of Beauvais from the sources I now have at hand. I will find all the walls and walk around them. But when I walk around these walls, I will try to embrace whatever

I meet, whether or not I think it has anything to do with Madeleine or me. I will try to enjoy the unremarkable evidence of human activity in the present.

BLUE

A blue pigeon it is, that circles the blue sky,
On side-long wing, around and round and round.
A white pigeon it is, that flutters to the ground,
Grown tired of flight.
. . . .
until now I never knew
That fluttering things have so distinct a shade.

—Wallace Stevens, "Le Monocle de Mon Oncle"

I am doing pretty well, all things considered. I have relaxed about my mission for one thing. I spent three afternoons walking around the walls. I believe I have found all of them, those still standing and those places they once stood that have been built over or paved. I have established the location of some of the gates, too, where Jeanne Hachette triumphed over the enemy, where Madame Brequigny tried to steer the bishop right. So I've done all I can about the story. I am trying to let it go. I am okay with turning this writing project into a notebook about my fabulous trip to France.

I don't worry about my marriage and what to do with Miles either. Well, I do a little. I should be glad he enjoys the art classes and the teacher. I'm sure it's all for the best. He wasn't home when I called yesterday. I don't know why he wouldn't be home on a Sunday. Kit said he wanted to sketch the water tower. It's March, for Pete's sake. No one in Flatfield willingly sits outside in March. It's still winter. Kit said it was a sunny day and above freezing. Well, maybe so.

I did get to know La Perle and La Belle a little better this past week. They were pleased to invite me to dinner one evening. I think they found their table shrunken with Soeur Luci away and hoped I would add dimension. It is Lent, of course. La Perle made a hearty lentil soup as good as anything I could have cooked up in the little staff kitchen. Conversation was convivial, although the minds of the Soeurs Béatrices are more heavily cast and move less lightly than Soeur Luci's.

I learned a little about their origins. La Perle came of age near Beauvais, amidst the sirens and bombs of World War II. She told me how in the worst days of the war her family still dressed up to go to church on Sunday. They had to take their chances, dodging guns and heavy trucks and wagons and horses on the way. The church bells pealed while anti-aircraft shells crackled overhead and guns thundered just beyond the far side of the last hill in the village. Yet she talks about her youth with fondness.

The small village in south central France where La Belle grew up was less affected by the war, there being little strategic importance to the area. She is a modern Wilgeforte. Her family were anxious to see her married to a wealthy neighbour who courted her with unsavoury appetite. She escaped by taking the veil. I asked her if she prayed that God would make her less attractive to this man. "Oh no. I wasn't clever enough to think of that." And apparently her father was not as ambitious as Wilgeforte's, so there was no need to spoil her natural beauty.

"Soeur Luci tells me she comes from this part of France."

La Perle had picked up her knitting and clicked away, adding, in the course of our conversation, a half-thumb's length to her knitting on the great green cape. "Yes, but she lived all over Europe when she was younger and playing the cello. She and her husband spent two years with a string ensemble in Netherlands before he died."

"Soeur Luci was married?"

"Oh yes. She didn't tell you that?"

"I had no idea."

"Well, it was a long time ago." La Perle concentrated on her knitting and left it to La Belle to fill me in.

"It is a sad story. They were very much in love, I think. They met at the conservatory. He was a wonderful violinist. I know this not only from Soeur Luci, but others who visit here from time to time who knew them both. They had been married almost three years when he suddenly died from an aneurism. Lucille was pregnant at the time, but under the stress of the terrible circumstance, she lost the baby. She grieved two great losses at once, the poor thing. Soeur Luci tried to continue her career in music but her heart wasn't in it. Four years later she entered our order. She's been with the order nearly twenty-five years now, and with the two of us here in Beauvais for five. We are so grateful for her."

*   *   *

Soeur Luci is back but I haven't seen her yet. The Sisters Beatrice will go on their retreat this coming Sunday. I have not found any joy in abandoning my search for Madeleine, although it is a sad relief to finally acknowledge that whoever she is and whatever the reason for her appearances, I have no power to conjure her and no responsibility to will her into existence.

I have become an ordinary tourist. I frequently drop in at the tourist office to get ideas for what to see or where to go. I think I may go to Paris after all. Back home it would be embarrassing to say that for three months I lived an hour away and never saw Paris. I will have to talk with Soeur Luci first, to finalize arrangements with her. In the meantime, I try to honour the abraded importance of the *genius loci* here in Beauvais.

The city is bigger than I thought. Because the centre is so compact and the streets so narrow, the places where they widen out into urban sprawl felt like a boundary to me. Now I realize much of the city's business goes on beyond the centre. As a tourist I am not obliged to learn how these parts of the city differ from Western suburbia. However, I have begun to notice many of the modern businesses downtown. The most prominent to me are the blue businesses across the street from the cathedral. On rue St. Pierre there are four with "bleu" in their name. I asked the aproned fishmonger standing at the door between the fish stands of L'ecaille Bleue "Why so many blue businesses here?"

He hesitated a moment looking a little perplexed.

"Parce que la mer est bleu—nous vendons des poissons."

"Ah, I see." I thought I did. "And the restaurants serve fish," continuing his line of argument. "Two seafood restaurants, a fish market. The sea is blue. Of course. Merci." I moved on, satisfied with his explanation, but the next shop down, La Malle Bleue, was a gift shop. *Oh well.* Around the corner on rue Beauregard is La Crêperie Bleue. I stopped there for a cider and lunch. I asked the waitress why there were so many blue businesses.

"Tous sont opéré par le meme propriétaire."

I should have thought of that. One owner monopolizing the tourist trade around the cathedral. "Do you suppose there is a reason they call their businesses 'blue'? Why 'blue'?"

"Je ne sais pas." She hesitated. "Bleu—c'est la vie—la joie." Then she brightened. "C'est l'espérance!"

I couldn't hear the last bit above the clatter of dishes in the kitchen and the noise of traffic. "Experience?" I asked. If blue represents life and joy as she said, I would be more inclined to give experience its opposite colour.

She shook her head, "Non— *l'espérance.*"

"Ah. Hope." Now I understood. She seemed satisfied. I do know the word, at least in theory. If I hadn't been told by someone who knew these things, I would have thought blue meant sadness, longing, resignation.

* * *

I didn't see Soeur Luci until today. It's Friday. I was walking up the stairs, coming back early to sit here in the long empty hallway and write. Although there's no urgency about the project anymore, I still like to hold my pen and let Soeur Luci crowd the space with sound.

Thanks to a break between tracks of exquisite music, she heard me coming up the stairs. She poked her head out the door. "Ah, there you are! How have you been? I have missed you."

"I have missed you too. Did your retreat go well?"

"Yes, indeed. I thought about you often."

"Not much of a retreat then, I guess. Sorry to have interrupted you!"

"Not at all. Whenever you came to mind I just prayed you a blessing and off you went. You were no trouble. Will you come to dinner Sunday? I will give the sisters a good meal to send them on their way."

"I would love to. But that's an extra shift for you, isn't it? Do you normally cook on Sundays?

"Oh, almost always."

"That hardly seems fair. La Perle and La Belle only have to cook twice a week and you, who have administrative responsibility as well as all the other work you do, cook three times a week."

"Ma foi! But it makes perfect sense! I am the best cook."

I had to smile. She was right, as usual.

"Besides, the work is contemplation for me. And I can be alone with my music. On Tuesdays I listen to anything I choose. On Friday, the day of Our Lord's suffering, I listen to chant or music of The Passion. On Sunday, I play cantatas by Bach and masses by everyone else. How could I do that if I didn't cook on Sundays?"

"You are so—intentional."

"Perhaps. Mostly, I find ways to keep the fire burning. I do not want to let the heart grow cold."

"Oh." I didn't know what to say. Before I knew her story, I may have thought she was quietly suggesting I attend to *my* heart which, in terms of my element, has in fact always been cold. But today I realized she was probably referring to her own struggle to sustain a rehabilitated heart. "What's today's music?"

"Pergolesi's *Stabat Mater*."

"It's beautiful."

"Yes." We stood listening together awhile. "And to think he was only twenty-six when he died. What depth and understanding from so young a man. But it appears heaven couldn't wait for him."

"Who?"

"Pergolesi, of course. The one who wrote this music."

"Yes—of course." For a moment I thought she meant her husband. I really want to hear her story. But we just stood there at the top of the stairs, listening. In any case, she was soon summoned by a pot bubbling on the stove. I said thank you and see you Sunday. Maybe I will learn more about it on Sunday, if I ask.

* * *

Sunday dinner was good. I did ask, and Soeur Luci told me about her early happiness. Her husband's name was Yves. She calls her lost daughter "Innocence." "Those two, they still breathe a precious fragrance over everything. I am very thankful to have them in my life." She sat back, folded her hands, nodded and seemed to disappear for a moment. We finished eating in silence.

Soeur Luci had to be back at the church for a baptism. She excused herself for leaving so abruptly, said goodbye to the Soeurs Béatrices, and suggested I join her for dinner on Tuesday evening. The sisters accepted my offer to clean up after dinner. I wished them a good retreat and they were gone.

I enjoyed it—washing the dishes. Odd how domestic patterns restore a sense of continuity. That's my problem. I'm camping out. I have never filled the staff-kitchen sink with water. I put a bit of dish soap on a rag, swish, rinse and I'm gone. I want to go home now. I want to see my sons. I want to set my own table. But in a way, I want to stay. I'm just barely getting to know the sisters. I would like to be in Beauvais for June 27. That's too far away. I want to get back in time to plant a garden on the drought-ridden prairie. I want to wait to see if Madeleine shows up. I think I miss Miles. I need to think about leaving Beauvais. I am feeling a little blue.

BLIND SIDE

'There is always a thing forgotten
When all the world goes well;
A thing forgotten, as long ago
When the gods forgot the mistletoe,
And soundless as an arrow of snow
The arrow of anguish fell.'

'The thing on the blind side of the heart,
On the wrong side of the door.
. . . .
There is always a forgotten thing,
And love is not secure.'

—G. K. Chesterton, "The Bellad of the White Horse"

I will give them one heart, and put a new spirit within them;
I will remove the heart of stone from their flesh and give
them a heart of flesh.

—Ezekiel 11:19

They don't really have weather in Beauvais. Winter is dull and
damp and chilly. Or chilly and damp and dull. That's about it. Winter in Flatfield is bright, but night comes early. It can be cloudy, or

threatening blizzards. The air is cold and crisp or soft with snow or biting with wind. What wouldn't I give for a little sparkle of snow right now. I walked a lot today in this inconsummate weather to clear my mind and prepare myself for quitting this place. I didn't think about Madeleine much. It's time to wrap it up, to bring it all to a conclusion, Madeleine notwithstanding. It's a fitting finale. Dinner alone with Soeur Luci tomorrow night, much the way it all began here.

Apart from Soeur Luci's musical interludes, I will be glad to be rid of the echoing silence of this place. That is one thing I won't miss at all. For awhile, Madeleine filled the space, but now all the sounds I hear come from outside my walls—except the floor creaks when I cross it, and the bed groans when I sit on it. I suppose I could have brought a radio. It's not easy to find peace and quiet at home. I never thought you could have too much of it. If I ever encountered any silence before I began to look for Madeleine, I don't remember what I did with it. Here the remedy is in my feet. I am wearing out my shoes.

* * *

Today I walked even farther than yesterday. I headed south into the St. Jean district. Things are a little more spread out south of the tracks. I walked down rue Colette in honour of Sister Colette. I haven't thought of her before today, but I wonder how she's doing. I wonder how things are going at the office. I don't really miss my job at all, but I wouldn't mind seeing Walter and Colette and Father Eugene. Can't say as much for BG.

I don't know how I ended up at Notre Dame du Thil. I must have got turned around on the Pont de Paris. At any rate, after walking for hours, I found myself there when Beauvais finally decided to come up with some real weather. The sky grew dark. I scanned the skyline for the cathedral since I know my way from there. Suddenly, a deafening blast of wind sent me reeling. Small white pellets pummelled from crouching clouds. People pulling coats up over their heads or sheltering under newspapers scurried everywhere. I kept

my head down and hurried along toward the cathedral. It was a long
way off. There seemed to be no public shelter en route. I was practically alone on the streets, the locals having been more resourceful
about finding refuge. I kept moving, buffeted by the wind, choosing
the green lights as long as they took me in the general direction
I wanted to go, which sent me east of the cathedral. Eventually I
found myself at the threshold of the tourist office and ducked in
there. It was on the point of closing. The girl at the desk recognized
me and let me in before she locked the door. I stood shivering and
wet, waiting with her until the torrent subsided. The storm settled
almost as suddenly as it began. I thanked my protectress, wrapped
my wet coat around me, and hurried off.

By the time I reached Maison Diocésaine the weather was dull
and damp and chilly again with no hint of the cosmic upheaval that
had just taken place. I had no time to recover. The days are getting
longer now and I had lost track of time. I put on some dry clothes,
pulled a comb through my hair, and went down the hall to dinner.
An energetic mix of piano and strings spilled brightly into the hall.
I tapped and poked my head through the door, hardly expecting
Soeur Luci to hear me above the music.

"Oh, hello!" She stepped away from the stove. "Come in! Come
in! Your hair's wet. Did you get caught in the *giboulée de mars*?"

"Giboulée de mars?"

"—what we call our sudden storms in early spring. It happens
because the air can't decide whether to be hot or cold."

"What a storm! I was coming from Notre Dame du Thil when
it began."

"You went so far?"

"I was a little lost."

"That's a long way to go in a storm! I hope it was worth the trouble. Did you make any great discoveries?"

"Not at all. I wandered everywhere but to no purpose."

"Here. Sit down. I'll only be a few minutes. Make yourself comfortable."

I did. I did not offer to help. I was so tired, too tired to give the attention Soeur Luci undoubtedly required to the arranging of the table and placement of silverware. There would surely be some ceremonious reason for everything and I wasn't up to it. I sat back and closed my eyes. I listened to the music and to Soeur Luci alternately humming along with the melody or pum-pumming with the bass, occasionally interrupting herself to talk to her creations, chatting away to the sauce—"How you spit! Is it too hot for you? Let me fix that." Then chiding the mushrooms for sogginess—"Mes jolis, you swim like fish!"

I could not ignore music so vigorous and playful—a colossal game of Snakes and Ladders. The instruments rambled step by step, sometime scrambling up a ladder only to plummet down again—a busy, nimble noise skipping along to who knows where. Then all but one sustained note in the cello tumbled into silence until a sweet song from some other place percolated to the surface. The piano coaxed the strings with punctuating chords and shimmering cascades, the strings gathered courage and the whole rigmarole played on, sometimes the game, sometimes the song. Soeur Luci continued her chatter. "There now, shining brown. Much better! Pumpee-dumpee-dumpee dum..."

Tripping merrily along, the instruments continued the chase. Suddenly a storm invaded, strident and grim, then a chastened retreat until a puckish rhythm teased them back into the game. At last, the instruments rushed to a gleeful finish and for a moment the room was quiet. There is no good reason why it left me feeling desolate except, by comparison, my afternoon's excursion had had none of the exuberance, none of the nimbleness, none of the tenderness, none of the joy, none of the triumph of arrival. Only the storm.

Next movement the piano set out with a simple pulse, a persistent footfall. The cello began a wistful melody. It completely drew me in, seeming to borrow the air I breathed. Then the strings took up the pulse and the piano carried the melody. In its turn, the violin did not take the melody. It just began to ruminate on two notes—like a sigh—from the melody, until those two notes became a question and assumed a life of their own. It all began innocently enough but with increasing urgency—still the relentless tread, the restless urging—the two notes continually asking an unanswerable question. I was overcome. I sat back and closed my eyes trying to contain it, but tears fell anyway. Odd. I never cry. I doubt I've shed a tear in fifteen years. I was so tired. I felt the air move a little as Soeur Luci sat down beside me. The melody wandered off on more urgent business. I could hardly bear it. Finally, Soeur Luci said, "I see you are captivated by this music. Isn't it lovely?"

"Yes. What is it?" I dabbed my eyes.

"Schubert. His second piano trio. The melody in this movement comes from a Swedish Folk song."

"I don't listened to the Romantics much. Sometimes I find them too—I don't know—too..."

"Too close to the bone?"

"Maybe. I'm not sure what it is."

"Perhaps it takes you places you don't wish to go. I think music maps the journey of the soul. And sometimes it uses tears to take you there."

"Oh, I never cry."

"Well, maybe you are finally learning how to do it. It's a great benefit, I think. No one lives long without losing some dear thing, or person, or dream. Tears are balm to sorrow. They water the soul. Without the tears, nothing new can grow. How else would we let go of our grief from sin?"

The intensity of the music grew until it erupted into a monstrous reiteration of the two-note motif. Then the implacable pulse resumed. I needed some distance from everything, Soeur Luci especially.

"I don't believe in sin."

"Moi non plus! What a thing to believe in!" She gave me one of her penetrating looks. "Better to believe in Love. —God is Love." Here she paused to be sure of my attention. "Sin is separation from God. To separate myself from Love! I don't believe in that at all.—So far we agree?"

How could I not? Soeur Luci has such a way of turning things on their heads. "I don't believe that beating oneself up with guilt is a good thing. That's what I mean."

"Be careful, Janine. Guilt may be the thing that helps you find your way back to Love. 'To the gates of the netherworld I shall be consigned for the rest of my years…' You don't want to get stuck there. If you are so far separated from Love, what will bring you back? Guilt is like a dog nipping at your heels. It doesn't feel good, but dogging the lambs until they rest in the fold, that's the goal. Of course, guilt snapping and snarling to no purpose is something else. But even in that instance, something probably needs to be remedied."

The inexorable pulse returned, the heart-wrenching melody breathed a final breath and the music died away, subdued and sad. I felt a sigh rise from somewhere deep inside me.

Soeur Luci stood up. "Come, dinner is ready. This next movement is lighter—see, now we dance. That is good for the digestion." Even so, she turned down the volume, which was a relief.

Dinner was fine. I know I was withdrawn, although I tried to be good company. I also intended to make arrangements to leave Beauvais, but I couldn't bring myself to talk about it. Soeur Luci kept the conversation light and friendly. I excused myself as soon as I properly could and went to bed early and exhausted.

* * *

I dreamed I finally had a visit from Madeleine. It was the strangest thing. She held out her empty hands to me. "This is what you came for." I found something hard and cold in my hands. I didn't want to hold it. It wasn't at all lovely. It was cold and stony, a bit triangular in shape and mostly covered with dry lumps of clay, the sable colour of the soil in that region of the Beauvaisis. And here's the weird part. I began to wash it with tears that started from my breasts. My breasts dripped as they did when my milk first came in for Adam and Kit. The tears miraculously began to wash away the stone leaving only the crusty, dried-up clay that gradually assumed the shape of the stone. I was astonished to feel the weight shift and become live. Not that the crusty old thing became alive itself, but that it was a live weight like the difference between holding a sleeping baby or one that's awake. By this time the tears streamed from my eyes as well and my whole body wept. The clay grew soft, and wet like phlegm. It didn't look pretty at all, but it became so precious, I clasped it to my breast. When I opened my hands to look at it again, it was gone, and my hands were clean.

I woke up. The sun was well into its course and glinting on the window glass. I just wanted to lie there looking at the sky. I didn't want to lose the dream. It made me sad and relieved and sorry and glad all at once. I rested a long time in the dream. I had no idea what it could mean. Finally I got up, determined to tell Soeur Luci about it. I ritually performed my morning ablutions, ate the nose of yesterday's baguette for breakfast, and went down the hall to the sisters' common room.

The door was closed—on the other side, a cello sounding solitary and vestal. I stood listening until the music stopped. I knocked. It felt like a great imposition but I just had to talk to her. Soeur Luci opened the door slightly, and stood there looking mildly annoyed, bow in hand. "Yes?"

"Oh, was that you playing? I'm sorry. I thought it was a recording. I'll come back later."

"What is it, Janine?" She quickly recovered her pastoral tone.

"Just a dream I had," I said, with what I meant to be nonchalance.

"I see. Well, come in then." She opened the door a little wider and motioned me in. I entered and stood hesitantly in the centre of the room. The cello lay on its side next to a straight-backed chair. Soeur Luci laid her bow across it and took her usual place. She patted the seat beside her saying, "Now, sit down and tell me about it."

I told her everything. When I finished she said, "What a beautiful dream." I was grateful for that. The dream was so precious to me. But I couldn't speak. Soeur Luci waited. Finally she asked, "Who is this Madeleine?"

"She's the main character in my story."

"She's quite a lady."

"I don't know why she's even there. She doesn't really do anything. And as I said, her hands were empty."

"And then what happens?"

"I hold something in my hands and I begin to weep."

"But you say you never cry."

"No, I never cry."

"That's strange, isn't it?"

"It's as if she made me cry."

"Hmh. A gift of tears. Do you know about the gift of tears?"

I was stunned. I had found Madeleine after all, and here she was, giving me tears. I thought about her miraculous appearance. I just couldn't figure it out. The more I thought about it, the more confused I got. Soeur Luci sat quietly by. At last I said, "But, it makes no sense."

"Maybe so."

"It's so strange, though. It has such power for me. I don't know why it affects me so deeply." Again we sat in silence. Finally Soeur Luci spoke:

"Have you ever lost a baby?"

"No." *What a question!* "I have never suffered that." Soeur Luci looked kindly at me but it seemed her deep eyes penetrated to the bottom of my soul. Suddenly, I started and caught my breath. I sat staring at nothing, beginning to remember. Soeur Luci leaned over and took my hand. I began to recall a whole history of events and thoughts and feelings that had somehow been quite gone—that I had not remembered all these years. Finally, I answered again. "Yes." And I began to cry. Soeur Luci sat with me, just being there. After awhile, I began to just be too—a little.

Finally she asked, gently. "How did you feel after you lost your baby?"

I tried to remember. "I think I was sad."

"Hmh. Yes. I think you were sad. I can see that. And what else?"

I took a deep breath that shuddered all the way down to my toes. "Angry, I suppose—" It seemed such a simple word for all that feeling I was beginning to recall. "—and resentful, and—" I really didn't

want to say it out loud. I had been so certain I was not depressed.
But I couldn't leave that 'and' unended. "—depressed." Now, as if on
command, all the tears stopped. I sat quiet and dry, recovering my
old self.

"And no one shared your grief?"

"No one."

"And you never nursed this baby at the breast?"

"Never." I stood abruptly to go. "Thank you, Soeur Luci. You are
very kind." I brushed past her, hurried out, and shut the door behind me.

NOTHING

One cried 'God bless us!' and 'Amen' the other...
Listening their fear, I could not say 'Amen!'
When they did say 'God bless us!
. . . .

Wherefore could not I pronounce 'Amen'?
I had most need of blessing, and 'Amen'
Stuck in my throat.

—Shakespeare, *MacBeth*

—*Oh, my God. What have I done?*
Down the hall and around the corner.
—*I had no choice.*
Into my room for my coat and back into the hall. Soeur Luci had taken up her cello again.
—*It's not my fault. I would have been fine with it.*
The fine tenor of Soeur Luci's music followed me down the stairs. It was no comfort.
—*I can't believe I forgot* that. *How could I have forgotten* that?
Out the door. Across the courtyard. Onto rue Jeanne Hachette.
—*It's nothing really. Nothing. I can just get rid of the whole business once and for all. Just forget it again.*
Up to rue des Jacobins.

—*I should never have talked to Soeur Luci. If it weren't for her, I would never have remembered. I wish it would just go away. Oh Lord! Here comes that man again. Dammit. He saw me.*

Head down. Eyes on the curb. Quick. He stands off the sidewalk out of my way. I pass him.

—*Bastard! Why doesn't he just leave me alone? What an idiotic charade.*

Too many people in my way. "Bon appetit!" they say.

—*Why did I come to this graceless place? This would never have happened if I'd just stayed home. It changed everything. It was not supposed to cause me grief. That was the point. It was supposed to liberate me.*

—*Dammit. I will not cry.*

On and on.

—*Endless. This endless ordeal.*

To the cathedral. Up the steps, into the building. To the choir. Past the serene Angadrême.

—*Smug. Not serene. She's smug. So fire can't touch her. Who the hell cares?*

Past the ridiculous men.

—*Hold onto your head, Denis. Don't want to lose it. Certainly not to a woman. Oops. You got bloody fingers. Well, blood happens.*

—*Haven't noticed any Saint James hanging out here lately—I hate Jim.*

Past the Holy Virgin, all the angels and saints, the painting of La Madeleine turning away from the mirror, the iron gates on the chapel.

—*Figures.*

The marble monument to The Maid.

—*Well, at least there's Jeanne. The bishop kneeling at her feet. It's about time.*

—*I have to get out of here.*

Out and down the stairs. It wasn't going away. I was stuck with it now, the horrible, sickening feeling. I prowled the city. *What to do? Nothing to be done. No relief in sight.* I walked around the walls again. I couldn't find them all. I couldn't even remember where they were supposed to be. *What's done is done. And it's all Jim's fault. If he had only asked about me. He didn't even ask how I felt about it. He just made his announcement without a care about how it affected me, or what burden I carried. It should have been his burden too. But he didn't ask. He should have been more forthcoming in the first place. If he had contemplated the priesthood up until he met me, he should have said something to put me on notice.*

—*The greater good. What idiocy. I was such a fool. Talk about privation. Talk about making nothing out of something. That's evil. No question. I was too busy trying to make something out of nothing. Trying not to ruin everything for him. Of course it's his fault. So what if he didn't know about it. He would have if he hadn't been such an ass. If he had cared at all about how I felt.*

—*Dammit. I'm such a doormat. He was so intent and steely eyed when he told me. He wasn't about to change his mind. I could see that. He was trying to tell me without seeing me. What else would you expect? How am I supposed to talk to someone when I'm not even there? That was it. If he had even looked at me once as he had before, as someone he knew and loved, or even someone he knew and used to love, I could have told him.*

—*It's not my fault. It's my right. It's my life. Yeah, my miserable, God-forsaken life.*

I had eaten nothing all day since that nose of the baguette. I began to feel light-headed and sick. The thought of food nauseated me. So many ways to feel sick. I had a caffeine headache. But the idea of sitting in a café with a cup of coffee galled. I sat and shivered awhile on a concrete bench in the square by the station. A recumbent figure on a fountain watched over an empty pool. Of course, the water doesn't run in winter. Finally I walked to St. Etienne's. The church was hardly warmer than outdoors. A priest was hearing confessions. I sat awhile watching the holy sinners waiting their turn. *Maybe I will confess it.*

—*I'm not sorry. I don't give a shit.*

I sat there anyway. When the last penitent had gone, the priest looked out at me. I shook my head and glared back. He left.

I made my way back to Maison Diocésaine. As I walked into the entry off rue Jeanne Hachette, I smelled fire. Dread overwhelmed me. I got a sickening sense in the pit of my stomach. I am terrified of fire.

FIRE

My barn has burned to the ground, I can now see the moon.

—Masahide

I have no memory of my father. I know he travelled a lot for his job. Just before my third birthday, he died in a fiery explosion at an oil well. My memory of the event is a haze, except the words that came around again and again *éclat, feu, incendie, brûler vif.* They still evoke the horror on my mother's face, her crumpled form at the kitchen table. And Gilbert's sobs and violent outbursts. Of course I cried then. But I mostly remember feeling confused and living on the edge of something I couldn't understand.

When I was six, the vacant house next door, by strange coincidence, burned to the ground just weeks before bulldozers were to have leveled it. The owner planned to build a bigger better house on the spot. The fire began about two in the morning. My mother got me and my brother out of bed, pulled on our shoes and jackets, and hustled us outside to the opposite side of the street and left us standing huddled together in the cold spring night, two solemn shivering shadows watching the flames snaking out windows, starting at the loud crackles and the heavy thuds when the joists and rafters gave way. We could see our mother reflected in flickering light, hauling the hose with her as she walked back and forth along the fence line drenching the fence, the roof, the walls as best she could, her resolute profile here and gone, here and gone in the coruscating glow. Sometimes it seemed the shadows would swallow her, that we would lose her to the fire. The words came back again and again—*éclat, feu, incendie, brûler vif*—bang, fire, burning, burnt alive. A hollow fear settled in my stomach. The fire fighters shouted orders to each other above the noise of the inferno. After an eternity, everything was dark and wet, except the sky in the east had filched those fiery reds and oranges and painted the edge of the horizon with them in thick bold strokes. When all but one fire truck had returned to the station, Mom took me and Gil back into the house and tucked us into bed. We each lay awake in our separate solitudes—the thick, dank smell of dead fire haunts me still. Neither Gil nor I went to school that day, and Mom didn't go to work that afternoon either. I have a great deal of respect for fire, for how quickly it consumes.

* * *

I hurried through the arched passageway of Maison Diocésaine to find the fire. I looked up to the window of my room. It was just as I had left it, propped open a little to let in the March air. The smoke in the courtyard was nothing to worry about. It came from a small pile of brush safely burning in the unlocked garden. No one was tending it the moment I entered, but clearly somebody had been doing a little spring cleaning. I stood in the recess of the entry watching it burn until Soeur Luci hurried back to attend it. She poked a few stray branches into the fire, then waited for the fire to burn itself out. Finally she shovelled a bit of dirt over it, tramped around it, brushed her hands together, left the garden, locked the gate, and went inside.

The fire changed everything. I became aware of how hungry I was. I emerged from hiding and went to the staff kitchen to make some supper. I scorched the chicken, undercooked my potatoes, the tomato I sliced into had a black furry core. I ate around the blackness and consumed what I could of a bad meal. Fear supplanted the horror of the afternoon. I could not stop thinking about the fire and worrying that it may smoulder and catch on the creaky wooden building where I sleep.

There was nothing worth doing in my room, and nothing going on anywhere else that I cared to do. I don't know if Soeur Luci went to the little chapel for Evening Prayer. I was not inclined to see her, regardless. I tried to be interested in something, anything I had on hand. I waited to hear Soeur Luci go into her room next door. When her room was quiet and she was safely settled, I carefully opened my door. There was no light from the crack under Soeur Luci's door. Her lamp was off. I tiptoed down the hall, walking close to the rafters where there is a little less movement in the floor boards, less squeaking. I went into the shower and wasted water. If you're wet enough, you won't burn. I took a long time. Someone, most likely one of the students, used the bathroom next door. I don't know if she was waiting for the shower. I didn't really care. In my own good time I turned off the water and found my towel. I dripped down the hall, close to the rafters, got to my room and put on my nightshirt—just the thing to have on in case of fire. Long sleeves, good coverage, but nothing to constrain movement. Then quietly, so as not to disturb Soeur Luci, I packed up all my books, all the documents and pamphlets I had collected, my passport, my return ticket, my money, my exposed film and photos, my notes and the whole story as far as I had gotten, into my knapsack and book bag and set them by the door. I made certain the straps were arranged in such a way that I could grab them without confusion. I didn't worry about the suitcases. Too much to move in a hurry. Beside my bags I placed my walking shoes, laces untied and the tongue far back to make them easy to put on in a hurry in the dark. I draped my coat across the bags, near the straps, but out of the way of the shoes. Then, I turned on the faucet to a dribble to keep Soeur Luci's plumbing quiet on the opposite side of the wall. I brushed my teeth.

I slipped in between the sheets, put my travel alarm within reach under the bed so the time would pass unmeasured by the tick, tick, tick. I turned off the light and looked into the darkness outside my window. I turned on the lamp again, silently slid out of bed, went to the closet and took my nearly-new jeans from the shelf. No sense in being left without a thing to wear. I tucked them into the space at the top of my knapsack, went to bed, and eventually slept.

I awoke at 5:15 to go down the hall to the bathroom again. Back in bed, I could not sleep. Feeling miserable, I tried to find some-thing enchanting to think about, just to help me settle. I could think of nothing. My bags still at the ready, I was unable to escape even into sleep. At 6:00, I heard Soeur Luci getting up next door. She tiptoed around the room, careful not to disturb me, I suppose. She turned her tap to a dribble to brush her teeth. I finally drifted off.

Next thing I remember, someone was pounding on my door "There's a fire! Come quickly, the plane is taking off." I jumped up, grabbed my bag, raced down the hallway and down several flights of stairs. The door at the bottom opened directly onto the tarmac. Breathlessly, I scrambled up the gangway. I got into the aircraft, found my seat, looked out the window. There, beside the tarmac, in front of an ancient building, sat Soeur Luci on a beautifully carved chair. Beside her was another chair, not so regal, but clearly part of the set. I rolled down my window and urgently called to her to come. She smiled a radiant smile and answered, "I do enjoy a good fire. Come! I have a place for you here." She patted the seat of the chair beside her.

"I can't. I don't want to get burned."

By now immense tongues of flame were licking her on every side. Soeur Luci just sat there beaming. She was in her element.

I quickly rolled up the window and prepared for take-off. I opened my bag to unpack it. In the bag were a few old nuns' habits, somebody's worn running shoes that were too small for me and a couple of plastic trophies like the ones they hand out to five-year-olds at soccer tournaments. I had escaped with the wrong bag. I hurried back to the door. It was bolted shut. I stood banging on the door "Let me out, let me out! I have to rescue my story!"

I woke up, my heart beating wildly. I looked around the room. Outside, a noisy garbage truck, grinding and tamping its load. Inside, my bags, packed and ready at the door, the story safely tucked within. I had escaped the fire, or so I thought. I should have been comforted by this. Instead I began to fear the fire would come another time unanticipated—with my bags unpacked and my papers strewn around the room. No need to worry. I was already burning.

SHADOWS

"Where is the Old Man of the Fire?" she said.

"Here I am," answered the child… "What can I do for you?"

There was such an awfulness of absolute repose on the face of the child that Tangle stood dumb before him. He had no smile, but the love in his large grey eyes was as deep as the center. And with the repose there lay on his face a shimmer as of moonlight, which seemed as if any moment it might break into such a ravishing smile as would cause the beholder to weep himself to death.

But the smile never came, and the moonlight lay there unbroken. For the heart of the child was too deep for any smile to reach from it to his face.

"Are you the oldest man of all?" Tangle at length, although filled with awe, ventured to ask.

"Yes, I am. I am very, very old. I am able to help you, I know. I can help everybody."

And the child drew near and looked up in her face so that she burst into tears.

"Can you tell me the way to the country the shadows fall from?" she sobbed.

—George MacDonald, *The Golden Key*

I felt weak, too weak to get out of bed. I lay there shivering, thinking about yesterday, trying to hang on to all the good things in my life that were now changed forever. I will say it again. I have lived a blessed life. Two beloved sons, a wonderful mother, a dear brother, good friends, good fortune, and, as far as husbands go, I could do worse, as Denise says. But I have spent all this time wondering about, wanting—something else—instead of embracing the something I already have—or had. And now I have the something else. Of course, the rest is still there. It's just me that's changed. I am someone different. I am someone different from what I have pretended to be. I have been living a lie. I tried to sleep.

* * *

A woman is standing beside my bed, talking, patting my shoulder. "Wake up, Janine. Janine? Can you hear me?" I groan. "There you are. How do you feel?"

"Mmmm." *Leave me alone.*

"Janine, open your eyes."

I strain to focus. A round, brown face. White smiling teeth. Inquiring eyes. My eyes fall shut again.

"Janine, look at me."

I try to look up to her face. Too hard to do. My eyes settle on her name tag. "Green."

"Good. That's right, Janine. I'm Mrs. Green."

"Just let me sleep."

"Janine, I need to know if you are coming around. Can you open your eyes again?"

I do. Her image fades away. I try again. Madeleine Green, the name tag says.

"Good, Janine. I am going home now. The night nurse will be in soon."

"Uh hm."

"I probably won't see you again, Janine. Try to be careful. You can deny life in one place, and sure enough it comes bubbling up in another. Life wants a 'yes'. It will find you, dear. Don't let me see you back here."

* * *

Well, that's over. Of course, it wasn't. I thought I would feel some relief at first. It was just over. It did not make me happy. I believed it was a good. It wasn't at all. It was evil. A big nothing. More nothing than anything else I've ever known. And when you live out of that experience of nothing, the something in your life gets sucked into a void. That isn't to say that something becomes nothing. Not at all. The something is the reality that casts the shadow that by the grace of God redeems life from the grave. The something carries you to the other side, over the abyss. I have known the grace of something in my life. Here in France, certainly. And my whole life at home. Still, the something loses radiance because of the nothing. Not the radiance of its reality, the radiance perceptible to me. Sin fractures the vision, not the fact. That's how Auden puts it. The facts are everywhere, the realities, and the light. I just couldn't see them anymore. And soon I couldn't remember why.

* * *

Both ends of the woolen blankets the sisters lent me are embroidered "MM" in large blue capitals. For a while I puzzled about this. The sisters don't know what it stands for. The blankets were here before they were. Maison something I suppose. Maison Diocésaine would be MD. Aumonerie begins with A. After awhile, I decided it would stand for Mary Magdalene because she kept disappearing—the only evidence of the church once named for her in Beauvais is the street name; Jeanne d'Arc now occupies the chapel originally endowed as the chapel of la Madeleine. People still don't know what to do with her. Legend identifies her with the woman who washed the feet of Jesus with her tears, because "her sins were many."

So she was a sinner. One legend says she was a prostitute. Prostitution inverts pride and wealth and power to self-loathing, poverty, powerlessness. It's probably easier to repent those things. The problem with prostitution is it separates an act of love from love. If she had lived today, I'll bet she would have had an abortion at some time or other before she saw the light. Whatever it was, La

Madeleine repented and when she wept she made room for love. Whatever else you can say about her, Magdalene had the fire of love.

Well, good for her. I'm no Mary Magdalene. I don't have her kind of fire. I'm not sure I love anybody that way. When it comes to me, fire just burns. My logical defenses, my disingenuous pretenses are burning. There's no gold to refine. If it doesn't stop, there will be nothing left but ashes. Well, bully for you, Augustine. You say moral evil is to choose a lesser good at the expense of a greater good. Who would have thought it was a greater good to say, "Sorry buddy, you're a real father now." Physical evil is nature falling short of its own inclination. Well, I was inclined to let Jim go since he wanted to—not to confuse the issue for him. Was that so bad? I chose the higher good—not my own good, but to honour Jim's vocation. Besides, there would be no support for me or the child any other way. Maybe it was pride after all—not choosing to be married to someone who would otherwise not have me. I just couldn't see any way around it. I started to cry. I don't seem to know how to stop it anymore.

I had a headache. It was probably getting close to noon. Time to pull myself together, get some coffee and a little fresh air. It was after eleven when I got to the staff kitchen. I made a weak cup of coffee with the last grounds of the bag. I haven't shopped in two days. I ate some stale bread, oily cheese and a boiled egg. It was tough and rubbery. I cradled my aching head in my arms and slumped on the table. I was crying again. *Oh God, let this pass.*

After some time I became aware of Soeur Luci, standing soundless beside me. I just couldn't lift my head to acknowledge her. She caressed my forehead.

"Tu pleur comme une madeleine."

"What?" I lifted my head.

"You weep like a Madeleine. You seem to have learned how to cry."

I thought she meant the Madeleine of my dream. Well, it's all the same.

"Come. You can't stay here. It will soon be noon. Let me make you a real cup of coffee."

I pulled myself up. Soeur Luci took my arm and led me across the courtyard. The lock to the residence opened readily. The stairs did all the talking as we climbed. We entered the common room. Soeur Luci shut the door behind her and motioned me to a chair. She put coffee on. I was more or less okay until she gave me my perfectly constituted cup of coffee and sat down beside me. Then I just lost it. I shook so much as I sobbed that Soeur Luci took the cup from my hand and set it on the side table. The coffee was no longer hot when I finally took a sip and looked into her quiet eyes.

"Your heart is broken."

I drank some more. It was still good. I wanted to finish it before it was cold. It seemed such a long time since I had lived in the world of upholstered chairs and easy conversation. For a moment I contemplated enjoying that cup of coffee and just carrying on as I have all these years. In my broken heart I knew that to be impossible. Soeur Luci put down her cup, leaned back, folded her hands and settled in her chair. I don't know where she finds the time.

I took a deep breath. "About that lost baby…"

The remarkable thing about Soeur Luci—she is never scandalized. She makes her observations, sometimes pithy, often extravagant, but never prescriptive. I told her everything. About how much I was in love with Jim, about how we were planning our future, how he went home for Christmas and after that everything changed. About how when he told me he would be a priest he was so direct and unfeeling and I was stunned and didn't tell him my news. And how I took care of everything without anybody being the wiser so things could go on as if nothing had happened. And how in a way it seems they did. Except I don't know how I managed to suppress it so thoroughly. And how at the same time it hounded me and made me its creature. I covered my eyes with my hands as if to block the vision, as if to stop the tears.

After some time, Soeur Luci said, "It's been a long journey, hasn't it."

I nodded and took in a deep shuddering breath, the way children do after a long, crying spell.

"And now you begin to take yourself home."

"I don't know about that. I feel as though everything is lost forever."

"Hmm. Only a few days ago you didn't think you had lost anything." She paused. "You can't recover something that doesn't exist. The first task is to find the shadow. You've done that. God forgives. Now you can follow the shadow to the place where its substance stands in the light, in the radiant mercy of God."

"I just can't figure out what that could be. I can't see anything good in all this. There is nothing to cast the shadow."

"It's your goodness, Janine, and your sorrow. You are inclined to love. But you confused comfort and ease with love. You tried to make both Jim and yourself comfortable. So for all these years you have been avoiding the love and forgiveness that will bring you back to the perfect human being you are called to be. You have had a lot of work to do, but see how far you have come. You have found what you came to discover."

"Oh no—I think I came here to escape it."

"Sometimes the heart has to beguile the mind in order to do the work. You brought your burden with you when you came. It was on your face the day I opened the gate to you." She smiled. "I even thought you may have exceeded the weight allowance for your flight. —Well then! I think we should have something to eat."

I was hungry. No question, I felt lighter and began to notice the normal pangs of living in the world again. Soeur Luci was already coaxing some delectables into a sauce pan. I thought about how thoroughly colonized I have been all these years by that abortion. I was so afraid to face it. And I never allowed myself to grieve the death, the loss, the shame, much less repent and confess it. Instead, I suffered a chronic dysphoria, a veiled depression that left me continually dissatisfied with so much of my life. I looked for someone to take the blame and mostly settled on Miles. Not that Miles has been a picnic to live with. He seems to invite hostility. He left me to deal with the demands of children and seemed to diminish the value of anything I tried to do. But I never gave him the benefit of the doubt either. No, it isn't all Miles's fault. I kept my distance. I think I always reserved a part of myself for Jim and the child, my aborted family, a feeble attempt to compensate for what I had done. Miles as good as said so the day after Jim's visit. I just didn't get it. And I married Miles partly because he wasn't Jim, then spent the better part of our marriage resenting him because of that. As a result, each of us sidestepped occasions for friendship with each other while happily welcoming other people into our lives. We needed a buffer to make us kind, which is why we got along better when Marilee and Jessica came to stay with us.

* * *

It was such a relief to tell everything to Soeur Luci. After lunch I took a long walk. The weather was mild, the air balmy. When I returned, I watched for Soeur Luci and went to Evening Prayer with her. That night I dreamt that I approached the throne of Grace—Grace was wrapped in light, as in a robe.

"Oh, my goodness," said Grace, "it's you!"

"Oh, Grace, I'm not your Goodness."

"Oh, but you are." Grace opened her arms and drew me to herself. I finally rested there.

COMMUNION

I thought I would feel better when I woke up. I do feel different. I am no longer sad. What I feel now is more akin to sorrow. It is not nameless. There's something redemptive in that. I have stopped worrying about what is wrong with me. Instead, I am thinking about my first pregnancy and what the child would have been like. I think she would have been a girl. She would have been different, at any rate, from Adam and Kit. They are already so different from each other. Adam is like his father—matter-of-fact, a person of few words. Kit is more likely to get caught up in the moment and rattle on about whatever comes to mind. I am often like that. I wonder if she would have been reflective or exuberant. She would have been both. I'm sure of it. I wonder about all that potential I willed into non-being. I wonder if it found expression some other way. I wonder if she is here somehow. Maybe in the air, or the rain, or the ground. I wish I could connect with her. Maybe she's in the mistletoe—uninvited but looking for life. I am so sorry.

* * *

I have never gone to Morning Prayer with the sisters. It would mess up the coordination of my breakfast timing in the staff kitchen. But I went today. I listened for Soeur Luci's steps in the hallway and got to the door just as she was closing it.

"Good. I am not alone. Come in."

I barely followed along. I sat there letting it wash over me. I wonder if Soeur Luci sings the hymns and psalms out loud when no one is there. I wouldn't. I suspect she does. But then, she has this beautiful voice. I'm sure God would miss it if she didn't. As for me, I mostly listen.

"Rends-moi la joie de ton salut." *Give me again the joy of your help.*

Joy. I have no memory of joy. —That's what I'll call her, my little girl. Joy. I am deprived of joy. —Deprivation. By the grace of God, I will heal. I think that's possible now. And some day I may be capable of joy. Amen. So be it.

I took breakfast with Soeur Luci. I finally made arrangements to go. I will leave Beauvais on Wednesday and go to Paris via Chantilly. That allows time for a farewell visit with La Perle and La Belle and I will still have a week to see Paris. Soeur Luci recommended a *pension* in the city centre that takes short-term guests. I asked her what to do about Jim.

"Should I tell him?"

"That's for you to decide. Will it make it better?"

"I don't know. I've carried it alone for so long."

"When will you see him again?"

"Possibly never. I have his address in Toronto. I have a three-hour stopover. I could call him then."

"And tell him by phone?"

"I guess that's a little insensitive, isn't it."

"It would be better to talk face-to-face with him. Or write a letter."

"Do I have to tell him?"

"Whatever is needed. You will know. You haven't said anything for twenty years. It can wait awhile longer. Take your time."

"He asked me to send a postcard from Beauvais. I can do that. I can tell him when I will be in Toronto. If he decides to come see me at the airport, maybe I will tell him then."

"Maybe so."

* * *

I have a lot to do. I called the *pension* in Paris and made a reservation. I called the airline to confirm my departing flight. Then I wrote a postcard to Jim. I tried to be proper since it will probably pass through several hands before it reaches his.

Dear Father Jim,

I have spent nearly three months here in Beauvais. The diocesan house has been the ideal place to stay. Thanks so much for lining that up for me. The trip has been fruitful, if not in the ways I anticipated. I will be coming home on Wednesday of Holy Week. My flight lands in Toronto at 11:15. I have a three-hour stopover but will have to clear customs first. I will try to call you at your office to say hello and tell you about my trip. I know you likely have other commitments, so if you can't be in to take my call, I understand.

God bless,
Janine

I wrote individual postcards to everyone in my family too. They are still asleep in Flatfield. I will have to wait until 8:00am Flatfield time to phone home. I am suddenly so lonesome for them, all of them. How could I have thought of going away for such a long time? Maybe I shouldn't go to Paris. I can go home tomorrow. I called the airline. The longer I spent talking, the more complicated and expensive it got. So I will go to Paris. That's probably for the best. I need to say goodbye to La Perle and La Belle anyway.

I mailed the postcards. I can't undo that now. I may end up telling Jim. I signed the one to Miles—"Miss you, Janine." I was trying to be friendly. I didn't say "Love" because I'm just not sure. I don't want him to make too much of it. Now I wonder if he will make more of the "miss you" than he would of anything else. I signed the others "Love." If I had signed them all "miss you" that would have been better. More generic. Well, what's done is done.

Beauvais is a beautiful city after all. It is raining again today, but I don't mind it. Spring must have come in the night. Everywhere there are shoots and buds, the trees are greening. The flower shops have set out positively lavish displays. I bought a huge bouquet for Soeur Luci. I stopped in at a little crêperie café off Place des Halles. I had a lemon crêpe. We sat watching the rain dripping down the window glass, me and the flowers. I'm doing what Soeur Luci does, talking to flowers. Perhaps it comes from spending a lot of time alone. You take your companions where you find them.

I went back to St. Etienne's. I am not so angry anymore. I sat awhile with Wilgeforte. Odd how it affected me, seeing her hanging there, not for love of me, but for the love of God—if there's a difference—and here's me, just making my way as if nothing ever separated me from life. But it's just not so. I should say *nothing* separated me from *my* life, which is more true when you think about nothing. I tucked a small bloom from Soeur Luci's bouquet by the red nail holes in Wilgeforte's feet.

On to Sainte Angadrême. In my case, her protection backfired. Well, thanks for the fire, I guess. A flower for her too. Just then the priest walked by. He must have been praying somewhere. I hadn't noticed him. I nodded to acknowledge him, and tried not to look like the person who glared at him two days before. *Surely I don't have to go to confession now. I told the whole story to Soeur Luci. That was cathartic. The redemptive cure, the wine and oil, is already poured into the wound, the remedy applied. I'm sure Soeur Luci will agree.*

I can't leave the church without a visit to Our Lady of Joy, the fifteenth-century statue of Mary, the Christ Child, and the dove he holds by the wing. Definitely one of the little roses belongs here. Light from the jewelled windows blushes with pleasure at the offering.

Outside the rain subsides. A hint of sunshine steals out from the hanging clouds. I walk toward the River Therain and turn onto the Pont de Paris. I throw a small sweet bloom into the water for Joy. I throw one for Innocence too, and one for Luci's Yves, while I am at it. It is her bouquet after all. On my way back to Maison Diocésaine I pass the place the Church of the Madeleine used to be and leave a flower there. I should get these flowers to Soeur Luci before they are all a memory.

* * *

You wouldn't know anything was missing from the bouquet. A bouquet is just a collection of perfection. Give or take a few flowers and it's still exactly what a bouquet should be. I filled a pitcher from the staff kitchen with water and took the bouquet to Soeur Luci's office. She was delighted. I told her I had been to the church and wondered about confession.

"It seems entirely unnecessary now. I wouldn't say anything to the priest that I haven't said to you."

"That's true. What could you possibly say?"

"So then, I have already been to confession. And God forgives. What more could I want?"

"Yes, God forgives. Do you want the blessing of the Church?"

"What's the difference?"

"The church is also your faith community."

"So you mean I should play by their rules?"

"No, I mean you have to decide how much you want to participate in that community."

"I didn't make the rules. I think someone who never spoke with a woman made this one. I would never have got this far if it depended on telling my story to a priest."

"I'm not saying the arrangement is ideal. I am saying it is the way it is."

"Well, I'm not up to it. I am already brought so low. I just can't do it."

"No one expects you to do more than you are able, least of all, me." She touched my shoulder.

"Well, thank you for that. I'll let you get back to work now."

"Very well. And thank you for the beautiful flowers. Would you like to join me for a bowl of soup this evening?"

"Yes, I would like that. I will buy bread and wine, I'm going out anyway."

"Oh, thank you. That will be good. —I will see you later then."

* * *

I step back into the courtyard, cross to the main doors, walk out onto rue de la Madeleine and head away from my earlier trek to the little garden square by the train station. I sit again on the stone bench and watch ripples forming from the drips falling as an afterthought of the morning's showers. There is water in the pool now, thanks to the rain. I have nothing to do until supper except find a nice wine to go with it. I don't need to go to confession to a priest. I, of all people. I know about these things. Soeur Luci is a lot like Gertrude the Great, really. Think about Jim's paper, about how in the vision Christ touched the tongue of Saint Gertrude and confirmed every word she may speak on his behalf. And then there was the debate among theologians about confessing to a layman, and Martin V's Bull in 1418 that sealed the deal against it. So, if I had confessed as I have to Soeur Luci in 1417, I would be more or less okay, if irregular, even in the eyes of the church, or else God help the poor souls who mistakenly died before 1418.

—I should go get the bread and wine.
—It's been a long time since I took communion. I would really like to take communion again. And do it here, in Beauvais, as close to Soeur Luci and Madeleine and Joy as I have ever been.
—I suppose I should go to confession.
No.
I can, in clear conscience, take communion without that.
—I'd better go shopping. I don't want to come running in at the last minute again.
—It's not even three o'clock. There's no rush. But I should get to the épicerie before all the baguettes are gone.
—Maybe I'll go to St. Etienne's for a few minutes.
—I have never taken communion in France. I will take communion on Sunday. That will be a fitting finish to the quest.
—I am feeling sad.

*   *   *

I went to St. Etienne's. As my luck would have it, the priest was hearing confessions. It is Lent, after all. I had wanted to pray in peace. Mercifully, penitents were few. Only three waited. I bowed my head and ignored them. I closed my eyes, prayed a psalm and rehearsed over and over why it should not be necessary. *Bless me, Father, I am sad again.* I looked up as the last penitent was leaving. The priest avoided my eyes. I stood up quickly. "Pardon, mon père—"

I don't know how that happened. I confessed everything, including being sad. It did not take nearly so long the second time. At the end I heaved a sigh and sat silent.

"C'est tous?"

Is that all? Isn't that enough? I've carried this over twenty years and you ask if that's all. "Oui. C'est tous."

*   *   *

I got back with the bread and wine in good time. I called home to Flatfield. Mom was still asleep, Miles already off to work. It was so good to talk to Adam and Kit, I could hardly bear it. I gave them my flight number and my ETA. They both talked excitedly about their daily goings on. I couldn't tell if they miss me. I can't believe I left them for this long. When I hung up, I wept for love of them.

* * *

A haunting melody sounded from the stereo as I entered the common room. Soeur Luci was chopping and cajoling vegetables by the stove. I set the bread and wine on the counter beside her.

"Oh, thank you."

"My pleasure." I hovered, trying to figure out if there was something useful I could do. Soeur Luci swept the vegetables into a pile. Finally I said, "Well, I went to confession."

Soeur Luci gathered up the chopped vegetables and dropped them into a simmering broth. She brushed her hands on her apron and looked sidelong at me. "You did? At St. Etienne's?"

"Yes."

I waited to see what she would have to say about it. She took a small sprig of tarragon and a bunch of parsley, minced them together and set them aside. She didn't seem to think further comment was needed.

"I thought you listened to chant and passion music on Fridays. This sounds like cello and orchestra."

"It is chant, in a way. The melody is based on the *Kol Nidre*, a Jewish chant for the Day of Atonement."

"Oh, I see." *Should have known.* I waited again but she didn't speak. Finally I couldn't bear it. "I don't think it made any difference, going to confession."

"You don't?"

"No."

"What did you expect to happen?"

"I don't know. It seemed almost mechanical."

"And he prescribed penance?"

"Only a few prayers."

"But you will do all you can."

"Exactly."

"Then leave the rest to God."

She stirred the soup then handed me plates and bowls to set on the table. I couldn't drop the subject. "I think the 'Inter cunctas' of 1418 missed the mark. Maybe people were making excuses and not seeking forgiveness in good faith. But I'm sure there have always been holy women like you who truly are confessors."

"Pardon me, but what is the 'Inter cunctas' of 1418?"

"The pope's—Bull—I don't know what you call it in French— that confessions must be made through a priest."

"I see." She arranged silverware at our places, then stopped, held up her hand, "Wait" and closed her eyes. The melody in the cello made a little skip, a little sparkle in a plaintive landscape then continued on more hopefully. "Oh, I'm such a Romantic." Soeur Luci smiled. "Now, where were we?"

"I was talking about how holy women serve as confessors."

"Certainly some have been confessors of sorts. La Belle knows of one here in Beauvais."

"Besides you?"

"Ma foi! No. Not anyone who is alive at present. I mean there is a legend of such a woman from Beauvais."

"There is? When did she live?"

"Oh, I don't know. You'll have to ask La Belle about that."

* * *

I had not expected to hear about her again. Not that I had any reason to believe this woman was Madeleine. I set the idea aside and enjoyed my time with Soeur Luci. Today, I can't help but wonder. It has made a long day, waiting for La Belle's return.

I went to church to pray my penance. It seems such a little thing to do. *But you will do all you can.* That's what Soeur Luci said. And there's really nothing else I can do except offer up my broken heart to God. I can have no regrets now. I cannot undo what's done. Even if I could undo it, it would unravel the lives of so many others. I doubt Miles would have married me. My sons would not exist, at least not as I know them now. I would be a different person too. Would I be better? Possibly. Or tired and resentful and trampled. Or hardworking with practical wisdom and good sense like my mother.

I'll bet that woman is Madeleine. Here I had just decided she was a full-flowered figment of an overwrought imagination, and she shows up again, where the shadows come from, where I finally stand in the light. I wonder why she—of all possibilities—presents herself to me. I have begun to think of her as a manifestation of grace. Sometimes when I think of her, I see Soeur Luci. I'm sure they are much alike. Madeleine's gift of tears took the weak and dying to a place where they could finally let go and offer up their sorrow and pain and repentance. Which is why I needed her. I couldn't seem to get there on my own. And Soeur Luci there to shine a light on the path, and calm my fears about following it. I don't know that I'm happier. In some ways, I feel more sorrow than I have ever known—not only for my foolish logic and my life-denying choice, but for my lack of presence to all the gifts of love that surround me. Here, on the other side, there is a new brightness and definition to life. At last I can see that.

* * *

It is just as well I confessed to a priest. For me, the most sacramental moment came at the end of my story when Soeur Luci said "God forgives." But the current dispensation does not recognize such a moment. So I will pray that someday they do, that God will turn their hearts. Or maybe an Act of God will take care of it—a lightening bolt or something. In the meantime, the point of confession is to restore things to a right relationship—with God and your community, especially those closest to you—which is why reconciliation is so necessary. Well, these are my people. I haven't made excuses. However inadequate the forms, I will not diminish them further by pretending they are meaningless. I have more to set right, mostly with Miles, which will be difficult, and maybe with Jim. But tomorrow, I will take communion.

NOW THEN

life is more true than reason will deceive
(more secret or than madness did reveal)
deeper is life than lose: higher than have
. . . .
futures are obsolete, pasts are unborn

—e.e. cummings, *1x1–LII*

I went alone to the late mass. I didn't see any face I know, except the priest's. I went up for communion. Of course, the tears came again. I do hope I settle down before I get home to Flatfield. I haven't seen the Soeurs Béatrices all day, but they are back. I don't know when they had Evening Prayer. Whenever it was, I missed it. It may have been eight o'clock when Soeur Luci tapped on my door. I am invited for a farewell supper Tuesday evening.

Today was my last Monday in Beauvais. I spent the day with train schedules and banking and taking pictures of places I want to remember. I went to the museum with new eyes. I was particularly drawn to a fire wagon from Madeleine's era—a boxed metal cart that carried live coals from place to place to restore fires that have gone out. I took pictures of some fifteenth-century carvings—of an armed man, of a monkey and a fool mixing mustard, and of the dogs and thistles on mouldings from the Church of the Madeleine.

I miss my family. I wish I had been less hostile to Miles when I left. I wonder how his classes are going. They should be wrapping up soon. I'm not sure that was such a good idea. I hope Miles knows the difference between loving a new interest and a new love interest. I hope he is looking at the moon and not the finger pointing to it. Of course it was a good idea. I've never given him anything like that before. It was a good instinct, to affirm something that lay buried under his heartless defences. I'm not such a bad wife.

*   *   *

I think Aline has gone home, at least until after Easter. She mentioned her plans awhile back. I will write a note to say goodbye and slip it under her door. I never told her I would be leaving. It seemed impossible at the time. This hall where I write is even quieter with her gone. The phantom students must also be away. At any rate, no one seems to venture past my door in this long hallway anymore. The creaks only whisper now. I wonder if the sisters like it better this way.

Somehow I managed to miss Evening Prayer again. I had hoped at least to do that today. However regular the sisters may be, they are not predictable. Usually they pray before supper, but I guess it depends on the day's events and what time they decide to eat. Well, I will go tomorrow for sure. I don't know how I managed to keep so busy all these weeks. I have nothing to do. I feel like I am treading water, waiting to begin again. I am not living happily ever after. I need to learn how to be living *now*. It will be so good to go home.

*   *   *

I spent all day Tuesday getting ready for dinner. I bought wine and a bouquet for the sisters. I wrote each of them a note of appreciation. I probably spent two hours figuring out what to say to Soeur Luci. How do you say thanks for making me uncomfortable—off-balance enough to make me finally fall into the abyss? I did the best I could. It was a little easier to thank her for helping me get to the other side.

La Perle and La Belle greeted me warmly when I arrived for Evening Prayer. I was glad to see them again. We sang heartily in the fullness of our restored ranks. With our amens, we withdrew to the common room. Of course Tuesday is Soeur Luci's day to cook so there was music—but not so loud as to drown a lively account of the Soeurs Béatrices' journey—and Soeur Luci pum-pumming at the stove. I will miss this spirited trio. I hope some day I come back for a visit.

The meal was as sumptuous as any holy person is likely to eat in the last week of Lent. It's always that way when Soeur Luci cooks, even though it's mostly pulses and vegetables. When we finished the first rush of serving and tasting and murmuring appreciation, I asked La Belle about the holy woman confessor Soeur Luci had spoken of.

"Dear old Madame Conteoise, such a woman! With every visit she had something to tell. I believe she knew the name of every family that ever lived in this region since the siege. Who knows what stories died with her? Peace to her memory!" La Belle stopped to chew a crusty bit of bread. La Perle passed a dish of morels and leeks to me. I took a second helping.

"This is so good. If I thought you had a recipe, I would ask for it, Soeur Luci."

"Mushrooms are always good," she shrugged, "there's nothing to know about it."

"So she says—" La Perle added, "but really, she means she can't explain it."

"Just as I thought." I passed the plate to Soeur Luci. "Have some more. I recommend it!" She smiled at the compliment but set the plate down. "And so, La Belle, what do you know about this woman?"

"Well, Madame Conteoise often spoke of a wealthy widow in the time of the Jeannes—you know, Jeanne d'Arc and Jeanne Hachette. She made her home a hospice for the desolate and sick and dying, people without any means or family to care for them, many of them vagabonds. She would care for them and hear their stories and weep with them."

Somehow I was not surprised. I looked over at Soeur Luci in time to see a wave of recognition cross her face. La Belle went on:

"But it was a terrible time you know—the long years of war and the epidemics—so many suffered. Beauvais was often cut off from commerce with other cities and her fields reduced to rubble because of the violence of men-at-arms and renegades and fleecers. Many times the lady would send for a priest to hear a confession and give the final sacraments. But the priests also suffered losses. After the old parish priest died, she sent to the cathedral, but no one would come to such a place for fear of the pestilence. She did what she could to help heal their bodies and souls, and to bless them. But when they needed a confessor, she could only listen and assure them of the forgiveness of God. Unfortunately, there was at least one canon in Beauvais who frowned on this.

"Do you know her name?"

"I don't really remember. It will come to me. Her family was in textiles—that's not unusual for this place. Anyway, Madame Conteoise told me the lady's story was published in the end—one of the first hundred or so books printed in France, she would have me believe! Except, all but one copy were confiscated and burned by this zealous canon. Can you imagine that! It sounds a little apocryphal to me. There was a report that one copy travelled with minstrels to England where it was translated more than a century later. But Madame Conteoise believed everything burned in the Great Fire of London."

"The story doesn't seem to be able to escape the fire. Why's that? Maybe it isn't meant to survive." I mostly wanted to find out what La Belle thought of it.

"Oh, no. I think it is just the opposite. The story will not be suppressed, no matter how hard some may try to do it. When she was dying, I visited Madame Conteoise every day. On my last visit we had such a beautiful time together, even though she often fell into confusion. We were expecting the priest to come to hear her last confession when she said, 'Sister, I have told you everything. But

I do not wish to put your story in danger. So we will wait for the priest.' It seemed odd that she should speak in such a way. It was her own story that she told, after all. I could tell Madame Conteoise wanted to say something more but she hesitated. She would begin to speak and then stop. She became restless, first asking me to stay with her no matter what happened then telling me to go quickly, before I was discovered. For awhile, I thought she would lose her spirit."

"She was dying of course."

"Yes, but I mean she would go mad. I finally realized why she was anxious for me. As she saw it, I now carried her story. She worried that it may do me harm. While she was fading in and out of consciousness she was confusing me with this Madame Mouton— that was her name!"

"Madame Mouton. Yes, I know of her."

"You do! How can that be?"

"Probably in much the same way as Madame Conteoise knew of her."

"Oh, I don't think so. You are far more rational than she ever was."

"I hope not. I am just learning how to let the story be, and not worry so much about facts or losing my mind. The Madame Mouton I know of was born Madeleine de Brout. Mouton is her husband's name. I came to Beauvais to see if I could find anything more about her." La Belle was astonished, La Perle sat forward with a quizzical look on her face, but Soeur Luci propped her chin in her hand as she so often does, leaned back and nodded slowly, seeming hardly surprised at all. Of course, Soeur Luci already knew of Madeleine's appearance in my dream—this character in my supposed novel.

In a short time we pieced together all we know about Madeleine. I am satisfied. In fact, once I understood the grace of her presence in my own story, my preoccupation with the details of Madeleine's story receded. The details are simply an appendix to the truth about Madeleine—that her story brought me to a place where I could be reconciled to my own story and reconciled to Love again. That is why the whole business became so desperate and urgent for me.

I told them everything I know about the beginning of the story and the way Madeleine came to marry Jacques and how it was Jacques met his death. La Belle was delighted with some of the particulars in my account—dicing for the *oublie*, Jacques's encounter with the preaching friar, and the turning Wheel of Fortune. She knew nothing about Madeleine from before the time she established her hospice, took in La Pauvrette, and adopted La Pauvrette's little newborn. She did not know how Canon Guy, who was nameless to Madame Conteoise, came to have a place in the pages of Madeleine's book. She did not know Jean Etienne was Madeleine's son by the canon. But she knew a great deal about Madeleine's last days.

This is what I know from La Belle. All Madeleine's daughters married except the youngest who made final vows as a nun. Jean Etienne became a canon himself, received a prebend in Beauvais, and lived near the cathedral. La Belle and I wonder whether he ever knew who his biological father was. Surely he read his mother's story.

Jacques Lucien, Madeleine's oldest son by Jacques, married and had children. On his father's death he took charge of the family enterprise and cared for his mother and his widowed half-sister, Marie-Josephte, in the family home. Madeleine's adopted son, P'tit Beau, who was known to Madame Conteoise as Thibeau, was an uneasy assistant to his brother. The family interests were doing well but did not require two men to manage them. La Belle suspects that Thibeau may not have cared for the work and had some of his birth parents' tendency to rootlessness. He always had a great fascination with the theatre. According to La Belle, Madeleine did take in troupes of players from time to time. One troupe, performing for their hosts as a payment for hospitality, gave Thibeau a small role in one of their productions. Thibeau got a taste for acting and was ready to join the troupe. Although Madeleine successfully dissuaded him the first time, this same troupe returned years later, when Beauvais was slowly recovering from the devastation and desolation of the war. It happened in 1472, when Burgundy was on the march and headed toward Beauvais, Thibeau, still single and now into his late forties or early fifties, said goodbye to his brothers and his mother, took a copy of her newly printed story on the pretext of getting it translated and published in England, and set out with the troupe, travelling northwest to the shores of the English channel at Dieppe, thus avoiding an encounter with Charles le Téméraire.

. Then the siege. All the able-bodied citizens of Beauvais rose to the city's defence. Madeleine was old and ill and kept to her bed. Jacques Lucien and the older grandchildren participated in the resistance. His wife, uneasy because of the upheaval, went to check in on her own mother, taking the younger children with her. There was no one to tend the hearth except the aging Marie-Josephte, Madeleine's step-daughter. So it was that as Madeleine lay dying, Marie-Josephte sent word to Canon Jean Etienne to come to his mother and offer her the last rites. Since Jean Etienne could not be found at the cathedral, the message was urged on Canon Guy, himself a man of many years, who reluctantly doddered along to the deathbed where he performed his priestly duties. Then, having said he would see his own way out, he passed through the main vestibule of the house and noted a quantity of neatly stacked books, printed and bound in the new fashion. The canon was one of those people of rank and taste who considered innovations such as printing to be common and unrefined. Disdainfully, he stepped over to examine the books more closely and was appalled to discover their pages alluded to his own history, however discreetly, and not without praise for the redeeming work of God, and remorse for the unbridled passions of the author herself. Just then, Marie-Josephte entered the room. The canon quickly recovered his dignity and said the books could not be considered safe in such a place, what with the assaults on the town and the turmoil in the streets. They would be safer in sanctuary at the cathedral. He sent immediately for a cart and a servant, and oversaw the removal of all the forty-nine little volumes into his care.

Although the canon later said the books were lost in transit due to a fiery arrow clearing the walls of the town and setting the cart and its contents aflame, it was the unvarying account of the servant that the people believed. This servant both delivered the books to the canon's private chambers and was later responsible for clearing an unprecedented accumulation of ashes from the fireplace. Thus, while Jeanne Hachette was doing her heroic work on the walls of the city and the relics of Sainte Angedrême were warding off attacks of fire, Madeleine's story was lost to flames within the secure walls of a faithless, defensive prelate. At that same moment, Madeleine died in the arms of Marie-Josephte, and the fire in the hearth of the Mouton household went out.

The final episode known to La Belle is of a heartbroken Jean Etienne, who, having finally got word of his mother's imminent death, hurried to her side only to find her lifeless in a cold dark room. His eyes wet with tears, he immediately set out in search of a fire wagon to find coals to kindle a new fire. This same son was reputed to have become the most compassionate of priests, a confessor with a gift of tears, who poured wine and oil into the wounds of sinners.

* * *

"Incredible, just incredible," said La Perle when La Belle finished her part of the account. "That the story should come together with two people who live such a great distance from each other. Just incredible."

"To think that you have been here all this time and we nearly said goodbye without knowing what the other had to tell. It is so strange." La Belle dabbed with her last bit of bread at a pool of marinade on her plate, savoured it, set her cutlery across her plate and nudged it away to put an end to supper. "I'm glad you asked. I would not have thought to tell you otherwise."

"Of course it is thanks to Soeur Luci, who mentioned it first."

"Voila! You found the story after all! You didn't expect this, I think."

"No. But you don't seem surprised, Soeur Luci."

"Ma foi! I have come to expect miracles. Still, this is a happy moment." She stood and pushed her chair under the table. "Now, as if the story isn't gift enough, La Perle has something else for you."

La Perle led us to her knitting chair and took a bulky parcel from her basket. "Here is something to remember us by, Madame LaFoy," she said, offering the bundle to me.

I pulled the string and out tumbled the deep green cape La Perle had begun knitting on Shrove Tuesday. "Oh, La Perle! It's beautiful!" I draped it next to my shoulder. It was absolutely perfect. "This is too much! I am already so deeply indebted to all of you. And I have nothing for any of you. Your gifts, all of them, are so much more than anything I could ever offer." For a moment I thought I should give it back, but I wanted so badly to keep it. "How can I accept such generosity?"

Soeur Luci gave me a sly smile. "Traditionally, it's done by saying 'Thank you.'"

"Oh, thank you, of course. A thousand times. Thank you." Predictably, tears started in the corners of my eyes. I embraced La Perle, and then La Belle, and finally Soeur Luci, and tried to settle down.

"Well, try it on! I want to be sure I got it right." La Perle began to wrap it around me. She adjusted the shoulder and smoothed the back. "Yes, it will do."

"La Perle, you are a wonder worker," said La Belle, who then pronounced the cape graceful and elegant and skilfully crafted, the colour well-chosen for my complexion, the length just where it should be, the detail on the collar a delicate finish...

"Yes," Soeur Luci continued, "it becomes you, Janine. You wear it well."

The rest of the evening we spent reminiscing about my arrival, and my impressions of the city, about how quickly the time had gone. We spoke a little of how life may unfold for the three of them and whether they would ever take a trip to Canada. La Belle told me I should hurry home because I am losing my Canadian accent and that would be a shame. It was hard to say a final goodbye to the Soeurs Béatrice, but at last I did it.

* * *

In the morning I packed up my nightshirt and toiletries, took my bags to the common room, ate a quick breakfast with Soeur Luci and had one last perfectly constituted cup of coffee. Then I put on my beautiful green cape and prepared to go. Soeur Luci chose the heavier suitcase again, carried it down the stairs and briskly led the way across the courtyard to the gate that opens onto rue de la Madeleine. There I thanked her again for her wisdom and patience with me.

"I will miss you, Janine. You ask good questions and have great faith." She set my suitcase outside the gate. Then she blessed me and kissed me cheek to cheek on either side, as any good French woman would do. "Adieu."

"Au revoir, Soeur Luci."

I picked up my bags and looked back one more time as Soeur Luci shut the gate behind me.

* * *

I remember to stamp my ticket. The train lurches onto a different set of tracks and heads east. Some fields are freshly tilled, the sable clods of clay lined up in small furrows, fallow fields sprouting green. Yellow forsythia bloom wantonly everywhere. Small trees in full leaf begin to flower, lilacs tangle garden gates. Larger trees vibrant with the first wash of spring wear feathery wraps of green vines on bare trunks. We pass through Villers St. Sépulchre. An old church stands in the distance not so grand, not so gothic as Beauvais' St. Etienne, but still communicating an ancient presence. A bombed-out building at Cires-lès-Mello offers a hollow epitaph to war.

I change trains at Creil. It is a short trip to Chantilly. The bus to the estate runs every hour and a half and I miss it. Seeing wheels on both my suitcases, the tourist officer suggests I walk. It's not far. Well, it is plenty far enough. Now I am sitting in the expansive grounds of the estate. I have taken a boat tour of the park and walked through the opulent halls and salons. I think you could fit the whole city of Beauvais on this property. The woman in the tourist office in Beauvais said I shouldn't miss an opportunity to visit here. It is one of the great houses of France. I've never seen anything so pretentious. I am not taken with it. I just wonder on whose backs this private wealth was produced. It's not even my era. I am impatient to go.

* * *

I took the next train to the Gare du Nord in Paris. I found my way to the platform for Line 4, crowded into the train with half the city's population and managed to squeeze my way out at the St. Michel station. I dragged my luggage to a long narrow escalator, perched my suitcases on one of the rising stairs then had to scramble to catch up with them. I climbed the last flight of stairs—another ride on an escalator seemed risky—and stepped out onto the Quai St. Michel. What a sight! *This—is a city!* I set my bags down. People threaded their way around me. Traffic buzzed like hornets. Great buildings lined the quay on one side, the monumental Notre Dame de Paris rose up on the other. I have not seen a vista half so grand in all my life.

I checked into the pension. The concierge was friendly and helpful. She gave me directions to take me to the Church of the Madeleine. Not that I'm on any particular quest anymore. I am satisfied with what I know of my Madeleine, but I was curious and the day was nearly gone. No time for any major excursions anyway. I took the wrong train at Châtelet and ended up at Place de la Concorde on Line 1. This was not really a problem. I just went the rest of the way above ground. Again I emerged from underground and stopped to stare. I was standing by the incredible Obelisk of Luxor. On one side of me stretched the famous Champs-Élysées up to the Arc de Triomphe, on the other the Tuileries Gardens and in the distance the Eiffel Tower. What a view! I found the rue Royale between two imposing stone buildings and made my way toward a massive pillared structure. It looked for all the world like a temple to Athena. I passed the houses of Gucci, Chanel, Dior. Not surprising, I suppose, that Athena would preside here, given her association with weaving. I could see nothing about this building on my map, but went to check it out before looking for the church, which according to my directions, had to be somewhere close by. I climbed an expansive bank of stairs. As I neared the great bronze portals, I realized the temple *is* the Church of the Madeleine. How strange.

Louis XV laid the foundation stone for the church in 1763. Work was suspended during the French Revolution until 1789, then slowly taken up again for ten years. Under the Consulate of the First Republic, work stopped until in 1806 Napoleon ordained the building of a temple to the glory of his Grande Armée on the site. However, after his disastrous defeat in Russia in 1812, he thought better of it, and with minor adjustments reinstated the plan to build a church. It doesn't look much like a church to me. It looks imperial and official. The building has variously housed a bank, a theatre, a stock exchange, and has served as a parliament building. Nothing about it suggests Mary Magdalene—except the usual confusion about what to do with her. What would she ever have done with fifty-two sixty-four foot Corinthian columns?

* * *

I am getting used to the seemingly endless grandeur of this place. Every day I walk or take the Metro in a different direction. I have spent a fair bit of time at Notre Dame. I went to the Sainte-Chapelle. It is exquisite—like the Sainte-Chapelle at Saint-Germer-de-Fly, only bigger and more resplendent. I have walked along the rue de Montmorency to see the stone house of Nicolas Flamel built in 1407. I visited the Eiffel tower and walked the length of the Champs-Élysées several times. I spent the better part of one morning standing in line for admission to the Louvre. It was worth it, but it is not possible to take it all in—not in a week, much less a day. I have seen the Gallo-Roman baths and the tapestries of "The Lady and the Unicorn" at the Cluny museum. This is not far from my *pension*. I am also close to some very old churches. On Sunday, I went to St. Séverin for Passion Sunday Mass and stood near the flamboyant palm grove of pillars during the blessing of the palms.

And I am visiting the full compass of my emotions. There are a lot of bellies and breasts and babies in paintings and icons and stained glass in Paris. I look at a Madonna and Child and find myself weeping. At the next one, I smile. I cannot predict my reactions to anything. I really didn't think I would care to see the graves at Père Lachaise, but I had a wonderful time there. The day was all April, mild and fresh with flowers. I felt so hopeful and eager to be home, so sure everything will be okay. The next day I plodded with a heavy heart around the light and blooming Jardin des Plantes.

*   *   *

I am unspeakably lonely. Nearly three months. It's absurd. People don't leave their family for three months if they can help it. I want to go home, to see my sons, my mother, my husband. My husband. I haven't thought of him that way for a long time. Now I worry about my marriage. Paris is a city for lovers. I don't remember a time when I could have walked these avenues easily, arm in arm with Miles. Maybe I could now. Maybe I've just forgotten how annoying Miles can be. We aren't at all compatible. What if I want to try again, and he thinks he'd rather be with that Vikki chick? I haven't been a joy to live with either. I wish I knew. I wish I hadn't been so insistent that Miles not pick me up. I didn't think we had anything worth keeping—I had nothing to lose.

I wonder if Jim will meet me for my stopover in Toronto. Of course not. Well, I hope not. I will know tomorrow.

I am finally going home.

STOPOVER

When you are old and grey and full of sleep,
And nodding by the fire, take down this book,
And slowly read, and dream of the soft look
Your eyes had once, and of their shadows deep;

How many loved your moments of glad grace,
And loved your beauty with love false or true,
But one man loved the pilgrim Soul in you,
And loved the sorrows of your changing face;

And bending down beside the glowing bars,
Murmur, a little sadly, how Love fled
And paced upon the mountains overhead
And hid his face amid a crowd of stars.

—William Butler Yeats, "When You are Old and Grey"

Return flight. I'm not fleeing. I'm returning. It is hard to settle. Why did I tell Jim about my stopover? I'd rather not talk to him right now. Well, I will call and say hello. I'll leave it at that. It was his idea after all, me going to France.

My seatmates are civil. So am I. Seven hours is a long time to be civil. I don't feel like reading any of the books in my carry-on.

I should have brought a murder mystery. I could have managed that. Instead I watched a half-hour documentary about the Easter Islands. I guess it was a seasonal piece. And apparently time does not stand still when airborne over the Atlantic, however contrary my sense of it. At last, we are landing in Toronto. I will have more than two hours there before boarding my flight for Edmonton. But I am almost home.

* * *

The Toronto airport is not anything like Paris, but busy enough. I was uneasy. I found a phone, called the school information number in the phone book, and asked for Jim's extension. My hand shook as I keyed it in. It rang several times. I was ready to give it up when a woman's voice answered "Dr. Peters' office—may I help you?"

"Oh, hello. May I speak with Dr. Peters? I am a member of St. Ignatius of Loyola Parish in Flatfield where he served last year."

"I'm sorry. Dr. Peters has a three-hour seminar on Wednesday afternoons and likely won't be in his office again until after Easter. May I take a message?"

"Oh, I see," I murmured.

"I'm happy to take a message."

"I'm just passing through. I have a stopover, that's all." I could barely speak. I thought I should be relieved. I did not expect to be disappointed. It had never occurred to me that Jim would not be available the whole time I was in Toronto.

The voice on the other end was sympathetic. "I'm sorry, dear. I'm sure he would have been delighted to hear from you. What's your name? I'll tell him you called."

"That's okay. Maybe next time. Thanks." Just as I hung up someone touched my shoulder. I turned and there he was, standing beside me. "Jim!"

"Janine!" He folded my hand in both of his.

"I just found out you have a three-hour seminar this afternoon."

"I asked a colleague to take it for me."

"Oh, I'm sorry. I didn't mean to disrupt your schedule."

"It's no disruption, I assure you. How are you? How are things with Madeleine? Here, let me take your bag. It's so good to see you." He took my arm and guided me to a quietish corner of the passenger's lounge. "Let me get you a coffee or something. What would you like?"

"You decide." I sank, shaken, into one of the chairs, surprised at how much I had counted on talking with him. And how grateful I was that he came—someone I know—someone who was part of my story, although not the happiest chapter. I collected myself before he returned.

"So, you went to Beauvais after all! I was so happy to get your postcard. And there for three months! Was it worthwhile?"

"Yes. —Yes, it was."

"Did you write up the story? Did you learn anything about Madeleine?"

"Well, it's more of a draft. Madeleine *is* known in Beauvais, but only by word of mouth. I found no written record."

"But they had heard of her! Well, isn't that something! So you found what you were looking for?"

"In a way. As you suggested, the story took me where I needed to go."

"And what did you discover?"

"Demons. My own personal demons." I did my best to give him an angelic smile. It may have come off as more of a grimace. Either way, it was enough to scuttle the investigation. I certainly didn't want to begin there.

Jim laughed. "You have no idea how good it is to see you, Janine. I've missed you. I often think about how much I enjoyed working with you last year. I'm not complaining. The people here are first rate, but I don't feel at home as I did in Flatfield. I guess it will come with time." He sipped his coffee and watched a young mother worrying three children along to an empty couch beyond us. He sighed. "And now my sister has separated from her husband."

"Oh, I'm sorry—"

"Yeah. It's quite a blow. She needs a lot of support. She's alone with the kids now. They're pretty much old enough to be on their own but it hit them hard too. So when I go to visit, I often come back empty. And my poor demented father hardly remembers why my mother never visits. That's all I have for family. Well, a few cousins scattered across the continent, but no place to go where I feel at ease. No place to be loved and ignored and let time spend. It's odd that Flatfield should seem so much more like home, since apart from college, I only spent one year of my life there."

"I've felt like that, Jim. That nobody would miss me if I disappeared. And I've never lived even a month away from home before now."

He seemed surprised at that. He sat back, folded his arms and studied my face awhile, maybe a bit wistfully. It made me uneasy, him looking at me that way. I really wasn't sure what I had said to induce such a response. Finally he spoke. "It's odd, Janine, that I do not regret entering the priesthood…" He hesitated, then continued "but I often regret not marrying you."

Oh, please. I dropped my head into my hands. *Not now.*

He waited until I looked up again, then said softly, "It can be very lonely, Janine. I think about you and wonder how it would have been if we had married." Then he began to recover himself. "But I know this is what I am called to be. If I'd never met you, I doubt I would ever even ask the question. You're a special person, Janine."

Good. "Jim, you're one of the best priests I have ever known."

He laughed. "'One of the best.' You'd think a friend would give a poor old cleric top billing just to humour him."

"You are not that old, Jim. And you never met Father Francis."

"True." He became reflective again. "Janine. There's something I need to say to you." He looked at me strangely, searching my face. I squirmed. This was not the interview I had imagined. Finally he spoke slowly. "It's taken me a long time to realize how ill-served you were by me. How badly I behaved. When I fell in love with you, I was not prepared for it at all. It came upon me so unexpectedly. I had been so certain of my vocation—then there you were." He hesitated and took a deep breath. "I didn't mean to deceive you or take advantage of you, Janine. I just wanted to be with you. Before long, I honestly thought we would marry. But by the time I went home for Christmas that year, I was uneasy and confused. I wanted to spend my life with you. I felt called to be a priest. I hoped for an academic career. I did not know what to do."

"That was a lifetime ago, Jim. Why are you telling me this now?"

"Just let me finish. I went to see Father Bernard—you may remember me talking about him—my mentor who knew me from childhood. I wasn't completely honest with Father Bernard. I didn't tell him how deeply involved I was. I couched it all in ambiguity. I only said we were as good as engaged. He said I shouldn't lead you on if I was having doubts about it—better to be clear for your sake."

"Hmh. He said 'clear'? Are you sure he didn't say 'cold'?" I was getting angry.

"Yeah, I know. You're right. I'm getting there. I was cold because I didn't believe I could honestly tell you how I felt without losing my resolve." He stopped and studied his hands. "I am so selfish. I only thought of my own difficulty and my own pain. I somehow figured you would just recognize the importance of my decision and support my lofty goals." He snorted. "What a cad! I was completely shameless. I can't believe it. I was so afraid of your feelings and my own. Fear blinds me, Janine. I become defensive and stop listening. It is taking me a long time to learn how not to respond from a place of fear."

"But you did come back later that summer."

"Yeah, I was pretty desperate by then. I knew something had gone wrong. I wanted to fix it without facing it. I was still completely self-serving."

"What young lovers aren't, Jim?"

"Oh, that's a little harsh, isn't it? I've seen many couples who care deeply and would sacrifice a lot for love of each other."

"I suppose. I'm beginning to think loving is learned. Of course falling in love—the initial attraction—disposes you toward it. But sometimes it's hard to forgive someone who knows your feet stink."

Jim laughed again. "Well, maybe you'll forgive me, Janine, since I had no idea."

I couldn't respond at all. Just like that, the whole thing had become a joke. And I did it. I was the one who changed the tone. I made excuses. As usual. Once again, I tried to make Jim comfortable even though I had no inclination to brush the matter off. After the misery of the past twenty years, thanks to my inability to be forthcoming and truthful, here we were, sidestepping again. I couldn't help myself. I buried my head in my hands and tried not to cry.

"Oh, Janine. I'm sorry. I didn't come here to make light of it. I came to finally ask forgiveness." He pressed my hand away from my face. "Janine—*please*. Please. Forgive me."

Weary and sullen, I crossed my arms and dropped my eyes. I stared at the floor awhile, tried to figure out why I cared, then sat back and faced him squarely. "For what?" *Good luck, buddy. Are you really going to be able to say you screwed me over?*

I have to hand it to him. He bit his lip and met my eyes. After looking at me thoughtfully for some time he said slowly, "For claiming intimacy without honour." Then he cradled his forehead in his hand and shook his head. "I am so sorry. It's taken such a long time, Janine, but ever since I left Flatfield, I have been haunted by it, by my failure to own up and ask your forgiveness. I am so glad you are here. I can finally come clean."

"Hmm. I see." All of a sudden I was very tired. My eyelids drooped. I just wanted to sleep. I sat silently staring at my shoes through half-closed eyes. I couldn't say anything.

"Janine. Are you okay?"

"I'm very sleepy, that's all."

"Can I get you another cup of coffee? And maybe a muffin or something? Are you hungry? Did you eat on the plane?"

"Coffee would be good. And something to go with it." I finally looked at him. "Thank you." I needed him to go away for awhile as much as I needed anything.

You would think I would be grateful that Jim finally took some responsibility. I tried to figure out why it rankled me. As far as he knew, we'd been lovers and he broke it off unceremoniously. That was all. That happens all the time. People get over it. I should be glad he cared enough to finally say, "I'm sorry." I didn't expect it. He preempted me. I expected to tell him about the abortion and watch him squirm. Yes, that was the thing. Some stubborn part of me wanted to pass the misery on, to make him bear the blame. I suppose that's the point of the crucifixion. The blame stops there. You don't have to pass it on. I'm not used to it, to being forgiven. Soeur Luci said to take my time. I would know what was need-ed. What was needed was for me to forgive him. For my own sake, come to that.

"Here you are, Janine. Coffee and a cinnamon bun fresh from the assembly line. As good as it gets."

"Thank you, Jim." I tried to smile up at him.

"Oh. You haven't been crying, have you?"

"Just cleaning my ducts."

"I didn't intend to make matters worse."

"You haven't Jim. It was unexpected, that's all."

"No doubt. And—you do forgive me?"

"Yes, of course."

He watched patiently while I broke a buttery layer off my cin-namon bun. "Can you say it, Janine? Can you say you forgive me?"

"I forgive you."

"Thank you." He squeezed my sticky hand.

I genuinely enjoyed the next hour with Jim. We talked about the Madeleine story and what could be done with it, and about his research and teaching. When it was time, he walked me to the de-parture gate. We hugged each other goodbye. Then he said, "Thank you for this, Janine. I am so glad you came. Sometimes, when I imagine you old and full of sleep and nodding by the fire, I wonder how you will remember me—if you do at all. I can't bear to imagine you thinking ill of me." It's just as well I didn't catch his allusion to Yeats's poem. All that came to mind when he said 'nodding by the fire' was that I've had my fill of fire for now.

He watched me away into the security area. When I turned to wave at that solitary figure of a man, a pang of tenderness overcame me. I left a good deal standing there with him at the gate. I left my regret. The biggest "if only" of my life.

HOME

What we call the beginning is often the end
And to make an end is to make a beginning.
The end is where we start from.

—T.S. Eliot, *Four Quartets*, "Little Gidding"

The last leg. It's been a long journey. I am thinking about what I said to Jim. That loving is learned. And how hard it is to forgive someone who knows your feet stink. I hope I'm not trying to talk myself into something with Miles. He's so hard to live with. I just don't know. I am anxious to see him, if only for a reality check. He'll probably be his old self, and all the grace of the last three months will dissipate.

It can't. I can't let that happen.

* * *

I believe I slept most of the way, just below the surface of consciousness—the way you do with a busy brain and an exhausted body. We landed. I pretty much sleepwalked toward the reception area, wondering who would be waiting for me there. Most likely my mom, maybe Kit. But as I rode down the escalator, I saw Miles standing alone off to the side. I could not read the odd look on his face. *O Lord, what's happened? Let everything be okay.* He walked quickly over to me as I stepped off.

"Janine—" so quietly I more read his lips than heard him. My heart rose to my throat.

"Is everything okay?"

"I hope so."

"What do you mean, Miles? Is something wrong?"

"No.—Well, yes. Of course. Or you wouldn't have gone in the first place."

"I didn't expect to see you here."

"You never said so."

"Never said what? Tell me, Miles! What is it? Why are you here?"

"Didn't you get the letter?"

"What letter?" His face fell. *O God keep us.*

"I wrote asking if you mind if I meet your plane."

"Oh, is that all? Thank God!"

"Well, that was the gist of it. There was more in the letter, though."

"But no bad news?"

"No. —No bad news except I asked to meet your plane."

I laughed. "I didn't get any letter. And it's nice to see you…"

He took my hands in his and kissed them. "Good."

We went to the baggage carousel to wait for my luggage. Miles asked predictable questions about my flight. He talked about what time it would be in France and I must be tired and did I sleep at all on the plane? My suitcases tumbled through the flaps and wound their way creaking and groaning to where we stood in the crowd.

Miles picked up both suitcases at once. "Whoa, that's heavy! I forgot, you took the library with you."

"Let me take one. They have wheels, you know."

"I'm good." He motioned toward the south exit with his chin. "This way." I followed at his elbow, happy to be free of my baggage for once. Miles seemed a little nervous but he was being so sweet.

The air outside was crisp and fresh. I could see my breath. "Oh, that's nice. I really missed winter."

"You did?" Miles turned to inspect my face as if I were some exotic creature.

"Yes. Winters in France are dull and damp. Alberta winters are so much more—explicit!"

He smiled. "You could say that. Not many would see it as a recommendation."

"Well, sometimes you have to do without to appreciate what you've got." *Oh dear. That sounds like a promise. I hope Miles doesn't take it the wrong way.*

Miles looked pleased.

*   *   *

It was a quiet ride home. We travelled along in silence, then we would both begin to speak at once. After some polite jockeying to make our observations, silence again. Occasionally I stole a look at Miles, so familiar and such a stranger. Mostly I looked out at the dim expanse of a predictable landscape. Every now and again, rain-glazed patches of unmelted snow caught light from the widening crescent of a nearly new moon. We passed the leaning silos. "Oh!" I breathed.

"What is it?" Miles asked anxiously.

"Whatever happened to the silos?" The silo on the east seemed to have twisted and leaned more toward the west.

"Just the wind. We had a big storm last month. The footings must have shifted. They'll probably settle again. Amazing how those silos keep standing."

Well, some things stay the same. We drove past the old Steadman place. An oil well, dueling dark against the sky, still stood in the field—one of the last of the old-style wells still pumping in our region. One of the last families in our area made rich by the boom, too. They sold their mineral rights and went somewhere else to be wealthy. The eastern edge of that property now forms one of the town limits of Flatfield.

Miles slowed down. As usual in spring, town roads are peppered with potholes. Miles manoeuvred slowly and carefully around them. I found that odd. Normally dodging potholes is a spring sporting event for Miles. He drives at the legal limit winding through the maze without slacking speed. Passengers hang on and brace for the bungle that never comes. He's good at it. But this night he took his time, as if in no hurry to get home.

Home. At last. Mom and Adam and Kit were outside before I could step onto the driveway. They swept me up and into the house in a flurry of hugs and chatter. Miles followed with my suitcases, interjecting a few remarks of his own. Inside I collapsed into the arms of my green Belgian mohair chair and sat in the centre of the excitement, entirely at home. I tried to keep awake, to savour the moment as long as possible, but sleep would come. I began to nod. The boys were both talking at once. Mom worried that I may have lost weight. I looked at Miles and smiled wearily.

"Alright guys. I think we need to let your mum get some rest. She'll still be here in the morning." Miles picked up my suitcases. "Come along, Janine. I made the upstairs bed for you. I'll take the futon tonight. You need a good sleep." I was so grateful for that. In a way I wanted to tell him he was welcome to his own bed even if I was in it. But I wasn't sure. Things can look a lot different from the other side of an ocean. I didn't want to lead him on.

The room was as neat and clean as it's ever been. Spit and polish—the mirror gleamed, the furniture shone, by the bed a clutch of tulips. Propped up on the highboy was a sketch of—I leaned forward to look at it—"That's the Beauvais cathedral, isn't it?"

"Good. It's recognizable. I drew it from the postcard you sent me."

"It's really well done. It's lovely. Everything's lovely. Thank you, Miles." I turned and hugged him. He held me close a moment then as if on cue we stepped away from each other.

"I should go," he mumbled.

"Yes, I need to get to bed," I answered, embarrassed. He headed toward the door. "Miles."

"Yes?"

"It's really good to see you."

"You too." He gave me a wan smile, walked out and closed the door behind him.

* * *

I slept until nearly noon. Miles was long gone to work and the boys to school when I got up. Mom was waiting for me in the kitchen. She had set a single place at the table, just so. Soeur Luci would approve.

"You woke up! I'll make coffee. How did you sleep?"

"Really well. I can't believe how much I love this place."

"You know, it's good you came back. I didn't know for sure you would."

"Oh, Mom. You knew I would be back. I had a round-trip ticket."

"I know that. I mean, come back to stay. You didn't seem to want that very much."

"You make it sound so bleak."

"It was, Janine. The boys did okay, but it was very hard on that man of yours."

"I don't own him, Mom."

"I think you do," she reproved. "Or you should. You'd better do good by him." She set out some warm bran muffins to get me going, as she said, and fried two eggs over easy. I changed the subject. I had a lot to tell her about France, all the places where I thought about her and how we should go back together someday. It was a good time but short. She had to be at work for the evening shift.

* * *

I am alone in the house. I haven't done much. Cleaned up my breakfast dishes, started unpacking, put in a load of laundry. Found homes for the books. Not sure what to do with my clothes. I never emptied the drawers in our bedroom before I left, but I feel strange putting my things there, as if I'm moving in on Miles. Don't know what to think about Miles. He was so careful and considerate last night. That will change. We could be back to normal in no time. He doesn't really know me. At least, he doesn't seem to know what the past few months have been about. Of course not. Neither did I.

Surely I don't have to explain it all to him. I can say it turned out to be personal and I realize he isn't responsible—well, not entirely

responsible—for our unhappiness. My unhappiness, I should say.
He was miserable enough, but I can't speak for him. I *don't* own
him. Why on earth does Mom think I should?

Oxford Universal Dictionary. Own:

†1. *trans.* To make (a thing) one's own; to seize, win, gain;
to adopt as one's own.

Not sure why that's considered obsolete.

2. To have or hold as one's own, possess.

There it is. That's my point. I don't possess anybody. To
have and to hold. Well, that would be what she's getting at,
not that Mom's given to consulting a dictionary for her opinions.

5. To acknowledge (something) in its relation to oneself…

That's pretty far down the list. I don't know if I'm capable
of that. This marriage business has always been a struggle. To
be expected, I guess, if you're hanging on to some other family you never had. Where has little Joy gotten to? Will loving
Miles honour her? How will *not* loving Miles honour her? I
have other children. I really wanted to sleep beside Miles last
night. I just don't know. Someone is at the door.

* * *

Adam came in. "Hey Mom! Howeryadoin?" He kissed me hello.
We spent a while catching up while Adam helped himself to an
apple, some chips, a glass of milk, then put two slices of bread in
the toaster.

"I guess I'd better start supper. I forgot how hungry you guys
get."

"Don't worry about it. It's Kit's night to cook."

"What?"

"It's Kit's night. He does Tuesdays and Thursdays, I do Wednesdays and Fridays. Grandma cooks on Monday because she's off then
and Dad does Saturdays. Grandma and Dad usually work something out for Sunday dinner. Mostly Grandma."

"Who figured that out?"

"Well, when you left, it didn't go so well at first because Grandma's gone in the evening and Dad usually doesn't get home until after six. So he worked out the schedule."

"You and Kit cook?"

"We have tacos and spaghetti a lot."

"I'm impressed. What about your dad?"

"He usually makes hamburgers or buys pizza. He's not really into cooking."

"Well, I already defrosted something. I thought I would make a chicken stir-fry."

"Oh, I'm down with that."

I cut up the chicken, put it in a marinade, started the rice, and found a few vegetables in the crisper. Adam hung around and kept company.

"Where's Kit?"

"Probably with his girlfriend."

"He has a girlfriend?"

"He thinks so. I haven't met her."

As if summoned, Kit tumbled in the front door. The door slammed, a backpack thudded. "Hey Mom! I'm home."

"So I hear."

"Here's the mail. You got a letter." He came into the kitchen. "Oh, are you cooking? Works for me!" He looked triumphantly at Adam and handed me the letter. It was the one from Miles, returned because of insufficient postage. *How strange. Miles is usually so careful about things like that.* I tucked it in my pocket to spend a few minutes with Kit, then excused myself and shut myself in the bathroom. I ran my finger under the flap, took out the letter and unfolded it.

Dear Janine,

First, I want to thank you again for the art classes. I am completely caught up in them. I'm sorry I was such a jerk about it. You're right. Surprises make me uncomfortable. I thought that once we were married, nothing much would change. The rest was just the ride—pretty much what you said the night you ran off into the cold. I'm sorry. More than you can imagine.

When you left, you said you didn't want to hear from me. At this point, however, much as I don't want to get in the way of working things out, I would like to meet your plane. I know this is not the kind of emergency you had in mind when you sent me your address but it feels urgent to me. Let me know if you really object. Otherwise I'll be there.

You have no idea how much I miss you Janine. I want to try again. I hope it's not too late. I'll do whatever it takes—even counselling if you want.

Love, Miles

I read it over and over again. That was a big risk for him, saying so much. The first paragraph was clearly written in a round hand, the rest of the page deteriorated into a scrawl as if he wanted to finish before he changed his mind or lost his nerve. It took me awhile to decipher "counselling." *Unbelievable. I have to talk to him. I just don't know what to say.*

I finished making supper. The boys set the table. It would have been a teaching opportunity for Soeur Luci, but I let it pass. Everything was ready to go. I suggested we wait for Miles but the boys wanted to start without him.

"He could be another hour. We never know when he'll get here."

"True enough. Okay. I'll make a salad, then we can begin."

"Salad with stir fry?"

"Yep. I always make a salad with stir fry if it's Holy Thursday."

The boys were skeptical, but I'd been away long enough to make them unsure whether I was having them on or not. I had used up most of the fresh vegetables for dinner. There were two red tomatoes in a basket on the counter which I sliced up and laid out alternately with shavings of onion. I slowly beat olive oil into a mixture of balsamic vinegar, Dijon mustard, pepper and basil. I couldn't stretch the exercise any farther. I drizzled the dressing on the tomatoes and onions and set it on the table.

"Alright then, we can eat."

Miles walked in the door. "You're just in time, Dad—for stir fry and Holy Thursday salad." Miles looked doubtfully at Kit who grinned back at him.

Miles turned to me. "Hullo." He pulled up his chair.

"Hi." I met his eyes then, like a child who stumbles onto a stash of Christmas presents, I quickly looked away, then down at my plate. I rearranged my silverware. Fork on the left. I couldn't think of a thing to say. Fortunately, the boys could. I heard about Kit's love interest. He taunted Adam for being too shy to initiate anything with a girl he likes. Miles said hardly a word. Nor did I. I needed time to think—alone. I really didn't want to mess things up. I didn't want to get in over my head either.

"I'd like to go to the Holy Thursday liturgy tonight. Anyone want to come along?" No one did. They seemed surprised that I was going—our first evening home together and all. "I won't be gone long."

* * *

I enjoyed the short walk to church. Light flakes of snow floated around me, accumulating on lawns but melting as they hit the pavement, as they do in spring. Evenings are beginning to stretch for the season but it was getting dark outside by the time I stepped into the lighted building. I immediately noticed Agnes, hovering near the entry to the nave. I was going to say hello to her when Sister Colette came hurrying up to me from the other side.

"Oh, am I ever glad to see you!" she exclaimed, "Are you wearing socks?"

What a welcome. "It's snowing outside, Sister. Of course I'm wearing socks."

"I mean, something you can easily remove?" she continued.

"Huh?"

"Rose and Mike can't come. Mike's not well. He had a stroke or something. Rose is at the hospital with him. So I need to replace them."

"Mike had a stroke? Is he conscious? When did this happen? What do you mean, replace them?"

"I need two more people for the *pedilavium*."

"What are you talking about?" I wasn't following at all.

"It's quite an honour, really. It's like having Our Lord Himself wash your right foot."

"Oooh! I *see*. You want to know if I am willing to have my feet washed."

"Foot."

"Sorry—foot. Well…" I wasn't very comfortable with the idea. After all, Father Eugene had been my boss. But I couldn't think up an excuse fast enough under the circumstances. I looked around for an alternative. There were only a few people in the entry area. I didn't know any of them except Agnes. I don't know what possessed me then. I said quite loudly, "Only if Agnes does it with me."

"Um…" Sister Colette seemed taken aback. "Uh…well…"

"Did I hear my name?" Agnes ambled over. "Hi, Janine. Welcome back. How was your trip?"

"Really good, Agnes. Thanks. But I'm glad to be home again. How are you?" Sister Colette started to back away. "Sister Colette needs two more people for the foot washing."

"Agnes is wearing stockings," Sister Colette objected.

"Are you willing?" I asked.

"I would like that," said Agnes.

"What about your stockings?" asked Sister Colette.

"Not a problem," said Agnes. "I'll be back in a second."

"Hmm—I'm just not sure about that," Sister Colette ruminated uncomfortably as Agnes hurried off to the washroom. "You know, Father Eugene… "

"How's Mike?" I interrupted. "Is he going to be alright?"

"I— I— don't know," said Sister Colette, "—I just don't know…" her voice trailed off.

I realized I wasn't going to get an answer. She obviously didn't know anyway. So instead I asked her what I was supposed to do to get my right foot washed. She briefed me on how to proceed, then told me where to sit. There were two pews cordoned off at the front. The other ten parishioners, carefully chosen to represent the face of the church—or at least the face preferred by the planners of the liturgy—were already seated, five in a pew. I took the last spot in the second pew. Within minutes, Agnes came rustling by, sitting directly in front of me. She turned around and smiled at me, saying, "Thank you." That was all. She settled in, bowed her head, and didn't move again until the service started. I have never seen her so still.

When the time came, the twelve of us stood to take our places in chairs arranged around the altar. Led by the person at the outside end of Agnes's pew, we processed onto the platform. Each person limped forward, left foot shod, right foot with only a sock on it. Until Agnes. She made her way to the front—barefoot. How like her, doing nothing by halves. I had to admire the quiet dignity of her surefooted approach. The person who followed her left the chair next to Agnes empty. When I got there, the only available chair was the one beside Agnes. So be it. She was there because of me.

Father BG and a server assisted Father Eugene as he began the ritual washing—BG held a pitcher, the other a supply of clean towels. When he got to Agnes, Father Eugene drew back as she put both her feet into the basin. I recognized the irritation in his face, I'd seen it often enough. I can't say if it was because of the two feet or because it was Agnes. It was probably both. But then the miracle occurred. As Father Eugene began to wash her feet, Agnes began to cry, inaudibly. But as she drew in a breath, she shook with a slight shiver, startling Father Eugene, who looked up at her in wonder. He didn't move for maybe ten seconds. The sleeve of his robe, which had been tucked up to keep it dry, slipped loose, covering his forearm and his watch. Still, he just knelt there, holding her feet in his hands. Then, carefully, he dried them. When he'd done he said, "Peace of Christ, Agnes."

It was good to be there. Father Eugene seemed surprised and pleased to see me. By then I was okay with letting him wash my foot too. Agnes sat quietly as Father Eugene continued around the circle. The rest of us busied ourselves replacing our sock.

* * *

I don't remember much about the rest of the service. I was trying to figure out what to say to Miles, trying to decide how to begin. *Of course, the important thing is to begin, just start somewhere. Then we'll see what happens.* I wanted to slip away quietly when mass was done, but couldn't avoid a few people who welcomed me back. That was okay too. Outside at last, I made my way home.

Miles was standing on the porch when I got home. "You're back."

"Yes."

"How'd it go?"

"Good. I'm glad I went." I stood a minute beside him on the porch. The snow had dissipated.

"Did you see the crocuses?"

"Not yet." We walked around to the side of the house. In the light from the kitchen window, I could see the fresh young blooms glistening with crystals of melting snow. "Very pretty. —There are a lot more this year."

"Yeah, I think so. They're doing well."

We turned back to the porch. "Miles—"

"Yes?"

"Can we have breakfast together tomorrow before everyone gets up? I need to talk to you."

"Guess so." He looked discouraged.

"It's a different story now, from what it was when I left."

"Hmh."

"I'm not angry with you anymore."

"But you still want to leave."

"I don't think so. We just need to talk and maybe then we'll know."

He sighed, exasperated. "Can't we talk now?"

"I can't. It's getting late and I'm tired. We'll talk in the morning." I rubbed his arm and went inside. Mom was home. She'd made camomile tea. I sat with her awhile. Miles came in, declined the tea and went into the family room. I went upstairs to bed.

SPRING

Grief melts away
Like snow in May,
As if there were no such cold thing.

Who would have thought my shriveled heart
Could have recovered greenness? It was gone
Quite underground; as flowers depart
To see their mother-root, when they have blown...

—George Herbert, "The Flower"

I was sound asleep when the alarm went off at seven. I would have been glad to turn over and sleep another hour. I sat on the edge of the bed staring through half-closed eyes. I looked over at the bold lines of the Beauvais cathedral softened by early light. The tulips were a little droopy, needing fresh cuts and water. I tried to think of a good way to approach Miles to make it easy on myself, not sure what I should tell him if anything, he's so uneasy.

—*He'll be fine if I just say everything's okay, I want to stay, and move back in with him.*

—*And how would you feel about that, Janine?*

Perfect. Now that Madeleine's safely put to rest, Soeur Luci's decided to haunt me.

I took out Miles's letter and read it over again for courage. "Whatever it takes." *So far he's been as good as his word.* I got up and dressed, picked up the vase of tulips and went downstairs.

Miles was sitting in the kitchen leafing through an art supply catalogue. The table was set—two places across from each other, our usual places at the head and foot. Not at all friendly to close conversation.

"Good morning."

"G'morning."

"I didn't mean for you to have to get up to make breakfast. I was going to do it."

"It's not rocket science, Janine. I've been up since five-thirty. No point in waiting." Echoes of the old familiar impatience in his voice. I tried to recall the tone of his letter. *This is the same guy. He's just afraid of what his incomprehensible wife is going to come up with next.*

I brought the tulips to the sink. "I thought I'd recut the stems and freshen the water so they last a little longer." Miles started the toast and poured coffee. Three boiled eggs already sat cooling in a bowl on the table. I set the tulips beside them.

"Do you mind if I move closer? It will be easier to talk."

"Go for it." Miles looked like a man heading for the gallows.

We ate to a percussive cadence—butter scraped on toast, egg-shells cracking, pepper mill grinding, cutlery on ceramic—the bare rhythms. No discernable melody at all. Miles finished his orange juice, took a long drink of coffee, wiped his hands and laid his napkin on the table. He sat back, crossed his arms and said: "So talk."

After spending the last day and a half trying to make me comfortable it seemed he was daring me to care. All my carefully rehearsed introductions scattered. I didn't know how to begin.

"I had an abortion."

"You what?" Incredulous, he pushed himself away from the table as if I had joined the company of untouchables.

I dropped my head into my hand. "Oh, no, Miles!" Shaking my head, I added hurriedly, "It was before I ever really knew you. It wasn't your child."

"Oh." He relaxed a little and heaved a sigh.

It took me a while to collect myself. Miles just sat there waiting. Finally I was able to summon the carefully thought-through recitation and tell him how I came to do it. Then I told him how it affected me. "It was more than I could bear. There was no one I was willing to talk to about it either. Eventually, probably because I just couldn't cope, I suppressed the memory of it entirely. But you know, I still carried it. I think it made me…unforgiving…and depressed and angry too. I don't know why I focused so much of my anger on you. I suppose I hoped marrying you would make it better and it didn't, and I blamed you for that.

—But it was unconsciously done. I didn't know how to fix it.

—And I'm sorry."

Miles looked at me thoughtfully. He was clearly relieved. This, at last, was not beyond his grasp. In its own perverse way, it made sense to him. "I thought we were pretty happy together at the beginning."

"Yeah, I think so. It was probably after Kit was born. Maybe it started with post-partum depression and I never really came out the other side after that. I don't remember. I know by our tenth anniversary, I was pretty miserable." I told him about my long journey to consciousness and about Madeleine's role in it, although I wasn't ready to let him know her ephemeral nature quite yet. I told him about how important Soeur Luci had been to the process. And how it was a good thing I had some time to think about it before I came home. But when I said I was in contact with Father Jim while I was in Toronto, that didn't sit so well with him.

"Whatever for? He wasn't involved in the decision in the first place."

"That depends on how you see it. Obviously he was implicated on some level."

"So you saw him." The edge had slipped back into his voice.

"Yes." I bit my lip. I tried to think of how to explain the importance of that encounter for me.

Miles fidgeted. He began to herd the crumbs on his placemat with his finger. "Well, what did he have to say about it?"

"I didn't tell him in the end. I couldn't have told you exactly why at the time, but I knew it wasn't a good idea. Now I'm beginning to see it's you I needed to talk to all along. You're the one who has had to live with the fallout."

Miles said nothing. He began to manoeuver the crumbs on his place mat into a little pile. I sipped my coffee. It was cold. "I need some more coffee." I got up, dumped the cold coffee in the sink, and brought the pot to the table.

"No thanks," said Miles.

I put cream in my cup and filled it with coffee. I took a long drink. "That's better." At least something was warming. *I shouldn't have told Miles about the stopover. Well, no. I had to. I'm done with secrets.*

"So why didn't you just have the baby and give it up for adoption?"

"Right. 'Just have the baby.' You just don't get it, do you Miles? It's not that simple. Where would I go? If I stayed in town, Jim would likely have found out eventually. Maybe he would have married me even though he didn't want to. Perfect! What a good beginning. Or carry it nine months and be done with it. How could I ever give away something so much a part of me?"

"Oh, I see. Better to destroy it."

"You jackass." I scraped away from the table and made for the door. Miles caught up and grabbed me.

"No, Janine. Stop. Don't go. I'm sorry." He locked me with his arms so I couldn't move.

I struggled to free myself. By this time I was crying. "As if I don't already beat myself up over it. I thought I could trust you. I counted on you to be decent about it."

"Please, Janine. I'm sorry. I shouldn't have said that. I don't know why I did. Please. Forgive me." He relaxed his grip. I stood sobbing in his arms.

"Maybe better to keep the baby and struggle along like Marilee."

"No, no. Janine. I can't say. I'm just sorry for all the lost years." He released his hold and led me back to the table. We sat down.

"I don't know what I should have done. I just wish I had done it differently." I mulled over the implications for the hundredth time. "Of course, then I would have been pregnant the summer before we were engaged. —Do you really suppose you would have married me after that?"

Apparently this hadn't occurred to him. Miles went back to work, expanding his little herding project to pick up a few crumbs that had missed the place mat. Finally he said slowly, "Probably not."

"Absolutely not."

"Would that have been better?" he asked stiffly.

"What do you think?"

He stared at the table awhile, probably wondering how not to offend me. "I'm glad I married you, Janine," he said softly, sweeping the pile of crumbs into his hand and brushing them onto the plate.

"Really?"

"Yes, really. But that's not the question, is it. I have nothing to say about it. You said as much."

"Miles—it's different now. What I said on Boxing Day—I didn't know what the problem was then. I didn't see how I could be my own person and stay married to you."

"But now you think it's possible to be your own person in a marriage?"

"Some marriages."

"Well, I thought that was your point—this has been some marriage."

I smiled. "You're not going to let me get away with anything, are you."

Miles stood and drew me up to him. "I'm just not going to let you get away." He held me tight. I laid my head on his shoulder. His chest heaved. A wave of relief washed over me. *Yes, something can grow here.* I can't remember when I ever felt so good.

* * *

I walked to the Good Friday service with my mom. A vigorous wind blew us along. It caught my coat and wrapped around me— prairie zephyrs blowing a new season in an artless new-world way. A few orphan patches of melting snow had settled into ice at the edges, thin glassy outcroppings over bare ground. I crunched along the glassy borders.

"You are feeling better, I think," my mother observed.

"Yep." *Crunch.*

"Good." She wanted more information.

"About that man of mine—" I grinned. Mom ignored it. "I'm going to keep him."

She smiled. "I thought so. He seems so happy today." A gust of wind nearly toppled her. I took her arm and we hustled along.

The church was crowded. It always is, since the three o'clock is the only service on Good Friday. We squeezed into a pew in the transept and waited solemnly. I felt like dancing. Needless to say, I was preoccupied. I have never found it hard to attend to the Good Friday liturgy. The texts are evocative, the story so large. But this day my mind flitted like a butterfly. To Miles and our morning—our good, good morning—to Soeur Luci—and La Perle and La Belle, of course—to Madeleine—to Joy—and back to Miles and me—to both of my confessions—*ex opere operato* as Soeur Luci would say. The unexpected grace was there for me, however irregular the avenue.

* * *

Saturday. Easter Vigil began at eleven. I wore my green cape. Miles came with us "to see you home," he said. Sister Collette and one of the lectors whose name I should know by now were handing out tapers in the narthex. We each took a taper and found our seats, just in time to be asked to move with the congregation to the back of the church again. When we had all gathered there, Walter put out the lights and Father Eugene began the ceremonial lighting and blessing of the Easter fire: "… Make this new fire holy, and inflame us with new hope…"

"Amen."

Then cutting into the wax of the new Easter candle with a stylus he formed a cross and two Greek letters saying: "Alpha and Omega—all time belongs to him—and all the ages."

All time and all the ages.

Several people lit their candles from the flame of the Easter candle, passing the light to others standing nearby. Gradually the church filled with a warm radiance as we followed the Easter candle with our own candles into the nave and up the aisle toward the altar. We found our places and stood holding the light for the singing of the *Exsultet.*

Rejoice, heavenly powers! Sing, choirs of angels! Exult, all creation... came the chant sung in a full sweet tenor from beside the ambo. I stood on tiptoes straining around a tall man in front of me to see who sang so beautifully. It was Father BG! *Who would have thought it? That someone so pedestrian could produce so exalted a sound? That's one mother lode of a redeeming quality. No wonder they ordained him.*

He sang on.
Of this night scripture says:
"The night will be as clear as day:
it will become my light, my joy."
The power of this holy night dispels all evil,
washes guilt away, restores lost innocence,
brings mourners joy;
it casts out hatred, brings us peace,
and humbles earthly pride.
Night truly blessed when heaven is wedded to earth
and we are reconciled with God!

The lights kept low for the seven cycles of readings, then at midnight with the singing of the "Gloria," all the lights, all the bells, all the voices. Quickening. Jubilant. Easter.

* * *

A peculiar brightness filled the room when I woke up Easter morning. I got out of bed, pulled back the curtain and caught my breath. Miles startled. "Miles! Come and see!" He got up and looked over my shoulder. A fresh, clean blanket of snow buried the back-yard, lining all the dark arms and hands and fingers of the trees. It was one of those amazing spring snowfalls—thick and wet and heavy.

Miles laughed and wrapped his arms around me. "Welcome home." I leaned comfortably back into him. "It will melt soon enough," he said "—and God knows we needed the moisture."

EVERYTHING

i thank You God for most this amazing
day: for the leaping greenly spirits of trees
and a blue true dream of sky; and for everything
which is natural which is infinite which is yes

(i who have died am alive again today,
and this is the sun's birthday; this is the birth
day of life and of love and wings: and of the gay
great happening illimitably earth)

how should tasting touching hearing seeing
breathing any—lifted from the no
of all nothing—human merely being
doubt unimaginable You?

(now the ears of my ears awake and
now the eyes of my eyes are opened)

—e.e. cummings, *XAIPE*, "65"

Even the farmers have had difficulty finding weather to complain about this spring. It has been dry enough for sowing and wet enough for good germination. Gilbert came down last weekend to help Miles and the boys frame the foundation for Mom's little suite. Amy and Giselle came along. It was quite a party. Miles continues the construction work mostly on his own, but he would like to have more time to draw. He plans to sign up for another class in September. I met Vikki. She's a lovely woman. You wouldn't know she's old enough to be his mother, except for the wattle in her neck. Marilee is back in town planning her next move. She finished her degree with honours. It looks like things probably won't work out for her with Shane, which is too bad. Jessica misses him, but she is closer to all her other people here.

I do not plan to go back to work at the parish and Miles is fine with that. It's been a while since we paid off the mortgage. He's less worried about money now. I will probably go to school in the fall. I'm not exactly sure which program I'll choose. I want to be useful. I'd like to be a person people come to when they need someone to talk to. I will have to learn to ask good questions, like Soeur Luci does. I don't see myself as a counsellor so much as a listener. Sort of what I imagine a deaconess would do. Of course, I won't be joining a religious order or anything. It may be I'll end up as a school counsellor or something in that line. It's not really a departure from my earlier discipline—it's still history—just a different approach to personal histories. And of course, the present will be my era.

I am rewriting Madeleine's story. I have yet to understand how I came to it, but through it I somehow arrived at the substance of things I didn't have the conscious good sense to hope for. If that still qualifies as faith, then faith certainly is a gift. As for the project, I'm sticking to the fifteenth century this time. Miles thinks it makes a good short story and I should try to get it published. We'll see. In the meantime, I make plans to observe the saints' days of friends: Magdalene in July, Angadrême in October, Gertrude in November, and Madeleine on June 27 since she died on that day in 1472. And I will bless Soeur Luci as long as I live.

Nothing seems to have dissipated. Amazing how foreign that feeling has become. Every day there's something. For once in my life I am glad to be married. Of course we have our moments. Miles is still curt and insensitive when he feels excluded. Sometimes he realizes that before I call him on it. And I am not so cold. I have warmed to him despite my element. We may not be soul mates exactly, if such a thing exists, but Miles and I are more compatible than I thought. We have learned to forgive.

* * *

Midsummer and the rosebush is in full bloom. Full bloom. The last fall Marilee lived with us she and I dug up my weevil-infested bush. We carefully eased the soil away from the roots. Jessica thought it a grand undertaking, playing in the dirt with her mother and me. Her tiny fingers tugged gently at the clods of earth clinging to the roots. She was so intent on keeping the plant whole that she wept bitterly when a small tendril broke away with the dirt. Marilee assured her the plant would heal. We rinsed the roots before planting the bush in the front yard, as far away as possible from its place of privation. The following summer—the summer Marilee and Jessica went away—the plant greened and grew but produced no buds. The season after, I picked that single blossom which I brought inside before the early frost. But this spring the shrub was covered with buds and all of them opened. The roses are perfectly full and perfectly fragrant. As Augustine says, nature inclines to express itself completely. And so it does. This is fulness of life. This is redemption.

ACKNOWLEDGEMENTS

I want to thank all of the following for their contribution, support and interest. From my experience it takes a village to write a novel.

In 2002, I began writing a short story exploring the idea of subjugated histories, and, being short of cash, thought it would be a promising submission for the CBC Short Story Prize. However, the word count rose, the deadline passed, the narrator, Janine, took over, and the story just kept growing.

In 2003, when I realized Janine was actually going to go to France, my daughter, Kirsten and her husband, Shawn Robinson, bought me an airplane ticket to Beauvais, so I could find out what Janine encountered there. My friend, Nicole Cleriot, who lives just south of Paris, arranged for my stay at the diocesan house in Beauvais, and sent me a train ticket from the airport to the Gare du nord, to help me on my way. Soeur Pierre-Marie Potier was my contact at the Maison diocésaine. She and the two other sisters who lived in residence, like the sisters Janine encountered, were gracious, animated and welcoming, but I don't know their stories. Any similarities between them and the sisters in the book are purely coincidental.

My daughters and sons, Kirsten, Hannah, Simeon, and Gregory Goa, and their spouses, Shawn, Roszan, and Tristan; my sisters Glenda and Diane Dennis; and my friend, Jinny Hilliard, endured continuing commentary on the progress of the novel and were good enough to ask time and again how it was going. Many of them read early drafts and gave me positive feedback. The quotations about Kierkegaard in Chapter 4 were lifted from a paper my son Simeon carelessly left on my hard drive. He tells me he is "glad it came to some use in the end."

Thanks to the internet, my brother, Rev. Bruce Dennis, often advised me on things French from his manse in Salies-de-Béarn in southern France.

David Gay commented extensively on early chapters and gave me valuable suggestions and encouragement. I am also grateful to Bev Curtis, Faith Farthing, David Gramit, Frieda Woodruff Gramit, Sr. Catherine Kroetsch, Kenna McKinnon, and Ron Chalmers for the time they took to read and comment on the work in progress. Ron Chalmers and David Goa put me in touch with Todd Babiak and Daniel Coleman respectively, who, with David Gay, took time to read the final draft and kindly wrote words of recommendation for the cover.

In 2014, I sent an excerpt of the novel to Margaret MacPherson, who was a Metro Writer in Residence that year, and who I knew from experience to be an excellent editor. We met, and she made some suggestions, but mostly encouraged me just to get it published. I especially want to thank Stonehouse Publishing for accepting my manuscript, and for their patience in working toward publication with a fussbudget like me.

And finally, I may never have finished this novel had it not been for Monique Nutter, who, when I spoke of my need for deadlines— "Nobody tells me, 'I want to have chapter nine by the end of April,'"—said, "I can do that, Della. I want to have chapter nine by the end of April." And she did. Monique and I met, month after month, from June 2008 until November 2009, when I finally finished my first draft. These encounters were always productive and enjoyable for me, and sowed the seeds of further collaborations. May the next chapter also reach completion.